DEMON IN DISGUISE

Bedeviled AF, #4

DEBORAH WILDE

te da media inc.
vancouver

Issued in print and electronic formats.
ISBN: 978-1-998888-49-8 (paperback)
ISBN: 978-1-998888-50-4 (epub)

Chapter 1

Even in a liminal wasteland ruled by chaos magic, where every second was objectively miserable and cartoonishly dangerous, this listing wall made of human bones, some with hair and sinew still attached, was, quite frankly, a bit much.

I grimaced at the eyeless skull jammed unceremoniously between two femurs. "Alas, poor Yorick! I knew him, Horatio."

My half sister, Maud Liu, uncapped her Nalgene. "A man of that infinite a jest wouldn't rock a toupee." The British notes in her voice were flavored by her native Hong Kong accent. "That low-budget costume piece stuck to his pate marks him a Boris or, no, wait. Shiny Jimmy." She took a long swig, blotting sweat off her forehead with her free hand.

The arid heat sandblasted our skin and had me swallowing every few seconds to keep moisture in my mouth.

I pulled out a finger bone that jutted out of the wall and touched it to the top of the skull like I was knighting him. "Shiny Jimmy. A petty thug with big dreams."

"A brawler of very little brain," Maud replied. "I may have dated him in my early twenties. Any protein bars left?"

I rummaged in the heavy pack resting in the dirt against the wall and tossed her a coconut-flavored one, grabbing a handful of trail mix for myself.

After nine hours of battling unpredictable weather, manic terrain, and distances with a maddening habit of contracting and expanding at will, our quest to find a secret fortress here in the Brink had led us to this single file dirt track alongside the aforementioned bone wall.

I squatted down and sketched a tic-tac-toe grid in the dirt with the finger bone. "Play you for the last trail mix with M&M's while we wait for—"

The ground rumbled so violently that my teeth rattled. Suddenly, the bones in one long section of the wall exploded out to fan themselves in a herky-jerky motion before fusing together in a nightmarish mélange, piling higher and higher until the creature's shadow blotted out the sun.

Which wasn't a bad thing, given how hot it was.

Less ideal was the giant wearing a kneecap like a jaunty beret, a waterfall of ribs on its left side, and arm bones sticking out every which way. He rocked on webbed feet cobbled together from a couple of pelvic bones and part of a spine.

A second skull, at about butt cheek height, worked its boney mouth. "I AM SHINY JIMMY."

Ezra Cardoso, sole remaining Prime among all the vampires in existence, blurred to a stop next to us, wearing a very human peeved expression. Streaks of dirt marred his T-shirt and jeans, his motorcycle boots were scuffed, and his jet-black curls were a riotous halo in this humidity. He raised an eyebrow. "You named it?"

Maud and I exchanged guilty looks.

"Only jokingly," I said lamely.

"YOU HAVE OFFENDED ME," Shiny Jimmy said. "NOW YOU WILL PAY."

Ezra huffed a sigh that was purely for show since breathing wasn't a requirement for my ex. "Please inform them how they have caused offense so they may grovel for forgiveness."

"Really?" I stepped forward, my hands planted on my hips.

"This is not the hill to die on," he muttered, snagging my damp shirt and tugging me backward.

"YOU DO NOT EVEN KNOW THE CAUSE OF YOUR OFFENSE?" Shiny Jimmy beat on the patchwork of bones forming his chest. His butt-high skull gnashed its jawbones together.

"Would you have preferred Boris?" Maud said.

Shiny Jimmy roared and swung a fist made of teeth and ropey muscle at her.

Ezra barely got her out of harm's way, only to be clocked in the side of the head. "What did you do?" he snapped, wincing as his fingers probed a tender spot.

"Nothing!" I flung my arms up in the air.

Light glistened off the fingerbone I clutched.

"Ohhhhhh." I held it out to Shiny Jimmy. "You want this back?"

Ezra dropped his head in despair.

Shiny Jimmy snatched it away, using it, so far as I could tell, as an eyebrow ridge. It really improved his glower.

Ezra jabbed me in the back.

"Oh, Shiny Jimmy," I said, bowing low with my arms prostrate, "please accept my most humble apologies for the offense I have caused. It was wrong of me to take your finger."

"WHO DOES THAT? I MEAN, WERE YOU RAISED BY SUPE-VULTURES?"

"She didn't have much of a father figure," Maud said.

I flipped her off. "Says the woman with the same dead-beat dad."

Maud swallowed her bite of protein bar. "Unlike you, I understand right and wrong enough to know that my path —and a lovely heap of cash—lay in professionally fleecing lesser card sharks. You keep trying to make a difference. For peanuts."

"I WANTED TO MAKE A DIFFERENCE," Shiny Jimmy said mournfully.

"So, being a wall wasn't your endgame?" I said.

"For fuck's sake, Aviva." Ezra pinched the bridge of his nose.

"I SOUGHT THE POWER WORD." Shiny Jimmy gingerly lowered himself into a sitting position with a lot of bone rattling and the loss of a couple of toes, which he scrupulously collected.

"Funny you should mention that," I said, attempting to throw my arm over the part of him that passed for a shoulder. I hit something squishy between two boney platelets but kept a friendly smile on my face as I wiped my hand off on my grubby jeans. "We're on the hunt for it ourselves."

"YOU'LL JUST FAIL AND BECOME A WALL." Shiny Jimmy sounded very much like Eeyore.

"If it's any consolation," Maud said, "you're not just some basic alley wall that people piss against. You're a fine cautionary tale wall."

Shiny Jimmy nodded, considering her point. "SINCE 1983."

Dayum. "How much of this"—I waved a hand at the bone mélange—"was actually you?"

"MY ENTIRE PARTY WAS ADDED TO THIS WALL, HERE TO WARN OTHERS OFF." He sighed deeply, the sound vibrating through the bones, along the ground, and up through the soles of my hiking boots.

"BUT GO ON. TELL US WHY YOU WANT TO USE THE WORD."

I swear he was smirking.

"We don't plan to use it," I began.

Shiny Jimmy cut me off with a disgusted huff. Quite the feat for an entity that one hundred percent did not possess lungs. "THAT'S WORSE. WHY WOULD YOU SUBJECT YOURSELF TO THIS IF YOU DON'T EVEN WANT IT?"

"Give a woman five minutes to speak," I said. "Here's the deal. There's this mystic Jewish concept of neshamah, the breath of life or divine spark connecting every living being to the source of all life."

"DO I HAVE THAT SPARK?"

Maud shook her head. "'Fraid not, pet. You're a wall."

Ezra facepalmed but Shiny Jimmy shook his head resignedly. "FAIR ENOUGH."

"Vamps," I continued with a stern look at my team to keep mum, "lack this essential spark and thus, the ability to procreate."

"Other vamps," Ezra said.

I raised my eyebrows at him, and he shrugged, unrepentant, kicking a stray bone aside with his boot.

"INFERNALS CAN PROCREATE. DOUBT THEY HAVE THE SPARK."

I did a double take. "You know about them?"

"I WAS ONE."

Maud and I stared at him, waiting for more, but that was all he was sharing. His admission threw me for a loop. Sure, I didn't want the power word that would turn vamps into Primes and allow them to procreate for my personal use, but "becoming a sentient wall" wasn't on my bingo card either.

Were Maud and I more at risk on this quest by the very

nature of our being? In the month since Ezra's father, Natán, had told me what vamp invincibility actually entailed, Darsh, Sachie, and I had uncovered everything we could about the ritual to achieve it.

Sadly, our progress had been limited by our workload. Darsh and Sachie were busy quelling a nasty spree of vamp murders (admittedly pretty fun), while I'd been busting my butt running my first (far more banal) investigation as a level three operative.

The infernal blood that was integral to this vamp ritual remained missing but finding the map with the secret exit out of Babel to this part of the Brink where the fortress was supposedly located was a much-needed win.

Ezra helped where he could, but the Copper Hell was its own trainwreck, not only because of the demon running it, but also because it now hid Silas, still deep in mourning over the Authority's betrayal.

Anyway, all of that had led to this moment with Ezra, Maud, and me in the Brink, searching for the fortress that was home to the keepers of the power word. Once we found it, I'd convince its inhabitants not to let the vampires have the word, get the name of the bloodsucker behind this dangerous scheme, then track them down and hopefully find the missing blood.

It wasn't as surefire a plan as I'd like, but it wasn't chopped liver either. Plus, I'd finally gotten to see Ezra in person. Our texts and occasional video calls over the past month were fun, but it wasn't the same as being in his presence. Even our dinner date had been pushed back three times.

Speaking of my maybe-not-totally-any-longer ex, he jumped into the dumbfounded silence now, correcting Shiny Jimmy about half shedim not having that divine spark. The proof of that was that while not all half shedim made it to term, those who did could have kids.

"HOW DOES THAT HELP VAMPIRES ACHIEVE PROCREATION?"

"The chaotic essence of a half shedim's demon magic disrupts the stagnant energies within vampires," Ezra said. "This allows the divine spark that is also in their blood to be transmitted to the vamps via the magic in the power word."

"DON'T THE HALF SHEDIM HAVE NEED OF THE DIVINE SPARK?"

"Sure do," I said tightly. "Be nice to keep our blood as well, but the ritual decrees otherwise."

Shiny Jimmy looked between the grim expressions on Maud's face and mine. "BRUTAL. MAYBE I PICKED A GOOD TIME TO BE A WALL."

"Chaos magic, divine spark via blood, and a power word come together to rekindle the life force within vampires, turning them into Primes." Ezra paused. "Or something resembling Primes. They aren't naturally born like I was."

"No substandard GMO for this vamp," Maud chirped.

"Exactly." Ezra ignored her sarcasm.

"This isn't the hill to die on," I said to my ex through gritted teeth.

"I'm just saying. Primes can have kids, but that isn't the sum total of my abilities."

Shiny Jimmy had been swiveling his head back and forth like he was watching a tennis match, but his patience must have hit its limit, because he shoved a hand between Ezra and me to keep us from bickering any further. "WHY NOT USE DHAMPIRS?"

"They don't have demon chaos magic," I said.

"They can't have kids either," Ezra said. "No divine spark for them."

"Even if they could," Maud chimed in, "we have no idea if any currently exist."

Shiny Jimmy squinted at Ezra. "YOU HAVE KIDS?"

"Fuck no."

Wow, okay. Did he not want kids? Not like I wanted them immediately, but I hadn't ruled them out decisively.

"No little Primes for you?" Maud needled him.

Ezra waved Brink grit out of his face. "I haven't had the lifestyle for them. I can't put one in a baby backpack while rock-climbing, and I don't think it's good parenting to have them fall asleep at celeb parties or shush them when I'm trying to assassinate someone. Somehow I can't see toddlers riding their tricycles at the Copper Hell." He glanced at me, then coughed. "It's not like I don't want—"

I raised my eyebrows.

"What's important," he said, "is that the only other Prime I knew of didn't have them either."

Shiny Jimmy shook his top head. The one with the kneecap beret. "STOPPING VAMPIRE BABIES IS A STUPID REASON TO BECOME A WALL. GO HOME. DRINK WINE."

That sounded great, however, I'd taken an oath to right the wrongs of the world, and stopping a plan that would tip the power balance in favor of vampires over humans fell under that vow. "No can do," I said. "We're fortress-bound."

"MAYBE." Shiny Jimmy grinned revealing a double row of pointed teeth that hadn't been there a moment ago. "AND MAYBE YOU DIII—OWWW."

Ezra had punched the giant in the solar plexus, sending those bones scattering.

Shiny Jimmy shook—exactly like you'd expect a pile of bones about to collapse to shake—and reached for his missing parts.

Maud and I grabbed the bones and tossed them away as fast as we could.

"Awwww," he said in a pitchy, more human-sounding

voice. "What'd you have to do that for?" He collapsed back into an inanimate section of wall.

Maud placed her hand on her heart. "Alas, poor Shiny Jimmy. I knew him, Horatio."

I loved having a sister.

Chapter 2

Ezra rummaged in the pack. "I left the two of you alone for less than ten minutes only to return to whatever the hell that was."

"Weren't you listening?" I said. "That was Shiny Jim—"

Ezra clapped a hand over my mouth. "No naming things in the Brink. Do we require yet another lesson on how to conduct ourselves?"

I bit his finger, batting my lashes innocently when he jerked his hand away.

"Does this use of 'we' mean Avi and me as usual," Maud piped up, "or are you actually including yourself this time?"

My ex stared at her deadpan, before once more searching through the backpack.

Maud gave an "ugh" sound and drank some more water.

I motioned for Ezra to hurry up. "You were AWOL from the one job you had, bodyguard. So, if you think about it, that little episode was on you for not being here to keep us safe."

Ezra pulled out a scroll. "I'm your guide. The leader and map reader, not the muscle."

"Not according to that poker game you lost," I singsonged.

"And it wasn't just any poker game, was it, pet?" Maud patted his cheek. "It was the much-touted tournament between the Crimson Prince, co-owner of the Copper Hell, and a five-time world poker champion."

Ezra pulled the elastic off the scroll. "Yes, well, I didn't expect your bluffing skills to trump my enhanced senses. You weren't even using a shielding device."

Maud mock-cried, miming with her fists on her cheeks for emphasis. "No one has better bluffing skills than a half shedim in a world that despises them."

I clinked my water bottle to hers.

Ezra flattened the map against the ground. "Five bucks says we're stuck on this path."

I brushed dirt off the parchment. "Can we go in literally any other direction?"

Appearances were deceiving here in the Brink, the boundary between earth and the vampire megacity. Six steps down this flat path and we could be buried alive in an avalanche. Or fall into a lake that didn't previously exist. Or just dally with another sentient wall.

Maud splashed water on her cheeks, drops flicking onto her red T-shirt with the Flaming Flapjacks dancing pancake logo that I'd been eyeing this entire trip.

"Incoming." Ezra shielded his eyes with one hand, tracking something in the sky.

It took me longer to clock the tiny black dots swooping down toward us.

Two supe-vultures, the only animal life known to exist in the Brink, landed with an odd grace about ten feet away atop the wall. They swiveled their featherless heads, lasering us with their beady-eyed stare like they could hasten our expiration dates.

Ezra unzipped his shirt pocket, carefully removed what looked like a jeweler's loupe, and set it on the map.

"Did you ever have those little toy dinosaur sponges when you were little?" I patted my damp curls. "The ones you put in water and they'd swell up?"

The clear glass of the loupe turned iridescent, and the band snapped open, segmenting into a lizard's body and face with beard: a tiny demon and our actual guide, despite Ezra's claims. The shedim was doing this job in lieu of a forfeit owed to the Copper Hell.

Maud snickered. "Your hair is sucking the moisture from the air. I assumed my eyes were playing tricks on me, but you'll be giving '80s metal bands a run for their money soon."

The wee shedim beastie's sticky little feet scuttled across the map.

Storm clouds pulsed darkly overhead, and while the air had grown hotter and muggier during our hike, there hadn't been a single drop of sweet, sweet rain.

Trust me, when a Vancouverite longed for a deluge, things were dire.

Ezra glanced up from watching the tiny demon's path and smirked at me. "I either transposed a number calculating follicle growth, or your hair will soon achieve black hole status."

I kicked a pebble at him. "Hilarious."

My sister winked cheekily. "At the very least, we'll be able to camouflage you as a shrubbery."

"Ni!" Ezra said.

Maud blinked at him. "Did the Crimson Prince just make a Monty Python reference?"

He looked down his nose at her. Amazing trick since he

squatted next to the map. "The Crimson Prince does not engage in such silliness."

"Prime Playboy?" she said.

I shook my head. "Not slick enough for him either. Mazel tov, Maud. You've just witnessed a pure Ezra nerd moment."

"Tell anyone and I'll be forced to kill you," he said.

The demon plopped its butt on the map and a trail of magic light appeared on the ground in front of us—sticking to the path along the bone wall.

I shook my fist at the tiny demon. "Screw you, Gimli."

Ezra cackled. "Told you I'd get you using his name." He extended his index finger and the lizard obligingly crawled onto it. My ex carefully deposited the little guy on his shoulder where it settled in, rubbing its tiny beard with its wee claws.

I sighed, gaining a new appreciation for my mother cautioning me against anthropomorphizing shedim, and followed my sister and ex, who were now tromping along the dirt path and bickering about at what point Ezra was to step in once we were in place outside the fortress (Maud: never, Ezra: cue sarcastic laughter).

"You're just sore that I won this map from Delacroix while you were stuck pumping the Bilge," Maud said.

Ezra shuddered. "I may never get the smell out of my nostrils."

"Next time listen to me," she chastised, "and don't get cocky with your forfeits."

"Hang on." My ankle wobbled on a pile of loose stones in my way. "Isn't everything on the yacht automated? Why would you guys have to pump your own bilge, whatever that is?"

Maud's lips quirked. "Bilge is one of Delacroix's shedim Brimstone Breakfast Club cronies. The one with the pompadour?"

She'd probably been properly invited to those gatherings by our demon daddy. Unlike me, who tended to be harassed into last-minute attendance, only encountering his buddies in passing.

Thin whisps of fog drifted toward us.

"Oh yeah. I met him." I scrunched up my face. "And pumping this Bilge involves…?" I mimed giving a hand job.

Maud roared with laughter, causing the supe-vultures to fly toward us.

Ezra smacked the birds away like volleyballs. "I'm not providing happy endings to shedim."

I shrugged. "Not with that attitude you're not."

"Bilge has two stomachs," he said, "one of which tends to get stuck and require massaging."

"Still a rub and tug," Maud chortled.

Ezra jabbed a thumb at her. "Between Michael, Delacroix, and now this one—"

"You mean the woman who managed to kidnap and torture another Prime?" she interrupted cheerfully. I was surprised she could joke about it, but she had pulled off the unthinkable. My sister was not to be underestimated.

He scowled at her. "Spending time with *my* family is looking pretty good."

"Rude," she muttered.

I waved my arms and growled at the supe-vultures who'd circled back. "Your father bribed me with the missing infernal blood to never see you again, and considering I have yet to be taken on this big date you were so eager to impress me with, discussions of family time is premature."

The birds fell into lazy circles above us, watching our every move.

"Maybe quit rain-checking me with important Maccabee stuff and let me astound and delight you." Ezra held out his hand to test the fog. "The rain checks aren't the problem. I just can't stand Delacroix gloating that you only did that to him once."

My father got me back by outing Maud as an infernal to Sachie, along with the fact that I'd lied to her about it. I hadn't seen Delacroix in a month, not since I'd told him to pull his head out of his ass and help the Authority find the shedim imprisoning other demons.

I didn't miss him.

"Trust me, Aviva," Ezra said, leaning close, "I very much want to take you on that date."

I shivered, but it wasn't desire. Well, not only, because I also coughed. The fog was growing denser, colder, and smellier—like chemical waste.

Despite finding the shedim jailers being in his best interests, Delacroix had thrown my offer back in my face. That said, he'd been surprisingly helpful (for him) assisting our search for the missing infernal blood that would allow vampires to regain procreation abilities.

Delacroix was totally against any more Primes—or Prime-like—vamps in existence. He'd maneuvered the only one into being his partner on the Copper Hell and helping to stabilize my father's siren magic. More would pose a threat to his power.

I coughed again, the fog now so thick it sucked in all light, and closed my eyes against its sting, my hands out in front of me. "Maud? Ezra?"

"Here." My sister fumblingly grabbed one hand.

"Steady on. I've got you both." Ezra placed a hand on my shoulder. "Walk slowly. Let me be your senses."

Maud's hand trembled. "Are the supe-vultures still with us?"

"Yes," Ezra said calmly. "But I hear them."

"You're assuming sound works properly," I said.

"Let's stick with that hypothesis for now," he replied, amusement in his voice.

The fog wrapped us in cold, sticky strands, pulsing and physically pressuring us to wander off the path and into unknown danger. After the third time corralling Maud and me back to his side, Ezra slung his arms around our waists, allowing us to resist the pull. He guided us carefully over loose stones while ensuring we all stuck close to the wall.

Until he suddenly knocked us flat onto our bellies.

I cried out, my knee badly scraping a rock on the way down. Thank goodness for denim.

"Avi?" Maud yelped.

"I'm okay."

Ezra kept his hand firmly on the back of my head. "Keep your eyes closed," he hissed. "And don't move an inch."

He didn't need to tell me twice. The light was a blazing orange that burned my lids and the only sounds over my hammering heart were wet smacks. It sounded like someone messily eating a burger and also soup all while inside an industrial car crusher.

I fought the urge to curl up into a ball because that required moving, but still, dirt flew up my nose. I wrinkled my face against the sneeze building inside me, squeezed my mouth and cheeks tight, and tried to hold my breath. I wasn't going to die from nasal tickling. For one blessed second, I thought I'd mastered it.

Some kind of barbed appendage scraped against my ankle, and the loudest sneeze in history exploded out of me, spraying a geyser of wet germs.

The fog funneled into a tornado and swirled away into the sky as if it was running late to meet a house from Kansas.

I blinked at the image before me, namely Gimli perched on the wall.

Thankfully, the bones in this section were dry and dusty, but the demon had blown up into approximately thirty-seven times his normal size, his flabby butt drooping over the edge, and a gnawed-up feathered appendage hanging out of his slobbery mouth.

I crept closer and Gimli growled. "Calm your tits, demon," I said. "Is that a supe-vulture wing?" I whirled on Ezra. "Why doesn't he require lessons?"

Ezra scratched the demon under the chin. "Because Gimli's a good boy who's just hungry and now he's scared off the fog. Didn't you, buddy?"

Maud pointed off into the distance with a whistle.

The small fortress stood at the top of a rocky hill surrounded by a moat. Its walls, lined with crenellations and guard towers, were made of weathered gray stone, while the entrance was a heavy wooden gate, reinforced with metal.

"Are we close enough for your magic to work?" I said.

"It's within my line of sight," Maud said, "but whether there are flames inside that I can use is anybody's guess." She pulled a lighter out of the back pocket of her jeans, her other hand creeping up to the Maccabee ring she wore around her neck. I'd taken her godmother's ring away once before, since using it would have killed my sister, but returned it after I dumped out the magic cocktail stored in the top compartment.

Maud flicked the lighter on and off a couple of times, centering herself. While we both had blue flame magic, her fire sight was much rarer and cooler than my ability to illu-minate weaknesses in people.

My sister could temporarily meld her consciousness with a flame, magically using it to spy. She didn't even need to see the second flame that she'd see and hear through. It was enough for the building that housed the flame to be visible. Even better than her spy powers was that when she extinguished the flames she saw through, she could erase everyone's short-term memories along with it.

If there were any lit candles or hearth fires inside the fortress, Maud would find them, get the lay of the land, and deliver any relevant information before our approach.

If there weren't any flames, well, that would suck, but we wouldn't be in a worse position.

Maud stared into the lighter intently, going slightly cross-eyed.

Ezra stood with his back to her, standing guard along the path, and even Gimli quit eating to watch my sister.

There were no magic words, just a slight pause before she smiled. "Lovely tapestry."

I was careful not to touch her and disturb the connection she'd made but I fist-pumped. "Fantas—"

Then, with no warning, her head jerked back, her face thrown to the sky, and she crumpled like all her bones had melted.

The lighter hit the dirt, but I caught my sister.

Maud's eyes rolled back to show the whites. Blood streamed from her nose and eyes, and she chanted some kind of gibberish.

"Maud!" I slapped her cheek, but when she didn't respond, I slid into my blue flame synesthete vision. She was a solid bright blue. "Ezra, heal her!"

His face was tight with frustration. "She's in the grips of some other magic. I don't dare add mine."

My sister sat up jerkily, her eyes totally purple. "Smart thinking, vampire." Her regular accent was gone in favor of sounding straight out of the depths of Brooklyn. "You really should have listened to Shiny Jimmy."

Chapter 3

I drew on all my training to beat down my panic. "The decision to spy on you was mine. It was wrong and I am willing to accept any consequence."

Ezra growled, his pupils going red and his fangs dropping.

I ignored him because Maud's eyes were still purple, and while the blood from her tear ducts and nostrils had slowed to a tiny trickle, her pulse was thready. The weight of her in my arms had nothing to do with her body mass. I swallowed through a thick throat. "Please help my sister or allow us to help her."

"Begone!"

The light faded from Maud's eyes, her pulse weakening under my fingertip. The ache of all our unmade memories pressed against my chest. I hadn't saved her from our father —hadn't just found *her*—only to condemn her to death.

"I don't want the power word!" I cried. "I'm not here for any test."

It was if time suspended. Maud's pulse was a barely burning coal, her life force almost totally gone.

I bowed my head, my grip on my sister my only firm hold on reality. "Please," I said again, more softly.

"I'll give you thirty seconds to explain." The Brooklyn-accented voice no longer came from Maud but from the air around us.

"Thank you." I carefully transferred Maud to Ezra's gentle hold and scrambled to my feet. "How should we—"

My sentence ended in a scream as the ground dropped out from under me and I plummeted into the darkness. It didn't end. I yelled until my voice was hoarse, but eventually, even my terror-fueled adrenaline dissolved into shallow pants. I kept trying to swallow and couldn't, too freaked out to do anything more than fall.

Eventually a tiny pinprick of light appeared far below my feet. I squinted at it, positive it was wishful thinking, but the light grew larger, until I tumbled out of the darkness, slowing to a stop on a cushion of air before being deposited onto a thick rug.

I lay sprawled on my back, catching my breath and gathering my wits. Neither Ezra nor Maud were present, but Cherry Bomb, my Brimstone Baroness, was. Not just in the way she always was, as a voice in my head either. I brushed crimson strands of hair away with clawed fingers, my skin hardened to an armor comprised of sharp-edged scales frosted in the same toxic green that my eyes now were.

I hadn't been forced to change; I'd chosen to while in that darkness. Might this be a bad idea? Maybe. I wasn't sure any antagonist would love having my demon-lite form on their nice rug. But something in my gut knew it was safe, that this would keep me from being possessed like Maud was.

"Well, this is a trip," said the person who'd hijacked my sister's vocal cords.

The woman lounging in the wing chair had patrician

features, her shapeless hand-spun robe the same cool hue as her blond hair. Nothing about her appearance matched her voice.

"What did you do with Ezra and Maud?" I said.

She smirked. "The vamp is shitting bricks, but both of them are fine. The woman's injuries are gone." When I narrowed my eyes, she held up two fingers. "Scout's honor. Milk in your tea or black?"

Her question felt like a test.

I sat up and gingerly surveyed my surroundings.

For an imposing, impenetrable stone fortress, the inside was surprisingly snug, with bright tapestries and multiple fireplaces, lush plants, and overflowing book-cases, as well as an inner courtyard visible through the picture windows with reflecting pools and a small arched bridge.

A supe-vulture sat on a dented cactus, its gaze trained on me.

I resisted the urge to shoot it the finger.

A long wooden table held a teapot covered by a colorful tea cozy, next to two delicate porcelain cups on saucers alongside a sugar bowl and small creamer.

How I'd fallen downward into this place when it had been visible in the distance from the path above was anyone's guess, but I put the question aside because my host was tapping one foot, waiting for my reply.

"Brandy." I stood up. "Neat."

She quirked an eyebrow. "That wasn't one of the options."

"Nope." I plopped myself down on the nearest sofa. "But it's the right answer." I pointed at the shoes peeking out from under her Handmaid's Tale robe. "You're wearing marabou feather slippers, likely with a satin-covered kitten heel. Those are brandy drinking shoes."

Her coarse robe shimmered and transformed into a silk

dressing gown in the same ivory as her slippers, with the same feathery trim at the cuffs.

She extended a foot and looked down at her slipper. Satin-covered kitten heel for the win. "They aren't to dress code, but no one ever notices the shoes. I'm impressed." She strode over to a cabinet and flung open the door, revealing a dazzling array of bottles, more styles of glasses than I could name, and several stainless-steel devices that looked like torture instruments but that I recognized from a high-end cocktail bar that Darsh, Sachie, and I sometimes frequented.

The woman poured us each a snifter of brandy then, handing mine over, settled herself into a round chair piled high with cushions, her legs tucked under her.

"Thanks, uh…" I raised an eyebrow in question.

"Daphne."

I nodded. "I'm Aviva."

She held the glass up. "Cheers. Here's to outside-the-box thinking and not drinking another damned cup of tea."

"L'chaim." The sweet alcohol was fruity with an undertone of oak. Really, I was more of a wine person, but any booze was welcome if it calmed my frayed nerves.

"We've got top-shelf brandy and your friends are safe." Daphne tilted her head at me, her green eyes icy. "You, however, still have to answer for your actions."

"I know," I said somberly. I cradled my snifter in my lap.

"I heard what you said to 'Shiny Jimmy.'" Her lips quirked. "You don't want the word yourself, so I'm guessing you're here to tell me not to hand it over to the vampires."

"Exactly."

She made a noncommittal sound, but when I tried to explain further, she held up a hand.

I sipped my brandy to avoid snapping back at her.

Darsh had estimated that the blood volume collected from the murdered half shedim was maybe good for a dozen vampires, tops.

"If my knowledge of dark magic is accurate," he'd said with a wink.

It probably was. Darsh had unplumbed depths. But that meant that whoever was behind this didn't intend for all vampires to be able to procreate.

I'd been told that person knew of my existence, so they could have added at least one more half shedim's blood to their stockpile. They hadn't, ergo, they had the amount they required.

A vampire not wanting to share power. Quelle surprise.

Thus, we'd followed rumors and breadcrumbs and whispers and gotten as far as the map and this fortress, where this mighty guardian resided.

However, if we'd found this place, then that vampire had as well, because they'd had months, if not years of looking for it. Yet, somehow, they'd been stonewalled.

Our conclusion? They didn't yet have the word necessary for the dark magic ritual to allow them to breed. We'd have heard if it had been attempted—or successful.

"Why are you wearing stretchy denim?" Daphne toyed with her glass. "You pegged my slippers but are wearing that?" She made it sound like I was an enigma clothed in sackcloth and dog shit.

Thanks to some demon forfeits at the Hell, Ezra learned that the closest Brink entrance to this fortress was via Babel. Specifically, a secret rift in a far corner of the vampire megacity. He'd created a portal into Babel from the yacht that placed us at the little-known rift.

The portal from Babel into the Brink would be monitored in some way by the procreation-seeking vamp, though we hadn't seen anyone there, but it was a risk we had to take.

As was that the second Maud and I stepped into Babel, we were forced into our shedim forms. Anticipating this, we wore stretchy clothes to accommodate the brief transition from human body to shedim and back to human. But we also required sturdier outfits than sweats for the rigors of the Brink.

Denim with give was our best option, and I succinctly explained as much.

"That's boring," Daphne grumbled, stroking the feather trim on her silk robe.

I barely refrained from rolling my eyes. "Look, I'm guessing since you've got a whole fortress set up to protect the power word that you don't want it falling into the wrong hands. And if vampires can procreate, that's a bad deal for humanity."

"What I want is irrelevant." Daphne sipped her brandy. "I don't even know the word myself, just that it has powerful healing abilities and anyone deemed worthy is capable of carrying it."

"Carrying it how?"

"At the back of the throat." She shot me a "duh" look.

"Like a stifled scream," I said.

She chuckled. "Kind of."

"The vampire intends to use it in a blood magic ritual. That's dark magic. Evil." Six half shedim had their lives cut tragically and horrifically short because of it.

"Blood magic is simply as benign or malevolent as the user's intention."

"Then healing isn't always a good thing. Not if it gives vampires this ability."

"Healing is healing." She said it in the rote, slightly bored tone of a speech uttered dozens of times before. "Once the power word is released, it's wiped from the user's memory."

"Is worthiness tied to intent?" Maybe I didn't have to worry. Maybe this test took care of things for me.

Her head shake dashed those hopes. "Survive the test. That's the only requirement."

"What's the test?"

"Damned if I know." She wiped a drop of brandy off the rim of her snifter. "That's literal. If I tried to find out, I'd be damned. I'm just a glorified administrator for the sentient fortress magic."

My shoulders slumped.

"There is some good news for you."

Wearily, I met her gaze.

"So long as one person carries the word, no one else can have it. And it can't be taken by force. If you took the test, survived, and never used it…"

"Then no one else could either." A simple solution. Except for the part where failed supplicants were turned into new sections of the bone wall, and that thing had stretched out as far as I could see. "Any chance of marking on the bell curve?"

Daphne snorted. "Magic sentience is more old school pass or fail."

"What are my chances of success?"

"Less than one percent of one percent." She pursed her lips. "That doesn't tend to deter people."

"When was the last time anyone was successful?"

"Nineteen thirty-two. What a grand day that was." She set down her glass. "Want to give it a go?"

"Can't you, I don't know, pause the test, or just refuse supplicants until we've stopped this vampire?"

"Funny. And no. This institution doesn't cater to the whims of mortals."

I wasn't taking this cockamamie test. Even if I passed (unlikely), I'd be stuck with a power word in my throat. The one time I'd had a breadcrumb stuck there over lunch, I'd almost gone mad. Would I have to direct all my energy into keeping from blabbing it like a juicy secret that was just too good not to share? No, thanks.

I drummed my fingers against the brandy snifter. Vamps were near indestructible, and yet procreation was so important to the person behind this that they'd killed all those half shedim. So why hadn't he or she attempted the test yet?

Employing video game logic, which was as sound as anything else right now, they'd sent a minion or a succession of them to attempt it before they tried themselves. You didn't need to know the exact odds to know that they weren't in your favor.

"Could you tell me the name of the most recent supplicant?" I said. "That's administration, right? Your area?"

"It is, but…" Daphne pushed the sleeve of her robe up, revealing flesh glowing with deeply carved magic runes.

I shivered.

She let the sleeve fall back into place. "The NDA is a bitch. But there is a way you can ask."

"To clarify, you mean ask the sentient force that turns people into bone walls and carved runes in your skin instead of sending you a perfectly harmless e-signed document?"

"Got it in one."

I swallowed. Somewhere in the multiverse, there was a version of me who'd become an accountant. Lucky bastard.

Chapter 4

I tightly hugged a cushion, visions of an eternity as a bone wall dancing in my head. "Is it another test?"

"Not like you're thinking. They'll still determine your worthiness, but either I'll be allowed to give you the information or I won't. No death involved." She paused. "Probably." She frowned. "I've never had this request before."

How reassuring. I sighed. "I'll ask."

A pair of brass scales appeared on the table, the left side sitting lower than the right, and I flinched.

Daphne peered at me, her brows furrowed. "What's wrong?"

I dug my fingers into the cushion, goose bumps exploding over my arms. I'd agreed to a game of three questions using similar scales with Delacroix. He'd abandoned the game when he didn't like my first question and beat me up with his fucking water magic. What would some magical protector of a power word do?

"You didn't say you worked for shedim," I said tightly.

"I don't. The magic protecting the power word is..." Daphne gently shook the scales, rattling them on their slender chains. A golden glow swam up from the base. "Something else entirely."

Nope. Still not reassured. I rubbed my forehead. "Do we each ask three questions? Should I think of a forfeit equal in weight to the importance of the question?"

"Ah." Daphne nodded sagely. "I see you've encountered this before. Happily, this isn't Demon Quid Pro Quo. One question for you alone. But yes to the forfeit. Lay your—"

"Yeah, I know." I placed one hand on each scale, the brass warm under my palms just like it was with Delacroix. I shuddered, my jaw set.

What forfeit would be equal in weight to the importance of the question? This mattered to me, but in the grand scheme of things, how significant was the name of the last supplicant to this magical force?

Best to err on the side of caution.

It wouldn't care about a memory or Maccabee intel. It was magic, so I'd bet the same. *I wager losing my blue flame magic for an hour.*

I'd placed this forfeit once at the Copper Hell. It had hurt like crazy to have it taken from me, but even if the hour started now, it's not like I could illuminate the weakness of a magic force. And I'd have Ezra to keep me safe for the return journey. Most likely, it would happen when I was sleeping and I'd be right as rain in the morning.

Daphne's chair hadn't turned around like Delacroix's had, nor had any hologram of my forfeit appeared over the left scale. This reassured me that this game wouldn't end like the last one had.

Keeping my forfeit firmly in mind, I silently asked my question. *What's the name of the most recent supplicant?*

Unlike last time, the scales didn't balance. I cursed softly; I wouldn't be allowed to ask my question. That said, I didn't feel any magic loss, and the glow didn't change in any way. I frowned. "Are you sure this thing is working properly?"

"Yes. It rejected your question and took your forfeit." Daphne started to rise.

I stopped her. "It's still glowing. Can I try again? Same question, different forfeit?"

We stared at the scales as if they'd provide guidance.

Daphne opened her mouth. Closed it. Checked the runes on her arms. "I guess?" She tensed as if braced for a blow.

Nothing happened.

She waved at the scales. "Be my guest. But just one more."

I'd been wrong about wager. The test for the power word involved proving one's worthiness. I'd do the same for this question.

Instead of wagering magic, I offered my ring.

I silently told whatever was listening all about my dreams of becoming the best Maccabee ever. How I'd be a force for change so no other half shedim would have to hide. I shared how putting on my Maccabee ring and saying the vow of tikkun olam, to fix the wrongs in the world, meant more to me than anything.

It didn't matter that we'd learned the magic cocktail we stored in our rings was corrupted, the ring itself was what was important. It was the embodiment of my dreams, my talisman, and the physical manifestation of my oath. I'd never taken it off, no matter how dire the situation.

I bit my lip. If my question was refused, I'd lose the ring and Daphne wouldn't give me a third try. I'd have failed.

Pushing aside my unease and the desire to snatch the words back once I bet the ring against the right to ask the question, I centered myself. *What's the name of the most recent supplicant?*

For one heart-stoppingly long moment, nothing

happened. Then with a slight creak, the left scale rose up under one hand and the right one descended.

I let out a breath; the scales had balanced.

Unlike with my previous try, the magic sentience had accepted my proposed forfeit as being of equal weight to the question. Thus, I'd fulfilled the condition and could ask my question without having to pay up.

I squeezed my hand, assuring myself the gold band was still securely on my finger.

A clear plastic bag filled with water popped into existence on the table next to the scales. It was sealed at the top with a twist tie, like a container for a goldfish from a pet store. The creature inside, however, was no cute coppery fish. It was a wriggling black maggot, pulsing and angry.

I grimaced. "What the unholy…?"

"It looks nasty on its own, but en masse, they're actually quite soothing to watch." Daphne handed me the bag. "There's an underground lake full of them whose shore is perfect for meditation after a long day of customer service." She shook her head. "Some of those supplicants whine like nobody's business. They knew the deal, the big babies."

Wow, lady. Five-star brandy but one-star compassion.

I hefted the bag in one hand. It weighed almost nothing, but the creature thrashed so violently that I almost lost my grip on it. "What am I supposed to do with this?"

"Crush it under your bare foot during a full moon and it will speak its name."

My mouth fell open, my face screwed up in horror. "This is the supplicant?"

"It's their name."

I shook the bag, disturbing the maggot and sloshing the water inside, icy sweat dotting the back of my neck. No wonder Shiny Jimmy took the moniker we'd jokingly bestowed on him. What kind of horror show did failed supplicants experience?

A million kinds of thankful that I hadn't taken the actual test, I asked Daphne to return me to Maud and Ezra.

"Come back and visit sometime," she said.

"I will."

She smiled wistfully, like we both knew that was a lie.

A card fluttered down onto the carpet. It had an illustration of an old-timey man with a bushy mustache and monocle surrounded by medieval devils, along with the words "Go Directly to Hell."

I hastily stepped back, but Daphne picked it up with a smile.

"That's nice of you," she said to the room in general, and held out the card.

I waved back and forth. "I'm good, thanks."

She laughed. "Toss it in the air when you get back to your friends and the card will transport your party back to the Copper Hell."

"Really?" I took it, flipping it over for any fine print. There wasn't any. "No strings?"

"None. Every successful supplicant gets a return ticket. You didn't take the regular test but you still qualified."

I didn't want to know how this magic force had our itinerary. "Thanks."

Daphne waved her hand and the room blurred and swum.

I blinked at the white spots in my vision, grunting when a hard body shoved me aside.

A loud buzzing interrupted my protest. Flies the size of poodles roamed like gangs invading a neighboring gang's turf. Though they had wings, they were flightless, scuttling at us in a side-to-side motion, their giant amber eyes as hypnotic as oncoming headlights, and their stiff bristles more like spikes than hair.

Supe-vultures were the only creatures native to the

Brink. These buggers must have come through a rift and been caught in the chaos magic.

Feeling no pity, I kicked away one of the dozen carcasses littering the dirt, their dried blood dark crimson rivers under an overcast sky.

Gimli, back to his tiny size, dozed on Ezra's shoulder.

Ezra punched a particularly aggressive fly in the face, knocking it back into two of its buddies. "Stay behind me."

Happy to stay out of this fight, I returned to human form and backed up, the ground sucking in each footfall like weak quicksand.

Over by the wall, Maud swung the heavy pack back and forth to swat the flies away.

The pack clipped one, blood trickling from the gash in its face. Three other flies immediately attacked, consuming the wounded one.

"What loyalty," I said weakly.

"What happened in there?" Ezra said, his eyes trained on the winged foes.

I double-checked that the plastic bag with the maggot wasn't damaged. "I got the name of the last person to fail the test."

"*And?*"

"And I'm fine." I kicked a fly that was getting too close. It backed up, but more like it was preparing to charge than fleeing. "Maud, how about you?"

"All good." She turned a half degree, brandishing the backpack menacingly.

Since that's exactly what I would have said, regardless of the truth, I asked her permission to illuminate any weaknesses. All my blue flame synesthete vision showed was normal fatigue and a slight strain in the muscles on her right side.

"I'm really sorry for getting you into this," I said.

"I'm a big girl. I could have said no." She hissed at a fly

who flapped its wings at her, buzzing. "It was an adventure, but now I want a hot shower."

Ezra killed another couple of insects, taking the numbers down to two of them and three of us.

"Everyone huddle up," I said.

It took a minute and we did it with our backs against each other's instead of facing in like normal, but once we were in position, I showed my team the Go Directly to Hell card.

"Catchy. We could use these for marketing," Ezra said. "But it's a little disturbing that they knew."

"Right? Argh!" I batted the fly that had headbutted me in the gut.

The card flew into the air, which constricted around us like a belt after a too-heavy meal, then snapped, flinging us all forward.

Between my second and third stumbling steps, I went from spongy ground to the moss-green carpet on the main floor of the Copper Hell.

Two flies, now normal-sized, came with us, buzzing in a dazed circle before soaring up to the yacht's ceiling.

Li'l Hellions, the vampire employees, rushed us. They were clad in identical uniforms consisting of fitted gunmetal-gray trousers and collared button-down shirts with the Copper Hell's logo embroidered above their hearts: a fat flame bound diagonally by a thin copper band.

In typical fashion, they didn't assist us; they badgered Ezra with business-related questions like he'd been gone for years instead of less than a day.

He was swallowed up by them, only his nose, bewildered eyes, and the top of his head poking up above the fray. The way they bobbed around him made me think of a drowning man. Poor besieged Prime.

Apparently, Calista had mostly left things in the hands of her very stressed employees. Ezra grumbled that taking an active role in running the megayacht was his personal "no good deed goes unpunished," but he'd agreed to run the Hell and so it would be done to his exacting standards.

The Li'l Hellions took to Ezra like a pack of unruly puppies falling in line with relief when their alpha dad showed up.

Maud removed her extra clothing from the backpack, cradling it in a bundle to her chest.

I sighed, wishing I could say bye to Ezra properly instead of a wave, and mouthed "Thank you." Hefting the pack, I looped my arm through Maud's and we walked back to the small foyer. Somehow the same mesh light portal would return Maud to the exit in Hong Kong and me to the Jolly Hellhound in Vancouver.

We hugged. Maud stepped through first, but before I could follow, I was hauled backward.

Ezra leaned in, the intensity in his eyes making my heart skip a beat.

The Hellions hovered about twenty feet away as if kept back by an invisible force that, if dissipated, would send them flooding toward us.

"Did you threaten them?" I murmured.

"Big-time." His cologne mixed with the natural scent of his skin, creating an intoxicating aroma that filled my senses. "That okay?"

"Depends on what you plan to do next."

He tapped a finger against his lip. "Do a thorough debrief of *exactly* what went down in the fortress?"

"That would be the smart play."

"And the reckless one?" he said.

I leaned in closer, my heart hammering. I'd told myself that I wouldn't decide whether or not to give Ezra a second chance before our dinner date, and here I was acting like things were already settled.

Ezra played all his cards close to his chest. It was a

survival tactic by a boy raised to be heir to a Mafia in a world where everyone wanted to take him down.

It gave me insight and empathy for how he'd treated me, but I wouldn't have forgiven him if he hadn't confided in me his determination to get to the truth of his mother's suicide. More importantly, he'd repeatedly proven he had my back and that he was trying to be a man worthy of my affection.

Case in point, even though we hadn't seen each other this past month, Ezra had dropped everything as soon as we had the map to come questing with Maud and me in the Brink.

That said, I'd argued both sides of going down this road with him again a billion times. Each time I tipped in favor of throwing caution to the wind and seeing where a reconciliation between us led, the giant divide between him partnering with my demon father at the Hell and me being a Maccabee swam sickeningly before me.

I raised my eyebrow, though I also made sure that no one other than his staff could see us before I issued my challenge. "Surely, you can figure out the reckless move on your own, Cardoso."

His lips met mine with a soft, dark laugh, one hand around my waist and the other coiling in my hair. Electricity shivered over my skin, and the scent of lemon and wood polish surrounded me as Ezra pushed me into the wall.

I rose on tiptoe, forgetting my schedules, my plans, and all the stressful things waiting for me back in Vancouver, to lose myself in this moment and make it last longer.

Even now, I couldn't believe that I could just have this. Whenever I wanted. I deepened the kiss, Ezra's heart shuddered against my skin and—

A cheer rose from the hallway.

I opened my eyes. It wasn't the Hellions encouraging

our public display of affection, since most of them glared at me behind his back for wasting their master's precious time; it was some game played at a nearby table.

Ezra rested his forehead against mine. "Do not bail on dinner Wednesday."

After certain Authority members almost railroaded me out of the Maccabees for a number of bullshit reasons, I'd kept my nose to the grindstone this past month, spending all my time on my first level three case finding an ugly heirloom vase that was stolen in a vicious inheritance dispute.

All the parties involved were horrible people and didn't deserve my every waking hour and near burnout, but I'd felt incredible pressure to hit the ground running. The emotions I'd communicated to the scales back at the fortress weren't fake.

I'd spent my entire career going above and beyond to prove myself as an exemplary operative for the day I went public with Cherry, and even if I was slowly trusting her to my inner circle, old habits died hard.

It was tough telling myself that I didn't have to spend every waking moment making myself indispensable. It was even tougher convincing myself that I deserved time off.

Especially when that time off involved rekindling a relationship with Enemy Number One to many Maccabee higher-ups.

Everything being what it was, I'd rescheduled on Ezra three times. He hadn't grumbled (much), but he'd insisted that our big romantic dinner date where he hoped his exgirlfriend agreed to reconcile happen on a Wednesday.

Hump Day. It was either comically unsubtle or the least romantic day of the week. Was he having similar doubts about us?

"I won't bail," I told him now.

"Ezra." This one male Hellion spoke tentatively, but the entire group had edged closer.

My ex's eye twitched. "Be safe."

I squeezed his hand and turned away, walking through the portal with a small smile and the maggot bag. I had the supplicant's name—more or less—and I hadn't even missed work.

I was nailing this level three gig.

Chapter 5

My mushy feelings quickly faded in the back of the taxi.

January in Vancouver always depressed me. Regardless of my frustrations having Christmas shoved down my throat the second Halloween was over, once the sparkle was turned off and the lights hung limply off eaves, with inflatable figures languishing like forgotten dolls in the rain, I almost wished for the anticipatory lead-up to the holiday back. Instead, I was left feeling trapped in a city-wide gloom, where future good times felt too far off to inspire joy.

It didn't help that shortly before the new year, posters and graffiti had exploded around the Lower Mainland, like the angry slogans illuminated by a sickly yellow streetlight in the dark night sky that we drove past.

"Fuck Trads" was spraypainted on the side of a low building, then crossed out in favor of "magic is the work of the devil" along with posters for the reelection of Jared Casey, featuring his fake smile and blond combover.

Video had recently been "leaked" of Jared during a hunting party with some buddies. In full regalia, he'd been caught sneering that "real humans don't need magic."

Then he cocked his rifle.

It went viral with a vengeance.

When pressed by media, Jared insisted his remarks had been taken out of context and that he'd been talking about hunting deer. Yeah, right. What a shithead.

I rested my head against the seat, my shoulders and neck tight, and placed the maggot bag on top of the backpack. Speaking of shitheads…

Ever since Ezra's dad, Natán, had tried to bribe me into staying away from his son, he'd set up minions to stalk me 24-7. They couldn't enter my home or workplace, and through a series of *Mission Impossible*–type maneuvers, I'd given them the slip for this side quest into the Brink. I didn't want them reporting back that Ezra and I had been together or where my investigation into this vampire ritual was at.

Natán had previously attempted to bribe me with insider information about the missing infernal blood that was key to vamp procreation. I refused to have him one-upping me on this investigation, manipulating events so my choices were either stop this ritual or stop seeing Ezra.

I'd given Ezra a heads-up about it, and he'd been understandably furious, ready to charge back to his father or take the vamp minders out himself, but showing that it bothered either of us handed Natán a vulnerability I refused to give him. I'd convinced Ezra to leave it be.

Sure enough, I exited the taxi in front of my condo tower and a figure peeled away from the shadows. She came only a few feet forward, her intent not to make contact or even scare me, just to let me know she was watching.

I hitched the backpack higher on my shoulder and strode up to the building's front door.

A few minutes later, I entered my apartment with a happy sigh. After setting the plastic bag down for a moment, I slid the backpack off and removed my hiking boots. "Honey, I'm home."

Silence.

I peeked in the kitchen, hoping the metal Moka pot sat on the stove, filled with espresso and ready to brew, but alas, my dreams of coffee went unfulfilled. Stomach grumbling, I peered in the fridge, but it was basically empty save for a troubling number of half-full pickle jars.

Sadly, I'd already polished off the Japanese potato salad that Sachie's mom, Reina, had sent over. Despite it being one of my bestie's favorite dishes, she "refused to succumb to creamy blackmail." I'd nobly consumed it in the interests of preventing food waste, but damn, it would have hit the spot.

I'd hoped that in the wake of Sachie's dad's heart attack, she'd resolve her argument with her parents about joining the Spook Squad, but the opposite happened. The health scare freaked Ben and Reina out, their fears of mortality manifesting as an overwhelming desire to protect their only child. Sach was understandably trying to help them out and keep an eye on her dad, but she always returned from the visits depleted and angry.

I was trying not to take sides, but they were treating Sach like a toddler about to run into oncoming traffic, and I felt for my friend.

I texted her that I was safe and home, wondering if she was out with Detective Olivier Desmond. The two of them were spending a lot of time together, which was wonderful. I wasn't jealous in the least. I was simply hungry and tired and would appreciate her making time for grocery shopping since she'd been in a reality with supermarkets and I'd been in a barren desert hellscape with the Great Bone Wall of Emo-ness.

When I didn't immediately get a reply, I decided that

the first order of business was peeing, then caffeine and any meal I could cobble together, and finally a shower.

I'd stowed the maggot in the bag of water in my room, emptied my bladder, and was walking back to the kitchen when I was tackled from above. I hit the ground with an "oomph," one arm pinned above my head. I swung my other arm backward and grabbed my attacker's hair, pulling hard.

The second their weight shifted, I threw them off enough to awkwardly roll out from under them.

Sachie jumped to her feet before I did, grabbed me in a headlock, and choked me out.

Wheezing, I slammed the palm of my fist backward into her nose, twisting her away and reversing our positions. "You like that?"

She stabbed me in the stomach, blood trickling from one nostril. "Die, infernal!"

I experienced a bright moment of panic until the realization that the blade was a prop knife whose blade had retracted on contact sunk in. Adrenaline thrummed uselessly though me. "Was that really necessary?"

"Yes, seeing as I'm trying to keep you alive." She tipped her head back, stanching the trickle of blood. "But you persist in remaining human when you're in mortal danger."

I spun on my heel and headed for the kitchen. "I *am* human. What I am not is in mortal danger from a plastic toy."

She followed right behind me, still plugging her nose. "You know what I mean."

"Sach, I can't armor up every time I come under attack."

"Why not?" She grabbed a rag from under the sink, wet it, and wiped off her nose.

I'd taken almost thirty years scared to tell her I was a

half shedim in case she recoiled in disgust or was furious that I'd hidden this from her, and I'd lose her. Instead, she'd leaned right into it as a means of self-defense. Of all the possible reactions, I hadn't seen this one coming—or how annoying she'd be, attacking me at all hours of the day and night (yes, even from a deep sleep) in her effort to have me deploy my shedim scales at the least provocation to stay safe.

"Because I enjoy walking down the street without someone trying to exorcize me between the grocery store and home." It was like trying to explain drowning to someone who'd never seen water—this bone-deep knowledge of what happens when you're different.

"Better outed than dead! It's a miracle you've survived this long. Especially with You Know Who always attacking you." She scooted around me to block me from the cupboard with the vacuum-sealed espresso tin.

I glared at her. "Right. No training or experience about it. Just divine intervention again and again. And Delacroix isn't Voldemort. Saying his name doesn't make him any more or less dangerous." I'd shared the truth of my demon daddy with her about a week after dropping my half-shedim form on her. Luckily, our apartment was warded against him.

She had the good grace to look sheepish. And better still, fill the Moka pot for me. "All I'm saying is that if I had this at my disposal, I'd use it and you should too."

I sat down at the table. "Can we have this discussion for the gazillionth time after I've eaten?"

Sachie flicked on the burner. "Pizza should be here any minute."

"Hawaiian?"

"Yes. I ordered your disgusting pineapple." She sponged the few bloody drops off her shirt.

"Wait. How'd you know I was on my way back?"

"Ezra texted me."

I smiled sappily. He'd been inundated by his employees and still took the time to make sure I was safe.

"Quit it." She tossed the damp rag in the sink, where it landed with a splat.

"Like I haven't seen that look on your face a time or two recently." My stomach grumbled again, but as if on cue, the intercom sounded.

Sachie went to get the pizza while I enjoyed the quiet hum of the kitchen and waited for the Moka pot to steam. She returned with two boxes while I was pouring myself a strong shot of espresso. She'd ordered from our favorite thin-crust place, and I shoveled three pieces in in rapid succession.

Only then did I have the energy to retrieve the maggot from my room and set the bag on the table between us.

Sach stared deadpan at the thrashing creature. "Our lease doesn't allow exotic pets."

"Oh damn. And here I had a sparkly collar picked out for it and everything." I checked that the bag wasn't leaking water. "It's not a pet. Out of curiosity, how long were you perched up in the corner of the ceiling like a gecko, waiting to attack me?"

My friend raked a lock of pink hair out of her eyes. "No time at all, but for the record, I prefer spider."

"I prefer you not be a giant weirdo who scales our walls."

"Aww. You're welcome." She flicked her finger against the bag.

The maggot freaked out, bashing against the sides of its plastic prison so hard that it rolled the bag a good foot closer to the edge of the table.

I moved it back into the center and filled Sach in on my adventures. When I got to the part about this maggot being the most recent supplicant's name, Sach grimaced but looked up full moons on her phone.

"There's one on Tuesday," she said.

"Then my social calendar for that night is set." I stood up and, yawning, reached for the dirty plates.

Sach was already dumping the coffee grounds in our counter composter. "I got this. Go sleep."

"Thanks."

My shower's hot water eased my tense muscles. I threw on the crimson sweater I slept in more often than not, and fell into a deep sleep, dozing on and off all through Sunday as well.

Monday morning, bright-eyed and bushy-tailed, I cornered Michael in the kitchen at Maccabee HQ, smirking as a level one operative insisted the director take the last apple turnover, then left looking crestfallen.

"Silly child," I said. "He hasn't learned that when it comes to food, it's every Maccabee for themselves."

"Mmm." Michael swallowed her bite of pastry and grinned. "But it always works out in my favor."

This playful side of my mother was new to me. I wouldn't say our relationship was suddenly perfect, but we were learning to trust each other, and there'd been more laughter than arguing in the past month.

Looking around, even though it was obvious that the closest operatives were a good twenty feet away from the open-concept kitchen, plus they were working with their headphones on, I leaned on the counter and lowered my voice. "Impressed that I didn't miss work?"

Michael and I had made an agreement about me taking time off to go into the Brink and find the fortress. She hated the prospect of vampires having babies as much as I did, and certainly didn't want that news getting out. Not on top of the low morale among the operatives over the corrupted magic in our rings.

I'd been certain that the Authority Council would make up some excuse for why we'd been banned from using the magic cocktail in our rings, or worse, not say anything at all.

However, in an astonishing move of transparency, the Authority had come clean about how when the cocktail was created in the 1600s, a shedim attack corrupted the foundational strain that allowed the five types of Eishei Kodesh magic to work in combination and destroy demons.

Using the magic in our rings didn't kill them, like we believed. Instead, it transported them to demon-created and -operated prisons that were disguised as love locks. The shedim jailers moved these padlocks around like batteries, leaching evil into the world and contributing to some of the worst events in history, both human-made and naturally occurring.

Apparently, there'd been a heated debate among the members of the Authority about whether to order the magic cocktail drained out of our rings, but they'd voted in favor of leaving it. Yes, it sent shedim into prisons that other demons could use to sow evil, but when facing a demon attacker, it was still a human operative's only chance of survival.

That said, we were no longer allowed to actively hunt shedim—that was left to vamp operatives whose innate magic let them truly kill demons.

While we discovered all this only last month, the Authority wasted no time putting their best and brightest on creating a magic formula that worked as we intended.

It wasn't even like the majority of Maccabees faced down shedim, and certainly not on a regular basis, but learning we'd been played by demons for hundreds of years had been a gut punch.

One more reason why this January sucked. And why Michael had me keep mum about going into the Brink.

I accompanied Michael to her office and was showing her a picture of the maggot when her guard dog—I mean, assistant, Louis—threw himself inside the room, his back pressed against the door. "Chief Constable Davis is on the war—"

The door was pushed wide, knocking Louis forward.

Keira Davis was the first female chief constable of the Vancouver Trad police force, running a tight ship with the same lack of patience for bullshit and corruption as Michael. With so much in common, it was surprising I'd never heard about my director interacting with the chief constable before.

The redhead had steel in her green eyes, striding forward with a purpose that dynamite would hesitate to interrupt.

Michael's expression hardened. "Thank you, Louis."

He bolted.

I rose out of my seat, but the director made a short sharp cutting motion in the air, and I dropped back down.

"I'm in a meeting," Michael said coolly. "You love your proper channels. Use them."

The chief constable saw me for the first time and stopped. I said hello, totally not expecting the broad smile she trained on me which was as vibrant as her purple and black heels. The ones I'd coveted forever at my favorite shoe store but couldn't afford. "Operative Fleischer. It's a pleasure to see you again."

"Should I leave so you can speak in private?" I once more half rose.

"You may stay." The chief constable took the chair to my right. "I understand you're a level three now. Congratulations."

I wasn't surprised that the commander of the Vancouver Trad police force was aware of me and I expected that Michael kept tabs on those officers as well.

My mother uncapped a small bottle of screen cleaner and sprayed liquid onto a soft cloth. "What's this about?"

"Sorry, quick question first, Chief Constable." I slid my phone in my suit jacket pocket. "When have we met before? I'm afraid I don't remember that."

"You wouldn't." She shot an almost sly look at my mother. "Seeing as you were a toddler the last time your mother and I spoke socially."

"We have more important things to discuss than a walk down memory lane," Michael said. "Like you getting to the point."

"I'd forgotten how much you suck at small talk."

"And I forgot how much you drag it out when it's entirely irrelevant to the situation at hand."

I covertly pinched myself to make sure I was awake, and this wasn't some fucking fantastic dream. "Chief Constable—"

"Call me Keira."

Uncertain about whether that was appropriate, I glanced at Michael. Her tight expression confirmed any qualms I had about taking the chief constable up on her offer.

That said... Sure, my mother and I were in a good place, but come on. Whatever was going on here was gold, and I was a prospector with a shovel and a get-rich attitude.

"Thanks, Keira," I said brightly.

Michael wiped her monitor screen with unnecessary violence. "Get on with it."

"You dumped a bullshit case on us." Chief Constable Davis wagged a finger at my director. "Bad form."

The bladed edge to her smile was immediately reflected back. "That's quite the accusation."

Front row viewing to a shark fight. Where was popcorn when you needed it?

"Cases are assigned according to the legal division of which community the perp is most likely to belong to," Michael said. She recapped the cleaning solution and placed the supplies in her desk drawer. "Tell me the vic's name and we can discuss why you feel this way."

"Chandra Nichols."

This was the matchmaker who'd released shedim from their lock prisons to sell to Eishei Kodesh criminals. I'd been questioning her when she was murdered and barely survived her shedim killer myself, but I hadn't reported witnessing that or even phoned in the death.

Certain members of the Authority at the time were looking to crucify me for my personal relationship with Ezra. They'd charged his best friend, Silas, on a bogus corruption allegation (I'd helped jailbreak him), and Silas had found Chandra for me.

Everything connected to Chandra Nichols was a giant spiderweb, albeit one that was stuffed in a high corner that no one had to look at. But now Keira had grabbed hold of a sticky strand and the whole thing could come tumbling down, secrets, dead corpses, and all.

I choked on my imaginary popcorn.

Chapter 6

Michael reached for her executive pen holder, and I held my breath. She bypassed her Montblanc, so she didn't consider this meeting super serious, but she also skipped over the ballpoint, which would have indicated (to me) that this conversation wasn't worth her time. She selected a rollerball pen that wasn't super expensive yet wasn't exactly cheap either. It was a solid pen designed for when you had work to really tackle.

That wasn't reassuring.

"Ms. Nichols was killed with a gun, not magic," Michael said.

"Eishei Kodesh can use guns too," Keira retorted.

We could; we just didn't tend to. When my people flexed, they did so with magic.

"That lent itself to a non-magic perp," my mother continued, "and put the file in your purview. I didn't 'dump anything' as you so melodramatically put it."

The general public weren't told about demons so as not to incite mass panic, but Trad cops were briefed. Maccabees couldn't force them to believe in the existence of those supernatural beings, since unlike vampires, most people went their entire lives without seeing a demon, however those officers were out there protecting humanity, and for about the last hundred years or so, we'd shared knowledge of that evil with them.

That said, there was a big difference between telling them that and them ever concluding that the suspect in a crime with no evidence of magic was a shedim. Michael had expected Trad officers to pronounce Chandra's death a cold case and be buried in some basement filing cabinet.

So much for that. At least Detective Olivier Desmond hadn't been one of the Trad officers investigating. I would have felt like an utter shit facing my friend, especially now that he was often over at my place visiting his new girlfriend, Sachie.

"This was never a workplace burglary gone wrong," Keira said. "Employment agencies don't have cash or anything valuable on their premises, and Nichols was Eishei Kodesh, yet you didn't fight jurisdiction at all."

"I no longer waste my time when non-magical weapons are involved." Michael grabbed a legal pad. "You have a high solve rate."

Keira crossed her arms. "Don't blow smoke up my ass, Mickey."

I choke-coughed. *Mickey?* Director Michael Hannah Fleischer had been called many things, but never anything as pedestrian as a nickname.

My mother glared at her…nope, not enough facts to supply an object of this sentence.

"What turned your suspicions to the magic community?" I interjected, my stomach aching.

I'd used the magic cocktail in my ring to destroy the shedim who'd killed Chandra. Little did I know at the time that all I'd done was send him into a demon lock prison.

I clenched my hands into fists.

Maccabees didn't have the locations of these locks, so it

wasn't as if we could use our rings to trap shedim and then hoard their prison cells until we had a way to destroy them. Nor could we differentiate the lock prisons from regular love locks.

We weren't sitting around with our thumbs up our asses though. The Authority stationed operatives around the globe to monitor places with the highest concentration of love locks. While we didn't want to give the demons a heads-up that we were onto them, at the slightest sign these prisons were being moved, or there was any unusual activity, we'd swoop in and take them.

It was the best we could do right now.

I unclenched my fists.

"We decoded an encrypted file on Chandra's laptop," Keira said. "Partially decoded. We got one name off it, then malware kicked in, corrupting the whole computer. Jasmine Bakshi."

I shivered, hearing that particular name coming out of a Trad cop's mouth, and wished for an umbrella for the shit about to rain down on me.

Michael quickly typed something in and peered at her monitor. "Ms. Bakshi had been arrested in a drug bust by the time of Ms. Nichols's death. As I'm sure you've verified."

Keira turned to me with an expression of mild curiosity. "Aviva, you worked that case."

My stomach dropped into my toes. No wonder she let me stay.

"You didn't find a single connection to Chandra Nichols while you were investigating the drug bust?"

"Sorry, no." I kept my breathing steady and my expression pleasantly bland, but I was a knot of tension waiting for Keira to drop her intel that I'd interviewed Chandra about the Bakshi case.

Michael cleared her throat, turning the chief constable's focus from me. "I'd never heard of Chandra Nichols or known anything about her until after her death."

That was true—and even disturbing in its own way. The matchmaker had managed to conduct these heinous acts of freeing demons and hooking them up with criminals right under our noses.

Keira pulled a thumb drive out of her pocket and dropped it on Michael's desk. "Consider this my official transfer of Chandra Nichols's murder investigation to the Maccabees."

Investigations did get switched between Trads and Eishei Kodesh when evidence warranted it. A muscle twitched in Michael's jaw, but she nodded.

"There is one other thing," the chief constable said, almost like an afterthought. "Roger Henderson."

Michael arched an eyebrow. "Jared Casey's head of security?"

The federal politician had pushed for anti–Eishei Kodesh legislation for some time. Casey's alt-right party was fringe enough that he'd never had any real power, but after a recent bank robbery gone wrong in Toronto where a teller was killed, his ideas lit a spark under some people.

It didn't matter that it was a knife, not magic, that ended the poor man's life, the murderer was Eishei Kodesh. Once that whole "real humans don't need magic" slogan went viral, Casey's proposed legislation gained a groundswell of support.

Sentiment between the two communities had grown tense across the country, but Vancouver was Casey's electoral district and it was especially ugly here. Both Maccabee and Trad cops had been called out on a regular basis to break up fights.

"Mr. Henderson isn't Eishei Kodesh if he works for Casey," I said.

"No, he's Trad like his brother, Brian. Chandra's employee," Keira said.

"The receptionist," I murmured.

The other two woman looked at me—Keira bemused and my mother in warning.

"It was reported her male receptionist was also killed," I said. "I assume that's Brian, but even if you suspect Roger went after Chandra and accidentally killed his own brother, that's still a Trad problem."

Keira crossed her legs, and even feeling anxious and slightly nauseous I couldn't help staring at those fabulous shoes of hers. "Remember the artifact thefts from the *Supernatural: Debunked* exhibit a while back?" she said.

Considering I had one of the stolen items in my possession, you could say I remembered it. None of them possessed Eishei Kodesh magic, but Sire's Spark was a shedim artifact allowing anyone with demon blood to find other things with demon magic, including half shedim. No one knew that and we were keeping it that way.

Michael and I both nodded.

"Roger Henderson runs a security company," Keira said. "He was responsible for transporting the items from their original owners to the Trad gallery for the exhibit."

"The theft happened at the gallery the night before the exhibit was set to open," Michael said. "That means it was long after he'd delivered them and not on his watch. It also doesn't tie him to Nichols beyond a family member who worked for her."

"Unless he was Nichols's inside man on the gallery theft?" Keira said.

My heart sank. Oh no. She looked like a dog with a bone.

"What if he helped steal artifacts for Nichols to sell to Eishei Kodesh on the black market? Jasmine Bakshi could have been a potential customer. After all, Sire's Spark, which is still missing, was rumored to be the strongest of all the ones originally stolen." Keira ticked items off her fingers as she spoke. "There's also the question of why George Green, the Trad thief who stole them, was killed? And why has a known collector of supernatural artifacts gone missing and is presumed dead?"

I could answer all those questions. The collector killed George Green, mistaking him for a man on my informant Rukhsana Gill's crew with the same name. This collector then attacked her, looking for the artifacts. Jordy said Rukhsana "dealt with" the collector, so knowing Rukhsana, she murdered the dude, but she had nothing to do with Chandra's death or the thefts.

My mother, meantime, stole the artifacts from the fence they'd been taken to and made an anonymous tip to the Trad cops about where to find all of them except the Sire's Spark crystal, which she'd locked in her safe.

I then made a dummy copy and switched out the real one for mine.

"You always did have such a powerful imagination," Michael said.

Except that truth was much stranger than fiction.

Keira furrowed her brow. "If it wasn't that, then why did Chandra have Jasmine's name in an encrypted file? The alternative is that the Maccabees missed Nichols's role in illegal drug production. Aviva? Could that be possible?"

"I didn't miss anything," I said evenly, cursing her out in my head.

"Do you have any evidence tying Chandra Nichols to that theft?" Michael said. "Or Roger to Chandra?"

"Phone records with multiple calls over the past year between Chandra and Roger," Keira said. "It's circumstantial, I know."

Michael danced her pen over her knuckles. "It's barely even that."

Unless he was transporting the released demon prisoners to their new, equally jail-like working conditions for shady Eishei Kodesh, like with Bratwurst Demon and Jasmine Bakshi.

Keira's instincts were sound, but Michael was also correct that this was super circumstantial.

"What did Mr. Henderson say?" I asked.

"We haven't asked him yet. One of my detectives was supposed to question him tonight, but…" The chief constable flashed an innocent smile. "It's a Maccabee case now."

I frowned. "Tonight is Jared Casey's big fundraiser."

There was an Eishei Kodesh counterprotest scheduled nearby with operatives on duty to keep the peace.

Keira slapped a ticket on top of the thumb drive. "The fundraiser is the perfect time to question Henderson for a couple minutes, seeing as he'll be distracted with a million little details. It's unlikely that a man in his position would risk that for whatever got Nichols shot, but due diligence must be exercised."

"Who's spewing bullshit now, Kiki?" Michael practically growled.

Kiki? My eyes bugged out of my head.

Michael flicked the ticket back at Keira with the tip of her pen. "Casey is buddy-buddy with the mayor. How fortuitous for you that if we do find something to pin on Henderson and shit hits the fan, it'll be the Maccabees and not the Trads in the thick of it. Since you're up for reappointment."

"I'm sacrificing the glory of solving the case for the greater needs of the city," Keira said with equally terrifying amiability. She returned the ticket to the top of the thumb drive. "Besides, Mickey, we both know how much you love a good subterfuge."

I white-knuckled my armrests.

Director Michael Hannah Fleischer had built her professional reputation on rooting out corruption and being scrupulously aboveboard. Okay, yes, she'd obfuscated a few things in the new very unchartered waters where we swam, but never at the expense of harming her beloved Eishei Kodesh community or Vancouver at large. She placed the well-being of the people above all else.

Ask me how I knew.

She was going to eviscerate the head of the Trad police force. I eyed the door.

Michael got a sly grin that made me blink. "Like with the Cameron case."

Keira barked a laugh. "That wig."

Michael cackled evilly. "The homemade catapult."

"No! Fuck you. I'd repressed that." Keira shuddered.

Tally up the new body count, people, because we were about to have another corpse on our hands in approximately five seconds when I died of curiosity.

I guess I shifted in my seat, or my "What the holy hell" wasn't in my head, because the two women snapped back into their professional faces.

"Fatal gunshot or not, I truly believe it wasn't a Trad who killed Chandra," Keira said. "She deserves justice."

She'd gotten vengeance when I killed her attacker.

Thought I'd killed her attacker.

Fine. Imprisoned him in a lock cell.

Did that count?

"She does," Michael said, "and we'll get it for her."

There was another few moments of logistical conversation about the handover, then the chief constable wished us good luck and left.

"What's really the plan?" I said when the door closed behind her.

Michael sat back in her chair, her fingers steepled. "I want to know beyond a shadow of a doubt whether the demon who murdered Chandra was the one she worked with to break the wards on those locks and free the shedim prisoners, or one she worked against."

I narrowed my eyes. "That's not all you want."

"The Authority believes Chandra told us about the magic in our rings. They've been resisting my demands that we track down other matchmakers because it suited them to believe that she was killed by a Trad with a gun and all further matchmaking was finished." She unfurled a cold smile. "Now Trads officers know that Chandra was up to something even if they don't have the details. Her actions can't be swept under the rug."

"Thanks to the chief constable we have leave to find the other matchmakers without anyone on the Authority being able to kibosh it." I almost gave a fist pump because this was a hell of a second case at my new promoted level.

Cherry purred in contentment that I was the best and only person to connect all the threads in record time.

"Exactly," Michael said. "Did she have partners and were any of them culpable in her death?"

"What happens when I conclude she was killed by a demon? One who I sent to a prison lock believing I'd destroyed him?"

Michael smirked. "Who said you'd be on this case?"

I shot my hand into the air. "Operative Fleischer volunteering for lead Maccabee on this, Director."

She made a tsking sound. "That's where I went wrong. I should have trained you to call me Director instead of Mom. Your teen years would have been so much easier."

"Or we'd be like Sachie, Ben, and Reina, reduced to potato salad bribes. And you don't even cook."

"I do, however, excel at takeout."

I crossed my arms.

"Yes, Aviva, you can have this investigation."

No kidding, since I was the only one with the complete backstory.

She winked at me. "To answer your question, if there were other matchmakers involved, they'll be prosecuted. As for the shedim himself, it depends on who we're dealing with."

"What happens if I conclude that it was one of the shedim who owned the locks and belonged to the group who corrupted the magic in our rings way back when? They'll get away with her death, won't they?"

"For now." Michael clicked her pen with a decisiveness more suited to starting the engine when an ax-wielding clown was chasing you. "But as soon as we've restored the magic cocktail to destroy shedim, the Authority will devote the lion's share of our resources and operatives to finding every demon involved. However, if Chandra's shedim partner murdered her, I'll send the vamps in the Spook Squad after that demon."

I looked around the director's office with its sound-proofed walls, and still lowered my voice. "If it ever gets out that we've known all along what happened to her…" I made a slashing line across my neck.

"You saved yourself from the shedim assassin," Michael said firmly. "We didn't tell the Authority at the time because there were too many other problems you had to overcome with Dmitri and his sycophants, yet we can't retroactively admit to what happened. I want this wrapped up once and for all." She wrote Chandra's name on her legal pad and circled it. "Nichols's murder isn't the Trad cold case I'd intended? All right. We control the narrative now."

I drummed my fingers on the armrest. "Chandra had nothing to do with the stolen debunked artifacts and I doubt Roger was involved with her death, but if he isn't totally innocent of wrongdoing, maybe those phone records are enough to make him pass me up the food chain." I made a big show of cracking my knuckles. "Leave it with me. I'll break Henderson."

"Absolutely not. This is just a friendly chat. To that end, meet Roger on your own, so we don't start off with an escalation." She passed me the thumb drive and fundraiser ticket. "Just remember, these people may not have magic, but they're either fanatics or opportunists. This is enemy territory."

I stood up, putting both items in my purse. "Don't underestimate them. I know."

"I meant stay safe."

I almost dropped my bag. Michael's open show of concern slid inside me with the warmth of stepping into a patch of sunshine on a lazy Sunday afternoon. Had I missed the other times the corners of her eyes tightened with worry or was this the first time she allowed herself to show it? Either way, it was…nice. "I will."

"Then scram. I can feel Louis hyperventilating outside the door, poor guy. He breaks out in hives when I'm late for my appointments."

I cracked my knuckles again. "I can take care of him too," I said hopefully.

My mother shot me a mock stern look. "Goodbye, Aviva."

I heaved a sigh. "You never let me have any fun."

Chapter 7

Had I not known the location of Jared Casey's fundraiser at Shaughnessy Manor, a historic mansion named after the old and very prestigious area in which it was located, I could have found it by sound alone.

The counterprotest in the park across the street led by pissed-off Eishei Kodesh could be heard for blocks. Bet the neighbors loved that. The right-wing Trad supporters inside the manor who'd paid $2000 a ticket (before any donations) to be at Jared's event tonight no doubt loved it even more.

Most of the Eishei Kodesh protesters (and "allies!" as one sign proudly noted) were congregated under trees and across the broad expanse of grass, but others thronged on the sidewalks and road, despite Maccabee operatives herding them back into the park with the patience of sheepdogs nudging their flock into compliance.

It was an exceptionally cold evening, especially by Vancouver standards, and everyone was bundled up in warm clothing.

The speaker at the podium decried Casey's horrendous proposed legislation in front of a cluster of Eishei Kodesh with flushed faces and raised fists. When they booed, their breaths formed white puffs in the air.

I shouldered through them and barely avoided being coshed by an overeager journalist's camera.

The mood was poised on a knife's edge of violence, as sharp and crackling as the frost lacing the ground and crunching underfoot.

Unlike the Maccabees on crowd control, the non-magic officers tasked with keeping peace had shown up in riot gear, including shields. Given my city's tendency to riot over hockey games, that decision wasn't unwise.

I continued down the road, past large properties hidden by tall hedges. They stood like handmaidens lined up in service to the massive estate anchoring the far end of the residential street.

Two men in black suits at the chunky stone fence provided the first line of defense. Their expressions were blank masks, their mirrored sunglasses adding a menacing vibe to their presence. More would be patrolling the grounds.

Let's be honest, the guns in their belt holsters did some heavy lifting as well. I hoped whichever of Natán's vamps was no doubt following me got shot. It wouldn't kill them, but it would still hurt before they expelled the bullet. No, wait. Let them be stampeded by the protesters. Really prolong the pain.

I didn't identify myself as a Maccabee when I presented my ticket to be scanned. Amateurs. Like a barcode couldn't be faked. True, biometric security would have been more expensive, but given the raucous protests nearby, it also would have been the better option.

My presence was verified, and the men stood aside to let me up the driveway.

Even in January, the grounds of Shaughnessy Manor were well-kept, with stately copses of trees and a winter-blooming garden. The wide driveway curved around a fountain to a shallow set of marble stairs, which led up to a broad front terrace set with imposing pillars. Graceful arched windows lined the first floor of the main wing, with quaint stone flower boxes affixed under the glass panes on the upper levels.

A bunch of chauffeurs stood chatting near the fleet of expensive cars parked to one side in a makeshift lot.

I strode briskly up the stairs, waving at the pair of muscle-bound men flanking the front door. My gold ring glinted in the light.

The blond guard narrowed his eyes. "Maccabees aren't allowed entry."

Finally, some eagle-eyed security bro was on his game.

"Operative Aviva Fleischer. I'm here to speak with Mr. Henderson."

"He's busy." The guard crossed his arms, bulging his biceps.

I was cold, this visit was a longshot, and my patience for his posturing was less than zero. I jammed my hands in my pants pockets and rocked back on my heels. "Lots of journalists out and about tonight. It would be a shame if any of them saw me being treated poorly or manhandled. What a PR fiasco. All I want is two minutes for a friendly chat, but you know the media." I laughed. "Always putting their own spin on things."

The guard tapped his Bluetooth.

I smirked.

While he called Henderson to the front door, his partner ran a metal detector wand over me.

I spread my arms wide. "That doesn't check for magic."

"We know where to find you," he said.

"You also know with total certainty that there aren't more of us inside?" I motioned from my face to his. "Newsflash. We look just like you."

"Anyone moves wrong, and we'll take them down before they know what's hit them." The guard sounded like he was hoping someone bust out their magic so he could wrestle them into submission with nothing but his bare hands and his hard-on.

This wasn't unexpected from a member of a high-profile security detail, but he sounded a little too certain about his odds. I slid into my synesthete vision, expecting a rapid blue dot of excitement over his heart, but he was a blank slate. Either this guy was really reaping the benefits of his stoicism journal and pre-dawn cold plunges or—no, there it was.

All the guards were wearing very rare, very expensive shielding devices.

Magic-shielding devices. Their protection didn't extend to a Red Flame touching and torching them, but the units blocked all psychological attacks on their person from Eishei Kodesh or vamps.

Their boss, Roger Henderson, had just gotten a lot more interesting.

"Operative Fleischer." A lean man in his late thirties with nondescript brown hair buzzed almost to his scalp, a military-straight bearing, and eyes that had seen far too much for his age, strode out of the manor. "What's this about?"

Diving into Henderson's past had revealed a stellar army career with no financial abnormalities, contentious relationships, or children. He was the picture of respectability.

"Just a quick chat about a case I'm hoping you can help with." I flashed him my most non-threatening smile.

He glanced back toward the protest. "I can give you five minutes."

"I appreciate it."

He led me through a stately wood-paneled foyer lined

with black-and-white photos of garden parties at the manor from bygone eras. "I've got a temporary office upstairs we can speak in."

Music and a buzz of conversation drifted into the empty corridor through the glass doors leading to the packed ballroom. Stylistic exterior details like the symmetrical placement of windows and Greek columns were echoed in this large room painted in shades of cream and peach.

I gave the crowd inside a cursory glance. How many of these civilized conversations held by people in elegant formalwear were as hate-fueled as the chanting outside?

The crowd shifted revealing a woman in an emerald silk dress, wineglass in hand, listening politely to her group. Her inch-long brown hair was on the shocking side of hairdos for this crowd, but less so than if she'd shown up with her skull snake tattoo popping against her brown skin.

Rukhsana Gill, chop shop owner and an informant of mine, was the last person I expected to see here, despite her having her fingers in all kinds of pies and traveling in many different social circles. Especially since I was positive she was Eishei Kodesh—though I'd never seen any sign of her magic.

As if feeling my gaze, she lifted her eyes to mine. My bafflement must have shown, because she gave a small, amused half smile before returning her attention to her party.

Roger and I continued up an expansive circular staircase, our footfalls muffled by the plush stair runner.

A roar from the park reached us through the windows, thin and old as they were.

Roger shook his head. "Tough times in our city."

"A lot of detractors out there," I said.

"Free speech is a wonderful part of our democracy." Roger brushed a hand over the smooth railing then checked his palm for dust. "We're happy to let Eishei Kodesh have their say."

"You took extra precautions though," I said. "Did Mr. Casey approve those shielding devices?"

"Jared has larger public appearances scheduled the deeper we get into this campaign," Roger replied. "He stands by his beliefs but also cares deeply about keeping his people safe while he shares his values."

"Keeping them safe using *magic* devices. Ones that are small, discreet, and probably unnoticed by any of his base tonight." I hit the top landing. "As opposed to venues whose nulling magic is a matter of public record."

"As the person in charge of his security, I didn't see any reason to switch our fundraiser from this grand old home just because the venue doesn't have nulling magic."

Roger wasn't stupid or naïve. Holding the event here was a calculated move to show Jared's strength. His guards were (secretly) protected from magic attacks, and any Eishei Kodesh who acted out would be swiftly dealt with—and fed into Casey's narrative of how dangerous magic was.

My escort turned down a narrow corridor lined with plain wooden doors instead of the fine craftsmanship found on the lower level. His office was a glorified storage closet, the desk crammed into it overflowing with files, half-rolled blueprints of the grounds, and his laptop. He sat on the edge of his desk.

There was no chair for visitors so I stood. "Chandra Nichols."

"My brother worked for her." Roger spoke with the careful detachment of someone holding grief at bay.

Wind howled outside, rattling the glass in the panes.

"We have her phone records," I said. "You two spoke on multiple occasions."

"Sure. Chandra was looking for advice about her home security system. Brian had hoped to score points with his boss." Roger's lips quirked into a half smile and he shook his head fondly. "He asked me to help her out with tips and some names of reputable alarm companies."

I couldn't read Roger with my magic vision because of his shielding devices, but he didn't look concerned about my line of questioning. His explanation sounded plausible, and neither Brian nor Chandra were around to contradict him.

There was nothing more to this lead. I was about to thank him for his time when a raised voice boomed through the connecting wall.

"…I don't have the time or the crayons to explain your job to you, you total fucking donkey."

Roger practically sprinted through the door. "Jared, enough."

I followed him. I almost felt bad for Henderson, but he'd chosen to work for this douchebag.

Casey stood in a charming light blue sitting room next to a young man holding a clipboard whose expression was so blank it screamed of disassociation. "Gibson can take it." He actually flicked his staffer's sleeve. "Can't you, Gibson?"

"Yes, sir," the young man said in a monotone.

"Go downstairs and get a soda," Roger said, brushing off the staffer's protest that he was working. "It's okay. Go, Derek."

Kudos to the young man, he walked out with his head held high, though the audible grinding of his teeth indicated he was going to require a good dentist.

I stepped into the room.

"Who are you?" Casey said.

I waved—with my ring hand. "Operative Aviva Fleischer."

"What the fuck, Roger?" he growled, pouring himself a drink from the decanter on the round table beside him.

"I've got a ballroom full of supporters wanting to donate to my worthy cause. Get her out of here."

Legislating a group of individuals out of existence. So worthy.

"You have no authority over me." I bestowed a wolflike smile on him.

He blinked, a crafty gleam entering his narrowed gaze. "Is that a threat? From a member of the dangerous magic community? One of their police representatives no less?"

"Not at all. I care about all the citizens in my city. Well, maybe not the hate-mongering, self-serving ones, but I would never abuse my position and threaten them either."

Jared snorted and swirled his drink around. "You have balls."

"Real humans don't need balls," I snarked back. *I'm a trained Maccabee, a half shedim, and have dealt with far worse men than you. You're kiddie league, asshole.*

Damn skippy, Cherry cheered in my head.

Roger stepped between me and Jared, who was visibly bristling. "I'll walk Operative Fleischer out then get you downstairs to the podium."

"Good." Jared set his glass down decisively and straightened his maroon tie.

I turned toward the door and—

A window blew open, hitting the wall with a loud rattle.

Jared clutched his chest. Taking a labored breath, he sank into a chair.

The temperature in the room plummeted too swiftly for it to be attributed to the winter wind.

"Roger," I said sharply.

He ignored me, already on the phone with 911 and answering questions from the paramedics.

If keeping Vancouver safe meant keeping the politician safe, then I'd do whatever it took to make that happen.

I crouched down next to Jared. "May I check you for

heart attack symptoms using my magic? It will help the paramedics and get you the appropriate medical attention faster."

"Fuck off," he rasped.

"Paramedics are coming," Roger said. "They don't think it's a full-blown heart attack, but I have to get him aspirin. The first aid kit is in my office. Back in a second." He raced out of the room.

Jared looked like he was about to protest but his skin went ashen and he broke out in a cold sweat.

Normally, I would never have violated the politician's decision, but my fingertips were white and my breath was coming out in icy puffs.

I slipped into my synesthete vision.

There wasn't any indication of chest pain, nor was Jared's heart beating rapidly. The opposite, in fact. Then there were his veins, which presented as a bright blue map through his body, the blood inside appearing as darker navy ribbons that moved sluggishly.

It was as if an Orange Flame was freezing him from the inside out.

My eyes tingled from an overabundance of adrenaline, presaging turning toxic green.

Stand down, Cherry. Thankfully, she did.

Two new guards raced inside, followed by Roger with water and aspirin. He gave his boss the medication, then ordered the other men to stay with Jared while he met the paramedics. Roger motioned for me to accompany him. "I'm bringing the first responders in through the back. I trust you'll keep Jared's medical condition confidential."

"This was orange flame magic." I held out my still-cold, numb hands. "The Maccabees should investigate."

"I took every precaution against an Eishei Kodesh threat." Roger hurried down a back stairwell. "There were no trees or hiding places close enough to the manor for one to hide and attack and there's no magic that can open windows."

"An Orange Flame could expand or contract those old locks causing the window to open." Line of sight wasn't as important for an Orange Flame as a lack of barriers between them and their target. "There is a park full of people with an anti-Casey agenda just down the block. The Maccabees will be investigating, with or without your blessing."

He ushered me down a narrow hallway. "If word of Jared's heart condition gets out, I will rain hell down on your organization and you personally."

"It won't."

Roger opened the rear door, greeting the two paramedics. "Our business is done for tonight."

That's what he thought.

Chapter 8

I circled back around the house and snuck into the ballroom to suss out any other Eishei Kodesh or any suspicious behavior in the wake of the attack on Jared. My magic vision didn't reveal anyone in an amped-up state of excitement or dread.

However, plenty of guests groused their annoyance that Jared's speech had been held up, appeased by servers out in full force with champagne and appetizers.

"Fancy meeting you here, chère." Rukhsana Gill sidled up beside me.

"I could say the same. How did you get an invite?" Tickets weren't for sale to the general public, offered only to a highly curated list of potential donors.

"I like to know my enemies," Rukhsana said.

"So do I, but that's not an answer." Was she Trad after all?

"Is it not?" She shrugged in a very Gallic way. "How did you get an invitation? Unless level three status comes with a significant pay bump?"

"Hardly." I scanned the crowd for any other Eishei

Kodesh. There weren't any familiar faces, but if Rukhsana was here, who's to say that others weren't?

Like Chandra's fellow matchmakers?

Orange flame magic was the second-most common type after red, but the level of power and control deployed in Jared's attack narrowed the list. Provided that person's ability was on record somewhere. Or that they hadn't lied about their magic type like Maud had. Hers was so rare that it would have made her a target.

Even if Rukhsana had magic, I didn't suspect her or any of her crew for this fake assassination attempt. It wasn't her style. Blackmailing him for information, sure, but this felt like a warning. For Jared? For Roger?

But from whom?

"Much as it pains me to miss Jared's big speech, I'm heading out," I said to Rukhsana.

She bid me good-night and joined another group.

I beelined for my car, texting Michael that I was coming to see her and getting a reply that she was at home.

I'd barely parked out front of her building when someone popped up from my back seat.

I screamed.

A sour-smelling male vamp with stringy hair slithered into the passenger seat, smirking. "Thought I'd introduce my—"

Still screaming, I grabbed the stake I'd taken to keeping in my cup holder and shoved it through his heart.

His eyes widened, then the fucker ashed all over my car.

I pulled out my phone and fired a text to Ezra. *An asshole minion just gave me a heart attack.*

I was cleaning up my vehicle when a portal opened and Ezra stormed through.

"Were you hurt?" His silvery-blue eyes blazed. He inhaled deeply, scenting me for wounds.

"I'm fine." I kicked at the pile of ash. "He's seen better

days though." I described him. "Any idea who he was? Will he be sorely missed?"

"Hunter. Total shithead who hasn't advanced up the ranks in forty years."

"Love that I'm getting the C Team now."

"How did he know where to find you?"

"He hid in my car." I shivered. "That better have been his idea and not a fun new policy from Natán." I peered into the darkness. "You shouldn't be here."

"There aren't any more stalkers around," Ezra said.

"But there will be. What if one sees you in this mood? Your father will have a field day."

Ezra laughed bitterly. "That's what you're concerned about?"

"Yes, and you should be too. Besides which," I continued, "I was on Maccabee business and I'm at the home of the Maccabee director. It's entirely inappropriate for you to be here."

"I was a Maccabee."

"Before you incinerated that bridge to be Lord of the Copper Hell." He tensed and I gentled my voice. "Look, I get why you did it. You want answers about your mom's suicide. But the very real fact remains—"

He held up a hand, his expression in the moonlight as hard as granite. "Operative Fleischer doesn't want to be seen with me."

I unclenched my jaw. "I don't have the energy for this tonight. Can we discuss it at dinner?"

"Is there still going to be a dinner?" he said sarcastically. "It *is* in a public place."

I was tired, anxious, and upset about whatever the hell had just happened at the fundraiser, and I slammed my car door shut. "Not if you're going to act like a little bitch."

Yup, that was entirely the wrong thing to say, but he'd

vanished through the portal before I could tell him I was sorry.

Mostly sorry.

Whatever. He'd be there Wednesday or he wouldn't, but if we couldn't figure out how to navigate us existing in two very opposing camps, then any reconciliation was over before it began.

Even though I had keys to Mom's condo, I pressed the intercom button as a matter of courtesy to let her know I was here and stomped into the elevator.

Michael was waiting for me in her kitchen with the kettle on. "Rough night?"

"Jared was hit with orange flame magic, which Roger refused to believe, blaming his boss's shock on his heart condition. He wanted to shut down any Maccabee investigation of it. Does that count?"

"I'd say so." Michael got out the cannister of decaf English Breakfast. "What did Henderson say about Chandra?"

"He helped her find a good alarm company."

"Any chance that Chandra was attacked with magic before she was shot?"

"I don't know. I'd been examining her through my magic vision for signs of a lie and she spiked bright blue, but I attributed it to fear at seeing the assassin. The simplest explanation for tonight is that one of the protesters at the park got riled up."

"But given all of Mr. Henderson's nice and neat explanations, there's still a sliver of doubt." Michael glared at the kettle like it was the poor appliance's fault for this mess.

"There is." I grabbed the milk and honey for our tea. "I couldn't detain Roger for further questioning tonight but—"

"Roger Henderson is off-limits." She poured boiling water into the mugs with the tea bags. "Until we have irrefutable evidence either that an Eishei Kodesh attacked his boss or that Roger had illegal business dealings with Chandra."

We carried our tea over to her sofa.

"Give me a few operatives to work both angles," I said. "And ask Keira for the fundraiser guest list."

Michael reached for her phone on the coffee table and fired off a text. "Anything else?"

"My first order of business is to find another match-maker." I cradled my mug. "With all our intel, we had no idea any of them existed."

"If any others do."

"As weird as it sounds, I'm hoping she wasn't alone in her bad choices. If that racket died with Chandra, it'll be a lot harder to wrap up her murder investigation. Let's assume for now she had Eishei Kodesh partners. That speaks to resources, deep pockets to cover their tracks. People who travel in circles I don't usually have access to and who'll be able to close ranks even more should a Maccabee start poking around."

Michael sipped her tea. "You want to go undercover."

"Yeah. I'm not a known element to the magic highfliers here in town. I can switch up my look and travel unde-tected. Attend various Eishei Kodesh events where our suspects would hang out. But I want another operative with me who can watch my back. We'll meet in a secure site away from HQ."

"You clearly have someone in mind."

"Silas." I blurted out the name.

Incredibly, she didn't kibosh the idea outright. She ran her finger around the rim of her mug, her lips pursed. "Why him?"

"He's a vampire who's best friends with the Crimson Prince and had a public schism with the Maccabees for the past month." These facts were good for my case to bring the vamp on board, but saying them aloud hammered home that dating Ezra would be so bad for my career. I caught myself rubbing a hand over my heart and dropped it into my lap. "Since we're doing this investigation under the radar, his reputation might open doors for us that are otherwise closed. Plus, he's tech savvy enough to get information from all sorts of places."

Michael drummed her fingers against her mug. "You think he'd come back to the Maccabees after the bogus collusion charges?" Her expression hardened. "And everything he faced after that?"

"With the right incentive." A juicy case beat listlessly playing video games at the Copper Hell. "And a huge freaking apology," I added.

Silas had found Chandra for me in the first place. His skills were invaluable, and he had as much of an interest in putting a bow on this case as I did.

"Let me ask him," Michael said.

I raised an eyebrow at her.

"Nicely," she added.

"Michael." I practically growled her name.

"The Maccabees treated him badly." She paused. "*I* treated him badly. He's been nothing but exemplary, yet I allowed personal prejudice to cloud my thinking. I should have stood up for him. Fought tooth and nail to secure his release." She gave a one-shouldered shrug, shaking her head. "I'd like him to know that. To know that I intend to do better and make sure the other Maccabees do as well."

"Can we get the Authority on board?"

"I'll convince the ones who require convincing," she said blandly.

My eyes went wide. "You'll blackmail them?"

"Please, Aviva." Her chuckle did not convince me otherwise. "Come in early tomorrow to get your team up to speed, but for now, it's been a long night and—"

I crossed one leg over the other, jauntily swinging my foot. "Oh, I think it can go on a bit longer, *Mickey*."

My mother pinched the bridge of her nose. "I'd hoped you were leaving that alone."

"You hoped wrong." I grinned cheekily. "Sneak attack."

"You really are very annoying."

"Yup. And I'm your only child, so you have to stay on my good side for when you're old and infirm. What's the deal with you two?"

"Kiki—" She caught herself with a rueful smile. "Keira was my best friend and roommate. We met in university in a criminology class, and we drifted apart when you were little. Life happens."

Life happened or *I* happened? Michael had been terrified of anyone learning what I was, so it wasn't exactly a stretch to think that extended to her best friend. I'd been the same way. I frowned. Keira was my mom's Sachie. The version of our friendship where I never told my best friend the truth.

I wiped my damp palms on my pants. "Okay," I said simply. Losing Sach would devastate me; I'd take no joy in forcing my mother to relive her own loss.

Besides, I had Chandra's murder to investigate and, if Jared's attack tonight was connected, solve before our entire city went up in flames.

Chapter 9

Sach greeted me like a normal person when I got home, not perched in a corner like a ninja gecko, but rather on the sofa sharpening her large collection of knives. Hmm. Normal for her anyway. Though the gecko impersonation might have been the better option. "Hi, honey," she said. "How was your day?"

"I need a shower to wash off vampire ash and my encounter with Jared Casey." I'd run into Sach at work earlier and updated her on my new investigation.

She dragged a thin blade against a whetstone. "Sucks to be you."

"Your concern is touching." I rubbed my throbbing temples.

Sach chuckled.

"Well, in one piece of good news, I've been given leave to convince Silas to work with me."

"He'd come back?"

I held up my crossed fingers. "Here's hoping."

I WOKE up Tuesday morning to a steady stream of sirens, but also a reply from Silas saying he'd meet with me though he wasn't promising anything.

I hustled to have breakfast and tidy up because first I had to pop into Maccabee HQ and brief my team. I smiled. My. Team. That was never going to get old. Sadly, there was no cool uniform or jewelry to denote my higher rank, more's the pity.

My good mood plummeted on the drive over because sound clips of Jared's slimy, hateful speech from last night were all over the news with nary a report of the attack. His fanatical delusions shouldn't have been given any platform, instead of free airtime that lent weight and credence to them.

I wrenched the radio button off. I should have held the bastard in place, chanting encouragement for the Orange Flame to ice him into oblivion. Instead, he'd recovered from his "heart condition scare" enough to double down on his hateful rhetoric, intensifying the mistrust in the city between the magic and Trad communities.

A car almost clipped me—honking at me like I was at fault—and it wasn't an isolated incident. My entire drive to work was one long hostile stretch of road.

The ratcheted-up tension had seeped into HQ. After the hit our morale had taken due to the corrupted shedim magic in our rings, Casey's brimstone oration added to the pressure cooker of stress and unease.

I greeted a couple of level two operatives holding a serious, subdued conversation, and made my way to the kitchen on the third floor.

At least my involvement in uncovering the corrupt magic and the existence of those love lock prisons had been kept mum. The Authority took full credit for that.

"Good job, Fleischer," Gemma sneered, placing her coffee cup in the dishwasher.

What now? Nope. Didn't matter. I walked past her and grabbed a mug from the cupboard, shutting it with a forced patience. *Do not engage. Do not engage.* Gemma had risen to a new level of needling since I became a level three, and she remained a level two, not even working with her mentor of choice.

She grabbed two water bottles from the fridge. "You should have stopped Jared Casey from delivering his speech. That Orange Flame attack was the perfect opportunity to shut that asshole down and you blew it."

"His camp refuses to acknowledge there was any magic —" I almost dropped my mug. Operatives were gossipy but that info was on a need-to-know basis. "Wait, *you're* on my team?"

Talk about her not working with her mentor of choice.

"Do you have any concerns that I can't do the work?" Crunching plastic sounded with each of her water bottle biceps curls.

"No, you're a smart operative." She was, though it galled that I had to bite back "just a massive bitch." I turned my back on her to pour my coffee.

"We're in Conference Room B," she said in a voice devoid of any inflection.

"See you there." I didn't turn around until she left. What was Michael thinking?

Half an hour later it was clear that my director was thinking I needed reliable people who could take instructions and run with them. And yes, that included Gemma, along with Albert and a recently promoted level two called Fyodor.

I started from the top, starting with why the chief constable turned the Nichols murder case back over to us. While I still didn't disclose my presence at Chandra's death, I did explain that she gave the Authority the info about our corrupted magic and the existence of the prison cells. I explained about matchmakers, using my previous case with Bratwurst Demon and the drug lab bust to illustrate that.

"We're hunting for any other matchmakers in addition to Chandra's killer," I said.

"What about Henderson?" Gemma said.

"Michael's ordered us to stay away from him until we have proof. That's where you come in. Gather all CCTV footage from the protest last night and manor grounds. Get reports from all the operatives that were patrolling in the park, run down local Eishei Kodesh criminals with anti-Trad sentiments."

"This is just for the attack, right?" Fyodor said. "Match-makers would be smart enough to not have a rap sheet."

"It's mostly for the attack, but keep an open mind because a seemingly inconsequential detail can be the thing to break a case open."

He nodded, writing down my words.

Gemma made kissy lips. She was the worst.

"We can also look into Eishei Kodesh who donated to magic politicians with anti-Trad stances," Albert said.

I tore my thoughts from the list detailing all the ways that Gemma sucked. "Good thinking."

Next, I tasked Fyodor with booking plane tickets and an all-inclusive reservation in Punta Cana as my cover story while I went undercover. Since I couldn't show up to HQ in my new disguise, I proposed an encrypted channel to communicate with Gemma while I was in the field.

She looked up from her laptop with narrowed eyes.

"You're in charge here," I clarified. For all her faults—and they were legion—she was smart and extremely capable. I'm sure Albert and Fyodor were as well, but I didn't have time to vet them.

Gemma held her suspicious stare for a moment longer like she was being pranked then shrugged. "Got it."

Oh joy. Still, we set up our communications, with

Gemma saying she'd check in before end of day with their progress.

I left them to it and headed home to meet Silas.

To kill the last five minutes before his arrival, I scrolled to the end of the text chain that Maud and I had going. Ever since I'd admitted to being her sister, we'd corresponded in a steady stream of snarky memes, sibling shit talk, and checking in, with the occasional video chat. Our Brink adventure had been the first time we'd seen each other in person, and while it had its dangers, deadly situations was our schtick.

Annoying Junior: *Your city is making news in Hong Kong and not in a good way - you okay?*

Me: *Shiny Jimmy is a fond memory right now.* I wanted to tell her about working this case, but texts weren't secure, and she wasn't need-to-know.

Annoying Junior: *Good thing you have dinner with E. You need to get some!* She added a gif of a cheesy cartoon character flashing his thong at a woman posed seductively on a bed.

I sent back a gif of a woman's mouth with her biting down on her bottom lip, but I wasn't feeling very light-hearted after the way Ezra and I had left things.

Speak of the devil, a text from Ezra (via a very secure channel that Silas had set up for the two of us) showed up moments after Maud's.

Count von Cardoso: *Spoke to Silas this morning. Mazel tov. Exposing the matchmakers will take your career to new heights once you crack it.*

I overthought all the hidden meanings in his message and whether he was being snarky before deciding to take it at face value like a normal grown-up. *I appreciate the vote of confidence. I just wish the whole situation was a little less horrifying.* And potentially explosive for me, you, Silas, and Michael.

I'm sorry about the other night, I added.

Don't worry about it. You were stressed.

Yeah, but my stress didn't give me carte blanche to be mean to you.

The three dots appeared, disappeared, then appeared again. *Delacroix is still disappearing on mysterious errands.*

I tapped my thumb against my phone. Was he still hurt over my comments? He didn't seem to want to discuss it, though, so I went with the change in topic.

For former royalty who rarely left the safety of the megayacht other than for Brimstone Breakfast Club, my father had been away a lot. Ezra and I couldn't pinpoint a reason for it, but whatever it was, it didn't bode well.

Delacroix had allowed Ezra to use Gimli's forfeit to track down the power word necessary for the vampire procreation ritual, but he also knew that Maccabee magic imprisoned demons in jail cells disguised as love locks. His comings and goings could be related to either of those things. Or something else entirely. I had too much on my plate to worry about it. Much.

I fired back my reply. *It would be so sad if Delacroix never returned.*

That seemed to be the end of the exchange except a moment later Ezra added: *Reschedule if you need to.*

I ran my thumb over the message. When I'd sent Ezra a screenshot during a playful text exchange showing that I'd changed his name in my contacts to Count von Cardoso, he'd replied: *The von implies more undead and teeth than the average vamp. I am very scary.*

To which I'd quipped back: *Or 50% more marshmallowy treat.*

His indignance that he wasn't cereal made me laugh, but for all that the world saw him as the Crimson Prince or Lord of the Copper Hell—for all that I saw him that way—my ex had a gooey center. I grimaced. *Phrasing, Fleischer.* I'd bailed on him three times and yet he was big-hearted enough to not just congratulate me but let me put my career above him with no hard feelings.

It was just that, right? And not him having the same doubts as me? Maybe that was a good thing, though, because then we could talk this out.

But only if we met face-to-face.

This is important to me. I'll be there, come hell or high water.

He hearted the message less than a second after I hit send, and a knot in my chest unwound.

My intercom buzzed. I shoved my phone in my pocket and let Silas in.

The vampire was so jacked that my arms didn't close around him, but he was also a gentle giant who softly patted my back with the hand that wasn't holding a laptop.

"I'm glad you've come back." I motioned for him to take a seat.

"I think I am too?" He dropped into a dining room chair and opened his computer. "This isn't a long-term decision yet, but Michael's groveling was a good start."

"Will you be traveling back and forth from the Copper Hell?"

"Not exactly," he hedged, running a hand over his short dark copper hair.

I sat back with a grin. "Staying at a hotel, then. Perhaps a rustic Airbnb."

"There are hospital corners," Silas huffed. "On his guest bed."

"Guest bed."

He crossed his arms. "The only one I've seen."

"Beds aren't a necessary component of—"

Silas shook his head. "You and Ezra deserve each other."

"I'm sure you mean that in all the best ways," I said.

"His level of fastidiousness is…" Silas threw up his hands.

Ezra's? Oh no, not him. Hospital corners again. "Sach

and I have our suspicions that Darsh is part cat. You couldn't pay me to live with him."

"Look, besides the laundry situation, the fridge rules for where I can stash my synthetic blood, and the standards he lectured me about for using the shower, he's not that bad."

Okay, besotted boy. "Michael gave you the file?"

"Yes, and I read through it already." Silas was aware of the love lock prisons, but I answered all his questions, including ones about Chandra, trusting him with the information that I was present at her death.

Silas raised his eyebrows. "Shit, Avi, you kept mum 'cause I sent you to her, didn't you? Bet you told the Authority it was an anonymous source."

"None of that was your fault," I said heatedly. "They railroaded you and would have killed you, just to get to Ezra."

Sorrow pinged through my chest but I locked the emotion down tight. "It is what it is. I didn't report the death, and by the time they knew I'd questioned Chandra, they also knew that our magic didn't kill shedim. Fair or not, they would have added that I'd sent her killer into a prison to my list of infractions."

I brought Silas up to speed on going undercover and my earlier team meeting. He laughed when he heard about Gemma.

Next, we started on the guest list I'd been emailed.

"Not all the attendees were Casey fans, or even Trad," I explained. "My informant, Rukhsana Gill, was there, and I'd swear she's Eishei Kodesh." She'd been to the Copper Hell and that wasn't somewhere Trads were invited. Or knew about.

"Magic isn't monitored," Silas said, typing in the first name on the guest list.

"Not unless Casey gets his way," I said bitterly.

My friend threw me a sympathetic smile. "I might be

able to get a bead on any other Eishei Kodesh who saw fit to attend. A suspect meaning to flaunt their presence."

"A suspect who wasn't Rukhsana," I said. "She didn't bother with a fake name and didn't try to hide from me. That woman is not someone to be messed with. If she intended to attack Jared, no one would ever find out."

"Could she be Trad and a supporter?"

"Trad is unlikely, though technically possible. Support Casey though?" I shook my head. "Rukhsana didn't use an alias but others might have. We need to verify every guest's identity."

Silas typed swiftly, his laptop keys clacking.

Roger's crew had vetted everyone quite well. We had names, photos, and contact information, but we had to compare it to security footage of the guests' arrival at the manor that I'd requested from Michael, and that took time.

Three-quarters of the way through the list, I was almost numb with boredom. This part of my job was the worst, but Silas was better positioned than my team to help me on this task.

He backspaced twice. "Aviyente with an 'E,' I think," he muttered under his breath.

"Wait. Who?" I squinted at the screen. "Mois Aviyente? Why do I know that name?"

"Beats me."

The timer on my phone went off and Silas smirked. "Dance break?"

"Yup. Shake off our brain fog."

I grooved around the living room while Silas did jumping jacks for the three minutes that "Crazy on You" by Heart played.

Silas sat back down at his computer. "Did that jog your memory?"

I paced around the dining room table. "No."

"Is this Mois an Eishei Kodesh suspect in a different case?"

"I don't think—oh!" I frantically did a Google search. "Fuck me," I muttered. "He's Chandra Nichols's ex-husband."

"That sure put a burr under the saddle," Silas drawled.

Didn't it just? Damn.

Chapter 10

"Mois Aviyente." Silas turned his screen around to show a corporate headshot of a white man with shrewd green eyes in a conservative suit. "Fifty-three years old, he parlayed a modest inheritance into one of Vancouver's largest real estate development firms. He's vacationing at his place in Buenos Aires, which explains why his RSVP on the guest list was marked as not attending."

"Location and lack of motive rule him out as Jared's attacker, but this is a hell of a connection between Chandra and Casey."

Silas clicked through a few links. "Mois is also Trad."

I flung my head back with a groan. "On a scale of tax audit to pumping the Bilge, how likely do you think it is that Mois or Roger is mixed up with the matchmakers?"

"Half a pump?"

"Half?" I grimaced. "Is that a thing?"

"Ask Ez."

"You found Chandra for me in the first place as a possible matchmaker. What led you to her?"

"A whisper of a murmur of a rumor deep in the dark

web about her off-the-book specialty services. At that point, I was ready to chase anything."

"Could you find that comment again?" Swinging my feet onto a chair, I phoned Gemma. "Mois Aviyente, Chandra's Trad ex-husband, donated to Jared Casey. Follow this up. Was their divorce acrimonious? And get hold of Mois. He's in Buenos Aires, but we need to rule out his involvement as a matchmaker."

"Will do," Gemma said.

This agreeable version of her was fantastic. I got off the call feeling buoyed.

Unfortunately, Silas was unable to find the comment that initially led him to Chandra, or any mention of her on the dark web. As disconcerting was that almost all of her digital footprint on the regular internet had also been scrubbed. The website for Express Recruitment, Chandra's employment agency, was "currently under construction" and the phone number had been disconnected.

"The matchmakers cleaned up," I said.

Silas scanned the screen for another moment, then grunted. "Mois and Chandra have a daughter."

Something about the way he said it, like he'd caught a tug on a line, made me sit up with a curl of excitement. "And?"

"Linda Aviyente, twenty-six. Owner of the Lions Gallery. Odd name."

"The Lions are the two tallest peaks of the North Shore Mountains. Solid local branding, though she's young for a gallery owner."

"Nepo baby," Silas replied. "Also a member of the Eishei Kodesh Leaders of Tomorrow as a teen."

I plonked my feet onto the ground. "Not a Trad, then, and not sharing her father's beliefs."

"You're assuming Mois supports Jared for his anti-magic position," Silas said. "He might like his fiscal conservatism or his stance on housing. Casey is a big proponent of urban development without any pesky social housing requirements."

"Big draw for a real estate developer," I conceded.

"Mois also set up a trust for his magic kid, so he can't be totally opposed to the existence of Eishei Kodesh."

"Or his daughter is the exception to the rule," I said. "Mois is a Trad. No magic and he isn't even in town." I got up to pace and think. "The *Supernatural: Debunked* exhibit was held at a local gallery. What does that get us?"

"Not much. That owner was Trad. Linda isn't."

"True, and the artifacts would have come with provenance and be acquired legally because that exhibit was too high-profile to do otherwise."

"Roger transported them, though, and knew Chandra," Silas said. "Does that also link him to Linda?"

"Is Linda a matchmaker? Did Chandra groom her future leader magic daughter to one day take over? And did that day come sooner than expected with her murder?"

"Too bad Nichols is a dead end," Silas said absently, his eyes on the screen.

"Phrasing," I coughed. "I still feel really bad about her."

"Sorry." He winced. "I meant that she's not around to question."

"No worries. I know what you meant. Now, how do we get into Linda's orbit?"

Gemma phoned back, which surprised me until I checked the time. Hours had passed since our last call.

"Starting from the top with the tasks you gave us," she said, "there aren't any Eishei Kodesh with a rap sheet or anyone the Maccabees are monitoring right now who makes sense for the attack on Casey."

"What about Eishei Kodesh donating to anti-Trad politicians?" I set the phone on the table and put it on speaker, not for Silas's benefit since he'd hear both sides of the conversation regardless, but because my neck and shoulders were tight from sitting here all day.

"We don't have any politicians who come close to Jared's hatred of our kind," Gemma said. "No CCTV footage of any protesters heading to the manor either."

That doesn't mean one hadn't. It just meant they hadn't been caught on camera. "And Mois?"

"We're still trying to get hold of him, but nothing in the court records suggests the divorce was messy."

I pushed away the dregs of the sandwich I'd been eating. The plate had been sitting on my incident report, and when I shifted the dish, a phrase caught my eye. "The guards last night wore shielding devices."

Silas looked up from his laptop with raised eyebrows.

"Didn't Roger Henderson confirm he'd purchased them as a precaution?" Gemma said.

"Yes, but from who? Those magic contraptions cost a bundle, and they aren't exactly easy to find."

"You think he got them from Chandra Nichols?"

"It would explain those phone calls better than consulting on some alarm system, but if not, perhaps her daughter, Linda, got them for Roger. Lean on him. The court of public opinion doesn't require hard proof. Neither he nor Jared Casey want any association with a murdered Eishei Kodesh to come to light."

Gemma stopped typing. "Michael said Roger was a no-go."

"Yeah, well, I'm making the executive decision other-wise. I'll take all the responsibility."

"And the blame?"

"And the blame."

"All right, then. I'm on it, boss." She hung up.

"Boss." I dusted my knuckles off on my chest.

Silas gave a pleased little hum. "Oh yeah. Linda will take this bait."

"What bait?"

He blinked slowly at me, like he'd forgotten I was there, then he blushed. "I have an art collection. Of sorts."

"Of sorts?" I raised an eyebrow. "Do you collect tasteful nudes in oils and acrylics, Silas?"

"Naw." His blush deepened. "Trains."

"Your model trains?"

"No, I branched out into train-themed artwork ages ago," he mumbled to his feet. "Linda's gallery focuses on twentieth-century art, and I really do want to sell some pieces."

I paced the room, picturing paintings featuring old-fashioned trains chugging through nondescript rural landscapes, depicted with sloppy brushstrokes in a thousand shades of brown and black. I grasped at a tactful way to ask why he thought she'd be interested. "Any artists I've heard of?"

I didn't recognize the first few names he tossed out, my heart sinking that I'd have to kibosh his idea, but my jaw hit the floor with Edward Hopper and René Magritte. "You—you—that's a serious collection, Silas!"

He crossed his arms, shifting defensively. "I bought them in the early stages of these artists' careers because I liked them. I got lucky that they're worth something."

I sat on the edge of the table and touched his arm. "I was a judgy asshole and I'm sorry. Art should bring joy, and trains are just as deserving a subject as anything else. You have provenance for them?"

"Darn tootin' I do. And photos."

"Now we're getting somewhere."

The plan was that I'd meet Linda at her exhibit opening Thursday evening, along with my boyfriend, Silas, who happened to have some prominent artwork he was looking to sell.

We'd connect with Linda on a social and professional level, spend time with her to gain her trust, and, fingers crossed, catch our first break in exposing the matchmakers and any connection with Roger or Jared.

I just hoped Darsh didn't get pissy at me for monopolizing Silas's time and attention. He wasn't the best with sharing. He was, however, phenomenal at disguises, and he agreed to help transform me into someone unrecognizable. Tomorrow—since he was working graveyard. Literally. The Spook Squad had definitively identified the vamps responsible for the murder spree last month and were moving in on the suspects tonight.

By the time Silas and I compiled a detailed profile on Linda, and he'd snagged us a spot on the guest list at her gallery opening, the moon was shining through the windows at the far end of my open-concept condo.

I did a double take. The *full* moon. Checking that we were done for tonight and agreeing to reconvene at Darsh's in the morning, I saw Silas off and prepared myself for a date with a maggot.

Whether it was the lunar pull or just its own vicious temper, the googly-eyed, fat little bugger that I'd gotten from Daphne thrashed around even more.

Once in the kitchen, I pulled off my sock, so I was barefoot as instructed, and prodded the bag with tongs I'd grabbed. While the maggot didn't appear to have a mouth, I still handled it gingerly.

Holding the open bag in one hand, I fished the dripping creature out with the tongs, but it slipped free and plopped to the tiles, wriggling back and forth. Steeling myself for the gross squelch to come, I smashed my bare heel down on it.

Sawdust scattered under my boot, my footfall a heavy thud on the worn stone. Whispers swept around me on the icy breeze, but I ignored them, refusing to be cowed. The others had been unfit, but I was specially chosen to carry this word.

Torches flickered over a face carved into a rough block of stone, its mouth hanging open in an "O" shape, like the Mouth of Truth in Rome. The empty eye sockets filled with an awareness, but I stared it down and the flames shifted, the illusion falling away. Tricks wouldn't work on me.

"I come as one of the Ashbishop's flock to reignite the spark of life. Give me the healing power to set things right." My voice rang out clearly, my entire vampire existence leading to this one moment. This one purpose.

The mouth twisted into a leering mass.

"Take my blood but know you will find me worthy." I thrust my left hand into the stone mouth.

The sentience chuckled, sending a shiver down my spine. *We shall see.*

A raspy tongue brushed over my fingers as the words brushed against the inside of my skull. A lake full of maggots writhed in my head.

I gritted my teeth but stood still, cloaked in my belief— in my desire—to heal our kind. To finally bury my sorrow like I'd buried my human child years after I was changed. To once more hold a child, *my* child, in my arms. I ran my hand over the scar on my abdomen.

Needle-sharp stone fangs dropped from the mouth's upper jaw and tore through my flesh.

I bit back my scream, my blood staining the sawdust.

Say your name and I shall hand down my verdict.

"I am—"

NO! A roar inside my head split my skull in two.

"My name—" I fell to my knees with a scream. My

flesh was ruined and my fingers... I gasped. I flexed my claws and a hot blaze shot up my arm.

Wake up. This isn't real.

Cherry! And I was— I slammed the brakes on even thinking my name, lest I be trapped in this memory for good.

The carved face zoomed toward me, its command to say my name lashing me like ropes.

Get out of this memory. Now. That supplicant is dead and if you stay here, you'll die too!

Flooded with a rush of adrenaline, I sprinted for the exit, the ground quaking and bucking under my feet.

The magic guardian of the power word nipped at my heels, demanding my name.

I tripped over the threshold—

—and snapped my eyes open, back in my kitchen, my face pressed to the tiles and my heel filthy with maggot goop. Trembling, I held out my hands. They were uninjured, the pain gone, but the ache of that supplicant's sorrow over her lost daughter lingered.

I sat up, pulling my knees into my chest, one hand resting on that phantom scar and the other clenched in a fist at having lost my chance at the supplicant's name.

She failed the test, Cherry said. *She was separated into bones for a wall and her name turned into a maggot. You were magically bound to that memory and the second she stopped existing, you would have as well. Whatever guards the power word never intended to let you live.*

I shivered and hugged myself more tightly. Now that I was out of the memory, I agreed with Cherry's assessment of the situation. I hadn't been found worthy to get the supplicant's name, nor was this a test.

It was a trap.

"Avi?" Sach crouched down next to me. "Move out of the wet patch."

"Heard that one before," I joked weakly.

Sachie kicked away the empty plastic bag, helping me to my feet and away from the maggot water. She kept an arm over my shoulder as we made our way into the living room.

I dragged the blanket draped on the back of the sofa over my shoulders. "I didn't get the vampire supplicant's name, but whoever she was, she wasn't doing this to fuck over humanity or change the power balance. She'd buried her human daughter." I clutched the two ends tight. "I never considered what it's like for vampires to outlive their children. She longed for another baby to fill that hole in her heart."

"That doesn't change the fact that vampires achieving procreation is dangerous for humanity," Sachie said.

"No," I said heavily. "It doesn't." I clutched the blanket tighter. "Her sorrow was why she was chosen to undergo the test for the word. She followed someone called the Ashbishop."

Sachie groaned. "I hate cryptic villain names. What's wrong with something sensible like Babel City Local #39?"

I mustered up a weak smile. "Any vamp going by the Ashbishop carries a fuckton of Catholic guilt."

"That's a place to start."

"Tomorrow, okay? I need to…separate myself from that grieving mother."

"Of course." Sach flicked on the TV, searching for something suitably mindless.

"Cherry pulled me out," I said. "Not with her armor, just her presence."

"So, you pulled yourself out," Sach said wryly. "Being her."

"Yes, but…" I shrugged. "I like thinking of her as a distinct personality."

"Whatever keeps you alive, weirdo."

"Darsh is going to create a disguise for me to go under-cover, except I left it up to Silas to tell him we're going in as romantic partners. Want to be there when Darsh inevitably announces his opinion to me about that?"

Sach stuffed a pillow behind her back as a show about renovations at a beach community began to play. "Now you're talking."

Chapter 11

Up to this moment, my life had been sadly lacking in brawny six-four vampires wearing booty shorts, cowboy boots, and flowing silky kaftans to a soundtrack of Ella Fitzgerald belting out "I'm Beginning to See the Light" complete with hisses and pops from the record.

Thank goodness that this stellar Wednesday morning had rectified that.

Sach and I cocked our heads sideways in identical movements to better study this fascinating specimen, but we turned at a loud choked noise.

Natán's female vamp minion from the other night was back on Aviva-stalking duty. She'd stepped into the middle of the street from wherever she'd been hiding to openly gape at Silas.

Our friend's eyes widened into saucers. "You're not Darsh." He slammed the front door shut, leaving Sachie and me stranded on the stoop under overcast skies.

Sach narrowed her eyes at the door. "That robe thing had no pockets. Nowhere to stash a weapon."

I checked, but the female vamp underling was gone.

Hopefully back into her hiding place and not running to tell tales. "Silas *is* a weapon."

"There's that." My bestie paused. "He did look fetching."

We both broke into snorted laughs.

The gate swung open with a creak and Darsh strode up his front walk carrying two bags from our favorite bagel place.

One look at my vampire friend with his slinky elegant lethalness and the reasonable guess would be that he lived in a penthouse apartment. Or a crypt. No one ever expected him to live in a crooked little character house, all slanted floors and jewel-tone painted rooms. Oddly, all the sharp edges and pools of sunlight through vampire-safe windows (filters needed only on the brightest of days for Darsh) suited our friend to a T.

"You're early." He sailed up the front stairs and unlocked the door.

"Yup," I said, following him inside and toeing off my shoes. "Like always."

"Time is a construct," Sachie said.

The music had been shut off, which was too bad, because that was a great album. Also, the idea of Silas dancing around unselfconsciously made me happy.

Darsh led us through the living room with its plush velvet furniture to the blue and white kitchen. The floors creaked when Sachie and I walked over them, but he glided silently along like he was part hoverboard. He shoved one of the bags into my chest, telling me to cut the bagels.

Sach was already opening the drawer for the bread knife.

Silas lumbered down the stairs and entered with a stiff bow. He'd changed into an ironed plaid cowboy shirt tucked into dark jeans. "Good morning."

Darsh shook his head. "You didn't need to put yourself out because of these two."

"I lost track of time," Silas said. "Not very professional of me."

No, Silas was always professional and appropriate. But he'd also confided in me about the dark shit in his head after almost two hundred years of being a vampire. If Darsh brought out a side of Silas that allowed him to live outside some rigid code of behavior and be in a place of color and silkiness and dancing around living rooms, then I was all for it.

"Sorry we startled you," I said.

Since Sach and I were as familiar with Darsh's kitchen as our own, we prepped the bagels, putting Silas on coffee duty for the in-need-of-caffeine humans, while Darsh went upstairs to get supplies for my disguise.

He returned hoisting a giant makeup kit and another bag with his hair-styling equipment like they weighed nothing, turning his dining room into a makeshift beauty salon. Admittedly, it was a very orderly salon. Darsh slapped Sachie's hand away when she moved his array of foundation bottles out of their neat line.

I was allowed half a bagel and two swigs of coffee before Darsh hauled me to the kitchen sink to wash my hair. I tuned out his litany of woes about the shameful condition of my follicles, which lasted until I was seated with a plastic cape around my neck at his dining room table.

My beauty guru, now wearing gloves, picked up the cup with the bleach cream and slathered it on the first hank of hair.

I'd agreed to change my hair color rather than deal with a wig, but I still grimaced at the sight of the bleach.

Sach looked up from her bagel. "That's going to take some adjusting."

"Aviva has put herself in my hands and she will look fabulous. Totally unlike her regular self."

"Was I just insulted?" I said.

"Go with yes," Sach replied, sneaking me another sip of coffee.

Darsh worked swiftly, half my head soon covered. "I'm still unclear about your role in this operation. You don't know enough about art to represent Silas and his collection."

A pit of dread formed in my stomach. I wasn't supposed to be the one to break the happy news to Darsh. For one, he was going to kill the messenger, and Silas was much harder to dismember than me. "I'm not his broker. I'm his girlfriend."

Darsh yanked sharply on my hair, and I flinched. "Whoops," he said with no remorse. "Silas," he trilled. "You left out an important detail about your triumphant Maccabee return."

Silas strolled into the dining room. "What's that?"

"The part where Avi is your girlfriend in this little scheme."

"Does that matter?" Silas watched him intently.

Darsh slapped more bleach cream on my hair. "I suppose it doesn't."

I shot Silas a look. *Dude, do not anger the man with the ability to bleach me into baldness.*

When he turned away, Sach raised an eyebrow in question at me, but it wasn't even 10AM and I'd had only a couple mouthfuls of coffee. I was nowhere near ready to deal with this drama.

I bit into a bagel. Crumbs scattered to the plate and Darsh glared at me. I glared back. I had a plate. I was in an eating-designated room. Trust me, I'd made the mistake of snacking in his living room once. Never again. His kvetching still rang in my ears.

While Darsh didn't like sharing (or messes), he also didn't like admitting that constantly hanging out with Silas meant anything. Sach and I hadn't gotten any sexual conquest details thus far, which meant that either: a) nothing had happened, indicating that Darsh was fighting feelings hard, or b) something *had* happened, and he wasn't dishing about it. See previous conclusion.

"Ezra is okay with this?" Darsh asked.

"What's not to be okay with?" I frowned. "We aren't actually dating."

"Please." Darsh waved one gloved hand. "This dinner date is just a formality, and we all know it."

"First off," I said snippily, "*we* don't all know anything. Second, if Ezra doesn't trust me, no matter what the situation, I wouldn't want to be with him again. And third—"

"She was talking about her and Silas," Sachie said. "The not-dating part."

"Yes. That. Thank you." I'd pointed at Sachie as I spoke, and light glinted off my Maccabee ring. I was going undercover on an awesome case as a level three operative and the great love of my life wanted to reconcile. I should have been ecstatic, but my ring felt tight because I couldn't see a way forward for both those things to have a happily-ever-after.

If I was being honest with myself, I hadn't simply rescheduled on Ezra because of work demands. Saying yes to him would set back my career dreams and years of hard work, but the idea of not taking this second chance made me feel sick.

Darsh snapped off a glove. "The bleach has to sit for half an hour."

Suddenly he gasped.

I touched a finger to my hair, not that I could see if something had gone wrong, but he was storming over to

Silas, who'd ripped a piece off a bagel and popped it in his mouth.

"What," Darsh said testily, "are you doing?"

Silas swallowed. "Eating? I like to try food now and again."

"Without a plate?" Darsh toed at the crumbs by Silas's foot.

"Guess I'm not a very good houseguest." Silas met Darsh's gaze, a challenge to the stubborn set of his chin.

Darsh broke the stare down first and stomped upstairs with the bleach and used gloves.

Sach slipped from her chair with a muttered, "I'll get the broom."

"Naw. My mess," Silas said wearily, heading for the kitchen. "I should have known better."

"You stay with this one, I'll go upstairs?" I said.

Sach nodded.

I got halfway up the stairs when my phone rang. I'd have ignored it, but it was Michael so I didn't.

Too bad that I didn't even get to say hello before she was tearing a strip off me for instructing Gemma to set up a meeting with Roger. The director had just endured the mayor's wrath for Maccabee insensitivity and the Casey camp was now off-limits to us entirely. To make matters worse, Keira was also furious because her decision to hand Chandra's murder investigation to the Maccabees was being called into question by the mayor's office as well.

Resisting the urge to compliment my mother's lung capacity since she had yet to take a breath, I cut into her rant. "I stand by my decision." I sat down on the stairs. "You've never given a shit about upsetting any of our mayors, so be honest about what's really going on."

"What's that supposed to mean?" Michael said testily.

"Gee, Mom, you and Kiki have some pretty massive unresolved history." I lowered my voice to avoid vamp eavesdropping. "Did you cut her out because of me? Does she know?"

"There was no point in telling her."

"I thought that about Sachie and she's handled it much better than I anticipated."

"You thought that about Ezra too."

I sucked in a breath. "Wow. Ouch."

"I'm sorry." She sighed. "That was uncalled for."

My jaw felt tight; I'd been clenching it without realizing. I relaxed the muscles, rubbing my hand over it to ease the discomfort. "Ezra didn't...well, not entirely. It doesn't matter. Is there anything else?" I said waspishly.

"No." Michael hung up without saying goodbye.

I buried my head in my hands, taking deep breaths until I'd calmed down enough to speak to Darsh.

He sat on the edge of his bed, which, like the guest room mattress, was made up with hospital corners.

I didn't tease him about it.

He fiddled with the beads on his black leather wrist cuff. For someone who enjoyed changing up his image as much as Darsh did, it was strange he never took that cuff off.

I sat down next to him, our arms brushing, and nodded at it. "That was Patrin's, wasn't it?"

"Yes." He gave a quiet wry laugh. "I'm not sure if it's a token of remembrance or the albatross I've condemned myself to bear."

I digested that a moment before speaking again. "Did you have any children when you were human?"

Darsh leaned back on his elbows, his brown hair spilling over his shoulders and his face wrinkled up. "Ew, no. Looking after my little brother was more than enough, thank you. What brought that question on?"

I told him about reliving the memory of the female vamp who'd taken the test to receive the power word. "The idea of outliving your child is horrific."

"It happens to humans too," he said gently.

"But vampires have to watch *any* human they care about age and die."

"That's why many don't make those attachments." He touched each bead on the cuff, almost reverently. "The loss is too much. It's also why vampires tend to flip out at around the two-century mark. Everyone we've ever known before as a human is long gone, and we finally feel well and truly alone. We have to figure out how to exist with the burden of immortality."

"You let humans in."

"Sachie is a rare and beautiful soul. I meet so few others of her caliber."

I elbowed him. "Ha. Ha. So, what's keeping you from admitting to whatever is really going on with Silas?"

"I could ask you the same question."

"I'm well aware of my feelings for Ezra. The idea of reconciling with him is…" I briefly closed my eyes, almost feeling Ezra's arms coming around me from behind like he used to when I was cooking, his chin settling into that perfect spot between my neck and shoulder. "Tempting. But it's a lot of other things too, and I won't just jump back into it. I need to be sure."

"Nothing is sure in life, puiul meu. Do you worry about Ezra watching you age and die?"

Not all momentous occurrences happened with a blaze of fanfare. Nor were they all car crashes that spun your life out of control and smashed its reality into a metaphoric concrete wall. Sometimes, you simply made a choice in the quiet of a moment.

"Not really." I let my frosted scales bloom over my skin, my eyes go toxic green, and smiled wobblily at my friend.

Chapter 12

Darsh leapt off the bed, cursing in Romani.

My heart thudded in my throat, but I kept my voice light. "I have a slightly longer life expectancy than most."

He crouched down next to me, his fingers hovering over my skin. "May I?"

I nodded, barely feeling his featherlight touch. "See," I said with a shaky laugh. "If I can be brave and out my most vulnerable self, you can too."

"Very sneaky of you." He dropped back onto the mattress next to me. "I'm glad you came to me for your disguise because those scales and your normal hair color would wash you right out."

I'd have shown my crimson hair but wasn't sure how that magic feature would interact with the bleach.

My relief swam down to my toes. Along with some indignation. "It's actually crimson in my half-shedim form."

"Like the sweater Ezra knitted for you?" He pressed his hand to his heart with a wounded look. "I take it Sach knows too?"

I lost my shedim features, human in appearance once more. "For the last month. And don't take it personally. It took me a couple of decades to work up the courage to come out to her."

He gasped. "Is Michael—"

"No."

"Holy crap! That's even better. She slept with a shedim?!" He fell back against the bed, one arm thrown across his face. "I'm slain. Truly."

Since the melodrama involved in learning exactly which shedim my mother had slept with (shudder) might finish Darsh off, I saved the news of Delacroix for another day. "You can't tell anyone. That includes no taunting Michael. You get away with a lot of shit with her, Darsh, but teasing her about this is off-limits. It wasn't easy for her raising a half-demon kid, especially as a single mom."

Darsh moved his arm away from his face. "I can't tell Silas? It seems unfair for him to be left out of the loop."

"Such concern for your houseguest," I teased.

He shot me the finger.

"I'm working up to it, okay?"

"Okay." He nudged me. "What was the woman's name?"

"What woman?"

"The vampire who outlived her child."

"I don't know. Cherry helped me shake off the magic before I heard the name." I rubbed my arms. "Good thing too. I would have been lost to it, otherwise."

"Who's Cherry?"

I blushed. "No one."

He sat up and booped the end of my nose. "That is absolutely not the case."

I sighed. "Cherry Bomb, the Brimstone Baroness. My shedim side."

"I love a woman who refers to herself in the third person. And with a divine name no less."

I always liked him, Cherry purred lazily.

"So the Baroness helped save you, but you're back at square one."

"Not exactly. The supplicant was there because she'd been chosen by someone called the Ashbishop."

Darsh went very still.

I turned to face him. "I take it that extreme reaction isn't due to how stupid that name sounds."

My friend stared into the distance, his voice thin and quiet. "I was turned at a time and in a place where the odds of my survival were slim. I didn't have the strength or violent urges of others like me, so I took a different route for survival, staying under the radar for decades while I slowly built an armor out of information. I made sure to stay in the shadows and not attract attention, and after more than a century, my reputation was formidable. Sometime in the mid-1800s, I was invited to the Copper Hell. Patrin…" His voice cracked but he notched up his chin. "Patrin had been changed by the same paragon who made me."

I'd never heard such contempt from him.

"Even though my brother was also a vampire and almost as old as I was, I'd protected him as best I could, allowing him to retain the innocence he'd had in life. Maybe I shouldn't have. Maybe then…" He shook his head wearily. "Patrin wasn't usually stubborn, but when he wanted something, especially from me, he always managed to talk me into it."

"He wanted to go to the Copper Hell?"

"Big-time. He swore he'd be happy with a single visit, but when he got there, well…" He touched his wrist cuff. "I tried to stop him, but I wasn't his keeper. Patrin made friends there and I convinced myself it was a good thing. He'd always preferred human company and, well." Darsh shrugged. "You know how that story always ended. It was better for him to have other vampire friends instead of being dependent on me as his one constant companion."

"Charming as you are," I said.

"Right? One of his friends introduced him to a powerful vampire who brought Patrin into his crew."

"At the Hell?"

"No. This vampire didn't gamble." His gaze went unfocused for a minute, then he shook his head. "Patrin disappeared into his new life, and I didn't see him or hear from him again until he was arrested for stealing from an Authority member."

I wrung my hands together. "He got caught, didn't he?"

"The only thing that kept him from being immediately staked was that they wanted his boss's name. I begged him to hand it over, but when he didn't, I took matters into my own hands."

"You found out the name?"

"I wish. No, I negotiated hard, saying it was Patrin's first strike and he'd return what he stole. Besides, I had something far more useful. Years of information about various vamp players. The Authority said they'd take my information, but they'd also take me. For one hundred years. Take it or leave it."

"Darsh—" I reached for him but at his flinch, dropped my hand, and schooled my voice into a matter-of-fact tone. "What happened to Patrin?"

"I saved him. Pointless really," he said blithely. "Whoever he was working for killed him anyway for betraying him by returning the stolen property."

I exhaled slowly at the tragic outcome. "You were never tempted to cut and run?"

"I'd made a deal and I intended to honor it."

"Honor or penance?"

"Does it matter? I played spy for the Maccabees for years. One of my jobs about ten years back had me cross paths with Michael. She was the first operative to know my situation yet judge me on my merits, and when the job was over, I stayed in Vancouver."

"You never found out who killed Patrin?" My gut was as twisted as my fingers.

"I did." He smiled sadly.

I exhaled hard.

"But I never found the Ashbishop. Eventually I heard he was dead, but if that rumor was untrue and he's back and gunning for vamp invincibility?" He clenched his hands into fists.

I closed my eyes briefly. Reopening Darsh's wound was cruel, but letting the Ashbishop roam unchecked was unthinkable.

Darsh gnawed the inside of his cheek. "I've never told anyone else the full story."

"I won't share it, but that's a lot of grief to have been carrying on your own."

"As is being a half shedim in this world, but sometimes the grief is easier than the words."

I inclined my head. Touché.

"You need to be very, very careful."

"Got it." I held out my right hand. "For now I have to concentrate on my undercover investigation, and for that, I'll have to remove my Maccabee ring." I tugged gently on the band, hoping it would get stuck on my knuckle like it had before. It slid over the joint and I stopped, the ring still on my finger.

"Does it help your decision that the magic inside is corrupted?"

"Honestly, I'm not sure if that makes it better or worse. It's been this talisman, the physical manifestation of my tikkun olam vow." I ran my thumb over it. "I didn't even take it off when I visited the Crypt, but I can't stay under-cover with it on."

"You could get it glamored," Darsh suggested.

"Sharnaz is on vacation for three weeks." The Maccabee glamorer was using up their banked holiday time for a trip to Thailand.

Besides, I was also hunting the shedim who Chandra worked with to break the wards on the prison locks and, as firsthand experience taught me, demons could strip glamors.

"Michael isn't too pleased with me right now. She's not going to approve the cost of bringing a glamorer in from another chapter on a time-sensitive basis." I steeled my shoulders. "The ring is not my vow."

I slid it off my index finger and was immediately assaulted by the itchy, uncomfortable sensation that I'd lost something. I tamped down my strong desire to put the ring back on and stuffed it into my pocket.

A timer went off on Darsh's phone and he checked one of the foils on my hair. "Time to make you beautiful."

"Beautiful in a different way from my normal beauty," I corrected.

Darsh wrinkled his nose, heading out of his room for the bathroom. "Since you're in a delicate state right now, yes."

I followed him into the hallway and down the first stair. "You suck."

"Kidding. But Avi? We're going to set some ground rules."

"For what?"

"Touching my boyfriend." He froze, his eyes wide, then he fled back into his bedroom and slammed the door.

"No take-backsies!" I screeched, flinging the door open and pouncing on him. "You said the words!"

He pushed me off. "I regret them already."

Silas skidded into the doorway, startling Darsh and me.

Damn his vamp hearing and stealthy stair climbing. "Making unilateral decisions, Rapunzel?"

"Like I'm not stating the obvious, cowpoke." Darsh stood up.

"Do I get a say in this?" Silas cocked his head.

Darsh's nonchalant "Knock yourself out" would have landed better were his gaze not locked warily on to the other vampire.

Sachie thundered up the stairs, poking her head out from behind Silas and scanning our faces. "What happened?"

"Darsh just declared Silas was his boyfriend," I said.

"Did he? Heh."

Silas looked down at Sachie. "I haven't said yes yet."

She elbowed him in the back. "Rude."

Darsh gave a ghost of a smile. "It is rather. Maybe I should rescind."

"No!" Sachie, I, and most importantly, Silas, exclaimed.

"Fine," Darsh huffed.

"Now that that's settled." Sachie squeezed past the huge vamp blocking her way. "What's next?"

"We're setting rules for acceptable touching," Darsh said firmly.

"For you and Silas?" she said, frowning.

"For Avi and me," Silas said. "What counts as acceptable touching?" He held out his hand.

I scrambled off the bed and over to his side. "Clear communication is important in relationships."

"Is this allowed?" Silas pressed his hand against the small of my back.

I shivered.

Darsh narrowed his eyes.

"What about this?" Silas clasped my hand in his, running his thumb over my skin.

"Oooh," I moaned.

Sach snapped her fingers. "Brush her hair off her neck so you can murmur in her ear."

I nodded eagerly. "Oh yeah. That."

Darsh crossed his arms. "You three are hilarious."

"Just understanding the rules, boyfriend," Silas drawled.

Sachie bounced on her heels. "He might have to kiss her."

"True." I closed my eyes and tipped my face up.

Instead of Silas's lips (which I never expected to feel), I got a hand pushing my face away. I snapped my lids open and blinked at Darsh's palm, held up mere inches from me like a stop sign.

He glared at all three of us, then spun and walked out of the room, his middle finger held up.

"Wait!" I scrambled after him. "You need to rinse out the bleach. This is chemical warfare!"

His voice floated back from the stairs. "Taunt the beauty expert at your peril. See where that gets you for your big date with Ezra."

"He's totally making my hair fall out," I said.

Sach nodded. "At minimum."

I poked Silas's rock-solid arm. "Why don't you get grief?"

He smiled smugly. "Because I'm the boyfriend."

Chapter 13

I gave Ezra's name to the hostess in the foyer of Le Demi Monde later that night, feeling smug at this little test of whether my ex would instantly recognize me. My strawberry blond hair took me aback every time I caught sight of myself in a mirror, but its pinky hue complemented my blue contacts. I'd leaned into lilacs and golds on my makeup palette, used shapewear to give me curves and push up boobs, and spritzed on a muskier perfume than I generally favored.

This wasn't just about pulling one over on Ezra. I had to get used to being in this persona—how she walked, her body language—for the gallery event tomorrow, so there was no time to waste. Plus, like it or not, there was so much pressure riding on this date that if things went horribly wrong, somehow the blow would be easier if I didn't look like myself.

At least, that was what I'd kept insisting during the embarrassing amount of time I'd spent getting ready. Cherry Bomb had used up her year's quota of snorts and Maud had insisted on photos of every single potential dress, providing helpful commentary.

That color reminds me of baby food. Yum!

Aw, you're so brave for wearing that. Good for you!

And my personal favorite: *That outfit is perfect if you want him to focus on your personality.*

Why had I wished for a sibling again?

Well, I was here now. I tugged on my ivory slip dress for the billionth time as I followed the hostess across the restaurant, its fabric clinging to my padded-out curves in a way that made me feel both sexy and self-conscious.

Le Demi Monde was a hidden gem nestled in the heart of the city. Whenever I'd driven past, I'd admired its elegant facade adorned with two discreet wrought-iron balconies and cascading window boxes that even now in January overflowed with vibrant flowers.

However, the one time I'd checked out its minimalist website, I'd noticed there were no prices on the menu and resignedly closed my browser. Happily, tonight was Ezra's treat, and I'd promised Sach that by the time I'd finished, my blood would be replaced by béarnaise sauce.

The gentle clink of fine china and crystal was a soothing percussion to the soft classical music playing in the background. Actually, everything about the space was tranquil, from the cream-colored walls adorned with British Columbia landscapes, to the tables draped in crisp white linens. Ornate chandeliers cast a warm golden glow over the space, their light dancing off the polished silverware.

I sniffed the heavenly aroma of boeuf bourguignon, my stomach rumbling, and stepped onto a slightly raised platform at the back of the restaurant. Partitioned off with enormous vases of orchids, it afforded guests more privacy.

Well, one guest to be precise, because this back area was otherwise empty.

Ezra stood up from a leather banquette, his athletic frame cutting an impressive silhouette in a tailored charcoal suit. His wild black curls were somewhat tamed, and my stomach did a little flip at the way his silver-blue gaze raked over me, his scrutiny intense.

Wait. My hand drifted to my hair. He did know it was me, right? I cursed myself for not sending him a close-up photo of my new look with the caption "AVIVA!!"

He schooled his face into a polite smile for the hostess. "I'm expecting my date."

My next step faltered.

The hostess glanced at me uncertainly.

"I'm his date," I said through gritted teeth.

The other woman smiled in relief. "A blind date."

Well, Ezra might end up blind once I poked his eyes out.

"How sweet," she said. "And romantic. He reserved this entire section for the two of you. Your server will be along momentarily. Enjoy." She left me there.

I crossed my arms, all the better to get those boobs front and center. "Like what you see?"

"Yes, but not because of your new look." Ezra poured a glass of red wine from the bottle on the table and held it out. "Because you're here. That glower when you assumed I didn't recognize you was adorable."

My stomach went squirmy at his fond smile. Point to Count von Cardoso.

Maybe don't use the villain name on the man you're reconciling with? Cherry said in an amused voice.

Considering reconciling with. The ongoing consideration is impor-tant to this equation.

Uh-huh.

Shut it, demon.

I sauntered past empty tables glowing with tiny candles. Barcly sparing a glance for the jaw-dropping view of the Vancouver skyline through the picture window next to us, I accepted the glass of wine.

Ezra's fingers lingered on mine.

"You clean up pretty well yourself," I replied, hoping my voice didn't betray the flutter in my chest.

The intimate seating in the banquette forced us to sit side by side rather than across from each other, and while Ezra wasn't nowhere near as muscular as Silas, he took up a lot of room. Oxygen too, which was no mean feat for a guy who didn't breathe. His rock-hard thigh brushed mine, and when he draped an arm along the back of the seat, I was curled into the crook of his arm.

I flexed my fingers like I could capture the easy familiarity of it.

In my head Cherry blew a raspberry at me. *You can, idiot.*

"What's with the disguise?" Ezra said with a forced lightness.

"I'm undercover."

"You certainly are." His smile sharpened into a butter-wouldn't-melt-in-his-mouth red flag. "Should I call you by a different name as well?"

"Undercover on a case," I said evenly. "I'm learning this new character. This is the perfect place to practice being her."

"I'm thrilled, as ever, to assist you in your career goals."

Keep it up, Cardoso. You're making my choice about us a lot easier.

No one thinks there is still a choice to be made, Cherry said.

There is if he's going to be a dick.

I sipped my wine, the flavor coating my tastebuds in silky grape ecstasy. "Goddamn that's good."

"It's a Chateau Petrus 2019, so I hope so."

"You're talking to a woman who buys her wine according to how funny the label is so you can skip your fancy names and dates, buster."

Ezra nodded somberly, though his lips were quirked. "Noted."

I picked up the handwritten menu sitting on my bone white china plate.

Which was merely the top plate upon a small stack.

I frowned at the plethora of dinnerware in front of me. And the staggering amount of cutlery. Also, what was that third glass for? I tightened my hold on my menu. Oh, for a burger where I wouldn't embarrass myself.

He tugged on my curl gently. "Stop overthinking whatever you're overthinking."

His touch sent shivers tumbling through me.

Get with the program and get to the good stuff already, Cherry snapped. *Any longer and you'll need a dictionary to remember what an orgasm is.*

Sex is not a reason to get back together with someone, I retorted.

Then pick one of the thirty other reasons off the list you made.

Point of fact, I'd made *two* lists and while the second one was short, its single point held a lot of weight. Shockingly it wasn't that Ezra had broken my heart. I'd processed our pasts—it was our present situation that was the issue.

I reached for the wine again.

Our waiter approached. "Are you ready to order?"

Ezra raised an eyebrow. "May I?"

Since I'd failed to see anything on the menu past the first hors d'oeuvres of stuffed squid, sure. "Been plotting the way to my heart, Cardoso?"

"You caught me."

I loftily waved for him to have at it.

Ezra ordered a meal in French with the easy confidence of someone who knew exactly what he was doing.

Once the server had left, I turned to my date. "I want to ask you something, to get all business out of the way before our delicious meal arrives."

"Shoot."

I launched into what happened with the maggot and the female vampire supplicant. I didn't tell him about

Patrin, but I did say Darsh warned me how dangerous the Ashbishop was.

"I doubt Darsh shared a fraction of his information. The Ashbishop disappeared long before I was born," Ezra said, "and no one's heard from him in decades. That was a good thing, but if he's back, he needs to be put down slowly and painfully."

"Can you ask around the Hell if anyone remembers him? Oh, and also ask about the female vampire who was the most recent supplicant for the power word on the Ashbishop's behalf?" I gave Ezra the few details I had— including that she'd become part of his flock because she buried a human child.

She'd died taking the test, but hopefully someone missed her.

Ezra agreed to look into both.

Our first course arrived. I got a beautifully plated appetizer; Ezra received a glass of chilled blood presented in an ornate crystal chalice.

I leaned forward, my mouth watering at the smell of flaky golden-brown puff pastry. I had to restrain myself from cutting it open to discover its treasures inside before the waiter had finished topping up our water glasses. Fortunately, I managed to keep my pace to that of a civilized person's and didn't moan or roll my eyes back into my head at the first taste of the goat cheese and caramelized onion filling.

"I love watching how much pleasure you take in eating," Ezra said. "It's so contagious that I feel like I'm sharing it with you."

I pointed my knife at him. "Well, this show isn't free. You know the price."

Ezra had been texting me hilarious anecdotes from the Hell every few days. "Nothing weird has happened today," he said.

"Bullshit." I coughed the word.

He gave an exaggerated sigh and pulled out his phone. "There may have been one instance involving a pinball machine and an Eishei Kodesh with a bad Botox job."

We fell into the easy rhythm of conversation we always shared. I found myself laughing more than I had in weeks, the tension of recent events melting away in Ezra's presence.

Ezra tapped the wine bottle, his eyebrows raised in question.

I held up my glass. "Drink me."

His pupils dilated. "Phrasing?"

"You know what I mean," I muttered, blushing.

He complied without spilling a drop. The man really did follow orders beautifully.

Idiot, Cherry scoffed.

He pressed in close to my side, his phone angled to take a shot of the two of us. "Smile."

I leaned out of frame, placing the glass on the table. "What are you doing?"

He frowned, fiddling with the image. "I'm capturing my dinner with a beautiful woman."

"You can't post that!" I lunged for the phone.

He pulled it out of reach with a scowl. "I wasn't planning to, but even if I did, no one would recognize you."

I peered over his shoulder at the screen.

The chandelier cast a honeyed light on the curvy blonde woman with flushed cheeks and sparkling blue eyes. Damn, my disguise was gorgeous.

Ezra had snapped the picture while he was almost in profile to the camera, his focus on me. A slight smile played on his face like he'd just recalled a cherished memory.

I stared at the woman who looked nothing like me. "Ezra."

"Is this where we fight again?"

I smoothed out my napkin in my lap. "Am I that transparent?"

"Only to those who know you well," he replied with a soft smile. "And I'd like to think I still fall into that category."

I took a deep breath, steeling myself. "This new case is going to be a lot, and I didn't want you to think I wasn't taking this—us—seriously."

Ezra placed a hand over his heart dramatically. "That warms my cold, undead heart. But the case isn't the issue. You don't want to date the Lord of the Copper Hell, do you?"

"I want to date *you*, Zee." I toyed with the stem of my glass. "What if we took it slow? Stay off certain people's radars—"

"Make me another dirty little secret?" His expression was thunderous. "Fuck that."

I'm not dirty, Cherry mildly commented.

My eyes tingled. I dug my nails into my palms, using the bite of pain to center myself and speak calmly. "Our friends would know. Michael, too, but she isn't going to tell the Authority. We'd keep it from our fathers for obvious reasons."

"Get real, Aviva. You think Delacroix hasn't figured out the truth? I've threatened to dismember him for hurting you. More than once."

"He knows you help me out, that we're friends. Anything else is none of his business."

"This has nothing to do with our privacy." Ezra reached for the chalice.

I squirmed in my seat. "Can't it just be about us for a while? You want all that other pressure?"

"Nice try, mi cielo," he drawled coldly. "You're retreating to your hiding-in-plain-sight fallback. I won't do it."

"At least that's a strategically sound place to be," I shot back. "You'd rather shove yourself—shove us—into the spotlight in the misguided belief that it keeps you safe." If we did this and then ever broke up, my cover was blown and I couldn't go back to hiding. Once I was outed to the world, that was it.

He crossed his arms. "I see it as being all in on this relationship, but thanks for your condescending opinion." He shook his head. "I'm not the same man I was, but you don't trust me. Just say it."

"This isn't about trust. It's about choices we've both made."

"And yours involves putting the Maccabees first."

"It involves putting *me* first. Not blowing everything I've worked so hard to achieve. If you cared about me, you'd understand that."

"I understand plenty," he muttered and fired back the rest of the blood in the chalice.

I slammed the table. "You got to dictate the end of our relationship, why can't I set some rules for the start?"

Ezra blinked at me, his expression an unreadable mask. Then he stood up and walked away.

I threw my napkin on the table. It was less satisfying than throwing my knife at his back. "For not being the same man, this looks awfully fucking familiar."

He stopped and turned around. His fangs had descended. "I'm not leaving you. I'm stepping outside to take a moment, so I don't say something I regret."

"You could have mentioned that," I sniped.

He didn't reply, his retreating footfalls feeling like a blow.

The waiter brought what should have been my succulent, decadent main course of Lobster Thermidor, along with another chalice of blood for Ezra.

I sawed listlessly at the sumptuous meal, not staring at the empty seat beside me.

Ezra finally returned and sat down. "I'm not leaving the Copper Hell."

I set down my cutlery. "Because of your mother."

"That and we have no clue what Delacroix is up to. Not only does this put me in the best position to find out, there's no telling what he'd do if his security system up and left. And if things get really bad with Natán, then you, me, our friends, we all retreat to the yacht where he can't get to us. I know you hate it when I do things to keep you safe, but this is for more than just you."

"That all makes sense, but..." I shrugged and spread my hands wide. "Is this our last supper?" I teased sadly.

"No." He leaned forward, his eyes blazing with intensity. "How about we simply be two people enjoying each other's company? No labels, no pressure. Besides, you don't even look like yourself right now and you don't even smell like yourself."

Right. Ezra and a busty blonde. My heart thudded hollowly in my chest. "Darsh gave me this pheromone-based perfume."

"Well, it gives us some breathing room. Ezra Cardoso is simply having dinner with..." He looked at me in question.

"Jackie." I used the short form of my middle name—Jacqueline—and flipped my hair off my shoulders. Too bad I didn't feel as lighthearted as I acted. "What happens when I'm not undercover anymore?" I said softly.

"We..." The corners of his eyes and lips tightened briefly. "Can't we have one thing that doesn't require a million strategies and contingency plans?"

That was rich coming from him. I downed the rest of my wine, my shoulders slumped.

"Ezra Cardoso, you naughty boy." A vaguely familiar Black man with a shaved head stepped onto the platform, his broad British accent at odds with his impeccably tailored suit.

"Alastair," Ezra said flatly.

The vampire who ranked only behind Ezra in Natán's Mafia hierarchy. My shitty evening was complete.

Chapter 14

Alastair placed a bottle of champagne on the table. "Here I planned to catch you in a little tête-à-tête with Ms. Fleischer, but you've found another lovely woman to charm."

"Who is this Fleischer? Are you seeing someone else?" I spoke with a Russian accent, grateful for the stupid high school play Sach had forced me to be part of where I'd honed that voice. However, while my voice was fake, my bristling was not. I wanted to finish hashing this out with Ezra.

"Of course not." My ex glared at Alastair.

The Brit pulled up a chair. "You're lucky I'm here, Ez, and not Remy. He bribed Eloise to take her shift so he could see his bestie again, but Aviva hasn't left the house, so I tracked you down." He chuckled. "Imagine Remy, here. Wouldn't that have been cozy?"

Ezra groaned, pinching the bridge of his nose. "Remind me to have a chat with him about boundaries."

"Now, now," Alastair said, clapping Ezra on the shoulder. "Don't be too hard on the lad. He's simply a card-carrying member of the Ezracurriculars. Helped him fill out the form myself."

"I hate you," Ezra said.

"No, you don't, because my presence means you and... Sorry, I didn't catch your name, love." Alastair draped an arm along the back of his chair, but there was a weight to his gaze.

My physical disguise was solid, and Ezra had assured me I didn't smell the same, so was the prickling between my shoulder blades warranted?

"You ruin our dinner," I said haughtily. "Take your champagne and go." I flicked a hand at him.

"Let's not be hasty, sweetheart." Ezra checked the label on the bottle. "There's no need to waste excellent champagne."

I sloshed more wine into my glass. Was parading me under Alastair's nose fun for Ezra?

The Brit laughed and crossed his legs, getting comfortable. "That's my boy. By the way, you haven't seen Hunter, have you? Natán sent him on a job the other day and he never came back."

I set the bottle down on the table with a too-hard thunk, willing myself to stay calm and keep my heartbeat steady.

"Probably on another one of his blood-drinking benders," Ezra said.

The other vamp huffed in disgust. "I wouldn't put it past him. Why Natán keeps him around, I'll never know."

"Alastair," Ezra said flatly.

"Yeah, mate?"

"Three's a crowd." Ezra made a shooing motion.

"True, true." He held up his hands in surrender. "Natán will be delighted to know you're broadening your social circles, Ez." He stood up and bowed. "Enjoy the champagne." Hands in pockets, he sauntered off.

I waited until he was out of vamp hearing range to speak. "Alastair knows it was me and now he'll run back to

Natán about our date. Your father will retaliate for my going against his orders to stay away from you."

"He isn't going to harm a Maccabee, especially not one whose mother is a director."

"Then why did he sic his vampire minders on me?"

"Intel." Ezra paused and shrugged. "And to mess with us. Be more worried about the day he pulls those vamps, because that's when he'll make his move. When we don't see him coming."

"That's super reassuring."

"Don't let Alastair or Natán wreck our evening."

"That's not all on them," I snapped. I exhaled slowly. "Sorry. Maybe we should call it a night."

"Come on. Get back in that dinner headspace, champ." Ezra threw a couple shadowboxing punches. "It's romance. It's sexy. It's fun." He looked at me entreatingly. "You don't want to miss dessert."

I didn't want to leave but I didn't know how to stay. I wrinkled my nose at my congealing dinner. Whatever. "Bring it on."

"Brace yourself, Fleischer." He caught the eye of someone beyond the potted orchids and nodded.

"I have pretty high expectations."

"I know," he said seriously.

At a footfall, I looked up, worried Alastair had come back, only to see a small army of servers carrying trays laden with desserts.

There were macarons in a rainbow of pastels hues, dark chocolate soufflé, crème brûlée waiting to be cracked open, delicate tulip-shaped glasses filled with layers of fruit, cream, and cake, and handmade chocolate truffles, all set out on the tables around us.

"Dessertapalooza," I breathed. "This is why you booked out this section?"

"Your answer was dessert dependent." Ezra tugged on

his collar, his nervousness sending butterflies dancing through my belly. "I feel ridiculous now."

I placed my hand over his. "Don't. This is incredible."

The servers turned reverently to a portly chef with a handlebar mustache carrying a tower, nay a golden pyramid of cream puffs held together by glistening strands of caramel.

I half rose out of my seat, dabbing at my eyes. "That is the most perfect croquembouche I've ever seen."

Ezra crossed his arms. "You have no clue what a Chateau Petrus is, but you can identify a croquembouche at forty paces?"

"It's like you know nothing about me," I said sadly. "Now hush and let me bathe in its magnificence."

"Mais, oui, c'est magnifique," the chef said in his thick French accent, carefully setting the dessert down in front of me. "I am the finest pastry chef in tous le monde. Monsieur Cardoso begged to fly me in from Paris on my day off."

"The money truck I offered didn't hurt." Ezra offered a bland smile.

"That's why we're doing this on a Wednesday?" I said.

"Duh. Why else would I schedule a romantic dinner on Hump Day?"

The chef wished me bon appétit and withdrew, taking the waitstaff with him.

"I...I don't even know where to start," I said, my eyes roaming over the desserts.

Ezra leaned in close, his breath tickling my ear. "That's the beauty of it," he murmured in a low husky voice. "You don't have to choose. You can try them all." His hand found its way to the small of my back, his fingers splayed possessively across the fabric.

I laughed off the starburst shooting through me at his touch, closed my eyes, and pointed. "That one first."

"That's a candle." He moved my hand a half inch. "How about that?"

I kept my eyes closed. "Feed it to me."

"You trust me to put something in your mouth without seeing what it is?"

"You trust me to have something in my mouth at a future date if you mess with me now?" I said sweetly.

Ezra barked a laugh.

My grin turned to a moan when I savored the sharp crunch of caramelized sugar, followed by the creaminess of decadent custard. I swallowed it and opened my eyes. "More."

Ezra's fingers tightened on the spoon. A slow, wicked smile bloomed across his face then he leaned in and licked the corner of my mouth. "You had some cream."

My entire body lit up, my nipples going hard. All right, Count von Cardoso, the game was on. My teeth grazed his fingers when he popped a chocolate truffle in my mouth; he wiped a macaron crumb off my lip with tantalizing slowness in retaliation.

We waged a war on a sugar-fueled battlefield of who would break first, every morsel he fed me intertwined with his touch and scent.

Until we hit the point where sexy tipped into "oh God, my stomach is going to explode."

"Mercy," I said, pushing away my third choux pastry puff tempting me like some creamy demon.

Phrasing, Cherry muttered.

"Have some water." Ezra poured a glass and pressed it into my hand.

We hadn't even made a dent in the desserts that had cost Ezra a small fortune, my fastidious ex had a dollop of something on his pricy shirt from feeding me, and now he was pouring me water, his primary concern my well-being.

"Aviva," Ezra said, his tone suddenly serious.

My stomach knotted up.

"I know things have been complicated between us," he said, "but I don't want to wait. If being with you means keeping us quiet for now, taking it slow, then I'll do it."

He was giving me what I wanted but damn. "You're giving me vertigo from this sudden change of heart. Our chemistry—"

"Isn't why I'm saying this. Alastair's presence made everything my father is forcing you to deal with hit me in a visceral way. And that's just one pressure you're facing." He leaned forward. "I don't want to be a stress in your life, though I can't promise your way will always be easy for me. Allegedly, sometimes, I like to be in control."

I snorted and twisted my linen napkin. It's funny how our encounter with Alastair had driven different things home for us. For me, it demonstrated that Ezra and I were always a hairsbreadth away from being discovered—if we hadn't been already. I hadn't calculated how much time had to pass before it was safe for us to come out about our relationship.

What if it was never? At least, not as long as Ezra remained at the Copper Hell.

"Avi?" He held out his hand.

"Fuck it." I placed my hand in his. "I'm in."

Finally, Cherry groused.

Ezra pulled away with a look of mock outrage. "'Fuck it, I'm in'? That's how you want to phrase our grand reconciliation?"

"I'm so full that if I was wearing pants, I'd have unbuttoned them, so I definitely do not have the energy to rephrase myself in a more romantic fashion."

"But you had the energy for that speech," he groused.

"In or out, Cardoso?"

Ezra held up his chalice. "To new beginnings," he said.

I mirrored the gesture with my water glass. "And old

friends. Who are also new friends. But also, not just friends."

Shut up before you drive him away, loser, Cherry said. No. Wait. That was my voice in my head. I mean, fair. "To new beginnings," I said.

We clinked glasses.

Ezra's eyes lit up with a mischievous glint. "I have an excellent bottle of Merlot back at my place. What do you say we continue this celebration somewhere more private? We'll portal directly to my accommodations. Delacroix will never know you were there."

I appreciated his forethought as much as I hated that we had to sneak around. Mostly, though, I was all fluttery at the prospect of making love again as a couple. "What happened to taking it slowly?" I teased.

"I plan to slowly explore every single inch of you. Does that count?"

"Okay," I squeaked.

The smile that broke across Ezra's face was radiant. "Yeah? We're really doing this? Us this, not sex this, though we will do that too. A lot."

I nodded and took his hand, trying not to laugh, but also so relieved that he was as nervous as I was. "Yes, Zee. We're doing this."

"We should probably kiss," he said.

"Only to make it official and not because we'd enjoy it."

"Not at all." He grimaced and slid his hand into the hair at the nape of my neck.

A gooey sensation speared my chest.

Ezra brushed his lips over mine, sighing my name and igniting a spark inside me that sent shivers cascading down my spine. His kiss was soft at first, almost reverent, his warm lips teasing and nipping.

I chased his lips, wanting to throw "slow" under a bus

and drive over it a few times for good measure, but he kept pulling back slightly, ruthless in keeping the kiss light.

Ruthless in driving me into a hot ball of need.

I lightly punched his chest. "I'm invoking my woman's prerogative. Enough of this."

He sat back with a half grin. "Enough kissing? Aw. Too bad."

"Ezra," I growled.

He leaned slowly toward me—then turned his head and nipped my ear, scraping his fangs along the side of my neck.

I sighed breathily.

He yanked me onto his lap, his lips claiming mine, and thrust his tongue into my mouth, tasting of wine and a darker copper note that Cherry flared to life at.

The kiss wasn't a slow ripple, it was a plunge into the deepest part of the ocean where only the brave dared swim.

I dove in headfirst, meeting him stroke for stroke, all lips and teeth and tongue, my fingers clasped in the curls at the base of his neck and my other hand gripping his biceps.

Ezra gave this sexy-as-fuck rumble that vibrated through me, curling my toes.

I tumbled between kisses that felt like the swell of waves, so lit up, I swore my buzzing was audible.

"¡Coño!"

Cotton-headed, I clutched at his shirtfront.

"Avi." Ezra nodded at the table. "Our phones."

They were buzzing simultaneously. We shared a look of disbelief before checking our messages.

Mine was a douse of cold water. "Some asshole smashed my car in my underground parking at home."

Ezra made a face at his screen. "Trouble at the Copper Hell that demands my attention."

"This was orchestrated," I said.

"Fucking Alastair." Ezra stood, offering his hand to help me up. "Rain check?"

I sighed, allowing him to pull me to my feet. In some ways, these petty strikes were reassuring. Natán could get to us anytime; he wouldn't do anything drastic while we were braced for it.

Ezra growled when his phone buzzed again.

We straightened our clothing as best we could, but his shirt was rumpled and my lopsided do was missing about seven bobby pins. There was no hiding what we'd been up to.

I followed him to the foyer with a longing glance back at all the desserts.

The hostess retrieved my jacket from the cloakroom.

"Darn. I forgot my scarf," I lied. "You don't have to wait."

He gave me a patient smile and nodded at the hostess, who produced a white bakery box tied with a pink ribbon. "A dessert sample to go."

"It's like you really know me," I said.

Even in our moments of frustration, there were sparks of magic, reminding us why we chose to fight for this reconciliation. As I held the bakery box with its brilliant satin bow, there was a familiar ba-bump in my chest—the one that always appeared when Ezra's thoughtfulness caught me off guard, making me fall for him all over again.

Half an hour later, I was home, sitting on the trunk of my car, eating macarons out of my take-home box of goodies, and staring at the wreckage of my plastic bumper on the concrete. Earworm from Hell Muzak played on the twenty-four-hour insurance claims line.

Sach strode out of the elevator, whistling at the damage. "Bet it was that asshole in 7D."

"It was one of Natán's crew." I put my call on speaker.

"I can't prove it, because they still haven't fixed the cameras down here, but I'm positive."

Sachie selected a chocolate truffle. "Are you and Ezra back together again?"

My fingers drifted to my lips and the memory of that kiss.

"That's a yes, then." Sach poked me in the forehead. "Make that dopey look go away."

I grinned. "Dopey is good. Better than anything requiring a Disney villain's karaoke playlist, right?"

"The jury's still out," she grumbled, then winked.

It meant everything to me to have her approval on this, since she'd dragged me through the darkness of that breakup and back into the world of the living.

My phone buzzed and I clicked on the photo of a demon caught mid-transformation. The half bat, half goat crouched by a Li'l Hellion who held a silver spoon like a makeshift stake, the two of them looking on with identical expressions of horror at Ezra, who was inexplicably covered in green goo from the knees down.

I showed the photo to Sach, who snagged another truffle and announced she was leaving before we started sexting.

I looked around. "In the parkade?"

"Public places can be sexy."

"While I'm on hold with the insurance adjuster?"

"Like I didn't have to hear the two of you more than once."

"When Ezra is covered in demon goop?"

"You define threesomes as you see fit, boo." She booped me on the nose.

I pointed to the elevator. "Go now."

Chuckling, she wandered away.

Count von Cardoso: *Wish you were here?*

I grimaced at the demon goo photo. *Not remotely.*

Fair. How bad is your car?

Didn't expect her to need a butt lift so early in our relationship, but here we are. How about next time we ignore our phones and run away?

I'm in.

When there was nothing further, I assumed he'd been distracted by more shenanigans at the Hell, but a final message popped up.

I miss you already.

I pressed the phone to my chest, like a giddy schoolgirl. *Back at you, Zee.*

My heart sank. I was already so far gone for him again. I crossed my fingers. *Please don't let this go wrong.*

It won't, Cherry said firmly in my head. *You're different people now and you both want this to work. So chill the fuck out and enjoy this.*

I ran my thumb over the message on the screen. *I miss you already.*

Okay, Aviva Jaqueline Fleischer, time to stop overthinking this and worrying about all the ways it could go wrong. Sachie and Darsh accepted Cherry, my mom and I were getting along better than ever, and now Ezra was officially back in my life.

I was allowed to be happy.

I *was* happy, and no one, not even my own dumb brain, was going to take that away from me.

And when the insurance agent answered my call, and I described the damage to my car? Well, even that didn't seem so bad.

Happy was kind of awesome.

Chapter 15

Thursday got off to a frustrating start.

Gemma still wasn't allowed to ask Roger about the shielding devices and Mois remained AWOL in Argentina.

To complicate matters, the press learned the Maccabees were investigating an attack on Jared, sending him scuttling to do a million and one interviews where he refuted that he'd been the victim of any assault, much less a magic one.

He called his buddy, the mayor, and the investigation was shelved.

Everything was riding on Linda Aviyente leading me to the other matchmakers. It was too many eggs in one basket.

However, just because we couldn't speak to Roger ourselves didn't mean I couldn't try a different tack to suss out his involvement with matchmakers.

I called Rukhsana while hand-washing my crimson sweater.

She had the inside track on what really went down with the debunked artifacts, and she'd been at the fundraiser. Too bad that when I asked her if she was watching Roger because he was part of that gallery heist, she laughed.

Apparently, about a year ago, Henderson caught a

young man stealing his car and had him arrested. Instead of calling his lawyer, the thief called Rukhsana, since he'd intended to deliver the car to her chop shop. Not a brilliant move on the young man's part, but if anyone could get him out of jail it was her. Rukhsana dug deep for something in Henderson's past she could, as she put it, "trade him for the thief's freedom."

Roger's worst infraction? He'd been late one year paying his property tax.

The thief went to jail.

Rukhsana couldn't believe that Henderson was that squeaky clean, so she made a point of running into him and, in her words, "tried to corrupt him one night with an excellent bottle of vodka."

The Frenchwoman had wryly added that unfortunately, the vodka was on a list of Russian items with sanctions against them and Henderson refused to partake.

"Whatever you think that Boy Scout has done?" Rukhsana said to me. "He hasn't."

I trusted her judgment.

That was that. Roger was innocent of the debunked artifact thefts and had only helped Chandra with her alarm system.

I draped my clean sweater over the shower rod to dry. Now to see what, if anything, Linda was guilty of.

Her new exhibit featured a group of sculptors working in the Cubist tradition and our host had gone to town with the theme at this opening. I'd just refused my third offer of appetizers cut into odd geometric shapes, preferring my coconut shrimp less blocky.

Silas and I circulated the large, packed space, my friend pointing out Cubist elements of various sculptures to me as we kept an eye out for the gallery owner. The west side crowd was a mix of artsy-bohemian and more conservative. Silas, in dark jeans and a fitted coral blazer that hugged his chest and biceps, hit the middle of the fashion spectrum nicely.

I shouldered through the crowd, holding Silas's hand in a tight grip.

Some people gave him a wide berth, but that could have been due to his size rather than any sense of him being a vampire, while a few others eyed him like they hoped he was for sale. Gross.

Regardless, I was perfect arm candy. I'd opted for a rarely worn black mini dress with black tights and a pair of high black boots that belonged to Sachie. Darsh had made a snarky comment when he'd first designed my new persona that I'd never be able to re-create his contouring mastery, but I managed quite well if I did say so myself.

The chunky silver pendant I wore on a thick chain that did double duty as a spy camera was a fantastic accessory.

I fanned myself with a flyer for an upcoming exhibit that I'd grabbed on the way in, while I surreptitiously snapped photos of the crowd. Silas and I would examine them in the morning.

I'd taken a taxi here, and while I'd spotted an unfamiliar vamp on duty outside my condo tower, he hadn't spared me a second glance. Had Alastair not recognized me (doubtful) or (more likely) had Natán issued orders to go along with the ruse?

Were we amusing that fucker?

I'd carried a low-grade tension from the succession of not-so-secret spies he'd set upon me, and being free from their prying eyes now, even in this crowded exhibit, allowed the tension to flow out of me.

A cool blonde in an asymmetrical linen tunic and trousers with a large turquoise ring on her middle finger gesticulated calmly while speaking to a small group of people. Linda Aviyente, our host and gallery owner, may have been younger than me, but she carried herself with unimpeachable confidence.

I watched her for a moment, then noticing an open window—hopefully with a breeze strong enough to cut the heat in here—I snagged Silas by the sleeve and tugged him toward the corner.

Amazing how people who didn't move at my repeated "Pardon me" were like Olympic runners off the starting block when they saw Silas bearing down on them.

A reedy man with a pencil mustache gestured broadly at a sculpture that resembled a lumpy frog, making his party laugh. His "ugh" was loud enough to carry halfway across the gallery.

I accepted a glass of white wine from a server, took a sip, and grimaced, catching the gaze of a man also holding a wineglass who was in the process of coating it in ice crystals.

The very pretty human with the incredible cheekbones grinned sheepishly and shrugged, bunching the shoulders of his fitted blue suit.

I saluted him with my drink, wishing I, too, had orange flame magic. Or some ice cubes.

"Aviyente is either an incredible salesperson, or she's using more than charm," Silas murmured, one hand under my elbow to steady me through the crush so I could see what he was talking about.

Linda had joined the reedy man who'd been so dismissive of the lumpy artwork. One of her hands rested lightly on his forearm and he nodded along with everything she said.

"White Flame?" I frowned. Linda was a former member of the Eishei Kodesh Leaders of Tomorrow, but there was no documentation on her magic type. "You think she'd be massively successful if she could use her magic to sell every piece she curated."

"She might be quite weak," Silas said. "Only able to affect people naturally disposed to big emotions."

Linda glanced at the bronze clock mounted above the reception desk, then shook hands with the reedy man and headed the other way.

"Help me find the washroom." I added a grimace like I really had to pee.

Silas glanced at Linda, then back to me. "Sure thing, babe. I think it's this way."

We followed the gallery owner, who had a smile or a quick word and a laugh for many of the patrons. Except if you looked closely, her smile was strained and she kept darting looks back at the man in the blue suit who'd iced his tepid wineglass.

Was he a friend or a foe?

"Damn," Silas said, stopping next to a life-size piece of two stocky figures embracing. "Maybe the restrooms are the other way?"

I peeked around the massive sculpture.

Linda slid a keycard along the mag stripe by a door reading "Employees Only." The statues blocked it from view of the other guests.

I rubbed the stacking rings on my right index finger, having blinged up with thin gold bands to cover my habit of playing with my Maccabee ring, which was back home on my dresser. I didn't feel itchy without it anymore, which was something, I guess. "Got an all-access pass to get us back there?"

"Let me see what we're working with." Silas circled the artwork, pretending to study it. "Amazing how kinetic stone becomes in the hands of a genius."

I nursed my tepid wine, trying not to tap my foot impatiently. Why had Linda left her own party? "I'm more of a photography fan."

Silas maneuvered himself behind the large piece and examined the door and electronic lock.

Correction: he manipulated the magnetic stripe with a plastic card.

"Jesus, Silas," I hissed, checking no one could see us.

"Relax. I'll scent anyone getting close enough to catch us." He bent the card slightly and fiddled with the mag stripe again. "They need to update this system. It's laughably easy to break into."

"For you maybe," I said. "Not all of us have your skills, pumpkin."

"True. I am what you might even call an edge case."

"Huh?"

"Coding joke." He jammed his shoulder into the door and snapped the card up the mag stripe.

The door unlatched with a quiet click.

Silas went preternaturally still, then he whispered "Incoming" into my ear. Making sure I caught the open door, he stepped out from behind the sculpture. "Any idea where the bathroom is?" he said loudly.

I slipped inside the back room.

I was prepared for something nefarious: bricks of cocaine that could be shipped with various pieces, indentured art school students producing fake copies of great works, even a wall of love locks, but the large space was disappointingly unremarkable.

Aside from travel cases, packaged artwork, and several dollies for transporting pieces, there was a nicked table in the center of the room with an empty padded carrying tray and a discarded pair of white cotton gloves.

I passed the half-shut door to a staff kitchen, heading for the light that shone out from another room at the back.

Linda's agitated voice clearly carried through the quiet space. "Please don't make me do this again."

The door from the gallery clicked open.

I dove behind a large wrapped canvas, barely even breathing, while steady footsteps crossed the floor. When they stopped, I crept toward Linda and the newcomer, hiding behind the door and peering through the gap in the frame.

The small office was comfortably cluttered with artbooks spilling off shelves and beautifully framed prints. Linda sat behind the desk, one hand resting on her closed laptop, and her phone cradled between her cheek and shoulder.

Pretty Boy slowly stroked her back. He leaned forward almost imperceptibly, body angled toward her, ready to offer support at a moment's notice.

I positioned my spy camera necklace to capture the two of them and touched the chain to activate it.

"I know," Linda said to the person on the other end of the call, "but…" Her voice was wavery. She listened a moment more then took a deep breath. "No, there's no issue. It'll be done same as always."

The second she hung up, Pretty Boy plucked the phone away. "You've got this," he insisted.

She leaned into him. "You say that, but it hurts so much. All the time now, not just when I use my magic."

I frowned. What was she being asked to do?

Pretty Boy brushed a strand of hair out of her eyes. "Where are your pills?"

"In my purse."

I flattened myself against the wall.

From the kitchen came the sounds of a bottle rattling and a running tap.

"Here," Pretty Boy urged, back with Linda. "Take them."

"You promised me the stronger ones." Linda's voice was shaky.

I clenched the pendant camera. Was he dosing her to keep her carrying out orders?

"Don't worry, sweetheart. I'll get them by tomorrow. Now put your game face on and go back to your guests. Act like everything is fine."

Linda's heels rang against the floor as the pair returned to the main gallery.

I remained where I was for another moment, my hand clutched around my spy camera necklace. What were they up to that required high doses of medication?

When I was positive the coast was clear, I did a cursory search of her office, but the filing cabinet was locked, the inbox on her desk only held invoices, and I couldn't figure out the password to her laptop.

I slipped back into the gallery and beelined for Silas, who stood a head taller than anyone, making finding him a breeze. Too bad we couldn't risk having him hack in to her computer at this event.

"Get this." I relayed what I'd seen. "Pretty Boy is an Orange Flame. You can thank the shitty wine for providing that detail."

"Pretty Boy?" Silas raised an eyebrow. "That's what you consider attractive?"

"His cheekbones are so pronounced. Objectively, yes, he's pretty. Also, not my type."

"Ez's fragile ego will be relieved to hear it."

"Back to the part where the dude is an Orange Flame? You know, like whoever attacked Jared?"

"Wasn't that file terminated?"

"Yes, but it doesn't mean Pretty Boy is not now a person of interest, given he's also doping up Linda. I got photos."

"Good. We'll run down every last thing there is to know about him, but first, let's corner Linda before someone else does."

She was placing a red dot sticker over a card belonging

to the piece that Reedy Man had disparaged, her smile once more in place. It didn't look like armor or a mask now.

"She made a sale," I said.

"And the meds kicked in," Silas said. "Her breathing has slowed down. She's stoned to the tits."

"She's okay though?"

"Yeah. Just very mellow."

I snagged a couple of glasses of tepid wine and headed over, Silas dogging my heels. "Fantastic exhibit," I said, handing her a glass. "You deserve this. Actually, you deserve better than this. Great taste in art." I indicated a stone sculpture of a woman standing in a puddle of her own tears. "But room-temperature wine? Not the way to go."

"Babe!" Silas cough-laughed. "Forgive my girlfriend who apparently has no filter."

"Not when it comes to wine." I shrugged unapologetically.

Linda laughed. "You're not wrong. It was supposed to be chilled, but there was a last-minute refrigeration issue. I'm Linda, but you already know that." She sounded perfectly normal, which made me wonder how often she took these drugs—or used her magic for whatever was happening tomorrow night.

"I'm Jackie," I said brightly and looped my arm through Silas's. "And this handsome hunk is Silas." I giggled. "He's very well endowed."

Silas blushed fiercely and mumbled "Dear lord" under his breath.

I squeezed his arm playfully. "I meant your art collection."

"I'm so sorry," he said to Linda. "Jackie's a lightweight when it comes to alcohol."

Linda winked. "But very entertaining. So, Silas, what do you collect?"

"Trains."

"I've not come across a collector with that interest before." The glaze in her eyes wasn't from the drugs.

This time when I squeezed Silas's arm, there was nothing playful about it. "I like the painting you have by what's his name again? The 'not a pipe' guy?"

"Magritte?" Had Linda been a cartoon character, her eyes would have bugged out of her head.

"I'm partial to the Hopper," he said, "but that's what's so great about art. There's something for everyone."

Linda nodded. "Exactly what I always say."

"That's why I want to sell the collection. It's time for others to enjoy those pieces."

I swear, dollar signs danced around her head. "You'd want them to find the right homes though," she said.

"Absolutely. I'll have to really know and trust whoever I hand them over to. Make sure their vision aligns with mine."

"I love how you put that," she said.

Silas, you genius. Playing coy was the perfect way to snag her interest.

Linda had to mingle, but as the crowd thinned, she returned more and more frequently to Silas and me. I'd like to say that my sparkling personality was responsible, but while the three of us got on well enough, the carrot was Silas's art collection. That said, even if Linda started the gallery with Daddy's money, she was savvy enough to charm me to secure my boyfriend's business.

We hung out with her as she closed up, then she proposed we move to Absolom, a members-only whiskey bar. More time together meant more opportunities to ply her for information about her parents, which we'd been unable to do with her coming and going at the exhibit opening, so we readily agreed.

Absolom was all art deco geometric designs and muted

earth tones with comfortable leather chairs and tableside humidors. Silas commented that it reminded him of the hotel bar in Singapore, where we spent our first vacation together. Linda had been to the place he meant. I hadn't, but I went along with it, adding fond fake memories that weren't place specific.

Excited over our shared jet-setting—she'd probably have a heart attack were the Prime Playboy to join us—she treated us to a private whiskey tasting.

I feigned interest in the very detailed explanations of each small glass and played drunk, though I was burning the booze out of my system via my shedim magic. My ruse wasn't just for Linda's benefit either, because Silas still didn't know about Cherry.

My partner remained sober. No surprise there. It took a lot to get a vampire hammered, especially one as big as him.

Linda, while she held her own, got very chatty the deeper into the tasting we got. We discussed magic types (a common new acquaintance topic for Eishei Kodesh), and I confirmed she was a White Flame.

It was a no-brainer to bring up Jared's speech, since that still dominated the news. Linda was of the unsurprising opinion that he was a "shitty little worm with shitty little prejudices."

We all drank to that, then I maneuvered the conversation to Mois.

The big twist of the night was that apparently her father shared her opinion of Jared. It took another whiskey and some delicate verbal dancing, but we learned that the only reason her dad donated to Casey was as a fuck-you to his ex-wife.

Did this fuck-you extend to Chandra's murder? She'd been killed by a shedim, but if Mois knew about his wife's matchmaking business—or was part of it—he could find a demon, no problem.

It's not like shedim took much convincing to commit murder. Breaking the Ten Commandants on the regular was hardwired into their DNA.

Frustrated, I shot back some top-shelf whiskey and started coughing.

Silas poured me some water and shook his head. "Yo, lightweight. Pace yourself." Once he saw I'd recovered, he offered a platitude about brutal divorces and asked what Linda's mother thought of her ex-husband's donation.

Linda replied with a terse "She died recently."

I wasn't supposed to know about that, nor could I just casually inquire whether Linda had knowledge of demons as a conversation opener to whether she was aware of what her mom was really up to.

How could I use Linda to flush out everything about matchmakers, including whether the shedim who murdered Chandra was a partner or an enemy?

Stymied, I invoked the time-honored Vancouver ritual of chatting about neighborhoods to buy time. (Me—west end, Linda—Southlands. Ooh là là.)

When she heard that Silas was a seasoned rider (I giggled knowingly, *loving* the bright red blush that produced in my fake boyfriend), she issued an open invitation to visit her place. She lived near one of the stables and some excellent trails in Pacific Spirit Park and we could saddle up together.

Since the closest I got to horses was a merry-go-round and I'd stopped riding those when I was ten, I said I'd come for the après ride drinks.

The night hadn't been a total bust. The invitation was a big win, since it would allow Silas entry into her home at a future date. We'd also filled in some details about Linda and Mois, and had some promising photos to comb through, starting with Pretty Boy. However, after a long night of faking drunk and conducting a subtle interrogation, I was ready for bed.

The second I got home, I peeled out of my shapewear, scrubbed all the makeup off my face, and tore out my colored contacts, peering intently at myself to feel a sense of connection to me, Aviva, not Jackie with her strawberry blond hair and blue eyes.

Maud phoned, replying to my hello with a disgusted, "Why aren't you having sex right now?"

I flopped onto my mattress. "Why did you phone if you thought I was?"

"It's been over a day, and you didn't give me details yet, sister dear. Are you and the Prime Playboy officially a thing?"

"Yes." I let the silence hang, grinning when she finally exploded with something said in Cantonese. "Did you just swear at me?"

"I insulted you. Slight difference."

"You suck." I rested my arm under my head. "Aren't you in Macao with your cousins?"

"I fly out tomorrow." A kettle whistled loudly through the phone. "Jenny's going to shove her fathead fiancé and perfect life down my throat."

"She's a dental hygienist. She has her hands in people's mouths all day, how perfect can it be?"

"My mother was convinced the sun shone out her ass."

Maud and I had commiserated over our mothers' respective disappointments in us and the scarily similar upbringings we'd had where keeping our shedim side a secret was paramount.

Michael and Chongying would have liked each other, or at least had a lot to discuss between their half-demon daughters and their questionable choice in baby daddy.

"Did your godmother know what you were?" I said.

"I told her." The sound of shuffling cards came through the receiver.

"How'd she take it?"

"Better than I thought, but she was dying so, you know, it put things in perspective. I think she was angrier at my mother for keeping this from her."

Just like Keira and my mom with all those lost years of friendship. "I get that. I'm glad you told your best friend years ago."

"What's up with all the melancholy? You're dating a hot dude. You're a level three. You have the world's best sister." There was more card shuffling.

"All true. Don't mind me. Melancholy officially banished."

"Hmm. I don't believe you. I'll just have to do something to knock you out of that headspace. Oh, I know! How about I post on one of Ezra's fan boards about the new love of his life? The Ezracurriculars will die of shock."

The words hit me like a bucket of ice water.

Ezra's reluctant agreement to keep us out of the spotlight would crumble. I could already see the hurt and betrayal in his eyes, thinking I'd allowed Maud to leak this for some Maccabee purpose when I'd banned him from doing the same thing.

My throat tightened as I imagined the flood of messages, the relentless whispered speculation among my colleagues, the paparazzi camped outside my apartment, and Natán's retaliation.

Would I be known primarily as Ezra's girlfriend, instead of for my own merits? I balled my fists. How long would the Authority even allow me to remain with the organization?

This was it, the moment where everything I'd worked for was shattered, including this fragile reconciliation.

"Maud! No!"

"I was kidding, Avi," she said in a hurt voice. "I wouldn't do that."

"Sorry. It's just, we need to keep our dating quiet for now."

The sound of shuffling cards abruptly stopped. "Ezra agreed to that?"

"He understands the reasons."

"Okay," she said dubiously.

"What's with that tone?"

"Reasons or not, I'd find it hard not to take it personally if my romantic partner wanted to keep us a secret. It's a lot of pressure to put on the start of the relationship, but again, that's just me."

I hugged a pillow to my chest. "Ezra and I are on the same page."

"Great!"

I loved my naturally upbeat sister but that was said with overkill peppiness.

Our call ended soon after, but my phone buzzed again while I was brushing my teeth. I picked it up with dread, worried it was Maud for round two, or Ezra with, well…

It was Darsh.

Silas had sent him a selfie we'd taken after we'd finished our first flight of whiskey. Silas had his arm around me in the photo and was nuzzling the side of my head, but from this angle it looked like I was half in his lap.

Darsh had forwarded it to me, making an exception to his dislike of texting.

I spit toothpaste into the sink, laughing at his accompanying message.

Next time, leave room for the Holy Ghost.

Chapter 16

Sach handed me coffee the next morning with a humph. "Why aren't you still sleeping, given how late you got back?"

"Are you bummed you didn't have time to lizard yourself up another wall and test my battle-readiness?" I joked.

She turned around to refill her own mug, back tense.

Uh-oh. That wasn't a good sign. I stirred in sugar and milk and pondered my next move. "Did something happen with your parents?"

"No, we're still in polite small talk territory."

"Did I wake you last night?" Odd, since she could usually sleep through anything.

"No." She pulled omelet ingredients from the fridge with the single-minded focus of an action hero choosing which wire to cut with five seconds left on the timer.

The cause of her grumpiness became apparent two minutes later when her bedroom door opened, and Detective Olivier Desmond strolled into the kitchen. In rumpled clothing.

Ooh. The boyfriend had spent the night for the first time.

"Good morning, sunshine," I said, the sight of Sach squirming doing more to perk me up than my first sip of caffeine.

Olivier, to his credit, did not backpedal or justify his presence. He cut through any potential awkwardness of this first morning-after encounter like a shark, walked straight over to Sachie, and kissed her.

Good man.

He took the mug from my gobsmacked friend's hand, then blinked at me. "Solid disguise. Morning, Avi," he said, in his calm Nova Scotian voice. "Heard the chief constable personally handed over the Nichols murder to your director. Those two personalities butting heads?" He made a "yikes" face.

I chuckled. "It was something else."

Sach peered at me suspiciously for a moment, but when she saw I wasn't going to get snarky (because I didn't have a death wish), she relaxed.

"We looked into the Ashbishop last night," Sachie said, shredding cheese.

I cracked eggs into a large bowl. "You did?"

She'd just shared this information with Olivier without asking me? I'd been the one determined to hunt down the missing half-shedim blood and find whoever had ordered those murders. I'd led every step of this investigation, and yes, I'd asked her to research the Ashbishop—with Darsh's permission to share what he knew of the vampire—but bringing her new boyfriend into it was a whole other matter.

I snatched a whisk out of the drawer.

"Vamp procreation poses a bigger danger to Trads than to Eishei Kodesh," Olivier said, splashing milk into his own cup of coffee.

"That's true," I said tightly.

"Olivier, do you mind seeing if there are any napkins on the dining room table?" Sach said.

"Sure." He left the kitchen at a fast clip.

She crossed her arms. "Do you want this vamp found or do you want to play team leader and invoke chain of command and a billion other bullshit procedures?"

I beat the eggs, working through how to phrase my thoughts without insulting the man she was in a first blush of feelings with. A man, whose intelligence and police experience were part of why I'd even matchmade them in the first place. Why *I'd* been interested in him at one point.

"Involving a Trad cop, when our communities are so ruptured, wasn't ideal in terms of timing." I frothed the eggs so viciously that yolk splatted onto my hand. Swearing, I grabbed a paper towel to clean myself. "I understand you're spending a lot of time together but—"

Sachie gave an incredulous laugh. "This is the Jessica King stupidity all over again."

I gasped, once more furiously attacking the eggs. "I am not jealous. Also, may I remind you that *you* were the one who freaked out about me still having contact with your parents when you first started fighting a couple months ago. And you're thirty, so don't throw an incident from when we were twelve in my face." I shook my head. "There's a lot at stake here and—"

"Don't treat me like I'm stupid, Aviva." She didn't unearth any weapon but her low, dangerous tone and the anger clouding her eyes were scary enough.

I dropped the whisk in the bowl and sighed. "I'm sorry. That's not what I meant. Look, I miss hanging out with you, but I've been busy with work so it's not just you." I looked up at the ceiling like a summation of the feelings swirling inside me would be helpfully inscribed there. "This all started with the murdered half shedim, a case that was very personal to me." I glanced at the doorway. Olivier was far enough away at the dining room table that he wouldn't hear this quiet conversation, still I was careful with my phrasing. "Now you and Darsh understand how personal it is."

"Olivier doesn't know any of that and I'd never tell him."

Still.

...retreating to your hiding-in-plain-sight fallback... Ugh. Get lost, Ezra's voice.

I was making great strides in terms of being more open, both with others and about my life in general, but prudence was wise, and I prided myself on working smart, not hard.

Ezra could let it all hang out in the spotlight because he was famous. Yes, he'd done a lot of legwork to make his strategy possible, but the structures I'd built were dependent on me being less obviously recognizable.

"I spent so long being so careful to keep any iota of Cherry hidden," I said. "It makes sense for you to bring Olivier's experience and intelligence to help find the Ashbishop but..." I exhaled. "It's hard for me to not control the flow of information."

"Okay." She dumped the shredded cheese in the bowl with the eggs. "I'm sorry too. I should have taken that into account. Olivier was just a second brain to help me research, not there in any official Trad cop capacity, but I won't ask again for his help without checking with you."

Should the multiverse be real, there was a version of me where I assured Sachie that I trusted her judgment and she didn't need to run things past me that would help us stop vamp procreation.

Instead, I quietly said thank you and made us the best damn cheesy omelets ever.

Over breakfast, Sach detailed the wide swath of senseless killing and terror done by the Ashbishop. He first popped up in Ireland about seventy years ago, slaughtering a small village, then spread like a blight, eventually making his way to North America and killing any human or vampire who got in his way.

"He had followers though?" I said, thinking of Patrin and wondering why the Ashbishop inspired loyalty to the degree that Darsh's brother wouldn't give him up, even when facing his own execution. It had to be fear-based. "What a brutal leader he must have been."

"On the contrary," Olivier said. "By all accounts, the Ashbishop was good to his crew of vamps."

"A real mensch," I said dryly. "Though Ireland fits. I figured his name stemmed from Catholic guilt."

"There wasn't a religious element to this Ashbishop's dealings," Olivier said, "and in fact, he burned down more than one Catholic church, but his desire to procreate could tie into a mutation of Exodus 13:2. 'Consecrate to Me all first-born.' He's not offering to God per se, but the devil." He frowned at my puzzled look. "What? Not plausible?"

"There's no single all-in-charge devil as described in the Bible," I said. "Not that we know of. It's more that we don't get a lot of quoting the Old Testament off the top of one's head around here."

Sachie salted her eggs. "Olivier was raised Baptist. It would be weird if he couldn't quote this stuff."

"Thank you for the helpful explanation of this very specific detail about Detective Desmond," I said, my lips twitching.

She threw her napkin at me. "Go find somewhere new to live."

I threw the wadded-up ball back at her. "Give me written notice and two months' free rent according to the law."

"I don't see why I should be out of pocket," she grumbled. "Stay. Whatever."

Olivier followed our exchange with a grin. "Back to the

Ashbishop. Where's he been all this time and why come back now?"

"I'm not so sure his return is super recent." I set my fork down. In for a penny and all that. "The missing infernal blood."

Sachie looked up sharply, but I shook my head that it was okay. I was only going so far with this, still, for someone who'd avoided all discussion of infernals *and* infernal-adjacent topics most of her life, it was a big deal for me to broach the subject with Olivier.

It was also a test to see how he reacted to that word.

"Infernal?" He looked between Sach and me, his brow wrinkled. "Is that another term for shedim?"

"Infernals are humans who are half-demon," I said.

"It's a shit slur," Sach said. "Don't use it. Refer to them as half shedim."

"Okay." Olivier looked lost.

I, however, smiled at my best friend. "We had a case a few months back where six half shedim were slaughtered in ritual killings. They were exsanguinated but their blood was never recovered. A vampire Maccabee called Roman Whittaker teamed up with an Eishei Kodesh to kill them, but the operative confessed to someone else being behind it."

I left out Roman's murder and that Dr. Metaxas was also a halfie. Even Sach didn't know that part.

"Somebody had to find those half shedim in the first place," Sachie said.

That had been Metaxas, but blood called to blood, and the Ashbishop had a way to find my kind. Or, the good doctor had provided the Ashbishop with a helpful list of names before she bit it.

It wasn't like the Ashbishop was a half shedim. Vamps didn't keep demon magic once they were turned, even if they'd been a halfie in life. Ezra had confirmed that detail through sources at the Copper Hell.

"These victims lived all over the globe so identifying them took time," I said. "But their blood is going to be used in the ritual to achieve procreation."

"Which also involves a power word," Sachie said.

I nodded. "Obtaining that word involves a magic test and the most recent supplicant was one of the Ashbishop's followers. Who knows how many other vampires the Ashbishop has sent to try and procure it? He could have been at this for years."

"We can't let this vamp have kids who he can raise to be an evil immortal army," Olivier said.

"Absolutely not," Sachie said.

Olivier offered to clear up the dishes, so I went to get dressed.

Silas and I were working at Darsh's place today. Silas had set up a bunch of computer equipment there and didn't want to lug it to my place.

I was applying mascara when Ezra texted me that there was a vampire at the Hell who was a longtime but infrequent visitor. He suspected she was acquainted with the Ashbishop and invited me to come to the Hell and ply her —or play her—for information. He added a "Hurry so you catch her before she leaves."

I replied he should open a portal in my back alley in about ten minutes and quickly texted Silas I'd be a bit late. I raced into the living room, throwing my hands over my eyes with an "Ack! Sorry!" at Olivier and Sachie kissing.

"Avi, you don't need to keep your eyes averted," Olivier said, laughing. "We can exercise self-control."

"Unlike some," Sachie said sweetly.

"At least I didn't drench you when I caught you." I glared at her.

She mimed firing a pistol at me. "My aim got really good that summer, but man, did I have to keep topping up that Super Soaker."

I slid on my boots and snuck out the fire exit of my condo tower to avoid Natán's minion. While there was no point pretending the cat wasn't out of the bag on my disguise, they didn't need to know Ezra was opening Aviva-only portals.

Too bad that when he opened this one, I simply bounced off the mesh light.

The portal shut down and my phone rang.

"I don't want to leave it open," Ezra said. "If you need more time, call me when you're ready."

"I can't get through."

"Huh. Okay. Hang tight. Let me see what's up."

I returned to the warmth of the lobby, sitting on the uncomfortable furniture by the front window while I waited for his call.

"Fucking Delacroix," Ezra said when he phoned back.

"What now?"

"He's banned all Maccabees from the Hell. No exceptions. Apparently, Director Abe and some of the Tokyo chapter Maccabees had a sting operation planned on the yacht."

I white-knuckled the phone. "Abe found out Silas came there after he escaped. If he has any proof that we were involved—"

"He doesn't. The Hell was the safest and most obvious place for Silas to retreat to. This was a fishing expedition. What's bothering me is that I had no idea this raid was in the works and Delacroix didn't see fit to inform me. He invoked a safety override on the magic security system which drains his powers. I can't get you in and I can't talk to him because he's disappeared again."

"There goes my invitation to come over for a glass of port."

Ezra gave a pleased hum. "I like that that's your first thought."

"Followed quickly by what is dear old Dad up to that he's paranoid enough to make himself even the slightest bit vulnerable by draining his magic to amp up security?"

"I'll sort this out. Meantime, I'll see what I can get from Irene."

"On a first-name basis with this infrequent visitor to the Hell, are you?" I teased.

"I am nothing if not a conscientious host," he joked back.

Even with my trip to the Hell thwarted, I was in a good mood as I headed out to my Uber, and the middle finger I threw to whichever minion was on shift was decidedly cheerful.

Darsh threw open his front door before I'd hit the top step. "You're lucky I'm reasonably fond of you," he huffed and marched past me to work.

"Good morning to you too?"

"That was fast," Silas said, walking into the foyer.

"Delacroix fucked things up." I stepped inside. "What's with Darsh?"

"There's something you need to see."

"Okay," I said warily. I toed out of my shoes and lined them up next to the closet.

Silas opened a browser on his phone and showed me a photo from the gallery event of us holding hands and laughing. It was posted on an Ezracurricular fan site, with people writing mostly positive comments that Ezra's best friend had found love.

My real name wasn't outed nor was there a ton of speculation on who I was. I was merely the best friend's new girlfriend. Yet, that "merely" embodied much of why I'd hate going public with Ezra. Ironic that I'd want to be recognized for my own accomplishments when my primary objective had always been to hide, but I was complex woman.

"The disguise holds up nicely and it cements your undercover persona," Silas said.

"True." The incongruence of my fake persona in this fake relationship was at odds with the memory of Ezra's kiss. I rubbed the back of my neck.

"Don't worry, Natán didn't orchestrate it," Silas said.

That hadn't even occurred to me, which was unsettling. I had to stay on my game.

"One of Ezra's fans was at the gallery and recognized me from photos taken of us before." He flexed a biceps, making a duck face. "They love action shots."

I gagged loudly. "Darsh knows this is simply work."

"He's not jealous," Silas said, leading me upstairs. "Just sad that we have to keep our status on the down-low until this is over. He gets it, it just sucks, right?"

Had Ezra seen this photo? I had no idea how much attention he paid to his fans' postings. Did I owe it to him to check in?

"The sooner we wrap this case up, the better," I said noncommittally.

"No kidding."

I entered the guest room and whistled.

Silas's set-up was impressive. Half of the space was taken up by a large desk cluttered with two cobbled-together computers and three monitors, while cables and spare parts littered the desk and floor.

I sat on the edge of the bed since Silas occupied the only chair that fit in the room. "Darsh doesn't come in here, does he?"

Silas wound a cable away from my feet. "I almost had to give him smelling salts the first time he saw it."

My partner had compiled a decent profile on Pretty Boy—aka Troy Abelman. The thirty-two-year-old was a former MIT grad student who'd dropped out during his doctorate on integrating magical cognition with AI to develop sentient machines capable of performing advanced magical tasks.

"AI and magic. That's not terrifying or anything," I said.

"I'm all for higher learning, but this is one time I'm glad someone didn't stay in school," Silas said. "And the school agreed. The project was kiboshed due to ethical concerns."

"Hence him dropping out." I tapped my finger against my lip. "How did Troy get from MIT to Vancouver? Was he already dating Linda and he moved here to be close to her?"

"It doesn't seem that way." Silas consulted the document on his left monitor. "Troy isn't even from Vancouver. He was raised in Milwaukee. His parents are still there, but there's nothing to suggest they're close. He started working at the Lions Gallery shortly after he left MIT."

"I wonder if that timeline coincides with whatever Linda is using her magic for?" I said. "Who else was at the event last night?"

Three hours, a stack of photos, and a delicious Thai food lunch later, Troy and Linda remained the only ones of interest from the exhibit opening.

Darsh phoned me with a terse command to make sure the big lug had some of the disgusting synthetic blood from the fridge since he hadn't stocked it for his own benefit and if Cowpoke got hungry and fed on me because I was running him ragged, Darsh would replace me as his second-favorite friend without hesitation.

I planted a hand on my hip. "Second-favorite?"

Silas gently plucked my cell away to say, "You take care of yourself too, Rapunzel." He listened for a moment before hanging up with a dopey look that made me grimace.

Should I have checked in with Ezra?

"Focus." I snapped my fingers in front of his face. "We're swinging by the address on file for Troy then we'll stake out the gallery."

If whatever Linda was using her magic for tonight was: a) illegal, and b) happening at her gallery, we intended to suss out as much intel beforehand as possible. If it was occurring elsewhere, then we'd split up and follow Pretty Boy and Linda until we had the location.

Sending up a silent wish to the universe that tonight's assignation involved love locks and matchmaking, I followed Silas to the SUV that he'd rented, fired up with purpose.

I ducked into the passenger seat, but instead of hitting comfy leather, I fell into a portal made of red and purple light, tumbling out the other side onto the hot concrete outside Flaming Flapjacks.

Rubbing my bruised hip, I sprinted for the portal to get back to the stakeout, but it winked out.

I was going to kill Delacroix.

Chapter 17

The clouds roiling over the jagged obsidian cliffs had nothing on my mood. I stormed inside the pancake house, shooting the dancing hotcake on the neon sign the finger for good measure. Why should it get to be happy?

The fly hostess was back at her podium. She'd gothed up her bulbous insect eyes with heavy dark liner, her bristly stick-thin legs that poked out from her black miniskirt rattling around in her shitkicker black boots with fat silver buckles.

"Where's Delacroix?" I snapped.

She appraised me with a bored look then pointed a wing out toward the back veranda.

I barreled through the restaurant, every maple syrup and brimstone–scented inhale ratcheting my anger up like a cartoon character with an internal thermometer about to blow.

The "Bring Your Appetite; Leave Your Grudges!" sign fluttered merrily under an AC vent.

My glower did nothing to it, but the shedim nearby who was unlucky enough to catch my eye swallowed nervously with one of its four throats.

I slammed the door to the veranda open, killing any conversation at the large round table.

Eight shedim with their stupid hats and varying degrees of old man human glamors looked my way, the party rounded out by one pissed-off Prime, who glanced at me then pulled out his phone and started typing.

My heart twisted at the sight of him. Was he upset about the photo? I wrenched my eyes away to size up the demons. The more pressing issue.

It was the same crew as the first time I'd been here. A person-sized bat with an old man face wearing an "I Went to Hell and All I Got Was This Lousy Cap" hat slurped porridge up with his tongue. He sat next to the demon with the Popeye biceps in a baseball cap with "Flame-Grilled for Flavor" on it.

Kangol Demon with a pompadour was also present, loudly sucking back iced tea with eyeballs floating in the glass. Oh yeah, he was the Bilge. The one whose stomachs Ezra had to pump.

There was Goat Demon with holes cut into his top hat to accommodate his curved horns, a pudgy tiny danger whose hat boasted the dancing pancake from the sign with "Devilishly Good Eats!", and the blue demon with one eye, four tusks, and a floppy hat adorned with sharp metal lures. A disturbing pile of what I prayed were chicken wings were scattered on his plate.

The last member of Delacroix's evil motley crew was Eeyore Demon, a gloomy-looking creature with a donkey's face and a mane attached to a sunburst of short hooved legs that sprouted from his neck. He looked positively miserable about the "Demon Tested, Hellfire Approved" cap perched jauntily on the top of his mane.

I hoped the extra helping of whipped cream on his runny waffles didn't cause lactose intolerance and shuddered, imagining splash zones.

At the head of the table (yes, he managed to make a round table feel like there was an alpha seat) sat Demon Daddy, resplendent in a shiny silver shirt. It had a moiré pattern with a hypnotic effect, like staring out at the endless expanse of ocean. He'd tucked his windswept salt-and-pepper hair under his black baseball cap with "Hotter than Hades, Cooler than You" in a jaunty white script.

He dropped a half-eaten piece of extra-crunchy bacon on a side plate and wiped his hands off on a napkin. "What's with the new look? Testing whether blondes have more fun?"

"Don't *ever* use your magic on me again," I snarled.

Delacroix flapped a hand. "Grab a seat and have some waffles, girlie."

I got a chair but the decision of where to put it stopped me in my tracks for a second. My first inclination was to sit somewhere other than next to Ezra so that Delacroix didn't get any ideas about us. But even as friends, obviously I'd sit next to Ezra since that was the safest place to be in this situation.

I shoved the chair between my boyfriend and my father.

"I've let Silas know you're here." Ezra's voice deepened menacingly, and his eyes narrowed as he added, "And that you will be returned unharmed. Soon."

Maybe he hadn't seen the photo?

Delacroix rolled his eyes at Ezra's threat.

I cleared my throat. "Get to the point of this visit."

The bat demon with the old-man face reached the bottom of his bowl, swiped at it one more time, then leaned over and licked up the side of Ezra's neck.

"¡Coño!" Ezra half jumped out of his seat and punched the demon in the face.

His nose caved in, but almost immediately it bounced back into place, and unconcerned, he licked crumbs off the table.

"Some people would give their right eye to eat here." Delacroix turned to the blue one-eyed demon. "Isn't that right, Zzzzanooz?"

The demon made a sound like a chain saw starting up that was either a laugh or a death threat.

Delacroix looked around. "Where's the waiter? You need a menu."

"I'm not eating," I said through gritted teeth.

"You and Lover Boy are the rudest guests ever," the shedim groused.

I opened my mouth to retort that he had it all wrong. I was dating Silas. That would have been the right response for my undercover investigation, but even if Delacroix did believe me, I couldn't bring myself to do that in front of Ezra.

To do that *to* Ezra, even if it benefitted a case.

My boyfriend snapped his fingers, startling me out of my unsettled emotions. "Guess I left my etiquette guide in my coffin. Why the fuck did you bring us here?" He practically vibrated with fury. It was a fair reaction; Delacroix abducting me was one thing, but Ezra was a Prime and his business partner. It shouldn't have been possible to do this to him.

Delacroix pointed at the single-serving bottle in front of Ezra. "Drink your blood and calm down. You're such a grouch if you don't eat."

Nope. I didn't need any new weirdness factored into this gong show.

"Delacroix." I practically growled his name.

"I'd like to propose a trade and I had to do it somewhere safe."

Ezra arched one eyebrow. "And that's here, is it?"

"It is, in fact."

Popeye Demon held out a claw for the small jug of maple syrup, which the Bilge handed over.

"A trade like the game you agreed to," I said, "where I give up all the information, and you just torture me?"

The shedim all snickered, Delacroix loudest of all.

Ezra draped an arm along the back of my chair. "Repeating that would be a very bad idea," he said.

Bat Demon nodded gravely. "You're right, Delacroix. They don't have a sense of humor."

"I'm not taking comedy tips from someone who taxidermies rats for fun," I snapped.

Bat-demon's old man face fell into a puddle of wrinkles, like a sad Shar-Pei.

"Your rats are unparalleled," Delacroix assured him. "As for you," he said, glaring at me, "I've located one of the Ashbishop's victims. Someone who can identify the vampire, since all of Lover Boy's flirting with Irene got him nowhere."

I yawned at his attempt to bait me.

Ezra laughed.

"Retrieve an item in Tuscany for me," Demon Daddy continued, "and I'll tell you where the victim is."

"Get it yourself," I said. "I'm busy."

Delacroix slapped his forehead. "Why didn't I think of that?" He jabbed a finger at me. "The house where the item is stashed is protected by a mezuzah."

"I'll do it." Ezra sipped from his bottle of blood, leaving crimson stains on his lips. "You don't need Aviva."

"Au contraire." Delacroix turned to me. "Cardoso can portal you to the grounds, but the safe requires Eishei Kodesh magic to reveal the panel. You'll punch in the code I'll provide. Cardoso will stand guard for the three minutes time delay until the safe beeps, then you open the door and retrieve the item."

"Back up," I said. "Stand guard from what?"

"There's bound to be a magic security system. Use your imagination. But you two can handle yourselves."

The other shedim watched me expectantly.

Finding someone who could identify the Ashbishop would help immeasurably, except I didn't have time for a side quest with an anything-goes magic security system.

On the other hand, Delacroix badly wanted whatever was inside that safe.

I crossed my arms. "What am I retrieving?"

"The brain of my enemy."

I laughed but at Delacroix's unamused expression stopped. Seriously?

"Do we have an agreement?" he said.

Getting a brain for some petty revenge wasn't worth any danger I'd encounter or a loss of focus from everything already on my plate. "No. Now return me."

I was getting antsier with every second not spent at the stakeout with Silas.

"Let me sweeten the deal for you," he said craftily. "I won't tell the Authority that you and Ezra broke Silas out of his cell with the help of a glamor. Personally, I can't stand the taste of that dark magic liquid crap you used instead of going to someone to create the disguise, but I guess it was an emergency. Beggars can't be choosers."

How had he found that out? I clawed my panic down. "Even if that was true," I said evenly, "that's blackmail, not a deal."

"It's only blackmail if you don't take the trade."

"You'll keep your mouth shut about what you think you know," Ezra said, "and let Aviva back into the Hell."

Delacroix made a buzzing sound. "New policy. No Maccabees."

Eeyore Demon said something in a series of brays.

Delacroix groaned. "All right, my friend. I won't stand in the way of true love. Girlie can visit but she's the only one."

Ezra shot me a sideways glance through slitted lashes at

the "true love" crack, but when I didn't object, he shrugged. "Your call, Aviva. There are other ways to find the Ashbishop's victim."

Delacroix snorted. "Good luck."

The sooner the Ashbishop was stopped, the better.

"You'll give me the Ashbishop's victim, allow me back into the Hell, *and* get me the name of the female vampire who last took the test for the power word that the Ashbishop needs for this ritual," I said. "Ezra will fill you in."

Delacroix and his buddies had a brief, intense exchange in some demon language, then he nodded. "You drive a hard bargain, but you have a deal."

"Wonderful," I said coolly. "Give Ezra the details. We'll do it tomorrow." The demon opened his mouth, but I held up my hand. "This is non-negotiable. You need me more than I need you right now, Delacroix, so we're doing this on my timeline."

That was true, but it was also true that I couldn't have him ratting me out to the Authority about Ezra's and my roles in jailbreaking Silas. Luckily, the demon nodded again.

"Now send me back." It sucked that I couldn't talk to Ezra about the photo that was posted or even squeeze his hand, because all eyes were on us.

The portal opened.

"I'll call you later," he said.

I was about to warn Delacroix not to send me into a moving car and that I'd give him the gallery address, when a blast of hot air propelled me into the portal.

"Byyyyyeeeeee!" the shedim called.

I tumbled onto the back seat floor of the SUV with a muffled curse.

"Shh," Silas said from the driver's seat.

Gingerly, I picked myself up and leaned over the console. "What'd I miss?"

We were parked in an alley painted in crazy wonderful fat black and pink stripes, next to a metal door with a sturdy security gate and a high narrow window with heavy bars.

I climbed into the passenger seat.

My partner wore a headset and in his lap was what looked like a ray gun with a plastic cone over the barrel.

"What's that?" I whispered.

"Parabolic mic." He tilted the end bit higher toward the window. "I'm listening to Linda and Troy but there's nothing of note yet." He rolled out his shoulder. "Delacroix fuck you over too much?"

"Less than usual," I said. "Hey, did you ever come across a piece of shit vampire called the Ashbishop?"

Silas whipped toward me so fast that the mic contraption fell to the floormat. "Please tell me you're not digging into him. Avi, he was…" Silas shook his head, his jaw tight.

"Did he hurt you?"

Silas huffed a soft laugh. "You could say that."

I curled my fingers into claws, wishing the Ashbishop was here so I could tear him limb from limb for harming my sweet friend. For killing Patrin. My heart sunk. Had Darsh mentioned his brother to Silas, and if he had, did it bring up fresh trauma? Telling Silas about my suspicions that the Ashbishop was alive was the last thing I wanted to do, but he deserved to know. "I'm worried he's resurfaced."

Silas flinched, his lips compressed into a flat line.

I explained about the vamp seeking procreation abilities and the woman who tested for the power word on his behalf. "Darsh said he was dead, but it doesn't appear—"

"Did the Ashbishop hurt Darsh?" Silas said in a strangled voice.

"No." Well, not directly, and Patrin's story wasn't mine to share. "Can you tell me anything about him?"

Silas picked up his mic. "He'd been a good man in life."

"You knew him."

"Much as I wish I hadn't." He rested his head against the window.

"I've heard of his rampaging and violence but also that he took care of his crew. Was there goodness left in him after he was turned?"

"His crew were tools. He liked to keep them sharp and in good condition. Don't mistake that for caring." His voice was tight with pain.

Had Silas been part of his crew? Was that why he spoke of darkness inside him and why he clung to pacifist ways now? He was deeply and profoundly scarred?

"Could you describe the Ashbishop?" I might be able to duck out of this stupid brain retrieval for Delacroix.

A sigh shuddered out of Silas, like there was this final human breath in him that had been trapped in his belly for centuries. "I've spent years blocking every detail of him from my brain. I can't go back into it. You aren't hunting the Ashbishop. He's dead."

"Are you sure?"

He wearily slid his headset off. "I'm pretty damn sure," he said in a voice thick with self-disgust. "Considering I killed him."

Chapter 18

I didn't press Silas for details of the Ashbishop's death, but hopefully, it involved prolonged pain.

"Someone has co-opted his legend." I stared out the front window, my lips pursed. "Any idea who?"

"Some of his vamp crew are still out there." He swallowed. "I couldn't bear it if one of those psychopaths found you. Please don't keep digging into this."

"I'll back off." I had absolutely no intention of doing so, but I'd tell Ezra, Sachie, and Darsh that we weren't to discuss the Ashbishop with Silas. I didn't want to distress him anymore.

Muffled sound came out of the headset and Silas started, pressing one side to his ear and angling the mic again. "Linda and Troy are going back to her place to await a shipment arriving in about an hour." He tossed his equipment in the back seat and started the engine.

Traffic was heavy and we got across town with only seven minutes to spare until this shipment arrived, but we still took the time to creep through the grounds instead of barreling up the driveway.

Linda had inherited her mother's house, a large property with lots of trees and multiple places to hide. I concealed myself in the branches of a gnarled oak where I could snap photos of the vehicle delivering this mystery shipment and keep eyes on Linda and Troy inside.

Silas hid underneath the living room window to eavesdrop on them.

Linda sat miserably on the sofa while Troy stuffed scrolls into fancy packaging shaped like large silver eggs. They weren't speaking so there was nothing for Silas to overhear.

The box that was dropped off was about the size of a dishwasher. I informed Silas through our comms that it was delivered by a local courier company.

I shifted and rubbed my numb butt, leaning forward with a firm grip on the tree branch to make sure I didn't miss anything.

Troy slit the top of the box with an X-Acto knife and began removing and unwrapping items from brown paper.

I frowned. Was that a hairbrush? Yes, yes, it was.

He handed it to Linda, who held it for a moment. Blotting her forehead with the back of one hand, she placed the brush in one of the fancy containers.

What the fuck con game was going on here?

"Silas," I murmured into the comms. "Meet me in front."

He cornered me before I hit the front stairs. "What are you up to?"

"Going in for better intel." I shook out my hair to be messy and shoved my comms in my pocket, motioning for Silas to do the same. I grabbed my lipstick and applied it with a shaky hand. "Day drinking is a beautiful thing," I said, and stumbled up the steps.

By the time I rang the bell four times, Silas stood beside me with his arm draped over my shoulder.

Linda blinked at us. She looked wan and her eyes were

glazed. She'd already taken whatever strong drugs Troy procured for her. "Wh-what are you doing here?"

"We've come for a ride." I giggled tipsily and nudged Silas. "I mean, not that kind of ride."

"Now's not a good time." She tried to shut the door.

"But you invited us." I pouted, lost my balance, and fell against the door, conveniently keeping her from closing it.

"Don't worry, Jackie isn't getting on a horse," Silas boomed cheerfully. "She is, however, going to hydrate. Where's your kitchen?" He swaggered forward.

Linda scrambled out of the way, leaving the two of us free to waltz on in. "Wait!"

Troy stepped into the hallway. "What do you think you're—"

"Ice guy!" I cried and flung my arms around him. "This is the Orange Flame with the best party trick that I told you about, remember, Si?"

"Yup. Down, babe." Silas chortled, removing me from Troy while managing to move us all farther down the hallway.

"That's enough," Troy said firmly. He flexed his fingers.

I dragged in a pained wheeze, feeling like my lungs had just been branded with a hot poker.

In my head, Cherry blinked at me. *Can I come out and play?*

Give it a sec.

"Drop your magic before I break your fingers off," Silas said pleasantly.

Troy didn't need a second glance at Silas to judge whether or not he was joking. He released me from his magic, however, Silas's skin went blotchy red.

The vamp paid it as much attention as a pesky mosquito flying around his head. He blurred down the corridor, Troy's hand suddenly bent backward in my partner's enormous grip. "That strain you feel is your distal radius," Silas said. "It's not my favorite bone to break but it makes a nice snap."

Linda grabbed Silas's arm.

He sighed and pinned her by the shoulder against the wall with his other hand. "Don't mess with people's emotions without consent, Linda. It's not nice."

White Flame. Thank you for the reminder, Silas. "Are we going to see horses or not?"

"I just need a sec, babe." He bent Troy's wrist back a hair more and the man whimpered. Huge red welts appeared on Silas's skin, but he continued to ignore them. "My favorite bone is the hyoid. It's the only one not connected to any other bone in your body, which I think is pretty cool. Just this V-shaped bone all on its lonesome at the base of your tongue. Think I can show you yours before you fry me?"

I almost laughed out loud. Instead, I left him intimidating Troy and skipped into the living room. "Oooh. Are you doing an unboxing video? I love those!"

Linda lurched into the room, her eyes wide. "I—we— Don't!"

I unrolled a scroll from its packaging—silver eggs engraved with intricate runes that were absolute gibberish.

She snatched the paper away from me but not before I started laughing.

"Omigod!" I cried. "You're totally faking people out. Silas! You gotta see this. There's a whole story about this haunted mirror," I said, waving the scroll, "but, like, look at it. It's totally a dollar-store find." I dropped onto the sofa, crossed my legs, and swung my foot back and forth. "Come on, spill."

Silas, who'd set Troy next to Linda like he was a chess piece the vamp was playing, motioned for them to stay put. He touched his finger to the back of his tongue in warning before he turned away from the duo.

Troy swallowed, all color draining from his face. Linda was probably scared but she just rocked a glazed zombie expression.

Silas moved slowly between the box with all the items, the silver egg packaging, and a number of scrolls that had yet to be tied up. He touched a cheap gold bracelet and shivered violently, dropping the jewelry.

I jumped to my feet, both Cherry and I on full alert. "Si? Sweetheart?"

"Sorry," Linda whispered.

"Why are you apologizing?" Troy growled. "They broke in here and—"

Silas absently shushed Troy and crouched down so he was eye level with Linda. "You're infusing your magic into these everyday inanimate objects, aren't you?"

She dug her fingers into the throw cushion on her lap.

"Wild! Like fear? That's why you shivered, Si?" I couldn't stop the barrage of "likes" and "totallys." Jackie turned into an '80s valley girl when she was drunk. Which did seem to be pretty often these days.

Silas nodded. "Your talents are weak on people but on objects?" He whistled. "Who writes the fake histories?" He pointed at Troy. "You?"

Troy glared defiantly at him.

I locked my frustration down tight. Serious as the crime was, I didn't give a shit about selling fake possessed artifacts. It was a second-rate fraud and not worthy of the match-makers. Linda wasn't one of those masterminds, just a nepo baby with an illegal side hustle.

I'd gambled everything on this stakeout and lost.

Troy was telling Silas if he thought he was going to muscle in on the action, he could think again.

"I don't want in." Silas nodded approvingly at Linda. "I want you to rep my art collection."

She stood up with a cautious smile. "Really?"

Enjoy your good fortune for the next ten seconds until I arrest you.

"Really." Silas rubbed his thumb and first two fingers together in the universal gesture of cash. "I want someone willing to go the distance and get me everything."

His acting was hardly subtle but he wasn't treading the boards. We were in a tense standoff, and from the way Linda prattled on about potential collectors, it had done its job.

At least these artifacts would be off the streets. Trying to be happy with that consolation prize, I stood up and stilled.

A metal case was tucked between the sofa and one of the side tables. What did we have here?

Noticing my pause, Silas pulled out magic-nulling cuffs. "By the power vested in me as a Maccabee, I'm placing you under arrest."

Troy swore and jumped to his feet.

I set the case on the sofa, my back to everyone, and clicked the locks open.

The spike of excitement that Cherry sent through me made my knees buckle. I hit the carpet, burning up and sweating, the colors in the room so painfully bright I swear they burned my retinas.

Silas was trying to cuff Linda while grappling with Troy. My discomfort wasn't the Orange Flame's doing.

I stared dully at the still-closed case, my heart in my throat. It was as if I'd touched my blood to Sire's Spark and was detecting a shedim, except that crystal was locked up tight in my safe, and neither Troy nor Linda had the shifting shadows in the backs of their skulls marking them as half shedim.

I reached for the lid with a hand covered in frosted green scaley armor. My panic over revealing myself was nothing compared to what I'd find inside.

Something heavy behind me thudded and cracked.

Linda screamed.

I didn't care, all my attention on the two silver love locks featuring initials engraved in hearts. Nestled in velvet padding, the locks were also wrapped in real runes of black and purple magic.

The more the runes pulsed like tentacles full of blood, the more the pressure in my brain grew, almost bowing me double. Sweat dripped onto the carpet.

I sucked in a ragged breath, yelling in my head at Cherry to stand down because my gut said she was making this harder on me.

These weren't empty prison cells like the one I'd taken from the drug bust.

There were shedim imprisoned inside.

The evil leeching out of them reached inside me like insects burrowing under my skin, all tiny feet and mandibles pricking me.

I vomited onto the carpet, the sound drawing everyone's attention.

"Aviva." Silas's voice was strangled. He had a cut on one cheek and a white-knuckled grip on the chain between Linda's cuffs. "Your eyes."

Dizzy, I rubbed a hand over them, my pulse spiking in fear that Cherry was now on display.

This isn't on me, she whispered.

My fully human fingers came away stained with blood. I gasped.

"What is that?" Silas frowned at the metal case. He stepped over the wreckage of a chair and then over Troy, who was sprawled on the ground, his arm bent at an angle that under any other circumstance, would have nauseated me.

Linda mewled.

Troy swung a panicked glance at the locks, then jumped

to his feet and shot his uninjured hand toward me in a sharp motion.

Ice crackled over me, but the more I tried to shake it off, the faster it built, until I couldn't move, and my teeth couldn't even chatter at the cold that penetrated down to the marrow of my bones.

I dimly heard a roar, my lungs burning from lack of oxygen. My vision wavered, my consciousness failing. *Save me.*

You wanted to be human, Cherry whimpered. *I can't do anything now.*

The light filtering through the ice grew narrower and narrower then—

CRACK!!

I pitched forward, shivering like I'd never be warm again.

Silas was jumping out the busted pictured window, its shards winking in the carpet fibers, and Troy was nowhere to be seen.

Linda was crying.

I glanced at the sofa, where the case with the love locks should have been—and wasn't—and shivered again. I wanted to scream and beat my fists on the ground. I had my connection to the matchmakers, but Troy had fled with two shedim prisons, and if he had a way to release a couple of furious demons and turn them on Silas?

Even Silas wouldn't survive that.

Chapter 19

The conference room at Maccabee HQ crackled with unspoken tension as Silas and I filed in. On the upside, Troy hadn't freed the demon prisoners, but on the very, very large downside, he'd gotten away—with the shedim locks.

Keira was next to Michael, her jaw clenched so tightly that a vein pulsed at her temple, while Olivier sat on her other side with his cop face on.

What were they doing here?

I slid into my chair, adding the commanders' barely contained anger and disappointment to the stockpile Silas and I felt at our failure to apprehend our suspect.

Michael's face was grim, her fist clutched around her Montblanc pen. "I've invited Chief Constable Davis here for a full debrief about the missing Orange Flame situation, as it poses a danger to both communities. Detective Desmond is the Trad officer taking point."

"Now that the operatives are here," Keira said, "what the hell is going on? Why does one Orange Flame require the combined efforts of both our police forces?"

"Aviva," my mother said, throwing me under the

proverbial bus, "why don't you explain about the magic in our rings?"

I probed my molars with my tongue in case one of them had suddenly sprouted a dental emergency that would get me out of this. No such luck. I pointed to Michael's right hand. The top of her gold ring's round pillbox featured an embossed flame, the design circled by five tiny gems: one each in red, orange, yellow, white, and blue. "Maccabees get these rings when we graduate to level one operative."

"We know all that," Keira said impatiently. "Vampire powers interfere with the magic cocktail in the ring which is why they don't wear one. They can kill shedim without it."

I nodded. "About a month ago, we learned that the foundational strain that lets all five types of magic work together to kill demons was corrupted, and unlike vampires, human Maccabees don't kill demons. Instead, we, uh, send them to magic prisons."

"So? Locked up is locked up, right?" Olivier looked between Silas and me. "Not right?"

"You ever seen a love lock?" I said.

"Sure."

"That's the prison," Silas said. "It's controlled by other shedim, not Maccabees."

Olivier did a double take. "Say what?"

"Think of them as batteries spreading evil vibes that can be hidden in plain sight and transported around to whatever fragile place is in need of exploiting." I almost threw jazz hands to cushion the shock with a bit of levity, but at Michael's glare, dropped them into my lap.

Keira gasped. "How long have you been helping demons create these batteries?"

"The Maccabees were never, at any point, willing accomplices to this," Michael said.

"How. Long."

"Since the 1600s," I said.

Keira looked apoplectic. Still, I wished I had vamp hearing to check her heartbeat.

Silas caught my eye and discreetly rubbed his thumb over his inner wrist, sliding his eyes to the commander.

Damn. Her pulse was elevated.

"What does this have to do with Troy Abelman?" Keira said through clenched teeth.

The director nodded at me to continue.

I scowled at my lap for two seconds before complying. "There are Eishei Kodesh, who I call matchmakers, who know about these love lock prisons. They have a way to break prisoners out to sell to the highest bidder. Eishei Kodesh criminal bidders," I clarified.

"Chandra Nichols is a matchmaker," Keira said flatly.

"Was," Olivier corrected, except he was glaring at me like this was my error.

I shrugged helplessly. "Yeah. Was. Past tense. What do you want me to say? It's a high turnover profession?"

"Knowing all that, you let my officers take the case." Keira smacked her fist against the table, sending a pen rolling off the edge and landing on the floor planks with a click as sharp as a gunshot in the charged silence.

"I did." Michael showed no remorse. "Chandra was murdered by a shedim who was, in turn, sent into one of those prisons. Your officers weren't ever in any danger."

The line of Olivier's shoulders had drawn tighter and tighter. "Maccabees kept this demon battery intel from Trad officers?" He shot me an accusatory look.

"It wasn't my call," I said quietly.

"Maybe not officially, but fuck, Avi, it's not like we haven't been hanging out shooting the shit when Sach and I —" He flinched.

I grabbed for his arm, but at the last minute pulled my hand back. "Please don't be mad at her."

Olivier half turned away from me.

"What would you have done?" Silas's tone was mild, and he kept his posture relaxed, but his question was pointed. "No disrespect to you, Detective Desmond, or Chief Constable Davis, but how would it have made any difference to the way you police?"

The room crackled with an electric undercurrent and no answer to that question.

"Both forces will put out an APB on Abelman," Keira said.

"And kick the media into an even higher pitch with a dangerous Orange Flame on the loose, after all of Jared Casey's vile speeches?" Michael held out her hands like she was balancing a scale. "Danger to the public versus our city not exploding."

"Fine. We'll keep the hunt internal," Keira said. "But top priority."

"Your officers are not to approach."

"How will yours?" Keira shot back. "Abelman has demon prisoners and your rings are useless."

"Vampires aren't," Silas said. "We'll marshal all the neighboring Spook Squads to find Abelman and kill any shedim."

"Good." Michael pointed at him. "You're in charge of that."

Silas eyed her like he expected a trap. "You sure?"

"Yes. Tell them about the missing locks, and for God's sake, make sure the press doesn't get hold of this. Go."

Silas booted it out of the room.

"I hate to be the bearer of bad news," I said.

"Never noticed," Olivier said wryly.

"But only a demon can break the wards on those locks."

Michael massaged her temple. "Troy likely knows where Chandra's shedim partner is."

There was a rap at the door.

"Come in," Michael said.

Gemma wheeled a dolly into the room with the box from Linda's house. Behind her were two unfamiliar women: one dark haired, tall and broad, and the other so petite she was almost pixie-like, with bright platinum hair.

Michael motioned the pair to empty seats. "Joan, Ruth. Thank you for joining us. I appreciate you giving us your take on the items inside this packaging."

Gemma, who hadn't seen my disguise before now, subtly twirled a lock of her own hair and grimaced.

I scratched my cheek with my middle finger.

The other two women reached into the box for a couple of silver eggs.

"Joan and Ruth were the ones who verified that the artifacts in the *Supernatural: Debunked* exhibit a while back didn't possess Eishei Kodesh magic," Michael said.

Just shedim magic on Sire's Spark, but hey, that omission didn't make what the director said any less true. Still, they were experts at this kind of thing, and verifying Linda's magic on the household goods would cement our proof.

Joan, or maybe it was Ruth, read one of the scrolls, while the brunette licked her fingertip and ran it around the glass of a hand mirror.

"Clever bit of business," the dark-haired woman said in a raspy voice. "The white flame magic contained inside is touch activated. There's enough power to give people a jolt of fear six or seven times."

Her colleague nodded. "Combined with the false provenances and cursed history, it sets into the brain as a cohesive whole. No one will doubt its cursed nature."

"Unless the owner tries to sell it later," Keira said. "Once the item's been depleted."

The brunette shrugged. "It's a scam. The White Flame who did this has been paid, and if anyone comes back to them, who cares? It's not like cursed items behave according to any scientific method."

"Thank you for verifying the magic," Michael said.

The experts nodded and stood up. Gemma, who'd been standing by the door, opened it like she was going to leave as well, but Michael asked her to remain a moment.

"Operative Huang, tell Chief Constable Davis what you reported to me."

Wait. She'd gone over my head to report something directly to Michael? I tried to catch Gemma's eye, but she deliberately avoided my gaze.

"Roger Henderson, Casey's head of security, purchased magic-shielding devices for his team from Troy Abelman," she said.

I crossed my arms to hide the fingers on my left hand that had busted into claws. I couldn't lay into my mother—my director—for deciding that Roger was once more fair game for questioning, so I focused my anger elsewhere.

"You mean my suspicion that I asked you to chase down?" I said icily. *Gemma, you brown-nosing cow.* She was happy to call me boss and then take credit for my ideas when it mattered. I saw how it was. "When did you confirm that?"

Gemma notched her chin up. "When you were staking out Linda's house."

Forcing my fingers back to normal, I slid my phone out of my pocket, making a big production of checking it for texts or missed calls. "Nope, no messages letting me know."

"Enough, Operative Fleischer," Chief Constable Davis said.

I blinked. What the fuck? The chief constable had leave to dress me down? I pressed my lips together, my angry retort lodging in my chest like heartburn.

Gemma smirked.

I narrowed my eyes at her, and her expression faltered.

"Will that be all?" She addressed both leaders equally.

"Will it, Michael?" Keira said with a hard edge to her voice.

"Operative Huang," my mother continued, "please provide Chief Constable Davis with a full report about Henderson and the shielding devices."

No mention of giving *me* the information. Was I even on this case anymore?

I waited until the door had closed behind Gemma to speak. "My hypotheses tied Henderson to Troy Abelman, who is connected to Linda Aviyente. A woman I also pushed to investigate. And, oh yeah, Abelman has two love locks in his possession, which circles us back to Chandra Nichols, Linda's mother, a confirmed matchmaker. Again, thanks to me." Screw modesty right now. "Could someone explain why I don't seem to be leading this investigation anymore?"

Michael clicked her Montblanc pen. "You lost Abelman and the locks."

I flinched, staring down at my feet with flushed cheeks.

"Why did you react so badly to those locks when the rest of us were unaffected, Aviva?" Keira said.

"My blue flame magic."

She shook her head. "That illuminates weaknesses in people. I may not have magic, but I've cracked enough suspects to tell when someone is lying."

There was another knock, and Silas slipped back in holding a form. "Spook Squad is good to go."

"Sachie?" Olivier and I said in the same worried tone.

"She's sitting this one out," Silas said. He handed the paper to Michael. "I need your John Hancock to transfer vampires from Seattle and Portland HQ here since all vamp operatives not on active investigations are on shedim duty."

Michael grimaced at the form. "More paperwork?"

"Louis sends his apologies but says it's absolutely necessary." Silas placed it in front of Michael.

While she signed it, Keira once again asked me why I was affected by the locks.

"I don't know," I said honestly. I shouldn't have been, not without Sire's Spark magic turning me into a shedim magic detector.

"She's telling the truth," Silas said. Vamp magic was pretty good at sniffing out the internal tells for when someone was lying.

I smiled at my friend, but he regarded me with a frown.

"Was that the first time you'd seen one of those lock prisons?" he said, the insanely polite vampire taking the signed form from Michael without thanking her for it.

It was like the molecules in the room rearranged themselves into new clusters: Silas, Olivier, and Keira in one, and Michael and me in the other.

"No," I said steadily.

"She saw one before," Michael said. "An empty one. As did I. She wasn't affected by its presence."

"Silas?" Keira said.

The vamp tilted his head. "Aviva isn't lying. Director Fleisher isn't either, but she's not telling us the full truth."

"How did deciding what I should and should not know work out for you back then, Mickey?"

I tugged on my collar, glancing at the door to measure how fast I could get out of here, while Silas took in the signed form like it was the most fascinating relic he'd ever encountered, and Olivier stared straight ahead, his expression an unreadable mask.

Michael threw her pen onto the table. "You could never accept the truth of my world. Has that changed?"

"What's changed is you can't refuse me full transparency," Keira said.

Michael raised her eyebrows. "Is that a threat?"

I fiddled with my Maccabee ring—except it wasn't my ring. It was the gold stacking bands I'd put on for this disguise. My heart sunk at the realization of why I'd reacted to the locks in the metal case as if I was driven by the crystal's magic.

Ignorance really had been bliss.

Chapter 20

I looked down at my right hand.

"I'm not wearing my Maccabee ring anymore," I said slowly. A fleeting dizziness swept over me, and I gripped the edge of the table. "That's why I reacted tonight." The idea settled into my bones, and, like it or not, took root.

Sire's Spark was infused with demon magic, which illuminated other demon magic either in people or on items like the prison cells. Blood called to blood. But only shedim or half shedim could use it.

I still couldn't suss out full demons, as proven by attending Brimstone Breakfast Club without any adverse effects. That meant that I could be surrounded by demons without knowing it—or being brought to my knees with nausea. I'm not sure if that was comforting, but it was no different from my current reality, so it was familiar.

However, for almost ten years, I'd worn a ring with corrupted shedim magic in it. Could it have suppressed my innate detection ability? It was likely that I'd never come into contact with either a shedim artifact or half-shedim before I first put it on, which explained why I didn't realize I was capable of this.

"How does your ring matter?" Olivier said brusquely.

"The corrupted magic in it must have a blocking effect on Aviva's Eishei Kodesh ability to illuminate shedim magic," Michael said.

It was a neatly crafted half-truth.

"Then why didn't those locks affect Linda or Troy?" Silas said.

"They're not blue flames," Michael said.

I flexed my right hand, exhausted by friendships torn apart by my birth, relationships ended over my truth, and secrets hidden for so, so long.

Telling Silas about Cherry was scary enough, but Keira? She wasn't just any Trad but the head of their police force and a woman who probably lost her best friend because of this secret. Then there was Olivier. We'd just repaired our own friendship, and he was dating my best friend. What would this confession do?

I'd said it myself. Hiding in plain sight was a sound strategic move. Why mess with that?

Except, I wasn't simply hiding in plain sight any longer. I'd adopted aspects of Ezra's strategy, outing myself to people I cared about, making sure I still mattered.

That despite being a half shedim, I was still too valuable to lose.

What if I took it a step further now, beyond those who already loved me to those who needed—who should— know for the greater good?

My heart raced as I imagined the domino effect of my confession—Keira's shock turning to rage, Olivier's trust shattering like glass, and the protective walls I'd built around my life crumbling, leaving me exposed to dangers I'd spent years hiding from.

"You want the truth?" I said wearily.

"Avi, no." Michael reached for me, but I shook her off with a sad smile.

"The ring *was* suppressing my ability to detect the shedim magic." Perhaps if our foundational strain wasn't corrupted, I'd always have had this ability. "But my blue flame powers were only partially responsible for why I reacted the way I did. Now that I've removed the ring, they work in tandem with this."

I unfurled Cherry Bomb like a prize being revealed in glimpses: a flash of claws, the bright toxic green of my eyes, a toss of crimson hair, then the stippling of scales. My short sharp horns popped out last like a crown at a coronation.

Fitting, since I was descended from demon royalty.

I held my head up, refusing to bow in shame.

Olivier dropped his hand to his (thankfully gunless) holster. His reflexive grab for his weapon stung, his deeply ingrained training cutting deeper than any verbal rejection could. His fingers twitched, hovering uncertainly before he forced his hand back on the table, but the damage was done.

Silas wore a small smile. "That's an awfully familiar shade of crimson," he drawled. "Think I saw it on a ball or two of yarn."

Blessings on the scales that hid my blush.

Sadly, Keira was as white as a ghost, fixated on me with wide eyes. She drew back as if struck. "What is that? An infernal?"

"*She* is my daughter," Michael snarled.

Keira dipped her chin with a wince. "That's not… Aviva, I didn't mean…"

Silas held up the form. "I'll get those operatives here ASAP," he said and fled.

"Yes, I'm half-shedim," I said, enjoying Keira's discomfort.

"Does Sachie know?" Olivier said.

"I told her last month."

"You waited decades to share this with your best friend?" Olivier sounded affronted on her behalf.

"Your first instinct was to go for your gun, Olivier, despite it still being me." I flicked my crimson hair off my shoulders. "So you can take anything you have to say about my decision to tell people about this and fuck right off."

Michael flashed the Trads a mean little smile. "Well put, Aviva."

Louis poked his head in the room. "Linda Aviyente is set up in—" His eyes widened into saucers at Cherry, then into dinner plates at Michael.

I dropped back to my human features like I'd been gut punched, my mouth working but no sound coming out.

Michael cleared her throat. "Louis—"

"Linda Aviyente is set up in Interrogation Room 2," he said in a tight voice.

"For the record," I stammered, "this is my normal body. My human side isn't a glamor. That's not how it works for half shedim."

He barely spared me a glance, his attention on Michael. "I've worked with you for seven years. I wouldn't have said anything. Ever."

"Right?" Keira muttered.

It was great that Louis wasn't horrified by me, but I was actually present and could have been included in this conversation.

My secret had always been that—mine. Every time I speculated about revealing it, I imagined the consequences I'd face. To my mind, fallout on Michael occurred only in a professional capacity as director.

I glanced at Keira and Louis. I'd been wrong.

Michael slumped back in her seat. She'd been wrong too.

Several very long, very silent seconds ticked by.

"Whenever you're ready," Louis said coldly and left.

The rest of us sat there in a loaded silence.

"Well?" Michael waved a hand at me. "Are you going to go question Linda or not?"

The last few minutes had done wonders to make me forget my hurt at being sidelined on this investigation. "Me?"

"I said I was leading this, not that you weren't integral."

Hope and anxiety battled in my chest as I grappled with this unexpected olive branch. *Hugely* unexpected, given what had just transpired. I stood up. "Yes. Of course."

"Detective Desmond and I are coming," Keira said.

I saw the exact second that Michael bit back her snarky retort in favor of a nod.

Keira and Michael gathered their things in silence, each darting glances at the other when they thought they were unobserved. I hoped they found their way back to their friendship when this case was over.

After Keira made amends for her reaction to me, that was. Olivier had a ways to go as well.

We all headed down to the interview room.

Linda was a pale, shaken figure, still she demanded her lawyer when I entered, rattling off his contact details. She'd already said this to the Maccabees who put her in the room.

"He's been notified." I spun a chair around and straddled it backward. "Interesting that you happen to have a criminal lawyer's phone number top of mind. What an exciting life you lead."

"No comment."

"Let me run a few things down for you. First of all, there's a manhunt for Troy Abelman. He supplied Roger Henderson, who is Jared Casey's head of security, with magic-shielding devices. Still no comment? Okay. The Trad cops are chatting with Mr. Henderson to ascertain whether Troy got those devices via you or your gallery."

Even if Linda procured them for Troy, it was perfectly legal. The question was whether she knew that.

"Jump in anytime," I said.

Her left eye twitched, but she didn't crack. Not verbally, though my synesthete vision showed her racing heart and sweat forming under her arms and at the back of her neck, along with amped synapse activity in her brain.

I sat on the edge of the table, crowding Linda's personal space. "Let's talk about the metal case Troy absconded with. The one containing locks with incarcerated shedim inside them. I personally questioned your mother before her death, verifying she was in the business of selling demon convicts to Eishei Kodesh criminals. How long were you working with her?"

Linda's eyes widened, her heart flared into an enormous blue dot, and activity in her amygdala went nuts. Profound shock. She shook her head, her gaze downcast.

"You weren't?" I said. "Then why did you have that case?"

She hunched into herself.

I placed a hand on her shoulder, forcing her to look at me. "Linda," I said gently, "you are in a lot of trouble. Give me something to help you face a lesser charge than shedim trafficking."

Truth be told, there weren't any laws about this, but only because it had never occurred to anyone that it was a possibility. I mean, the number of events that had to transpire for this crime to occur? Corrupted Maccabee magic, demon prisons, a shedim working against their own kind to break the wards on the locks? It was all too fantastical and improbable for even the Maccabees to imagine.

Chandra had died before those charges could become a reality, but the Authority Council would throw the book at Linda.

The silence stretched out.

I'd overheard Linda speaking to the person forcing her to produce these phony cursed artifacts. Troy had been with her. Chandra was dead. Mois was Trad and didn't feel right for this, and I still had no evidence any other matchmaker existed.

In fact, I was pretty convinced I was looking at one of the only two matchmakers left.

The artifacts Linda made were at a Con 101 level, but they went beyond ripping people off financially to having them experience levels of fear that had even gotten to Silas.

"Where is the shedim forcing you to commit fraud? Your mother's partner."

Linda's pulse points went nuts, rapidly flickering blue in my synesthete vision. She twisted her hands together so tightly I was scared she'd break a finger.

"Please stop!" Her voice cracked in pain, her heart hammering in a dizzyingly bright blue dot.

That's when her lawyer arrived, demanding to speak privately with his client.

While I waited to be called back into the interview room, Michael explained that the lawyer had been legal counsel for Mois Aviyente's company for years.

"Daddy bailed Linda out?" Olivier glanced at the one-way glass. "That was fast."

"Almost like he expected trouble," I said.

On the other side of the glass, the lawyer calmly spoke with Linda, who nodded her head in nervous bobs. Unfortunately, the audio was off to ensure their privacy.

I was called back into the room and informed that Linda would cop to the fraud charges.

"What about the locks?" I said. "They were at her house and tie her to her mother's illegal activities."

"Circumstantial. She inherited the home. Who's to say that metal case wasn't there the entire time?" The lawyer smirked.

I turned to Linda. "Give me something to find this shedim. Something to keep you safe."

Linda shied behind her lawyer, who blocked my line of sight. "She can't help you," he said.

Michael opened the door. "Judge granted bail. She's free to go."

The lawyer escorted Linda out. She was careful not to meet my eyes.

"She's a flight risk," I said, watching them get into the elevator.

"The judge saw it differently. Ms. Aviyente has her gallery to run and isn't going anywhere."

Keira tasked Olivier with working all their foreign contacts to bring Mois Aviyente in for questioning in Buenos Aires as they left.

Silas was already off putting together his crew of vamp operatives to hunt down Troy Abelman and those lock prisons. Hopefully that net would close soon.

Michael sagged against the wall, rubbing her eyes.

"Troy and Linda are the only matchmakers," I said.

"The Authority will be pleased you concluded that. Now all we need is the identity of the shedim who killed Chandra."

"Linda doesn't want to say anything about her mother's shedim partner or any shedim," I said, "because she's terrified. But *Troy* is the one with those locks in his possession. He's the one facing trafficking charges and he's the one that will crack this open once and for all."

I brightened. There was a way to find Troy that only *I* could pursue. And I'd get to see Ezra in the process. Sure, I'd be using him to charm Rukhsana, but she could flirt with him all night so long as I wrapped this case up in a timely fashion.

I'd get what I could from my informant, and then? I

was taking my boyfriend back to my place and locking the world out.

Chapter 21

Ezra sat alone on his balcony, every inch the Lord of the Copper Hell from his crisp suit that was black as pitch to the sharp gold glint of cuff links and his jet-black curls ruthlessly slicked off his forehead.

The floor of the gaming hall wasn't visible through our video call, but an excited cheer from one group of players rose above the chime of slot machines and the whir of spinning roulette wheels, then a sudden pained roar cut through the symphony of sound.

My boyfriend didn't flinch at the noise; he didn't even glance over. He stifled a yawn, his lids heavy.

I pushed out the door of the autobody repair shop, waiting for my car to be brought around. "When's the last time you slept?"

"And here I was hoping for some sexy talk," he said with a wry smile.

I frowned at him. "Ezra."

He looked up at the ceiling as if searching for the answer there. "Yesterday? Seeing you energizes me."

"Points for sweet-talking, but you need to take care of yourself. Fit in those catnaps of yours."

The mechanic rapped on the window and held up my car keys.

I motioned I'd grab them in a minute. Much as I longed to see Ezra, asking him to come with me to charm Rukhsana was placing yet another burden on him.

"What do you need, mi cielo?"

My insides went gushy at the nickname that was being used in sweet seriousness instead of like a weapon. Then they turned into a pretzel because I was making him keep us a secret.

"Nothing," I said. "I just miss you."

"I miss you too, but I recognize that look. Out with it."

I sighed. "I was hoping you'd come with me to Rukhsana's."

He pulled a mock aghast face. "You're pimping me out? So soon into our second act?"

"Yes." I walked around to the side of the garage. "But also, I want you with me tonight when I fall asleep."

Our call went fuzzy, the screen filling with static before it went black.

I swallowed. Had Delacroix decided to be a dick and mess with our cell reception or had another crisis happened at the Hell?

"Ezra?"

A familiar mesh portal opened up and Ezra strode toward me, his trench coat swirling around his legs. He planted a hard kiss on my lips.

"Best idea I've heard in ages," he said.

"I'm sorry about the photo," I blurted out.

Ezra furrowed his brow, then shook his head. "The one with Silas? Documentation is good. It helps your mission."

I probed his words for any subtext or snark, but he appeared to be genuine. "It does, but I'm sorry I ended up in that public position. With Silas," I repeated.

"That isn't a chargeable offense," Ezra said wryly. "Seriously, the photo is irrelevant."

"You're sure?"

"Positive."

A vise around my chest loosened. "Okay, I'll go get my car."

He leaned against the brick wall, sin and sensuality wrapped in cashmere. "I'll be waiting."

I looked back only three times, amazed that this gorgeous incredible being—that the former love of my life —was mine again.

While I gritted my teeth and paid for the repairs, I texted Sachie, Darsh, and Michael that I had proof the Ashbishop was dead, though I left out Silas's role. I added that we were searching for a copycat vampire, from here on out to be called Ash Lite.

Forty-three percent less evil, Cherry joked. *For a smoother, less cloying, evil chaotic taste.*

Moments later Ezra and I were on the road, making excellent time to Rukhsana's new chop shop.

After also filling my boyfriend in about the Ashbishop, I glanced over at him. "Are you really okay with keeping us on the down-low?"

He hit a stereo button, skipping songs on my playlist. "I said I was."

"Yeah." But there was a difference between truly accepting something and capitulating. I returned my attention to the road.

The scent of motor oil and the rhythmic clanking of tools greeted us as we stepped into Rukhsana's new chop shop. Ezra's eyes darted around, taking in the organized chaos of partially dismantled vehicles and gleaming parts.

"Avi!" A booming voice echoed through the garage. Jordy's coveralls were smeared with grease, his beard once more growing in dark and bushy. "Didn't expect to see you today." He saw Ezra and stepped back with a nervous bob. "Crimson Prince."

The one other time they'd met, Ezra had almost choked Jordy out. My boyfriend had an amused glint in his eyes, but just in case, I muscled between them and tossed Jordy a paper bag. "I brought you a little something."

He caught it deftly and peered inside, his eyes lighting up. "Apple fritters." He yanked one out and took a bite, closing his eyes in bliss. "They're still warm. Uber Eats has nothing on you. You here to see the boss?"

I nodded. "Is she in?"

"Up in her office." He headed toward a rusty intercom on the wall and pressed a button. "Hey, Rukhsana. Avi's here." His expression turned sly. "She brought a variety of treats."

I winced.

"I better rank above the doughnuts," Ezra murmured into my ear.

A honey-rich French-accented voice crackled through the speaker. "Send them up."

We climbed the metal staircase, the steps creaking under our weight, and entered a plush office that stood in stark contrast to the gritty garage below.

Rukhsana Gill sat behind her desk, her multiple piercings catching the light. She'd dyed her inch-long hair since the fundraiser. The blue more thoroughly obscured the snake tattoo on her skull than her natural color. "Ezra Cardoso, how delicious."

Her sultry smile packed the force of a nuclear weapon.

I clasped my hands behind my back against the urge to hustle Ezra out of here, lest he succumb, and took one of the two chairs across from the Frenchwoman.

"That color is horrible on you, chère." She patted her hair. "Maybe use a brush now and again? Let me give you the name of my stylist."

I caught a glimpse of myself in the window overlooking the shop below. My hair was a mess, and my makeup was mostly gone. I smoothed my locks down, more upset that I'd let Ezra see me this way than that Rukhsana had.

Screw self-consciousness. I had more important things on my plate. I dropped my hand. "I'm good. Hope you don't mind us stopping by unannounced."

"Mind? How could I possibly mind when you brought such exquisite company?" She wagged a finger at Ezra. "Though it's unfair of you to show up when I don't have a shot at you."

My heart stuttered. *She knows.*

Ezra's expression smoothed out into a polite smile. "I beg your pardon?"

"Don't be coy." She looked at him with her eyebrows raised, but at his baffled shake of the head, smirked. "Check the web, chèr."

Ezra and I reached for our phones at the same time.

Photos of him cozying up to a gorgeous redhead in a 1940s-inspired dress were splashed all over gossip sites with headlines like "The Perfect Couple" and "Two Vampires; One Heart."

I couldn't make sense of this. Had they pulled out some old pictures of Ezra? Why publish them now?

"Irene and I are just friends," he said.

This was the Irene he'd met with? I practically strangled my phone. Then I kept reading. Oh good. It got worse.

She wasn't merely some random beautiful vampire, she was a famous ballet dancer with a slew of star performances to her credit. She was poised, elegant, and exactly the kind of public figure Ezra would have on his arm.

The logical part of my brain piped up that this was great. It threw Natán a curveball and helped hide any trace of my reconciliation with Ezra.

Cherry had a different take.

A cold, irrational jealousy slithered through me, coiling around my heart and whispering doubts about my place in Ezra's world.

My boyfriend hooked an elbow carelessly over the back of his seat. "If anyone has a shot with me, it's you."

"Flatterer," Rukhsana said. "I hope you're not just here to tease me with promises you won't keep."

"I never make promises I don't intend to fulfill," Ezra replied, his voice low and inviting. He added something in French that resulted in her husky chuckle.

I tried not to gag. Or stab them.

"You're terrible." Rukhsana trailed her fingers along her décolletage.

"And you're brilliant," Ezra replied. "Perhaps the only one who can help us."

"Don't overdo it, chèr." Rukhsana winked and grinned. "Go on."

"Have you heard of Chandra Nichols?" I said, taking back control.

Rukhsana shook her head. "Should I have? Is she missing?"

"No, she's dead. What about Linda Aviyente? She owns the Lions Gallery."

"She is missing?" Rukhsana made a face. "It's not much of a loss to the art world, but if you really need to find her—"

I leaned forward. "Not her. Her lover and employee, Troy Abelman."

"The one with the magnificent cheekbones?"

I clapped my hands together. "Yes!"

"They can't be that special," Ezra said without ever having seen the man. "They're cheekbones."

Rukhsana and I turned twin looks of pity on him.

Ezra crossed his arms, throwing in an eye roll for good measure.

"Why is Troy of interest?" Rukhsana said.

"He's disappeared with some sensitive items."

Rukhsana's eyebrows shot up. "How sensitive are we talking?"

"Sensitive enough to cause a lot of trouble if they fall into the wrong hands," I said carefully.

She smiled slowly. "Now that," she said, "is much more interesting than a pretty face. You want me to put out feelers?"

"If you could. We need to find him fast. But warn anyone about approaching him directly."

Rukhsana tapped her chin, her lips pursed. "It'll cost you."

"Of course," I said.

"Not money. Information. Tell me specifically what these artifacts are."

I hesitated, my mind racing through the potential consequences of revealing too much.

Troy was on the run with two prison locks. A shedim had been incarcerated in each one, but who knew if that was still true?

Rukhsana was resourceful, as was her network of spies, but if human operatives didn't have a way to kill demons, regular people, magic criminals or not, didn't either.

Plus, I didn't want Rukhsana interested in those locks and telling her they were demon artifacts would set her on their trail. "That's above your pay grade. What if I triple your fee?"

She sat back and crossed her legs. "Not interested."

"You want information," Ezra said, "I'll give it to you. A one-time favor where I'll obtain information for you. Not about this case though."

I shook my head at him, but he ignored me, his focus on Rukhsana.

"Do we have a deal?" he said.

She drummed her fingers on her desk. "Yes, but I'll also take triple my fee."

"Done," I said, opening the app to transfer money to her offshore account. The Maccabees could pony up for this bribe.

"I'll put the word out," she said. "If anyone's seen or heard anything about your man Troy, I'll get it out of them."

Relief washed over me. Even if Silas and the other vamps found Troy first, I didn't consider this gamble a waste of money. "Thank you."

She nodded and opened an old-fashioned leather accounting book, the two of us dismissed.

Ezra and I walked downstairs to the garage.

Jordy rolled himself out from under a car, lying on a mechanic's dolly, and threw me a big wave, whistling cheerfully along to the Rolling Stones song playing on a battered radio.

I grinned and waved back before stepping into the night and taking a deep breath of fresh air.

"That went as well as it could," Ezra said.

I pulled my car keys out of my coat pocket. "Did it?" I said waspishly.

He stepped in front of me. "You're mad at me? The only reason I was with Irene was to help you."

"I figured you'd play her for the info, same as I was supposed to."

"She insisted on having a drink while we spoke. We never even left the Hell and I didn't have any fans on board, which means Natán got to one of my staff." He curled his hands into such tight fists that blood dripped from one palm. "How about you focus on that?"

It pissed me off even more that that hadn't been my first thought. "I can multitask."

He glared at his bleeding hand, where the skin was already healing, like it was the force of his anger, not his magic, that was closing the wound. "What do you want from me? I can't help people taking photos of me without my knowledge or consent, and I can't set the record straight because that's what *you* wanted."

"Finally, the truth comes out. You hate keeping our relationship quiet. You're a fucking Prime, Ezra. You don't need the spotlight to keep you safe." I stepped around him and continued on to my car, feeling hollow.

I nursed my anger and hurt—rational or not—all the way back to my car, where he caught up with me.

"When I was a kid, Natán did this bullshit interview about our happy father-son dynamic."

I opened my car door but didn't get in.

"He showed the article to all his cronies, so proud of how I'd answered the questions. How well I'd conducted myself." Ezra gazed off, his jaw tight. "It was shortly after Mamá died and I got it in my head that here was a way I could make my father stick around."

I reached for him, but he brushed away my hand.

"Somewhere along the line, wanting to make him proud turned into wanting to keep myself safe from him. Maybe it's childish and I should have outgrown that long before I did, but for someone so smart, you got what was happening here all wrong." His lips twisted and his gaze held no trace of softness. "I don't want the world to know about us because I'm scared. That ship sailed a long time ago." He brushed his fingers over his pec, his tattoo hidden by his coat. "I was hoping that the person I saw as *my* world thought enough of me to openly acknowledge I was hers."

I pressed against the cool metal of the car door, the weight of Ezra's words overwhelming me. A mix of shame and regret churned in my gut. I'd profoundly misunderstood his motives and wounded him in the process.

"I want that too," I said quietly. "I'm sorry for hurting you. For putting this investigation above us."

"You put *yourself* first. And you had every right to. I love that you refuse to give up your dream of making this world better for half shedim, and I'm sorry for how I behaved."

I caught his hand. "You do mean the world to me, Zee. I'm all in and—"

He gently laid a finger against my lips. "Hearing you say that is enough." He ducked his head, a shy smile on his lips. "It's everything."

Chapter 22

The air between us softened, charged with unspoken understanding. We were two people who'd found solid ground amid the chaos, and in that moment, the world around us faded, leaving only the connection we shared—fragile, precious, and more real than anything I'd ever known.

I wrapped an arm around his waist. "Come on, Zee. I'm taking you home."

"Home," he said softly with a wistful smile that made my heart twist. "I like the sound of that."

Nasir, Cécile, and Darsh were with Silas tracking Troy. That left Sachie working the night shift.

A sugary anticipation danced through me at being alone with Ezra.

When we got back, I herded him into the lobby instead of going directly up to my condo. "I showed Cherry to Keira and Olivier, and they reacted in the way I feared most."

"I'm so sorry, Avi."

"It's okay. Well, no, it was horrible, but I lived through my worst nightmare and I'm still standing. I'm done running scared. I'm allowed a private life, and if the Authority or Natán don't like it, tough shit." I laced my fingers through Ezra's and tugged him out the front door, "Hey, minion!" I yelled into the night. I held up our joined hands. "Take that back to your boss."

"That was incredibly…" He shook his head, an unreadable expression on his face.

"Stupid?"

Ezra slammed me up against the wall and kissed me breathlessly. "Brave."

I rose on tiptoe for another kiss. "It was rather."

My night got even better with the discovery of an envelope addressed to me on the dining room table. Inside was a beautiful card with a handwritten heartfelt apology from Olivier—and a gift card to the Fluevog store.

"What's that?" Ezra said.

I smiled. "Sachie making sure that her boyfriend treats her bestie properly."

The delighted expression that bloomed across Ezra's face when I slipped on my favorite sleepwear—the crimson sweater he'd knit me—made my heart do a little flip.

I ran my fingers over the careful stitches at the cuffs, remembering how many nights I'd done this while missing him.

We stayed up talking, the two of us curled under my covers, with me in the crook of his arm. Mostly we chatted about fun inconsequential things, but as the hour grew later, our discussion grew more serious. I told him about my new magic trick detecting demon artifacts without needing Sire's Spark, and he shared where things were at with the quest that had driven his every action.

"All these years of searching for why my mother walked into the sun that day," Ezra said, "and I still don't have an answer. Maybe it's time to stop looking. It's not like it'll bring her back."

"True." I traced my fingers over the tattoo on his left pec. *Cuando era niño soñaba con conquistar el mundo. When I was a kid, I dreamed of conquering the world.* It was a reminder to him of the rest of the quote: *ahora me doy cuenta que tú eres mí mundo y me has conquistador. Now I realize that you're my world and you have conquered me.*

Not gonna lie, I got a little thrill every time I saw it. "What will give you closure? To keep searching for answers about your mother or to stop?"

"I don't know. I'm worried I'll end up feeling worse about what I find."

"How so?"

"I tracked down the rabbi who led the Sephardic synagogue that Mamá and my father attended when they were human. He had some things to say about her that I'd never heard before."

I frowned. "He broke the confidentiality of his position?"

Ezra coughed into his shoulder. "The man was very old and may have believed he was speaking on the phone with Natán."

"You're terrible."

"Then you don't want to know what I learned."

"Oh no. I'm terrible too. Tell me everything."

"It turns out Orthodox Judaism doesn't prohibit artificial insemination. My parents went through all the hardship of trying to conceive, but my mother suffered a miscarriage."

I squeezed his arm. "What a tragedy. I'm so sorry."

"Imagine going through that, only to get pregnant with me a year later and then be turned into a vampire partway through the pregnancy."

It was too awful to contemplate. "Still, she must have been overjoyed when she got pregnant with you," I said. "Her miracle baby."

"By all accounts she was. My father was too." He paused. "Does it make me incredibly selfish in the wake of their loss to think about how I might have had a sibling?"

I stroked his arm. Ezra had grown up so alone. "Absolutely not."

"Learning all this just makes it harder to understand how she chose to die instead of stick around for her kid. And to do it in front of me?" His voice cracked with pain.

"I wish I could say something to make it better or help you decide," I said. "But whatever you choose, be it learn why or let the past stay in the past, that decision is valid and right. You get to do what's best for you, Ezra."

"I know. I've just been searching for so long that…" He scrubbed a hand over his face. "New topic."

We jumped into a discussion of what Ezra had learned about half shedim. Not all had physical demonic features like Maud and me. Some had a heightened resistance to magic attacks, kind of like an inherent shielding device.

"That tends to only happen for half shedim who are White Flames," Ezra explained. "Whereas some Yellow Flames heal faster."

"What about the downsides?" I rested my head on his bare chest. "My Eishei Kodesh magic lets me illuminate weaknesses in people, but my shedim side likes to exploit that and push it as far as I can, even if it means hurting them."

"Hmm. I'll ask." He idly massaged my scalp, the stress of the day falling away under his sure touch. "But you all have an extended lifespan." He paused. "I know you think about outliving Sachie and your mom, but you'd still have Maud."

"And you and Darsh and Silas." I shifted to look up at my ceiling, blinking away moisture. "I try not to dwell on it and just appreciate the time I have with the regular people I love." I rose on my elbow and looked at him. "Is that why you've packed so many skills into your life already? Knitting, multiple languages, skiing, rock climbing... Because you're going to be around for a long time?"

"I didn't see it that way," he said. "I just enjoy learning new things, and I'll have a lot of time to do so. As do you."

"I never considered what I wanted to do with my life beyond be a Maccabee and further my Cherry agenda."

I'd read this article about college admissions interviewers discussing how they met all these kids with perfect GPAs and tons of volunteer experience. But when these students were asked what they did for fun, they looked at the interviewers blankly. When your world revolved around achieving perfection to move your life forward, it didn't leave any room for hobbies.

I'd had fun, sure, but if my life was a pie chart, how tiny would the wedge of my outside interests be?

"Well, it's definitely something to consider now," Ezra said. "Maybe we could learn something new together?"

"I'd like that." I yawned.

"Get some rest," he said.

"You can sleep too, or at least do your catnap thing. Sach won't be home tonight."

"I'll try," he said.

The thing about a vampire boyfriend was that I couldn't exactly fall asleep to the sound of his breathing. He offered to give it a go, but his Darth Vader impression only made me laugh. I tumbled into dreamland with a smile on my face.

What felt like five minutes later, I half woke up, sprawled on top of him.

"Go back to sleep," Ezra said.

"Mmmm," I mumbled, pressing a drowsy kiss to his mouth.

Moonlight filtered in through a gap in the curtains,

casting a gentle glow on his face as he nuzzled closer to my neck.

I sighed contentedly, feeling the soft brush of his lips against my collarbone. His hand trailed up and down my side, tracing patterns that kept me caught in this dreamy state of half-wakefulness.

Ezra nipped lightly at my earlobe. "I love how you taste."

I turned in his arms, my lids still closed, and nestled into him like a puppy.

He kissed me, just the barest tease before deepening it, his hand sliding up to cup my breast through the sweater. His thumb brushed over my nipple, circling it gently.

I pulled him closer and wrapped my arm around his hip.

"Got me where you want me?" He trailed tiny bites and nips down my jawline.

"Not quite," I said with a gasp as he hit the spot in the hollow of my neck that drove me wild. My body woke up with a zing, and I leaned over him, my eyes wide open.

Ezra's heated gaze had Cherry sit up and take notice, her excited spike making me shiver. He pushed a knee between mine, slowly drawing my legs apart.

"Presumptuous of you," I said.

"You're right," he said. "I probably shouldn't do this either." He ran his hands up my arms, pushing me onto my back and locking my wrists above my head with one of his hands.

"Definitely not," I said, squirming. The world could have ended outside my bedroom door and I wouldn't have noticed. Here, under his hands, I was finally where I belonged.

"Noted." His tongue grazed my lower lip. "This is likely right out, then." He pushed my sweater up and caressed the stiff peaks of my nipples.

I pressed closer to him. "Totally banned. We wouldn't want more of that."

"Hmm. Would this be less presumptuous of me?" Ezra crushed his mouth to mine, pinning my hips to the bed with his. His rock-hard erection demanded my attention.

I slid my hand under the waist of his boxer shorts and gripped that velvet steel, stroking him.

Ezra growled and pressed me deeper into the mattress.

My chest rose and fell raggedly with each breath, my body demanding more of his touch, more of him. I bit down hard on his lip.

Ezra pulled back, the silver in his eyes mercurial, and his pupils dilated. "Now who's being presumptuous?" His voice was raspy with desire.

"Want me to stop?" I rubbed my thumb over the slit in his cock.

He flared his nostrils. "I'll try to power through it."

"Big of you."

He bucked his hips, his dick hardening even more. "Oh, sweetheart, you remember." I laughed and he gazed down at me with a tender expression.

I caressed his jaw. "I missed this."

"Me too. Okay, enough small talk." He slapped my hip. "Get naked. I'm going to fuck you."

"You charmer," I said, already pulling the sweater off.

He pitched his boxers in the corner and made a big show of positioning himself on top of me. "Ready?"

"Ready, Coach."

Ezra grimaced. "How about 'Ready, tiger'?"

"Get reaaallll…" My words turned to a breathy sigh as Ezra thrust inside me.

"All good?"

I shrugged. "I'll try to power through it."

"That sounds like a challenge to me, sweetheart."

"I double dare you."

He rocked against me, watching me moan with a delighted grin.

I dug my hands into his curls, my breathing shuddery and uneven and my body spiraling higher and hotter with need.

Ezra gave a hard, fast rock and I forgave him his smirk. That said, I also shamelessly rubbed myself against him, making him lose his freaking mind.

His fangs grazed the skin on my neck and I moaned, pressing my bare throat against the points, my pulse thudding and my chest rising and falling in a ragged motion.

"Bite me," I demanded. I'd wanted it again since that first time a couple months ago.

He hissed a "Yeesssss" and swiftly bit down. Two sharp points blazed on my skin. He lathed the spot with his lips, but the pain was already fading, replaced by a euphoric high that sent a zing down to my toes.

I surrendered myself completely to it, reveling in the thrill that surged through my veins.

Ezra kissed the bite, then shifted onto his knees, grabbed me by the hips, and jerked me toward him. His eyes were two brilliant orbs, captivating me, while his strong fingers kept me anchored under his unleashed passion.

I shattered, stars exploding across my vision.

Ezra followed with my name on his lips.

We lay there in happy silence.

He ran his fingers along my arm. "I always meant to count the freckles on your body."

"There you go," I said, trying to untwist the tangled covers with my feet. "Something we can learn together."

Ezra smoothed the sheets out. "You'll just be shoving your feet out of the blankets in another five minutes and messing them up again." He did an ab curl, half sitting up for a moment. "I never noticed your pinky toe is crooked."

"I fought a coffee table when I was a toddler and lost."

"Poor baby. I hope you got back at it later?"

"I did actually." I chuckled. "I spent years banging my toes against that stupid monstrosity. Then one weekend, when Michael was out of town for work, I must have been sixteen because Sach was driving her mom's car that year, we decided to make crème brûlée."

"Doesn't that involve a blowtorch?"

"A baker's torch, but hush. You're getting ahead of things."

"My bad."

"We spent the entire weekend making batch after batch to get it right. We finally perfected it, but we were really tired, so we flaked out on my sofa bingeing this show while the ramekins cooled in the fridge."

Ezra stared at me with a half fascinated, half horrified expression. "The show matters, why?"

"You have to understand that it was a really good program. We didn't want to pause it for a second, so we decided we'd torch the desserts right there on the coffee table."

Ezra groaned.

"The new one that Michael came home to was much nicer."

He patted my head. "Good spin."

"Thanks."

"Aviva?"

"Yeah?"

"Will you make me crème brûlée sometime?" He sounded so hesitant, like a little kid scared to ask for what he really wanted.

I hugged him. "Of course, Zee."

"Aviva?"

"Yeah," I said with a smile.

"Will you change your hair color back?" he said with studied indifference.

I sat up, the sheets pooling at my waist. "Are you saying you were two percent less attracted to me just now?"

"I mean, I wouldn't go that high."

I swatted him and he laughed. Truth was, I wanted to look like myself again as well, but I snuggled into him with a humphed "We'll see," and let sleep take me.

Chapter 23

I woke up on Saturday and snagged an early appointment with my longtime stylist. "To be clear," I said to Ezra, "I'm doing this for me, not you." I tossed my fake contacts in the trash.

He hung out at my place while I was gone. We were going to retrieve "the brain of my enemy" for Delacroix when I returned from the salon. Ezra had argued that there was no point helping Delacroix anymore when we'd agreed to it in exchange for a victim of the first Ashbishop, not our copycat.

However, I pointed out that we had nothing on Ash Lite, other than Silas being worried that it was one of the original crew. Thus every scrap of information on the Ashbishop and his vamps was essential to help us find our current suspect.

More importantly, back out now and Delacroix would tattle to the Authority about our role in Silas's escape.

Besides, I wanted to see this brain for myself and figure out what the shedim planned on using it for.

While I was sitting under the dryer with the foils on, I checked in with Michael.

None of Keira's colleagues in Argentina had made contact with Mois Aviyente yet, and Linda remained in her house, with no unusual activity and no one else coming or going.

I hid in the salon's bathroom to make an encrypted video call to Silas. "Where are you now?"

"Just outside Calgary."

"Troy crossed the border into Alberta?"

"Yeah. We caught him on CCTV footage in Banff. Pretty place."

"Never been," I said, "but I've seen photos." The tiny town was nestled in the majestic snowcapped Rocky Mountains near crystal blue lakes. "What makes you think Troy continued on to Calgary?"

Darsh edged himself into the frame, draping an arm over his boyfriend's shoulder with a look that dared me to comment on it.

I made kissy noises at them.

"You colored your hair back already?" Darsh said. "It would be *such* a pity if all those chemicals made it fall out."

Silas pushed him out of the frame. "If you can't say anything nice…"

Darsh instantly reappeared on-screen. "That's what you're for." He smacked a kiss to Silas's cheek.

The other vamp blushed, his freckles darkening. He rubbed his hand briskly over his short copper-colored hair. "Back to Troy," he said pointedly.

Darsh grinned.

"I left the Seattle Spook Squad running down leads north of us in Edmonton," Silas said. "The Portland bunch doubled back into British Columbia, and Nasir and Cécile went south into Montana, but since the Trans-Canada Highway runs from Banff to Calgary, Darsh and I are hunting Troy here as the most likely city where he can go to ground."

"All work." Darsh threw the back of his hand to his forehead.

"You could find ways to play in a nuclear disaster," Silas grumbled affably.

"It's one of my many talents."

Someone knocked on the salon's bathroom door.

"One moment!" I lowered my voice. "Much as I would love to stick around and induce myself into a diabetic coma gorging on the sweetness of you two, I must dash. Keep me posted?"

"Of course," Silas said.

Darsh blew me a kiss and the screen went black.

WHEN I GOT HOME, Ezra nodded in approval at my return to regular Aviva. I made a note to dump the padded shapewear I'd purchased to transform into Jackie's curvier body, then followed him into the elevator.

Ezra had gone back to the Hell to change. He now wore his gorgeous cashmere trench coat over dark jeans and a fitted black sweater while I had on a short puffy winter jacket that made me vaguely tomato shaped.

"Whatever happened to that cool gothic hunter jacket of yours?" I said, watching the floor numbers and tapping my foot impatiently.

"Because you want it?"

"Vampire detective badge unlocked."

Ezra laughed. "We can discuss you *borrowing* it."

"Borrowing, huh? What would it take to upgrade to ownership?"

A wicked grin blossomed over Ezra's face and he reached for me but the elevator chimed.

I ducked under his outstretched arm. "Duty calls."

We bypassed the lobby and exited out the fire door into

the alley. A soggy bag of trash had been tossed next to a dumpster, and a rando vampire leaned against the wall, smoking a cigarette. Two bags of trash, then.

"Where are you lovebirds off to?" He spat out a phlegmy glob and I shuddered.

Always nice to know Natán had efficient underlings.

"The happiest place on earth," Ezra said. "Fuck off."

In half a heartbeat, the strange vamp was behind me, his arm wrapped around my throat. It happened so fast that my brain was still processing the glowing tip of his cigarette discarded on the concrete. "Think I could get mouse ears?" he said.

Ezra's fangs descended. "You're about to have no ears if you don't let her go."

The other vampire tightened his hold on me, my air supply almost cut off. "I don't think you understand what I'm willing to do for those mouse ears, bud."

Ezra's smile unfurled in much the same way that the glacier must have appeared to the *Titanic*: sharp and cold, promising danger and death.

I sighed. There wasn't time for the boys to play. I morphed my left hand to claws and stabbed my captor's eyes out.

He screamed and released me, spinning around with blood spurting out of his empty sockets.

I ducked out of the splatter zone and shook my hand to dislodge his eyeballs. Only one fell off.

"Need some help?" Ezra said, amused.

"You fucking bitch!" The vampire flailed around attempting to grab me. A milky film with green dots appeared in his sockets, his eyes already healing.

I flung the other eyeball against the wall and nodded at Ezra. "Have at it. But quickly."

The still-blind vampire snapped his head up, spinning

around to block Ezra's attack, but even with sight he wouldn't have been any match for the Prime.

Ezra snapped his neck before Natán's minion completed his ninety-degree turn, the crunch echoing in my ears.

Catchy, Cherry said.

The vamp's face grotesquely contorted in surprise in the split second before he crumbled into ash—a fun little snapshot to carry with me.

I wiped my hands off on my jeans. "My magic kingdom for some hand sanitizer."

A mesh portal shivered into existence.

Ezra offered me his arm. "My lady?"

I looped my arm through his. "Thank you, kind sir."

We stepped into the foyer of the Copper Hell and immediately back out onto manicured grounds, the silhouette of a grand Tuscan villa looming against the star-studded sky.

"It's a bit much to clean on a regular basis," I said, "but it also doesn't scream 'this way there be evil.'"

"That's not true." Ezra scanned the darkness. His heightened senses would pick up anyone—or anything—long before I did, so I remained relaxed until signaled otherwise.

"The place seems pretty tasteful from out here. Are you getting an evilcore vibe?"

We avoided the gravel path leading to the circular driveway, sticking to the grass.

"I was referring to the 'bit much.' There's a cleaning staff," Ezra said in an "obviously" voice.

"Oh, sunshine," I said, patting his arm. "It must be so nice in your reality."

"It is rather."

We jogged up the front stairs.

I eyed the large brass knockers adorning the high wood doors, then shook my head. "Too easy."

"Your restraint is admirable." Ezra ran a hand over the mezuzah mounted to the doorframe and raised an eyebrow. "This is top-of-the-line." He rattled the doors, but they didn't even budge. "There's rebar in these. Majorly reinforced. Even I'm not busting the doors down."

The heavy bars on all the windows also proved resistant to Ezra's super strength.

"Think all this security is merely for some pickled old brain?" I said.

"Only one way to tell." Ezra shrugged out of his trench coat and dumped it in my hands.

"You're going to break in?"

"As that's the first step in this theft, yes."

I swatted his arm. "Ha. Ha. I meant how? This is a private building, and you haven't been invited inside." I frowned. "How did Delacroix think this would work? There's no way he didn't consider every little detail."

Ezra screwed up his face. "About that…"

I took a step backward, my eyes wide. "Vamps don't have to be invited?!"

He waved his hands. "Breathe, Avi. That's still a safeguard." He paused. "Against other vamps. Primes, not so much."

I smacked him. "So, you were just paying lip service to me the first time you asked me to invite you into my home?"

He wagged his eyebrows suggestively. "As I recall, you had no complaints about said lip service."

"Ugh. Delacroix knew this, didn't he?"

"Yeah."

I swatted Ezra's arm again. Harder. "Begone."

He chuckled. "Back in a moment." He dug his fingertips into some barely visible crack in the wall of the villa and hauled himself up, climbing it like a gecko.

Good thing Sachie wasn't here to take notes.

I admired the tight clench of my boyfriend's glutes and the flex of his biceps until he got too high up for me to ogle him anymore, then I hopped down the wide shallow stairs to see where he was going.

Ezra pulled himself over the lip of the roof and vanished from sight.

Less than two minutes later, the door was opened by a very sooty vampire. "The place is empty." He reached for his trench coat, then grimaced, and opened a small portal that hovered above the stairs. "Toss the coat in."

I pitched it through the portal into Ezra's living room at the Copper Hell where he could retrieve it later, and entered the villa here in Tuscany. "You went down the chimney? How did you fit?"

The villa's interior was a maze of opulent rooms filled with sheet-covered furniture and winding corridors that smelled of mold.

"I may have broken it open in a few places." He brushed soot off himself, then just gave up. "It was my only option."

"No. You also had 'we turn around and go home without the brain' as a choice."

"Sure, but"—he flashed me a sheepish grin—"my mom and I used to watch *Mary Poppins* together and there's this one song with chimney sweeps that I'd make her replay."

"'Chim Chimeree' or whatever?"

"No. The dance one. 'Step in Time.' They made being a chimney sweep seem like so much fun." He did a little two-step.

I got a pang in my chest. That was sweet, but also incredibly sad that he'd stuffed himself down a chimney to feel connected to his dead mother.

We descended a spiral staircase, the air growing thick and oppressive. Cherry whispered at me to be careful.

"Thoughts?" I tapped the toe of my boot against the stone wall at the bottom.

"Delacroix told me about this." Ezra ran his hands over the smooth surface. "It should be right about…"

There was a soft pop and the wall rippled like water. Symbols appeared, glowing an eerie green, then the stones parted like they were curtains, revealing a corridor bathed in a bloodred light.

"Who can resist an invitation like that?" I said.

Ezra took my hand. "We'll be fine." But he quickly tugged us through the gap in the wall before the curtain came down on us.

The rocky, uneven corridor was so narrow that we had to walk single file. Ezra went first, keeping a tight grip on my hand.

My hair stood up on the back of my neck and every step wound my shoulders higher into my ears. I'd have jumped at every little sound but there weren't any. Even my breaths felt stolen away before they left my lips.

I blotted my forehead with my sleeve because our passageway was growing hotter and drier.

Ezra stopped suddenly.

I bonked my nose on his back. "What is it?"

"Wind. A faint whisper."

I strained to hear it but couldn't. However, should it come with a cooling breeze, I was all for it. I prodded Ezra between the shoulders to get him moving again.

Six feet later, we turned a corner, and I blinked up at the wash of stars in the vast night sky, a sea of reddish sand cascading away from us in undulating dunes. Far in the distance was a single cactus.

"Rich people," I said. "They have cleaning staff *and* their own private indoor deserts."

It was magnificent, but neither Eishei Kodesh nor vampires could create an illusion like this. Either we'd been transported to an actual desert (not great but the better of our options), this was a demon illusion (Danger! Danger, Will Robinson!), or we'd accessed some demon realm (see Will Robinson comment).

"How are we supposed to find the safe?" I shifted my weight to keep my balance against the pull of sand on my feet.

Ezra pointed off into the distance. "I think it might be that cactus."

"Oh, fuck right off."

We trudged toward it. I tried not to think about quicksand, lest I invoke anything. Our journey was slow and sweaty, but we arrived at the cactus without incident.

The very prickly, scarred motherfucker of a plant was a solid ten feet in circumference.

I gingerly touched one of the fat, sharp thorns. "Ready?"

Ezra nodded. "Three-minute time delay once you punch in the code. You remember it?"

I tapped my head and nodded.

"Stay vigilant."

"Really? Because a nap seems like such a good idea right now." I pressed my palm against the thorn, swearing as it sliced my flesh.

A holographic keypad shimmered into the air, and I punched in the eight-digit code.

The cactus shuddered like a cat blinking off sleep. It didn't have eyes, but I felt something wake and study me.

A three-minute stare down? No problem.

Two large hands made of shifting grains magically reached inside me, their knuckles scraping abrasively against my organs.

I gasped and doubled over.

Ezra tried to pull me clear, but his hold slipped right off like I was a greased pig.

Abomination. The magic hands snapped out of my body with a sharp sting, grabbed my ankles, and flung me into the desert.

Screaming, I squeezed my lids closed against the hot, gritty wind scratching my face. I hit the ground, bounced four times, then rolled down a dune, bruised but unbroken.

"Ezra!" My voice echoed mockingly around me, but I was alone.

Chapter 24

Cursing Delacroix—and my own stupidity for agreeing to this—I headed off through the endless sea of red sand. Conventional wisdom dictated that if you strayed off a trail you stayed put, but those were hiking rules on an earthside mountain. The only rule applicable to magic deserts with bad-touch sand hands were GET THE FUCK OUT NOW!

I trudged over dunes for an eternity, my throat parched from the relentless heat.

Nothing ever appeared, and the dark didn't give way to daylight though I'd been walking for hours. My steps grew more laborious, my thighs burned, and my body was slick with sweat. I wiped myself down with the jacket that I'd tied over my head, and sucked on the fabric, desperate for moisture.

"Ezra!" I called out for the thousandth time, my voice cracking. The sound was swallowed by the vast emptiness around me.

The landscape shifted constantly, dunes rising and falling like waves. I'd hobble to the top of one, hoping to spot something—anything—only to find my view obscured by another, larger dune that hadn't been there moments before.

I'd flipped into my shedim form for protection and added stamina, but the effort of maintaining it outweighed any benefits, and I soon reverted to my normal body.

Sand cascaded beneath my next step. I stumbled, rolling my ankle with a hot shaft of pain, and sank to my knees with a cry.

Get up, Cherry snarled in my head. *We are not dying here.*

Just let me rest. One little nap with dreams of cool water and shade. That sounded nice.

Don't you dare lie down! She screamed at me until I pressed on, precious tears running down my face from the hell that each weight-bearing step caused my left ankle.

As I crested yet another dune, my heart leapt. In the distance, I saw a flash of green—the cactus! *I'm coming, my pretty!* I threw myself down the hill, rolling faster and faster, my heart soaring. There had to be a way out once I got… whatever it was I was here for.

Or I found… Wasn't I with someone?

I tumbled to a stop at the bottom, but the cactus shimmered and vanished, leaving me alone once more. A sob of frustration escaped my cracked lips.

Suddenly, the sand shifted, pulling me down.

Panic surged through me as I sank deeper, the grains rough against my skin. I thrashed, but it only made me sink faster. The sand was up to my waist now, threatening to swallow me whole.

In desperation, I reached for Cherry. She responded sluggishly, like I was trying to grasp smoke, but my arms transformed, frosted green scales glinting in the harsh moonlight. With renewed strength, I dragged myself out of the quicksand's grip and lay on solid-ish sand, panting.

Cherry went quiet, barely a spark inside me. I was fully

human and totally exhausted, every part of my body throbbing. My eyes burned with sand, and tears streamed down my cheeks. When my vision finally began to clear, there was another flash of green nearby.

The cactus's flesh was torn apart like a jagged smile to reveal a metal door.

"No," I moaned. "Not another mirage."

This one didn't vanish.

I wish it had, because the sight of Ezra fighting an enormous man made of sand, one arm dangling limply from the Prime's shoulder and his skin a mix of soot and blood from dozens of cuts that weren't healing, would have been a nightmare I could wake up from.

Delacroix appeared out of thin air, a cigarette jammed in the corner of his mouth. "Ah. Perfect timing." He stepped over me, rubbing his hands like a cartoon villain.

The sand creature punched its fist down on the top of Ezra's head.

My boyfriend collapsed like a balloon that had lost all its air, crumpling facedown in a heap.

I grabbed Delacroix's pant leg. "Help him!"

He dragged me across the sand, not even slowing his pace.

"Anything happens to Ezra and your magic at the Hell goes to shit." I spat out sand. "You won't be safe."

Delacroix growled an annoyed sigh. "Then get up, girlie, and open the safe door. That brain isn't going to steal itself."

Hating the demon with every fiber of my being, I rose, keeping as much of my weight as possible on my uninjured leg, and hobbled over to the cactus. I couldn't let myself look back, because if Ezra still hadn't moved, I'd shut down.

We hadn't overcome everything thus far for my fucking father and some sand creature to destroy us.

I glanced over my shoulder.

My boyfriend was bathed in a silver glow, fighting alongside Delacroix to shred the sand creature into ribbons with a brutal thoroughness.

The demon had lost his human glamor in favor of majestic silver scales that rippled over his thick serpent's coils. His strikes recalled the swell of waves, while the sand monster, roughly ten feet tall and humanoid, felt rooted to the earth's core. Delacroix shot forward and sliced off a ribbon of sand using the heavy black horns that curved upward off his head.

The monster lunged for the demon, but the serpent bobbed out of his grasp and opened the crimson spike that protruded from his neck into blades that shredded his opponent.

The sand creature reared back with a howl, bleeding granules.

Ezra tore his attacker's head off, and the creature dissolved into a pile of sand.

Delacroix slid toward me, shrinking back to his human glamor. His skin and hair were dusted in sand. He snapped his fingers at me. "Don't just stand there."

I wrenched on the safe's handle, grunting and pulling with all my might to release its top edge from inside the cactus. The cut from the thorn I'd first stabbed myself with tore open, and a smear of blood stained the metal.

The door flew open, almost smashing me in the nose.

Inside the safe was nothing more than a two-by-three-foot hollowed-out section of the cactus cavity. Impaled on a single large thorn was the brain Delacroix sought. It wasn't a dusty, almost quaintly desiccated lump, but a fleshy pulsing monstrosity covered in strange dot-like growths that didn't correspond to any anatomical structure I'd ever seen.

Ezra gaped at it, the silver glow of Delacroix's magic boost gone. "Qué mierda?"

A demon brain. My curiosity almost made a dent in my panic and pain.

Being around it didn't incapacitate me with nausea—more proof that this innate demon magic detection that I manifested since taking off my Maccabee ring didn't work on full demons—or their parts.

I reached for it with a grimace, the brain quivering like cold jelly under my palm. Shuddering, I adjusted my hold and tugged, but the brain didn't come loose, and now I was stuck fast as well.

I couldn't move, and worse, something was assessing me, creeping through me.

It poked and my magic freaked out.

Scales to skin, crimson locks to brown, claws to fingers, my features flipped back and forth as if something was puzzling me out. My transformation slowed like a slot machine window, landing on the winning prize of all shedim parts.

The brain quivered and plopped into my hands.

A second later, I was knocked aside. The brain was ripped from my grasp so brutally that a burst of scales tore free.

Delacroix seized me by the shirtfront and lifted me off the ground with one hand.

"Let her go." Ezra ran toward us.

Delacroix froze him in his tracks and leaned his face close to mine, his eyes glittering dangerously. "Keeping secrets, girlie? Frankly, I'm a little hurt it took a cactus to facilitate a proper family reunion."

"I'm not. You always were a prick."

My lungs suddenly felt like they were filled with salt water. They weren't actually, yet I couldn't breathe. Coughing, I thrashed uselessly in my father's grip. He was drowning me in the middle of a desert, and every part of me burned from the lack of oxygen.

Ripples rose up from the red waves cascading out to the horizon. I tried to touch them, but I couldn't lift my arm. I was numb.

My soul drifted down to a place without panic. Without pain. I was surrounded by a swirl of colors and beauty.

Fuck that, a voice growled in my head.

The numbness tore away like a sheet ripping off a line. Fire seared every one of my nerve endings, my vision flecked with giant black dots, but the magic drowning sensation subsided a fraction—just enough for me to drag in a gasping breath.

"I don't like being tricked," Delacroix said.

"Should have earned your demon detective badge," I snarled and swiped my claws across his cheek, drawing blood.

Delacroix was so startled that he dropped me.

I landed on my bad ankle with a howl, instinctively reaching out for something to grab hold of.

My fingertips sank into one of the growths on the brain and my vision exploded into chaos. I went rigid as a torrent of information flooded my mind, streaming numbers and letters that blinded me. Then I sagged to the hot sand, my thoughts blurring in a feverish haze.

The barrier keeping Ezra from me must have fallen away in the demon's shock because my boyfriend reached me and slid his shoulder underneath mine to take the weight of my bad side as he helped me to my feet. "She'll kill you for that," he said to Delacroix, "and I'll take great pleasure in helping her."

My body felt light, almost floating through the heat shimmering off the sand, but my skin was cooking. "Plus codes," I gasped.

Delacroix froze.

The gentleness of Ezra's grip was belied by the menace

he directed at Delacroix. "The brain contains the locations of the prison cells?"

I'd given them to Delacroix? My legs buckled but Ezra kept me upright.

The demon touched a finger to the blood on his cheek. "Keep your mouths shut about this or I'll tell its previous owners where to find the Maccabee and Prime who stole it."

Salty sweat burned my eyes. "You mean you'll tell the shedim how your daughter took it thanks to very precise instructions from her father?"

He flipped the brain over to examine it. "There are other shedim who look similar to me. Who's to say you're not one of theirs?"

My eyes flared so bright green with rage that Delacroix blinked and looked away. After all he'd done to me, it shouldn't have been any big surprise that he'd toss me away like trash if it suited him.

I clenched my fists to keep from rubbing away the sting in my chest, then stepped up toe-to-toe with the asshole demon. "Free those prisoners and there won't be a corner of any reality that's dark enough or far enough to hide in." I could barely get the words out because my brain felt like it was melting, plop by plop disintegrating in my skull.

"Who said I planned to free them?" Delacroix cast about in his shock of hair for another cigarette, which he jammed in his mouth.

"Something worse, then," I retorted. Though I couldn't imagine what that was.

"Aviva," Ezra said insistently and tugged my arm up.

My scales were a sickly gray.

"I'll stop you," I said to my father. "Whatever you've planned."

"Yeah, I'm terrified. You look like a guppy some two-year-old caught," Delacroix said with a mean smirk.

"Get us out of here," Ezra snarled at the demon and swung me up in his arms.

I tried to speak but my mouth was dry and tasted of sand. The bursts and swirls of colors dancing around my head were pretty, though.

Well, they were until they swam around me in a nauseating blur.

The world bounced twice, then Ezra pressed his wrist to my lips.

I tasted copper. I savored it, drinking greedily, the healing magic in his blood flowing into me.

He finally disengaged his wrist with a wince. "Stop," he said gently.

As my senses returned, I saw that we sat outside under a tree with the villa in the distance.

"How long was I gone?" Off his confusion, I clarified. "When I first disappeared in the desert?"

"Only a few seconds. I turned around and you'd vanished, then you just reappeared."

I stared at him in disbelief. Seconds? It had felt like days of torment. "Time was different there."

Ezra's expression darkened. "Whatever Delacroix is up to, we'll stop him."

"Sure. Just add it to the list." I sat up with a muttered curse. "He didn't give me the person who can identify the Ashbishop or anything on the vamp supplicant. Take me to the Hell."

He did as I asked but didn't let me leave the foyer. "I'll corner Delacroix and get that information myself right now. Unless you want me to come home with you."

"I do, but no. Keep an eye on him."

"I will." Ezra kissed me softly.

I sighed in relief when I returned to the alley behind my condo tower and there wasn't a vampire waiting for me, but the emotion was short-lived because Alastair sat in the lobby, swapping gossip about the British royal family with Mrs. Carson from the fourth floor.

"Ah!" The Brit waved at me. "Here she is now. Thank you, my dear, for keeping me company until Aviva got home."

The older woman, a notorious grump who always side-eyed me, ducked her head with a blush. "The pleasure was mine." She passed me with a frosty glare and got into one of the elevators.

"Did you compel her?" I said.

"I'm hardly old enough for that." He tutted me with his finger. "A word of warning, luv."

"Do tell."

"Make it easy on yourself and leave your watchers alone."

I crossed my arms. "Your concern for my well-being warms the cockles of my heart."

"It's just laziness, innit?" he said, straightening the couch's throw pillows. "You or Ez move against Natán and then I've got a mess of trouble to deal with. One missing vamp I could explain away. Two's a coincidence. Three is a nasty, nasty pattern, and I'd hate for the box man to have to intercede." He rose fluidly, strode out the door, and out of view.

I'd hoped that after sand monsters, my father's wrath, vampire minions, and a demon brain that I'd get five freaking minutes to catch my breath, but I'd just gotten into my bedroom when my mother phoned.

"Linda's home burned down," Michael said. "Fire-fighters couldn't find her when they went inside."

"Oh my God. Did Troy do it?" I chucked my socks into my hamper.

"We don't know. There haven't been any sightings of him. Forensic techs will check for a body when the house cools down enough. Let's hope she got out and will reach out to us." She ended the call.

I was all for Linda making contact, but her lover was still on the run with two occupied prison locks in his possession, and her mother had worked with a shedim who freed jailed demons.

Linda might indeed get in touch soon, but with who?

Chapter 25

I'd have to tell Michael that a brain existed containing the locations of all the lock cells in the world, but one thing at a time.

First up was a long shower.

Troy Abelman was missing, along with two locks. It would have been nice if I could do more than passively recognize the plus codes, like attach those coordinates to specific shedim. Unfortunately, the locks in Troy's possession could have corresponded to any of the hundreds of locations I'd seen when I touched the growth on the brain.

Or, they could belong to none of them, if those cells had somehow been removed from the system by the matchmakers.

Sadly, Rukhsana's network hadn't yet sighted Troy or learned anything new about the man to help us find him.

Ezra, however, came through as always. He not only got the location of the Ashbishop's victim from Delacroix, but also that the power word supplicant was Evelyn Rue. Of course, my father had held to the letter of the agreement and not troubled himself to learn anything more than the female vampire's name.

I crashed out on my sofa.

What if I was too late and Ash Lite had all the elements required for the dark ritual to give vampires procreation?

No, I had to trust that I'd stop him, the same as I had stopped other nefarious players. I stuffed a pillow under my head. Wasn't everything in my life nowadays about living in a place of trust, not fear? There were times that worked out the way I wanted and times it didn't. But I kept going. I was still standing and living to fight and laugh and love another day.

Besides, a lifetime of living with a massive secret had honed my instincts and sharpened my training and experience. It made me the excellent operative I was.

I'd find Ash Lite and once again, I'd do my part to make this world a better place.

Tomorrow I'd pay a visit to the Ashbishop's victim and pray that he gave me something concrete—like the names of the brutal vampire's crew.

Are you going to deal with the fact that Daddy Dearest knows about you?

Well, Cherry, I'd been planning to save that trauma until morning, but thanks so much for bringing it up now. Delacroix hadn't exactly liked me, but I'd amused him, and at times, I'd swear I'd impressed him. So why hadn't any of that mattered now?

I struggled to take a deep breath, but it wasn't the memory of drowning, it was a wave of hot fury—followed swiftly by self-loathing that I cared. I calmed down by reminding myself he'd also attacked Maud after he realized she was his kid.

Mentally calculating the time difference, I phoned my sister. At least I had someone to bitch about our shitty sperm donor with. "Delacroix just learned he has another daughter."

She tsked sympathetically. "From the sound of your

voice, you didn't get waffles with a Flaming Flapjacks T-shirt?"

I rubbed a hand over my chest, then clenched it into a fist and dropped it to my side. "I foresee more torture in our dynamic."

"Sorry Dad's playing favorites?"

I laughed bitterly. "Me too. Fuck him."

"Is it fuck Ezra too?" she said, not unkindly. "I saw the photos with that ballet dancer."

"They're irrelevant. We're good."

Maud teased me about announcing my girlfriend status to the Ezracurriculars so I threatened to have Silas dig up the most unfortunate photos of her ever and post them on websites advertising the next poker world championship she was entered in.

Perfectly normal sibling stuff. It didn't erase the sting—or the danger—of my interactions with Delacroix, but if erasing him from my life meant losing Maud, too, I'm not sure I'd take that deal.

I WOKE up Sunday morning to a spate of texts all amounting to the same thing: there was nothing new to report on Troy Abelman or Linda Aviyente.

After a fortifying cup of coffee, I logged into the Maccabee database (valiantly resisting the urge to check the gossip sites) and spent the next hour digging into Evelyn Rue, the female supplicant for the power word.

She'd been registered with Philadelphia HQ for her feedings when she was initially turned twenty years ago but had moved to Babel before joining the likes of Shiny Jimmy as a wall in the Brink.

I forwarded the info to Ezra for him to track down anyone who knew her, and drove out to the address in the

Fraser Valley where the original Ashbishop's victim, Rylan Quinn, lived.

About eighty minutes later, I buzzed in at a high gate. Seaside was an in-patient facility that provided physical therapy and counseling for accident and fire victims, people suffering from PTSD, and, when necessary, survivors of vampire attacks.

It wasn't like they advertised that particular service in their commercials, but Maccabees were certainly aware of the private clinic, which had locations around the globe. Hell, we sent people there.

Seaside wasn't a long-term living facility, and the Ashbishop hadn't ever been sighted in Vancouver, so it would never have occurred to me that one of his victims might be cared for here.

I'd threaded my Maccabee ring on a slim gold chain around my neck, which I held up to the video screen now to identify myself as an operative. I was still undercover and couldn't openly wear it, but I wanted to keep it close.

Once my official presence was verified, Cara, a bubbly nurse, escorted me past bright exercise rooms with balls, bikes, and all manner of physio equipment, smaller meeting areas with couches and posters with inspirational sayings, a yoga room with mats laid out in neat rows, and an activity room where patients in loose cotton shirts and pants gathered around board games, chatted, or sat on window benches reading.

Patients generally lived here for three to six months before moving into the community and switching to weekly visits until they were well enough to go home.

Seaside was fortunate in that there were some wealthy anonymous donors who supported the global clinics in addition to the regular fundraising they did. No one was turned away based on financial need.

Cara held the kitchen door open for me.

A badly stooped elderly man was wiping down the stainless-steel counters. His thinning yellow hair was tucked under a hair net, and he shuffled on two state-of-the-art prosthetic legs.

"Rylan, a Maccabee's come for you. You troublemaker." Cara wagged a finger at him.

Rylan regarded me with green eyes that were clear and alert. "Are you here about my cyberfraud or the seven husbands of mine who died under mysterious circumstances?" he said with an Irish accent.

"Last week it was six," the nurse teased.

He rinsed his rag out in the sink. "Belvedere sleeps with the fishes. Sorry, Cara. Know you were fond of him."

She laughed. "When you're done chatting, Darleen is getting back from physio early. She'll be wanting to play chess, then."

"Our tie-breaker match. I've got my strategy ready." Rylan waited until Cara had left. "To what do I owe the pleasure of your company, Operative?"

"Fleischer. Aviva." I looked around. "Is there somewhere we can sit down?"

The older man regarded me shrewdly for a long moment. "Is he dead?"

"The Ashbishop?" I said with a frown.

All the color drained from Rylan's face, and he staggered backward into the counter.

I steadied him. "I'm so sorry. I thought that's who you meant."

Rylan allowed me to help him to a table in the empty cafeteria and bring him a glass of water, though he didn't drink it. He ran a gnarled thumb around the rim. "I'd hoped to never hear that name again."

"The Ashbishop is absolutely very, very dead. Forgive me for scaring you, but who were you referring to?"

"My patron." At my confused head shake, he sighed.

"When I was a wee lad, the Ashbishop slaughtered most of the people in my village, including me mam." He stretched out one of his prosthetic legs. "They thought I was dead too. But I wasn't. I lived a miserable life until I was about ten, when Dr. Ellis came to see me. He'd been sent by a mysterious patron who knew how I'd suffered and wanted me to be treated and cared for. On behalf of the patron, who'd pay for everything, the doctor offered to take me to this facility in Canada."

I did the math in my head. "None of the Seaside clinics were established until after vampires came out to the public in the 1960s. You would have been one of the first patients here then."

"Indeed." He lifted the glass with a shaky hand and drank.

"Why Canada? Why not Ireland? How did the patron learn about you? Who was this doctor?"

"The clinics started in California and moved up the west coast. Ireland didn't get one until years later. I don't know how this patron found me, but I wasn't the only one. Years later, I learned there were others who'd been brought to different Seaside clinics. All of us with one nightmare in common."

"The Ashbishop," I said grimly. "You think he had a change of heart and was repenting for his actions?"

Rylan rubbed his collarbone. His movement shifted his shirt enough to reveal thin white scars like crosshairs. "The devil doesn't have a change of heart. The Ashbishop was evil incarnate. A monster of a creature, big as an oak, with hair of fire and the face of an angel, who feasted on our blood and our flesh, and laughed while he did."

Awesome. This did not bode well for the kind of vampires he gathered around him. "You were brought here, cared for, and chose to stay?"

"Another condition of our care. We're provided with a

generous monthly stipend, so long as we give back by volunteering at one of the clinics to help other people who've suffered. Not just from vampires but anyone who comes here."

"How many people have taken that offer?" Where was all this money coming from?

"Only a few." Rylan shrugged. "Most want to put it behind them and move on with their lives once they're physically strong enough."

That was understandable. However, would the mental scars from these nightmarish tragedies ever fully heal, even with the best Eishei Kodesh magic or latest medical technology?

"I wish I didn't have to tell you this but some other vampire has taken his name."

Rylan's grip on the water glass tightened. "Are they like him?"

"They're looking for a way for vampires to procreate." I left out the half-shedim murders Ash Lite had sanctioned.

"Vampires don't care about children," Rylan scoffed. "Those urges die along with their beating hearts."

I flashed on the memory of Evelyn Rue and couldn't say I agreed. But I hadn't come here to argue that point. "It might be one of his crew."

"Each as bad as the next." He crossed himself. "Dragomir, Emeric, Baylor, and Zuberi. There were others, but those were the worst. The ones we feared almost as much as the Ashbishop himself. I pray they're in Hell."

Cara entered the cafeteria. "Sorry, Rylan, but Darleen is getting antsy."

There was nothing more he could add, so I thanked him and followed Cara back to the foyer with photos of past doctors. The center position was reserved for Dr. Ellis, a man in his forties. "Is he still alive?" I said.

"No. He passed away years ago. I never met him. Wish I had."

A woman snorted. "You're a deluded idiot."

Cara sighed and turned to the thirty-something patient with bandages on her face and hands. "Dr. Ellis was a good man, Nancy. He implemented procedures and championed techniques that's allowed you to get the best care."

"Now you help people, but that wasn't always the case," Nancy said.

"What are you talking about?" I said.

"Demons." Nancy's eyes gleamed.

"Don't exist," Cara said firmly.

Beg to differ. Cherry smirked.

Nancy jabbed a finger at Cara. "Yeah? Try telling that to the women they strapped to tables and used as human incubators. God, just imagine being forced to carry those… those infernal abominations."

I flinched. I'd heard a lot of shit about half shedim, but this was a new one.

"Three heads," Nancy said. "Hearts of stone."

Cara shot me a look of *See what I'm dealing with?*

The infernal stuff was clearly bullshit, but was a grain of truth buried in there? Had vampires tried to achieve procreation before and covered that up in the same PR campaign back in the 1960s that made them so irresistible when they first went public?

Which, coincidentally, was around the time Seaside was founded?

I narrowed my eyes at the photo of Dr. Ellis. Could Ash Lite have tried this before?

"What about vampires?" I said insistently. "Did they do these experiments?"

"Vampires?" Nancy practically swooned the word, fanning herself. "They don't have to force anyone. Take that Ezra Cardoso, for example. Or better yet, let him take me."

"Thanks for your time," I said sharply.

I sent Ezra the four names that Rylan had given me, then spent the drive back rearranging the precious few facts about Ash Lite to accommodate the new information about the crew or the clinic.

I was almost back at my condo when Silas called.

"Troy's dead." His swore viciously. "And it's all my fault."

Chapter 26

I crouched down next to Troy's corpse in the woods behind Linda's home. His lifeless eyes seemed to stare back at me, holding secrets I wasn't sure I wanted to uncover.

The man's body was contorted, his limbs twisted at unnatural angles and his charred, blackened skin split and peeled to reveal scorched muscle and bone. His face was a half-ruined mask of gruesome agony, his mouth agape in a silent scream over empty sockets.

He'd died from an intense burst of heat from an Orange Flame, because had a Red Flame torched him, the forest would have caught fire as well.

The attack was so intense that wisps of acrid smoke still drifted off the body, even hours later, carrying the sickening stench of burned flesh.

The metal case with the prison locks was nowhere to be seen.

"Fuuuuuuuuuck!" My scream sent two crows winging away from a cedar tree.

Silas placed his hand on my shoulder. "If I'd found Troy two hours sooner, then…" My friend shook his head, bleary-eyed with exhaustion.

"Then you might have been killed as well. Vampires are just as flammable as humans." I stood up, looking past the tree line to Linda's fire-wrecked ruin of a house. "Was orange flame magic responsible for that too?"

Silas nodded at one of the forensic techs speaking with Darsh by the plastic fencing that had been erected around the home. "That's what Gaitan believes, but Malika is on her way over to examine the body."

I paced the muddy forest ground. "Jared's attack by another Orange Flame wasn't a coincidence. The same person is responsible for Troy's murder."

Silas nodded. "I suspect they burned down Linda's home to flush Troy out and when he showed, killed him."

"And took the metal briefcase."

Silas frowned down at the corpse. "Now that I'm less sure of. The amount of magic that was poured into Troy? It's like his killer was furious and vented on him. Likely they would have eliminated Troy even once they got the metal case, but not this brutally."

I rubbed my pounding temples. "Could Linda have gotten the metal case back from Troy?"

"There's no body and no evidence that she died in that fire," Silas said. "So maybe."

"Which our Orange Flame suspect may very well know." I sat down on a fallen log, avoiding a patch of moss.

"Michael has been trying to reach Linda since the fire," Silas said. "But she hasn't answered and her mailbox is full."

"Just fucking great." How was it possible that we now had a corpse on our hands, plus a missing person, and two demon prisons complete with occupants still out in the wild?

Silas went to speak with Darsh and Gaitan and I phoned Rukhsana.

"Aviva," she said. "I was just about to call you."

"Troy's dead," I said curtly. "Did you find anyone who'd seen him in the last couple days? Anyone who helped him while he was on the run?"

"No one. He was very cautious."

Not cautious enough. "Is that what you meant to tell me?"

"No," she said. "Mois Aviyente snuck back into the country."

The Trads didn't know that yet or I'd have heard, but it didn't surprise me that Rukhsana had the information before we did.

Mois had ample money to procure an alias and a fake passport we knew nothing about. With Linda missing, her house burned down, and Troy dead, the older man would be operating at high alert paranoia.

"Is he with Linda?" I said. "Do you know where they are?"

Rukhsana tutted me. "My question first, chère. Those dangerous artifacts of Troy's that you mentioned, are they demonic?"

"Where did you hear that?" I said blandly.

"Fool."

I planted a hand on my hip. "I beg your pardon?"

"Not you. Mois Aviyente, and I'm not outing my source."

"Give me more than that, Rukhsana." I stood up. "Things are serious."

"I heard he was trying to trade some artifacts to shedim for his life."

"And his daughter's?" I crossed my fingers, hoping she was alive.

"No idea. But it's a stupid plan and it won't work."

"Why not?"

There was a long, weighty pause. I checked my screen, but the call was still connected. "Rukhsana?"

She exhaled hard and then my phone chimed.

I opened the photo she'd sent me and flinched. Her stomach was covered in angry raised scars. Rukhsana had a healer in her contacts, which meant these scars defied magic mending.

"Demons lie about making deals," she said bitterly. "I was very, very lucky to escape with my life. Mois shouldn't count on the same. You have to find him."

"Thank you for telling me, but…why did you?" Rukhsana was not one to share vulnerabilities and this one was a whopper.

"I'm tired of Vancouver. I want to start somewhere fresh with a few of my crew and you're going to help me." She named an outrageous sum.

"I don't have that kind of money."

"Ezra does," she said flatly. "Convince him."

"How——"

"Did you think batting your boyfriend's eyelashes at me would butter up poor, old Rukhsana?"

Intellectually, I'd always appreciated the Frenchwoman's reputation and how she'd gained such power in the relatively short time she'd lived in Vancouver, but right now was the first time I felt it in my bones.

"You got me." I cradled my phone between my chin and shoulder and threw up my hands. "You're young, hot, powerful, and clearly a totally pathetic human being. So yeah, I brought Ezra around to foreplay you up before the paid main event."

She actually chuckled. "Get me the money."

"You know you're supposed to negotiate before you show your cards. I could refuse."

"You won't. You care too much. Even about a criminal like me."

She was right. I did.

While I didn't plan to hit Ezra up for the cash, I agreed

to the amount, giving my word that she'd have it once Mois was found.

Let the Maccabees pay for catching Mois. One of the privileges of being a level three was my ability to authorize stuff like this, though I wished it wasn't necessary because the paperwork was still a nightmare.

Silas waved me over.

Malika had arrived, along with a few of her team, and they were zipping into protective suits.

With our deal in place, Rukhsana bid me à bientôt. I headed to my friends, greeting Malika and the new Maccabee arrivals.

They tromped off to examine Troy's body, the coroner issuing directives to her people while she tucked her head-scarf more securely under the hood of the suit.

I shared what Rukhsana had said as Silas, Darsh, and I hurried back to our cars. "It might be a long shot, but will you follow me to the Lions Gallery?" I said. "Mois has the money for them to hole up anywhere, but this is Linda's home turf, and I'd want to be somewhere familiar."

"We'll be right behind you." He and Darsh peeled off to the rented SUV.

I barreled through traffic with the gas pedal floored and a liberal use of my horn, parking in a restricted spot down the block from the gallery and slapping my Maccabee permit on the dash.

The operatives who'd been watching the business had been replaced by Trad officers. That was less interesting to me than the heavy security bars on all the windows that hadn't been there the night of the exhibit opening.

God, was that really only last Thursday? Three days ago?

The officers reported that the bars had been in place the entire time they'd staked out the building.

Silas and Darsh arrived to hear that.

I did a thorough walk through of the entire front of the gallery, pulling up short when I reached the doors.

Someone had installed a mezuzah on the frame.

I sprinted into the alley, where, sure enough, another one was on the back door with a sticker bearing the name of the security company. "The deal with the shedim wasn't because Troy died. He took off with the case because the deal was in place. It was set up already."

"Who are these shedim?" Darsh asked.

"Either the demon who was partnered with Chandra connecting prisoners with Eishei Kodesh criminals or the owners of the prison locks themselves." My stomach twisted and I glanced at my hands but the wound from the cactus heist was gone.

"What is it?" Darsh laid a hand on my shoulder and I jumped. "Easy," he said.

I couldn't tell them about the brain here. We were too exposed. "I'm worried about Linda and her dad hanging on to those locks. Chandra must have had them in her possession when she was killed, and for whatever reason, her family couldn't get to them until recently, while Mois was out of the country."

"Then he knew about her matchmaking gig."

I nodded. "I'd say so. As did Linda."

Silas and Darsh wrenched on the bars securing the back door.

"They're too strong for me to break," Silas said, "and the front door was also reinforced to defy vampire strength. Add in mezuzah wards and nothing supernatural is getting in there."

"Nothing human either," I said. "Our only hope is for Mois and Linda to come out." I pounded on the alley door, calling the gallery owner's name.

Silas and Darsh glanced at the high narrow window, then Darsh jerked his chin to the barred glass.

I stepped directly under it. "Linda, please listen to me. You can't trust shedim. If you and Mois won't cancel the meeting, then let me have operatives in place to protect you." I rose up on tiptoe, attempting to peer in through the glass. "Linda?"

"Whoever was there is gone," Darsh said.

I dialed the number on the sticker for the security company but held my cell out to Darsh before I hit call. "Can you compel someone over the phone?"

He eyed it thoughtfully. "I haven't ever tried it."

"But you're old enough to compel so give it a shot." I shook the phone at him.

"That's not a good idea," Silas said. "Call and ask like a normal person."

"Silas," I said with forced patience, "no employee will be allowed to divulge when they installed these bars, and I don't have time to go through proper channels. If this security was planned before Troy's death or the house fire, then maybe Rukhsana was wrong about meeting up with shedim. But if it was a last-minute addition, it's verification. That means we have a chance to stop the demons and get that case. Besides, we're not compelling the employees to divulge their innermost secrets."

"It's not right," he insisted.

"Fine." I whipped an elastic band out of my pocket and yanked my hair into a ponytail so hard that my scalp burned. "Go sit in your car and pretend it's not happening."

A gleam flashed in Silas's eyes, a cold and calculating darkness that sent shivers down my spine. He radiated an aura of menace, every muscle in his face taut with an unsettling intensity.

I took a step back, fighting my overwhelming urge to bust Cherry out, but before my heel even struck the ground, the expression had disappeared, replaced by a hurt look. I could almost believe I'd imagined it, because this was Silas, the vamp who didn't even fight back when he was arrested.

But I hadn't.

A monster of a creature, big as an oak, with hair of fire and the face of an angel, who feasted on our blood and our flesh, and laughed while he did.

Silas, my copper-haired friend, telling me about the darkness in his head…

"You—you're the Ashbishop," I whispered.

"That's not funny, Aviva," Darsh growled. He blinked at Silas, who'd gone as white as a ghost. "Tell her she's wrong." His voice was questioning and demanding at the same time.

"I…" Silas hung his head.

A sound like a wounded animal punched out of Darsh, bouncing off the trees and feeling like a net trapping the three of us in this unthinkable new reality.

Darsh locked eyes with Silas. "Say it." His voice was low and deadly.

I edged behind Darsh, my pulse racing, my mouth filled with a metallic taste and my chest tight.

"Darsh." Silas held out his hand, then suddenly stiffened.

"Say. It." Darsh strode toward Silas in slow, measured steps.

"He's dead." Blood trickled out of Silas's tear ducts and nostrils.

"Say it!" Darsh screamed and punched Silas, knocking the larger vampire backward.

His legs buckled and he crashed to the dirty concrete. His mouth twisted in pain and his ears bled along with his eyes and nose. "The Ashbishop is all on me."

Darsh pounced, landing to straddle Silas. He locked one hand around his throat.

Silas closed his eyes, accepting his fate, but his so-called confession didn't make sense. Did I have this wrong?

Darsh's grip tightened, his fingers leaving white marks against Silas's skin.

"No!" I ran at the pair, pulling Darsh off.

He swung his wild eyes to mine. "Don't make me compel you."

I dropped my hands and stepped away from him. "You almost pulled Silas's brains out through his nose with your compulsion, yet he didn't admit to being the Ashbishop. Silas," I pleaded, "explain what you meant."

The vamp opened his eyes, his face etched with sorrow, but he remained silent.

I'd set something awful in motion, but if Silas wouldn't clear this up and Darsh wouldn't listen, I didn't know how to stop its inevitable tragic conclusion. "Please."

Darsh ground his knees into Silas's arms. "Did you get a thrill fucking me after what you did?"

Silas jolted up, pushing Darsh off him. "What are you talking about?"

Darsh laughed mirthlessly and snapped his fingers. "Right. You killed so many people that my brother's death wasn't even memorable."

"Patrin?" Silas reached for Darsh, but at his flinch, held his hands up. "I never met him."

"You're lying."

"Then compel me, but I swear to you, Darsh, when you showed me his photo the other day, that was the first time I laid eyes on him. And if you'd said that the Ashbishop killed him, I'd have set you straight." He wiped the blood off his face, his injuries already healing. "I'm not that vampire," he said softly, "but I'm the reason he exists. All that death, it's all my fault."

"How so?" I said.

"I created that monster."

Darsh dropped his head into his hands and bent over double, sitting there on the ground like he no longer had any strength left in his body.

Silas rolled a pebble under his finger. "I was changed almost two hundred years ago." His Southern accent had grown stronger, either in distress or because he'd reverted to a past version of himself in order to tell this story. "Notarized consent wasn't required. Vampires hunted and fed, and sometimes they left their victims alive, even making them companions."

"You were angry that you were changed," I said.

"No, I loved it," he said sadly. "I didn't have much of a life as a human, but as a vampire? The world was this glorious, magical place." His boyish face lit up.

I looked around the alley as if seeing it through his eyes, somewhere wondrous, alive with color and texture and scent and sound.

"I fled my parents' farm." He gave a small self-deprecating smile. "I rode trains for the first time. I traveled the world. It was a wonderful life."

"So what happened?" I said.

"A century is a long time," he said. "I felt stuck in an endless night, without purpose. I went to Ireland to drink my way through Dublin and ended up attending a philosophy lecture on existential crises. It was like the professor was speaking directly to me. Fintan had the gift of gab, he did." He snorted. "I approached him after, and one beer turned into dozens of conversations. Fintan not only became my best friend, he was my brother and only family. One day, I showed him what I was, and he was fascinated. He kept asking questions and…"

Darsh still hadn't looked at Silas, though he'd turned his head slightly to listen. I took it as an encouraging sign.

"He asked you to turn him," I said.

"I didn't do it right away, I kept making him think on it,

so he wouldn't have any regrets." He winged a stone against the alley wall.

Darsh's head jolted up at the sound, his shoulders tense, but he didn't move.

"Best laid plans, right?" Silas said. "Fintan's change was difficult and I braced myself to lose him, but he survived. He viewed it as a curse from the devil." He raked a hand roughly over his short hair. "Fintan now believed the religious dogma he'd eschewed in life."

A blazing red dragonfly fluttered past.

Silas followed its flight with an almost pained expression. He tentatively reached a hand out to it and the insect flew off. "In Fintan's opinion, his humanity had been burned to ashes. His bones were barbed wire, their marrow replaced with vengeance. Since he was now soulless, condemned to an evil existence, he'd embrace that. He unleashed the Ashbishop on the world."

"You created a killer, then you stood passively by," Darsh said viciously. "Just like you always do."

"I tried to help him see his life differently. I believed I'd helped him find peace with this." Silas flexed his hands against the pavement as though drawing strength from the earth itself. "But it was a ruse. Fintan escaped my watch and butchered his first village. I hunted him down but he stayed one step ahead of me, collecting others as twisted as himself."

"The more the merrier," Darsh said snidely.

"Is he dead or not?" I said.

"He is." Silas shook himself out of his reverie. "I loved him, I turned him, and in the end, I killed him. Darsh, if Patrin's death—"

"Don't say his name." Darsh pushed to his feet.

It was fair that Darsh needed time to process all this, but it wasn't fair to put the Ashbishop's sins on Silas.

"You found Rylan and put him in Seaside to be healed,

didn't you?" I said. "You've been supporting the survivors of the original Ashbishop's attacks. It's why you intended to sell part of your art collection. Money to keep supporting them."

"I could donate the proceeds of the entire collection, hell, spend my life financing every single Seaview clinic, and it wouldn't be enough." Silas stood up. "But I don't know what else to do for the people Fintan harmed."

Darsh pressed his hands against his eyes for a brief moment, then blurred out of the alley.

I sighed. "Does Ezra know?"

Silas shook his head, his gaze trained on the mouth of the alley, but Darsh didn't return.

I wouldn't be angry with Ezra for keeping that secret from me; my worry was how he'd take the news.

"Tell him," I said gently. "Darsh needs time, but Ezra should hear this from you."

"I'm sorry," he said. "I should have told you before."

I squeezed his hand. "I'm the last person you need to apologize to for keeping secrets. And nothing that monster did is your fault. Stop paying penance."

"Yeah," he said with absolutely zero conviction.

I shook my head. "I do have a question though. You brought Rylan to Seaside decades ago. In all that time, did you ever hear about them working on vampire procreation?"

"Not Seaside," he said, "but their umbrella company owns other medical franchises around the globe. One of them is a fertility clinic. I don't remember the name, but it's human fertility, not vamp."

"At some point could they have worked with vampires?"

"I never heard that, but who's to say?" Silas scrubbed a hand over his face. "I can't lose him." He didn't specify if he meant Darsh or Ezra, but it didn't matter.

"You won't," I said firmly. My curl of excitement about

this fertility clinic possibility fizzled out hard with my next breath, because the thought of Ezra brought an awful hypothesis with it. "I'm coming with you to the Hell."

I desperately hoped I was wrong, but if I wasn't? Ezra had to hear this from me.

Chapter 27

I followed Silas's rental car to the Jolly Hellhound. I left Linda a voice message while I drove, begging her to let us be present for the meeting and telling her that she could send me the details anytime. Day or night.

I made one other call, this time to the rabbi who'd warded up my condo. There was only one security company in town that handled that and probably only one rabbi. When I explained the urgency of the situation, she told me that she'd installed the wards at the Lions Gallery yesterday, once Shabbat was over.

Pieces were slotting into the puzzle—at least where the Aviyente family was concerned. They were putting all the precautions they could into place for this meeting. Though which shedim attacked Jared and murdered Troy was yet to be determined.

Silas had already gone through the portal by the time I made it into the back room of the pub. One bright spot of all my frequent travels to the Copper Hell was that I'd been allowed to dispense with ordering that gross Bitter Abyss drink.

The three bartenders who worked there were familiar

enough with me that when any of them saw me, they buzzed the portal door open.

I stepped into Ezra's living room, smiling because the portal took me directly into my boyfriend's private quarters and not the general foyer. When he was nowhere to be seen, I wandered over to the chessboard, which had been reset. I'd never played much chess. Maybe one day Ezra could teach me.

I selected a book of Pablo Neruda's poetry off the bookshelf, which was next to a sumptuous watercolor of a couple caught in an erotic embrace. The poems were in Spanish, and although I wouldn't understand them, I wanted to experience them in their original language. I opened the book and settled in on the sofa to wait for Ezra.

He showed up a half hour later and sank down next to me, resting his head on my shoulder. "I hate this."

"Me too." I shut the book and placed it on the cushion. "What a thing to live with."

Ezra threaded his fingers through mine. "Thank you for encouraging him to tell me and for being here with me now."

"I wish this visit was that selfless. First, though, did you find anything on the names Rylan gave me? The Ashbishop's crew?"

"Dragomir and Baylor are dead. I'm still tracking Emeric and Zuberi down." He paused. "I dealt with the employee who took the photo for Natán."

I squeezed his hand. "Shitty. Sadly, what I have to say isn't going to make you feel better."

Ezra's expression turned more and more inscrutable as I recounted Nancy's allegations of demon experiments and my suspicions that they contained a grain of truth—except pertaining to vampire procreation.

When I got to the part about Seaside's parent company

owning fertility clinics as well, Ezra made a distressed noise at the back of his throat.

A cold weight settled in my chest. "Your mother received her artificial insemination treatments at one of those clinics, didn't she? For her pregnancy before you?"

"Yes. Does that mean…" Ezra shook his head. "My mother would never have gone along with any plan to create vampire babies, but my father? Me being a Prime is somehow *his* greatest achievement," he said bitterly. "Is this why Mamá killed herself? She found out she'd been used in some sick trial and it's also why she miscarried?"

"Natán despises dhampirs," I reminded him, heartsick and wishing I'd never brought this up.

"Because his own was too weak to survive being carried to term?" Ezra said.

"Natán wouldn't have been the father, though, because he was still human, and even if he had been a vampire, he's not a Prime. Were there any male Primes in existence when your mother got those treatments?"

Ezra shook his head. "There was only Calista, but the copycat Ashbishop is trying to achieve procreation via a magic ritual. Who knows how these clinics attempted it?" A muscle ticked in his jaw. "Natán will never admit it if it's true."

"Then this becomes something else you have to decide if you want answers to," I said. "I hope I'm wrong about your mother, and I'm sorry for causing you pain."

"You haven't. Any pain is on my father's head and will be returned a thousandfold if this is true." Ezra narrowed his eyes. "I'll look into the fertility clinic in Caracas."

"Okay, but do it in a way that doesn't scare the answers out of them or traumatize them? Please?"

He kissed my knuckles.

"That wasn't an answer."

"No? Is this?" He hauled me to him for a hard, hot kiss

that left me clutching the front of his shirt and my hair disheveled from his fingers. "I wish we could make time stop for a few days," he said. "No crises, no cases, no secrets. And especially no fathers. Just the two of us."

"That sounds amazing." I nuzzled into his chest. His cotton shirt was soft against my cheek, and when I inhaled the trace of his cologne, the anxiety that had been clawing at my chest since Silas's confession loosened its grip. Five seconds more. Three. One. I made myself pull away. "I have to go. Michael needs to be told about that brain."

Ezra gave me a sad smile. "Be safe."

I'd dealt with a lot of really crappy things in the past little while but leaving Ezra right now was one of the worst. Still, I had my game face on by the time I returned to the pub.

I left a voice message for my mother while I grabbed dinner at the Jolly Hellhound, because my stomach was growling. Damn it. I should have loaded up at the Copper Hell's buffet. Ah, well, next time.

While I ate, I checked in with Malika, who confirmed Troy's death occurred via a violent burst of orange flame magic. He hadn't suffered for long, which I guess was a blessing.

Michael hadn't phoned back by the time I was getting ready for bed, nor had Linda replied to my request to let me protect her. I texted both of them again but was too tired to stay up waiting.

I was having a very nice dream involving swimming with a magic otter when I was shaken awake before dawn on Monday by my boyfriend frantically whispering my name.

"Whazzup?" I muttered groggily.

He dropped onto the mattress next to me and laid his hand on my hip as if testing if I was real. "I had to make sure you were safe."

I yawned and sat up, pushing my hair out of my face. "This place is mezuzah warded, there are weapons—including Sachie—stashed approximately every five and a half feet, and the only vampires with leave to come in here are you, Darsh, and…" I grabbed Ezra's shoulder. "Silas?"

"No." He was quick to reassure me. "Nothing like that. I couldn't reach anyone yesterday at the fertility clinic in Caracas where my mother had her IVF treatments because it was Sunday and they were closed, so Silas and I did some digging."

"And?" I covered my mouth, acutely aware of morning breath, and hopped out of bed.

Ezra stayed in my room while I brushed my teeth. "Nothing nefarious came up about them, and their patient records were encrypted, but Silas hacked into the patient records for the Seaside clinics. Idiots have them all linked in one database."

I spit toothpaste into the sink. "What did you find?"

"A patient record for a baby boy delivered forty years ago. Alastair Walker."

I rinsed out my mouth. The name sounded familiar, but I couldn't place it. "Who?"

"Dad's enforcer."

I returned to the bedroom and sat down next to Ezra. "He looks thirty, tops. Good genes."

"Just you wait. Why do you think he was delivered at a Seaside clinic?"

My eyes bugged out of my head. "Oh shit. Is he a Prime?"

"That would almost be better. The father listed on the record was some guy we verified as an Eishei Kodesh, and his mother?" Ezra paused. "Emily Astor."

"Calista's alias?" I gasped, which turned into another yawn. "He's a dhampir? Natán is going to lose his freaking mind." I headed into the kitchen.

"Aviva." Ezra followed close behind. "You're not following. Dhampirs can't have kids."

The penny dropped. I spun around, almost dropping the coffee cannister in my hand. "Alastair is Ash Lite."

Ezra nodded. "I headed into Babel last night and spent four hours finding a friend of Evelyn Rue's who confirmed that she'd been hanging out with him."

I was going to kill that half shedim murdering bastard. Slowly and thoroughly.

"Get in line," Ezra said at my obvious train of thought. "I went to Natán with this and to say he's furious is an understatement."

Good. Maybe he'd quit being such a dick to us about dating. "You believe him?"

"About this? Yes. He had no idea Alastair was Ash Lite and no part in the murders of the half shedim."

I filled the espresso basket, shoved the holder into the machine, and hit the button for a double shot. "Did you ask him about your mother?"

Ezra paused. "There's no point. Not while Alastair is missing. Natán has put out a reward for his capture and return." He leaned against the counter, the kitchen light catching his hair. "I don't know how I feel about being on the same side as my father."

I patted his arm consolingly. "You think Alastair went to the fortress in the Brink to try for the power word?" Espresso flowed into my small cup. "He was too chickenshit to do it himself before, but is his desperation enough to try it now?" I fired half the coffee back, the caffeine a delicious rush to my brain synapses.

"That's the million-dollar question, so I sent Silas there while I came here," Ezra said.

I grabbed the bread from the fridge and popped a couple slices into the toaster, telling Ezra about Alastair waiting for me in the lobby of my building the other day.

"He warned me to play nice," I said, "but he didn't abduct me or harm me, and it's not like there was anyone around to stop him. A lot of people would mobilize to find me if I went missing, so did he leave me alone because he thinks I'm not a threat to his plans or because his plans aren't in place yet and he didn't want to be exposed?"

"The latter," Ezra said immediately. His confidence in my ability earned him a peck on the cheek.

"I do still get one 'I told you so,'" I said. "Hiding in plain sight *is* a sound strategic move."

He wrinkled his nose. "Just because you're safe for now doesn't make you safe. Natán denied killing Roman Whittaker, and given Alastair lied about why he was in London when it happened, I'm inclined to believe him." My boyfriend relaxed slightly. "Best-case scenario is that he's at the fortress, in which case, Silas will find him."

The espresso cup slipped from my hand and shattered on the tile. "Maud," I whispered. "Zaven Barsamian, the vamp who was blackmailing her."

"The one you believed was doing it to impress Natán." Ezra punched a cupboard, denting it and breaking the top corner off its hinge. His fangs had descended.

Sachie ran into the kitchen, holding a stake and a Taser, both of which she almost fired at Ezra.

He stilled, his fists clenched, and wrestled his very pointy teeth into submission.

I stepped between them. "Everything is fine. We're all good. Yes?" I made sure both of them nodded.

"Something set you off though," Sachie said to Ezra.

He updated her on his findings, while I swept up the wreckage of the espresso cup.

Sachie whistled. "Ballsy of Alastair to cozy up to Natán. His focus and determination must be off the charts."

"Why?" I ignored the toast that had popped up, my

appetite gone, and dumped the ceramic shards into the trash.

"Alastair is the most powerful vamp in the Kosher Nostra after my father," Ezra said.

"And you, Crimson Prince," Sachie said, taking the broom and dustpan from me. She returned them to the narrow cupboard by our fridge.

"In reputation, not practice," Ezra admitted. "Alastair is smart enough to have seen past the lie that Natán and I keep up."

Look at the man with a thousand masks being all forthcoming. I smiled.

"But Sach is right," he continued. "Alastair has a formidable reputation, and for him to achieve that much power when he doesn't have the same abilities as the other vampires in the Mafia? It's impressive in a fucked-up way."

"We need to get to Maud," I said. "He could force her to take the test or just want her blood."

"I'll go," Ezra said. "You stay here behind wards."

"No way." I was already heading for my bedroom, Ezra behind me arguing.

"I'll stay with Avi." Sachie followed us. "Stash Maud with Delacroix. He'll keep her safe."

When I looked doubtful, Ezra placed a hand on my shoulder. "Delacroix is territorial. He's publicly claimed Maud and won't allow anyone else to hurt her. And she's no threat to him."

Unlike me. "Is he even around, or is he still leaving the Hell on errands?"

"He hasn't gone anywhere since he got the brain," Ezra said.

Sach frowned. "Did he get a heart and courage too?"

Smirking, I entered my bedroom, picturing Delacroix as the Scarecrow. "I stole a demon brain for Delacroix, learning after the fact that it contains the locations of all those love lock cells."

"I am not caffeinated enough for this." She smacked the inside of her elbow. "Just mainline the espresso right in."

"Am I bringing Maud to Delacroix or not?" Ezra said.

I opened my closet. "I don't trust Delacroix, but I do trust you. No one can get through your security at the Hell to target Maud."

Ezra staggered back in mock shock. "Are you saying I was right to maintain my position there?"

"I'm mildly conceding the point," I said.

Ezra crossed his arms. "Then mildly concede that I'll keep you safe there too."

"That wasn't ever in doubt, but I'm not sitting here like some damsel in distress." I grabbed my phone. Linda had read my text but hadn't answered it or returned my initial call. "I have to find out when the Aviyentes are meeting with the shedim to hand over the prison locks."

After a quick debate with myself about whether it was right to break this confidence, I messaged Linda again, this time with the photo of Rukhsana's demon-inflicted wounds.

Me: *This is what being very, very lucky looks like when dealing with demons. This person has far more experience with dangerous individuals. You and your father are lambs leading themselves to the slaughter. Let me protect you!*

"I don't see you for one day and all this happened?" Sach peered over my shoulder at the photo, shaking her head.

"Go have breakfast," I said. "Then you can come with me to HQ while Ezra, you get Maud. Check in the second she's safe, and whether Silas finds Alastair at the fortress in the Brink."

The two of them graciously allowed it (i.e. did not get

in my way when I busted Cherry out on them and reiterated that I was going).

I wasn't being stubborn or reckless, I truly didn't believe that Alastair was coming for me, and more importantly, he had no idea yet that we'd unmasked him. This was a valuable window of opportunity.

Sachie drove us to HQ like the devil himself was on our heels, so in her normal fashion.

I approached Louis with trepidation, receiving his usual disdain and disinclination to accommodate my request in a timely manner. It was weirdly reassuring, though I tugged on my sleeve to straighten out a wrinkle, taking his reaction as a personal challenge. I mean, what was the point of a demon reveal if he didn't jump to do my bidding?

I loomed over his desk. "Announce me or try to stop me. I'm happy to play out either choice."

He glared at me, but at my hard smile, hit the intercom buzzer to tell Michael I was there.

Since Sachie wasn't part of the Chandra and Troy murder investigations, she headed down to the basement to do some work. I promised I'd come find her right after this meeting.

"Where were you last night?" I sat down across from Michael, twisting my chair to give me a clear view of her around a stack of folders on her desk.

"Dinner with a friend."

I leaned forward. "A Trad friend, perhaps?"

"Yes, Aviva, I was with Keira."

"Making up?"

"Sorting through things. Don't get all excited that we're going to be some version of you and Sachie."

I could hope. I'd love for my mom to have a ride-or-die person.

"What did you need to tell me?" she said.

Oh, where to start?

Michael was annoyed that Mois had snuck back into Canada. She proclaimed that this trade of the locks for his and Linda's safety was deluded and misguided—to say the least. "I'll call Keira to pull her officers off watching the gallery and put our vampires in place."

"Silas is in the Brink right now," I said.

"Why?"

"Short version? Natán's third-in-command, Alastair Walker, is a dhampir."

"Second-in-command," Michael said.

"That's Ezra."

She shot me a flat stare.

"When did you figure that out?" I said.

"The moment I learned he worked for us. Continue."

"Alastair's mother was Calista, and he's the Ashbishop copycat."

"Until Alastair is apprehended," Michael said, "I want someone with you at all times." Her concern both warmed and annoyed me, but it felt good to be in a place where I *could* see it as concern and not my mother thinking I couldn't handle myself.

"Sach is playing bodyguard until Ezra can take over," I grumbled.

"Good." Michael flipped open the top folder, the pages adorned with "sign here" stickies. "It wouldn't be illegal for a dhampir to seek out treatment to try and conceive, unlikely as it is, so why did Alastair go to such lengths to hide this?"

"We assumed that in order to achieve his goal, Alastair had to become a Prime, since they're the only vampires who can have kids." I shook my head. "Achieving Prime-hood is impossible for a dhampir."

My gaze drifted over to the living wall of bamboo to my left as I listened to my mother's pen scratching across the paper. The thick round stalks and lacy leaves were beautiful and surprising pieces of nature set amid the form and function of Michael's office. It wasn't all that dissimilar to what Alastair was attempting. In the same way that bamboo left unchecked would overrun an area, vampires having kids would trample the human garden called earth.

"Our understanding of this ritual is that it's based on the idea of neshamah," I said. "The divine spark connecting everyone to the source of all life."

"Which vampires don't have," Michael said.

"True, but half shedim do. We can have kids just like most other people, because we're half human and our demon magic doesn't suppress that ability. In fact, the chaotic essence in our shedim magic is what disrupts the stagnant energies in vamps."

"Vampires no longer have the human capability of procreation," Michael said, "so they require the divine spark in your blood to be transmitted to them via the blood ritual, with that power word providing the healing magic to facilitate it all."

"Yes. They don't regain any human life force but instead are sparked into a higher form of vampire, one capable of having children. But what does this ritual do to a dhampir?"

"When you put it like that..." Michael closed the file folder. "Are we sure the ritual works on full vampires? Or is this higher vampire form an impossibility and the ritual only works on those who still possess human blood?"

I raised my eyebrows. "You think the fake Ashbishop lied to his flock? Shocking."

She tugged the folders into a neat stack. "He required supplicants to get that power word, and who'd sign up for a deadly magic test if they wouldn't benefit from the outcome themselves?"

"Okay." I drummed my fingers on the armrest. "Let's run with this theory. The ritual *only* works on dhampirs because it restores their human ability to procreate. It also amplifies their vampire magic. Not to the point of where Primes are, because they've started from a lesser place than a regular vampire would, but in terms of strength, speed, and enhanced senses, they're finally placed on equal footing with all other vampires."

"A desirable outcome for a dhampir," Michael said. "It eliminates their weakness, and given they can have kids like only a Prime can, there's no way for anyone to dispute that status."

I stood up. "I'll let Ezra know all this."

Michael nodded absently, toying with her Maccabee ring.

"What are you thinking?"

"How did you find out about Alastair?" she said.

I shared my suspicions that Seaside was doing experiments into vampire procreation, and how that led me to their fertility clinic. It appeared as advertised, but Silas hacked into the main database of patient records for all the Seaside clinics and found Alastair.

"When you were a baby," my mother said, "your pediatrician worked at one of those Seaside clinics in the States, after his residency. It's why I chose him. With his experience treating vampire-inflicted injuries, he'd know what to do should there be an incident with you changing in front of him."

"Was there?" I perched on the arm of the chair. He would have been under a doctor-patient confidentiality, so I wasn't worried about that.

"Once. Two tiny horns and these fierce green eyes." Michael sat back, her fingers steepled together. "I was so relieved at how he took it in stride." She frowned. "It never occurred to me that maybe his experience wasn't simply with vampire-related injuries, but dhampir births as well."

I pressed my lips together. "Okay, this is so stupid and awful—"

Michael reorganized the pens in their stainless steel cup holder. "Out with it."

"When I spoke with one of the original Ashbishop's victims at the Seaside clinic here, I met another patient. Nancy. She wasn't there because of any vampire, but she mentioned the clinic's history hid demon experiments. Women forced to birth half shedim. Ridiculous, right?" I said weakly.

Michael leaned forward. "You may have been a surprise, but I was a willing participant that night."

I covered my ears. "Ew. Stop."

The last thing I wanted to do was give the idea of demon-human experiments any credence, but my pediatrician hadn't reacted to me going shedim and Nancy said the clinics' history was steeped in these experiments. My mother hadn't been forced into anything, but she was certainly tricked about Delacroix's true nature.

So was Maud's mom.

Demons willingly created half shedim to help spread chaos, but were there humans who took advantage of that? Or at least profited from it in some way, like Seaside would through its patient fees?

"Delacroix knows I'm his daughter," I said.

"Are you worried about that?"

He'd tortured me more than once, but he hadn't killed me. Not that I was holding my breath for our dynamic to improve now that he was aware we were related, I just didn't think it would worsen. "No. I'm not worried. See…" I smiled brightly.

Michael crossed her arms. "Aviva Jacqueline Fleischer, that look is just as unconvincing now as when you were sixteen and had just torched my coffee table."

"Calm down, it's great news. Do you know what plus codes are?"

"Sure. They're addresses for places that don't have them, based on latitude and longitude but displayed as a string of numbers and letters."

"Right. It turns out, there's a record with the plus codes of all the demon prisons on earth."

Michael narrowed her eyes. "And?"

"And they're contained in a living demon brain that I sort of stole for Delacroix, not knowing what it really was, and now he has it, but claims he doesn't want to free the prisoners." I took my first breath of that entire blurted confession.

Michael dropped her head in her hands and massaged her temples. "Couldn't you have just told me you smashed my car?"

"I mean, I might have if you ever let me drive it. As a teen, or say more recently, like after my first car was blown up or my current one was vandalized."

Her fingers flexed against her skull.

"All that to say," I pressed on, "is how about you question my pediatrician about demon experiments?"

"He died a couple of years ago." She looked up. "Delacroix hasn't gone after the locks yet. We'd know if any significant numbers had been moved. And there's no point in confronting him about it now. All that notwithstanding…" She set her mouth in a determined line. "It's time Delacroix and I had a little chat."

I gave a defeated sigh. "I was afraid you were going to say that."

Chapter 28

We didn't storm the Copper Hell. For one thing, Linda phoned me back.

"Troy's…" The whispered name was infused with pain. "He's dead, isn't he?"

"Yes. I'm sorry."

"Was it a shedim?"

"I believe so. Is your father with you?"

"Yes."

"Okay. Good." They were hunkered down together. "When is the meeting happening?"

"It was supposed to have happened already but the shedim changed it to tomorrow morning at the gallery."

"Do you know how many are coming?" I said.

"No."

"Are these the shedim your mother worked with or the ones she defied by releasing the incarcerated demons?"

Linda swallowed. "Defied."

"The same ones who murdered her?"

"Yes. They threatened Dad and me with the same fate if we ever told anyone about the locks."

"Are you and Troy matchmakers as well?"

"No, there was only ever Mom."

"No other matchmakers," I said for Michael's benefit. "Good. Let me negotiate at the meeting."

My mother raised an eyebrow.

Linda was reticent. She was scared enough about allowing hidden protection when the demons had insisted no one other than her and Mois be there. Having another party inside might sour the deal entirely.

I wanted to scream at her that there was no deal. The shedim weren't going to let her and Mois walk away. "What if I pretend to be the shedim that your mother worked with?"

Michael mouthed "Speakerphone" at me with a hard glare.

I rolled my eyes but hit the button on my cell.

"Why would they buy that?" Linda said.

"They know Chandra had a shedim partner who was finding the locks and breaking the wards on them. I'll pretend to be that shedim and we can pass it off as that demon wanting safe passage as part of this deal. Did you ever see them? Either in their demon or human form?"

Linda swore she hadn't. "But that's who I was making those fake cursed artifacts for. It was part of my mother's deal with them."

"Then you spoke with them," I said.

"A growly voice from a blocked number." Linda didn't know their name, what gender they preferred to glamor as, or anything else about them. Her mother had been careful to keep that information from her.

"What about Mois?" I said. "How much did he know?"

"Not much. I didn't even tell him about the briefcase with the locks until after Mom was murdered. It was her insurance. He threw all his resources into retrieving it, which took a while, and then we had to make this deal."

I paced the director's office. "If the shedim your mom

worked with is still alive, then it stands to reason the demons you're meeting with don't have its identity. This gamble will work."

"What if there's a situation where they expect to see an actual demon?" Linda said. "What will you do then? Your cover will be blown."

"Let me worry about that." Should push come to shove and I had to deploy Cherry, the element of surprise would be stupendous.

Michael had an operative who could wipe Mois's and Linda's memories about Cherry, the other demons would be dead, and my team had seen what I was. No one was going to blab about me.

Cherry listened with a smug satisfaction that we once again had a unique role in this investigation.

My mother, on the other hand, crossed her arms.

I got the rest of the meeting details from Linda, then hung up and faced Michael. "Can we skip the part where we argue about this? Linda and Mois will think Cherry is a glamor, and then you'll wipe their memories and it won't matter anyway."

"You think that's what I'm worried about?" Michael snapped. "You're pretending to be the shedim who jailbroke those prisoners? Are you insane?"

"Someone with experience needs to control the situation and get a confession. I want to determine whether the shedim at this meeting killed Troy."

It made sense that our killer was a demon. First of all, shedim magic manifested in all kinds of ways. One could easily draw heat into or out of someone like an Orange Flame. Second, we'd ruled out all the Eishei Kodesh possibilities.

"If it wasn't one of them, we need to hunt down the demon who worked with Chandra. Besides"—I flipped my hair off my shoulders—"this always was an undercover investigation."

Michael, uncharacteristically, slammed two desk drawers and swore three times before agreeing with a sigh. "Have Silas marshal the Vancouver Spook Squad."

"Not Cécile and Nasir," I said. "They don't know about Cherry." Michael would never agree to wipe their memories. Not that I'd ask that of her.

In my head, Cherry snorted.

"You should have considered that before you offered to play demon," Michael said. "I'm not removing two valuable weapons."

"Please, Mom."

Michael blinked at me calling her that at work. It had just slipped out, but I really needed my mother in my corner right now.

"Please," I repeated. "I barely ever ask you for anything, but I'm begging you not to make me out myself to them. I can't go into this worried whether that changes them having my back."

"Which would be an argument against doing this in the first place."

"I'll have a Prime, Silas, who has the strength of two vamps, and Darsh as backup. That's enough." The Portland and Seattle vampires had been sent home when Troy's body was found.

"No. I'm sorry, Aviva, but this is my call. I'm putting all my vamp operatives on this. I trust every single one to protect their fellow Maccabee, regardless of the situation. It's on you to do the same."

The weight of Michael's decision pressed down on me. I'd professed to be full steam ahead when it came to trust, and yet, here I was, back in hiding. I took a deep breath…

And nodded resolutely. "Tell them. I'll make sure we succeed in this mission, no matter what."

Her gaze softened slightly, a hint of pride flickering in

her eyes. "I know you will, Aviva. Just remember, you're not alone in this."

She didn't argue about Ezra being there. That was a win.

"Sachie stays out of this because she'll want to fight. It's too dangerous," Michael said. "Clear?"

"Clear."

I was already working through a million strategies. The best option was to talk my way out of this situation without Cherry ever making an appearance because that would escalate things to a physical fight, and I'd never killed a shedim without my magic ring.

Technically, you never killed one with it either, Cherry unhelpfully said.

The point was, I didn't know how to kill a demon, and the vamp cavalry would be stationed outside the gallery. They might not arrive in time to assist me.

While Michael phoned Keira, I got Silas on the line.

He was reluctant to contact Darsh, but I insisted. Silas was leading the vamps and it was important that Darsh respect that. Not that I honestly believed he'd let personal feelings get in the way of work, but still. They had to trust each other as much as I trusted them both.

I explained that the vampires were to start watching the gallery now but not attack the demons when they showed up, which shouldn't be until tomorrow. However, even if they arrived early, it was capture only. We required a confession about who killed Troy.

Meantime, Michael got Keira's agreement that other than the two commanders, only vampires, Olivier, and myself would be present, though I'd be the only one at the handover.

Ezra texted while Michael and I were finalizing details. *Got Maud. Safely back at the Hell. No sign of Alastair yet, but*

Natán has his vamps on it and my staff are working the clientele here for information.

I thanked him, relieved that Alastair couldn't get to Maud. This would have been the appropriate moment to inform my boyfriend that I'd be inside negotiating with the shedim, but Silas was in charge of vampires and chain of command dictated that I tell him first.

Nice loophole, Cherry scoffed.

I told Michael there were no Alastair sightings yet. "Still interested in reuniting with your baby daddy?"

She grimaced. "Never say that again."

"Well, I don't know what name you called him by."

"Since that person doesn't exist, Delacroix will do." She stood up, her expression all business. "I always meant to try a Bitter Abyss. Your car or mine?"

That was a no-brainer. It was January, and she owned a Mercedes with heated seats.

First, we stopped downstairs at the Spook Squad. Sachie agreed to let me accompany Michael to the Jolly Hellhound, provided I returned to HQ immediately after and back under her watchful eye.

"You're such a good friend to Aviva," Michael said. "That's always meant a lot to me. I only wish you could be there for her when she pretends to be the shedim working with the matchmakers at this handover meeting."

My best friend turned a shade of red unseen outside of cartoon characters with steam erupting from the tops of their heads.

"Thanks for that," I muttered.

Sachie crossed her arms. "That's not happening."

"Yes, it is." I uncrossed them, arranging them in a cute pose on her hips. She smacked my hands and I grinned. "This was delightful," I said, "but the Hell awaits."

"I'm going to speak with Delacroix." Michael headed for

the door then turned back. "Aviva told you he knows she's his daughter and that he's in possession of a demon brain that has the locations of all the prison cells which she stole for him?"

"The brain part, yes." Sachie unearthed a mini blade from behind her ear. "But she's playing fast and loose with the information she shares."

I threw up my hands. "In my defense, there's so much shit going down, I can't keep track of who knows what."

Sach danced the blade over her knuckles. "Don't care. Do better."

"Also, Mother," I said through clenched teeth, "I didn't know what the brain was when I stole it. Motive is important."

"So is having all the facts when dealing with a shedim."

"Like you're one to talk," I fired back.

Michael waved a hand through the air. "If you do stab her, Sachie, do it outside the building so it doesn't have to go through HR. Spare yourself the paperwork."

"Happy to follow orders," Sachie said.

"You're an excellent operative." Michael hit the elevator call button.

"Are you two having fun?" I said.

Sach ran a finger along the edge of the blade. "Getting there."

The elevator pinged and Michael stepped into the empty car.

"Don't quit your day job for the comedy circuit," I said to my on-probation best friend and headed after my mother, wondering if I was too old to apply for emancipation.

"Was that really necessary?" I said to the closing doors.

Michael pressed her finger to her cheek and tilted her head. "Yes, I believe it was."

We made good time to the pub. My mother spent the drive humming while I gnashed my teeth. She enjoyed the disgusting drink and inspected the back room with a delighted curiosity since she'd never had reason to be there before.

It was hard to stay mad—even mock mad—at her.

I let Ezra know that Michael and I were coming through the portal, and was reminded that Delacroix had banned all Maccabees from entering the Hell except for me. I cursed silently. I'd been dealing with so many fires that I'd forgotten that salient detail.

Before I could break it to Michael that this trip to the Jolly Hellhound was pointless, Ezra messaged that it was good thing he'd been working on a way around that, just in case he had to spirit our friends to the yacht for safety.

Me: *We're good to go?*

Zee: *In theory. I haven't tested it yet, so it's up to Michael.*

I relayed this information, watching her swirl her drink while mentally turning over every angle of the risk.

"We proceed as planned," she said.

"Solid vote of confidence in Ezra's abilities, but perhaps another operative should go through first?"

"Are you implying that any of our Maccabees are expendable?" my mother said wryly.

"I mean, would we mourn Dmitri's loss into some magic void? Would that not be an opportunity for a more forward-thinking operative to assume his place on the Authority?"

She shot me a deadpan look. "I'm going now."

"Yup." I waved a hand at the metal door. "Have at it."

My pulse jumped when I stepped into the foyer at the Hell and didn't see her. I raced into the main gambling area on the lower level and stopped.

Ezra had descended from his balcony to personally greet Michael. She appeared uninjured and didn't sport a haunted expression from her travel through the portal, instead laughing at something my boyfriend was saying.

I allowed my dopey smile for a second, then briskly strode forward.

His eyes warmed at my approach. "Hey, you."

"Hey, yourself."

"Where's Delacroix?" Michael said.

"In his quarters." Ezra escorted us outside.

A crescent moon peeked out from behind clouds rippling across the night sky and the sea was calm.

I took a deep breath of salty air, the tension in my body unwinding. Wow. How messed up was my life that being on a demon-owned yacht in the middle of some ocean counted as relaxing?

"Tell Ezra your plan," Michael said as we wound around the side.

"Oh no." The vamp came to a dead stop.

I shook my head. "I should respect chain of command."

Ezra's left eye twitched. "That would be a first."

"I am the command," Michael said. "Tell him."

I notched my chin up and spilled about going in as Chandra's demon partner to trade the metal case for Mois's and Linda's lives.

Ezra blinked twice then headed up a narrow metal staircase.

"Where's your growly displeasure? The part where you portal me into a locked closet?" I said in a miffed voice, jogging after him.

"I'm saving my energy for making sure you walk out of that meeting alive. Trust me, I'll say plenty after the fact." He stopped next to the round abode resembling a shimmering iridescent silver bubble and knocked on the door.

"I'm busy," Delacroix said, cracking the door. He squinted at Michael. "Who the fuck are you?"

Dude was a shedim, and he'd only known my mother for one night, but still, bad form. I'd have said as much except I was busy dry heaving from the hard burst of magic that had sussed out something demonic nearby. Other than my father, that was.

"Michael Fleisher. Aviva's mother," she said coldly.

"Huh. You didn't age too bad—"

Michael socked the demon in the gut. He doubled over with an "ouf," his fangs dropping.

You go, Mom, Cherry cheered.

I blinked, surprised that my Brimstone Baroness thought of Michael that way, and swallowed hard, focusing on the crisp sea air to clear my nausea. What was inside Delacroix's place?

"Feisty," he said to my mother, his fangs vanishing. "Here for an encore?"

My heaving worsened.

Ezra muttered some bullshit about having to be elsewhere, but I clamped on to his arm like a vise. There was enough trauma here for both of us to partake.

"Since the event itself was entirely unmemorable," Michael said, "not on your life."

Delacroix grinned and scratched his belly through his wool fisherman's sweater. "You know that's not true, Mickey."

Please kill me now. He did remember her, and given the gleam in his eyes, I really wished he didn't.

"As for you…" A watery tentacle rose out of nowhere and slapped Ezra's ankle. "Don't undermine my orders."

Ezra stomped on the tentacle but it vanished before he made contact.

"A word of warning, Delacroix," Mom said, interrupting. "Hurt one hair on my daughter's head and I'll end you."

"Bravo," a familiar voice enthused.

"Maud!" I pushed past my demon parent, but the second I stepped through the doorway, I clapped a hand over my mouth at the bile rising in my throat, spun around, and ran for the railing.

Dimly, I heard Maud asking if I was all right and Ezra replying to her in a gentle voice.

My mother came up beside me and stroked my back like she had when I had stomachaches as a little kid.

Delacroix laughed meanly and said, "Boo hoo. The sisters can't play togeth—*ouf!*"

"Mock them again," Ezra said, "and I'll do worse than that."

I took another couple of deep breaths. "I hate this," I whispered miserably.

"Here." Michael slipped off her Maccabee ring and slid it onto my finger. It was a bit of a tight fit, but it killed my negative reaction to Maud's half-shedim nature.

The sucky irony was that I didn't even need this extra ability to detect half shedim. After all, I saw their shifting shadows with my blue flame magic, and even if I chose not to use my synesthete vision, there was always Sire's Spark, whose effects were, mercifully, only temporary.

"You've never taken that off," I said sadly.

"Well." She glanced back at Delacroix. "I might have. Once."

The night they'd… No wonder he didn't immediately figure out who I was. Not-a-Maccabee-Mickey was nothing like Director Michael Fleischer.

I removed the ring and handed it back. "Still," I said. "Not since then."

"You're my daughter and you're suffering." She tried to press it back into my hand.

I shook my head and unfastened the necklace with my own ring. "I've got mine." I put the ring back on and my nausea instantly vanished.

Whether it was the knowledge of the corrupted magic in it or not having worn it for a while, something had changed about the way it fit me. Not physically, but it was no longer the comforting talisman it had been.

We entered Delacroix's bubble and Maud waved tentatively at me from the wingback chairs grouped in front of the hearth.

The fireplace wasn't lit today, but the demon had added another framed photo of underwater life to the stunning collection adorning the walls. Like the others, the close-up of a bug-eyed fish smiling derpily for the camera was imbued with heart and humor.

I beelined for my sister and hugged her tightly.

Michael examined each photo slowly. "Very nice."

Delacroix smirked, almost preening.

"Maud." My mother stopped next to the other woman. "This is rather a different meeting than our first one."

"Well, no handcuffs," Maud said nervously, edging close to me. "So there's that."

I shook my head slightly to indicate that Michael didn't know that our story about Maud being compelled to abduct Calista was a total fabrication.

My sister relaxed and Delacroix didn't out us. I'd been pretty certain he wouldn't, since Maud being locked up would have put a crimp in their breakfast get-togethers.

Michael held her hand out to Maud. "Welcome to the family."

Chapter 29

Maud shook Michael's hand. "Thank you."

Delacroix groaned. "If I want cloying sweetness, I'll eat the chocolate mousse cake at the buffet."

I planted my hands on my hips and glared at my boyfriend. "Why is this the first I'm hearing of that dessert?"

"I was respecting chain of command," Ezra said unrepentantly, dropping into a chair.

I made a snarky face at him.

"My promise about Aviva?" Michael said to Delacroix. "It extends to Maud."

My sister beamed at my mother.

"Now that you've made your puny threats," Delacroix said. "Leave. I'm busy."

"Yeah," Maud said, sitting down once more. "Losing."

An in-progress poker game lay on the end table that had been dragged between the two wingbacks.

Michael jabbed a finger at Delacroix. "I have questions, which you're going to answer."

"You want answers, you'll play for them." He opened the cabinet with the brass scales.

Other than my lingering horror from the last time I'd seen them, I didn't react to them now. "Put those cockamamie scales away. You owe me answers from our last game of Demon Quid Pro Quo and I'm transferring that to my mother."

"It doesn't work that way." He sat down in the remaining empty chair and waved a hand at me. "But I'm feeling generous. One question only."

The conclusions that Michael and I had drawn about Alastair being the only one this procreation ritual would work for because he was a dhampir held little interest for Delacroix, but Ezra's attention sharpened like a blade.

However, when Delacroix learned that Alastair was Calista's son, I could practically hear the gears in his brain working out a way for that to benefit him.

"Alastair is still AWOL, but he won't stay that way for long," Ezra said. "The reward Natán offered for his capture is too tempting."

Delacroix snorted. "Played by one of his own, was he? Not even an equal. That's got to smart." He rubbed his knee. "That it?"

"Since I haven't asked any questions yet," Michael said, "it is not."

I toyed with my ring. If my or Maud's existence was due to some experiment, it was vital that we know this had happened and who was behind it, but my stomach roiled at the idea of having that verified.

"Aviva?" Ezra said warily, coming to stand beside me.

I pressed my lips together and shook my head.

"Was getting me pregnant part of some bigger plan?" Michael's voice was steely. "Some experiment?"

Maud gasped.

Delacroix laughed loudly. "You been hitting the conspiracy blogs, Mickey?"

My sister scooped up the cards and shuffled them with trembling hands. "Why do you think that?"

"We heard a rumor about the Seaside clinics originally used for that purpose," I said. "And Mom's pediatrician, who showed no surprise when I displayed shedim features in front of him, had trained there."

"Shedim arranged for other shedim to be locked up and used like batteries," Michael said. "It's hardly a stretch that you'd want demon babies."

"You got me. I seduced some breeder into a night of passion and knocked her up. Mwah ha ha." Delacroix twirled an invisible mustache like a cartoon character.

Michael's glare was glacial enough that the demon ducked his head, muttering about people being testy.

"You said it yourself," I rebuked Delacroix. "Demon kids help spread chaos."

"I'd have been delighted to use you both that way, except I didn't know either of you existed. Why else would I have skipped molding you during those formative years?"

"Maybe you did know that you knocked up a Maccabee," Michael said. "Maybe having a half-demon child with that parent was enough chaos for you."

"What about the other one?" Delacroix pointed at Maud. "Her mother was just some…" He looked blankly at my sister.

"She was a professor, you rat's bunghole," Maud said tightly.

"Calm down, Junior," Delacroix said. Jeez, we had the same nickname for Maud? "Whatever your mom was, there's no conspiracy and no experiment. Not demon ones anyway. If those fertility clinics were up to something with the bloodsuckers, then more power to them." He tipped an imaginary hat. "I've answered your question, now scram."

I narrowed my eyes at him. He *had* answered our questions and let me live, despite me knowing about the plus codes, yet I wasn't chalking this up to fatherly love.

Delacroix didn't let Ezra roam around with insider knowledge because he enjoyed their business partnership. He required the Prime to keep his magic stable, thus it was a good bet he intended to use me further for something as well.

But what?

"Avi." My mother nudged me to the door.

Maud opted to stay at the Copper Hell and win a few hands of poker with some of the high rollers. After the tournament where she'd wiped the floor with her other opponents, including Ezra, idiot patrons were eager to beat her. She gleefully recounted that she'd won cash, a magic painting allowing its owner to spy on people (which she'd sold for cash), and an hour of vampire magic enhancing her senses.

"Disappointed you couldn't sell it for cash?" I teased.

She shot me a wicked grin. "Nope. I put it to good use."

I laughed.

Michael insisted I take the rest of the day off to psych myself up to play intermediary between the Aviyentes and the shedim tomorrow. Ezra would have rather stayed with me, but I pointed out that that would hardly be restful, and besides, I was being returned to Sachie's care.

I got a kiss and his reluctant agreement.

Since Sach still had some work to wrap up, I hung out in the Spook Squad, cuddling Bentley, the unicorn stuffie mascot.

Provided all went well tomorrow, Mois and Linda would be safe, the demon representatives would be dead, and the metal case with the two prison locks would be in the Maccabees' possession.

There were no other matchmakers to apprehend, and I could inform the Authority that one of Chandra's shedim enemies murdered her, letting them believe that demon got away.

I adjusted the cap that Ezra had knit for Bentley, listening to Sach typing away in the conference room.

It bothered me to go into this meeting unsure of who murdered Troy—Chandra's shedim partner or the ones coming for the locks.

It was worse not having a bead on the scope of any of the shedim's magic.

While the shedim at the trade were the lock owners, it would be foolish not to expect a surprise visit from the demon who'd worked with Chandra. Would "the enemy of my enemy" apply here or was I just doubly fucked?

For a hot second I wondered if Delacroix planned to show up and take the two locks in the metal case. Was he waiting for me to deal with the other shedim and bring the locks out from behind the wards for him?

I shook the fanciful notion away. He had the plus codes —the locations of every single prison lock in existence. Should my father want the ones in the metal case, he'd come for them at his leisure.

One less thing to worry about.

Inquiries into Jared Casey's attack were closed, but in my mind, it was still a loose end. He'd been attacked with orange flame magic, same as Troy.

I returned Bentley to his customary spot riding the stumpy planted palm tree and pulled out my phone. Henderson could make things difficult for me if I pestered him about those shielding devices he'd purchased.

Yeah, well, that was before I had to face shedim who nearly murdered his boss. If he had anything to give up that could help me steer this meeting tomorrow through all the landmines, then a slap on the wrist was worth it.

His first comment after answering the call and hearing

me identify myself was to inform me he had nothing more to add.

"Here's the thing, Roger," I said, wandering around the room. "Troy Abelman was murdered with the same type of magic that your boss was hit with, and you're connected to both men."

"I don't have magic," he protested. "I didn't do it."

"That's not it," I said. "I'm worried you might be next."

There was a very long, very weighty pause. Got your attention, did I? Good.

"Is there anything else you can think of, no matter how seemingly inconsequential, that might help me out?"

"No, I swear, I've been upfront about everything I know." His voice shook with conviction.

"Okay," I said, though I still harbored doubts. "I'd like to put you into protective custody until we've caught Troy's killer. Would you prefer this happen with the Trad officers or the Maccabees?"

"Maccabees," Roger replied with no hesitation.

I put him on speaker so I could text Michael to make this happen ASAP. The danger to Henderson was slight but better to be safe than sorry. "I'm arranging it as we speak. Director Michael Fleischer will reach out to you directly. Go with the operatives she sends."

"Thank you."

"We'll keep you safe." I paused, then offhandedly added, "Out of curiosity, why did you buy those shielding devices?"

He specialized in personal security, so his knowledge of them wasn't surprising. Sure, it was a precaution in the face of Jared's proposed legislation, but his boss, the one most at risk for an Eishei Kodesh attack, hadn't been given one.

Roger had gone behind his boss's back, and it wasn't merely to protect his crew.

"See, uh… There was this woman."

Oh, brother.

"An Eishei Kodesh. I wanted nothing to do with her."

I rolled my eyes. Magic bad. "Uh-huh."

"But she was smart and beautiful and charming and she was interested in me."

I smothered my face with a cushion.

"I tried to be the exciting guy she thought I was," he said. "The hero I'd been, helping save the world, instead of a former solider reduced to running security for guys like Jared."

That was rough. I slid the cushion off my face. "You bought the shielding devices to impress her? To make your job seem more dangerous?"

"Not exactly, though I stretched the truth about some of my jobs."

"You shared confidential details," I said flatly.

He paused. "Yeah."

I let the silence stretch, though I was now annoyed along with impatient.

"You're judging me." He exhaled hard. "I would too. I'd spent my life adhering to a strict moral code, but I let the rush of dating her sweep that aside like it didn't matter." He gave a wry chuckle. "I mean, her first approach was over a bottle of contraband booze. Should have known then it was my first step down a slippery slope."

I sat up so fast I hit my knee on the coffee table, but the pain barely registered. My heart thudded against my ribs.

I tried to corrupt him one night with a bottle of vodka....

Cherry woke up with a gleam.

I dug my fingers into the armrest. "What was her name?"

"Roxie."

"Roxie *what?*" Maybe it wasn't her.

He didn't answer me.

I throttled my phone since I couldn't choke sense into him. "Don't tell me you want to protect her."

"No. Well…no. A couple months ago," he continued, "I woke up and Roxie wasn't in bed. I figured she was in the bathroom, and I headed down into the kitchen to get some water. I— She…"

I white-knuckled the phone, psychically willing him to get on with it.

"Roxie had this tattoo, and well, this is going to sound crazy, but it came to life. It looked like it was made of fire."

That wasn't Eishei Kodesh magic. Not a vamp ability either.

Roger Henderson was dating a demon.

A strangled noise punched out of me.

"You don't believe me," he said.

"I do." My voice was laced with sorrow. "Did Roxie see you?" I had to understand the exact nature of the danger he was in to pass that on to Michael.

"I don't think so," Roger said.

Pray she didn't, Cherry said.

"But it freaked me out," the man continued. "I broke up with her a few days later saying work was too busy for me to have a relationship."

"How'd she take it?"

"She was sad, but said she understood. Except she started showing up to different functions I was working. That's why I bought the devices. She was clearly there as a mindfuck, and combined with that freaky tattoo magic, I thought…well, she might try to mess with my head in other ways. Or my team's minds. The devices would shield us from any magic psychological attacks."

Sachie exited the conference room with her messenger bag slung over her shoulder but remained quiet since my call was still on speaker.

"Tell me her name," I said sharply.

He didn't answer, but his silence said it all. All the pieces rearranged themselves with horrific clarity.

"Let me tell you what I think," I said in a hard voice. "You went way beyond telling Roxie about your clients. Yeah, that tattoo trick freaked you out, but it wasn't your first glimpse of what you were dealing with. It was the terrifying kick in the pants that made you run. Roxie had you transporting freed demon prisoners for her, didn't she? That was the reason for the calls with her partner, Chandra Nichols."

"Shit." Sach sat down hard on a chair.

"I—" Roger began.

I death-glared at the phone screen like he could see it. "Yes or no."

"Yes," he replied in a broken whisper.

"Say. Her. Name."

"Rukhsana Gill." The words left his mouth in a breathless rush like he was equal parts relieved and terrified to say them. "Her name is Rukhsana Gill."

Chapter 30

I finished the call with Roger on autopilot, then spun in a circle. "Where's my bag? I need to talk to Michael and—"

"Avi," Sachie said gently and plucked the phone from my hands. "Sit down."

I shook my head. "I can't."

Rukhsana, my informant, the person I'd started to think of as a friend, was a demon. No wonder I couldn't determine whether she was Eishei Kodesh or what kind of magic she had.

No wonder she always came through with the intel I required.

She'd been playing me all this time.

"Fuuuuuuuuck!!!!" I winged a cushion against the wall.

Sachie tugged me onto the sofa next to her. "Table your anger for a moment and talk me through this, because I missed the first part."

"Roger dated Rukhsana, who's a demon. Whether she insinuated herself into his life specifically to get intel on his client base or because she and Chandra required secure transport for their operation, I have no idea. She attacked Jared as a warning. That's why he wasn't actually injured."

"Her initial plan might have been to kill Casey," Sachie said, "but this worked out better. Jared's still around to spew hate and do the heavy lifting keeping tensions high between Trads and Eishei Kodesh. The shedim version of 'work smart, not hard.'" She slung her arm along the back of the sofa. "How does Troy fit into it?"

I buried my head in my hands with a moan. "I'm the fucking idiot who told her Troy had dangerous artifacts. God, I bought her worried act when she asked me after his death if they'd been demonic. She knew what they were the second I mentioned them." I raised my stricken gaze to my friend. "I got Troy killed."

"So Chandra didn't share her insurance policy with her partner and Rukhsana wants those locks back?"

"It's more than that," I said. "The shedim who own the locks know that Chandra had a demon partner. They're after her identity. The way Troy was murdered, the anger and force of the magic poured into him. Rukhsana tortured him to find out whether he, or Linda, or Mois had her glamored identity."

"She's a demon. Switch glamors. Disappear."

"She needed money to hide herself so thoroughly that they'd never find her." I sagged, overwhelmed by my stupidity. I'd agreed to give it to her.

Sachie snapped her fingers. "The brain."

"What about it?"

"It's the plus code location of all the locks."

I slumped even more. "The ultimate insurance policy."

"Could Rukhsana know it's missing and that you stole it?"

"Missing, yes. That I took it?" I shrugged helplessly. My blood felt replaced by ice.

Sachie sent off a text.

"What are you doing?"

"Ezra needs to stay with you until we catch Rukhsana."

I stood up, stuffing my panic into a tight box. "She can't breach HQ so, for now, I'm safe. Let's go upstairs to see Mich—*ouf.*"

Ezra had blurred out the stairwell door and into me, crushing me to his chest.

I hugged him back tightly. Sachie didn't even make any snide comments about him getting through the portal, inside HQ, and down here in seconds.

My boyfriend finally released me. "Whatever guilt you're torturing yourself with over Rukhsana, stop it right now."

I gave a wavery laugh. "You don't even know the full story."

I'd pointed Rukhsana at Troy, and I'd have to live with his murder. I prayed I didn't have to live with the deaths of Linda and Mois on my conscience as well.

"I don't have to," Ezra said. "I know you, and I'd bet everything I have that even now, some part of you still cares what happens to her."

"No," I lied miserably.

Sachie clapped her hands together. "Time to gather the troops, kids. Let's take this to the director."

It was after 9PM and Michael had left for the day, but upon hearing that Roger's demon was Rukhsana, she came right back.

We were soon gathered in one of the large conference rooms on the fourth floor, along with Keira, Olivier, Silas, and Darsh, who took up position at the farthest point in the room from Silas.

Silas kept shooting glances at Darsh like he was a bomb on a ticking timer.

It wasn't unwarranted. Darsh's skin was brushed with purple under his eyes, his normally silky hair lay lankly against his skull, and his dark blue nail polish was chipped.

I peered at his hands. Was that blood crusting his nails?

He glared when he caught me staring and I looked away with a sigh.

Cécile, the leader of Vancouver's Spook Squad, had also been invited, along with its final member, Nasir.

Sachie wasn't on the case, but I was on Ezra's watch, so she stayed downstairs until it was time to take me home.

Olivier leaned over. "Am I forgiven for being a dick? I truly am sorry."

"We're good." I crossed my arms. "You're lucky you have a very smart girlfriend who helped you fix things with that gift card."

"No kidding."

"It would have been so awkward if you'd had to wonder whether tonight was the night Cherry murdered you in your post-coital glow," I added.

"Yeah." Olivier nodded sagely. "That would have put a real damper on things."

Keira and Olivier, to their credit, didn't freak out being enclosed in a room with this many vampires, though I couldn't tell if the chief constable was still disgusted by me and just putting a professional face on it.

I shoved my chair closer to the table with a grating scrape while Michael did the introductions.

Cécile frowned. "Chief Constable Davis, why are you here?" the Québecois vampire asked.

"Be patient and all will become clear," Michael answered. She nodded at me. "Take it from the drug bust."

Everyone in the room had pieces of this case, and while some had the full story, I started with the drug lab and the imprisoned Bratwurst Demon who'd killed herself.

I took everyone through finding the matchmaker, Chandra Nichols, though I still edited out my presence at the murder.

Admitting the discovery of the love lock prison cells was my find and not the Authority's barely got any reaction from Cécile or Nasir, though I could tell they were still puzzled about Keira and Olivier being present.

They both got "aha" expressions once the story turned to Casey and how Chandra's ex-husband, Mois, was one of Jared's donors.

I took a moment to drink some water because I was parched.

Ezra squeezed my hand under the table.

I launched into the phony artifacts that Linda and Troy were manufacturing, the discovery of the metal case, Troy's escape and subsequent murder via orange flame magic, and Mois and Linda's proposed trade with the shedim for their safety in exchange for the two locks.

"That's not going to happen, right?" Nasir looked to Michael for confirmation.

"No. That case is to be secured at all costs," she said.

"This is all very exciting," Darsh drawled, "but why this emergency meeting? We already had our marching orders about the handover tomorrow."

Glad as I was that he was participating, he lingered at the edge of our group, shoulders curved inward. Across the room, Silas traced patterns in the carpet with the toe of his shoe, his chin tucked to his chest.

I uncapped my water bottle but didn't drink from it. "The shedim we'll face tomorrow are part of the bigger group who first corrupted the magic in our rings. The ones who ensured Maccabees sent demons into the cells for them to use. But I expect Chandra's shedim partner to blindside us as well."

"Did you identify that demon?" Keira said.

"Linda has no idea who it was," I said, "but new information has come to light." I dropped the entire ugly story on them, including who Rukhsana was to me and that I'd told her about Troy and the dangerous artifacts.

I'd *led* her to Troy.

I was the reason he was dead.

"I don't ascribe to the 'guns don't kill people' beliefs," Olivier said, "and I don't believe this either. A demon murdered Abelman. End of story."

Everyone save for Darsh and Silas (who were stuck in their silent beef with each other) weighed in on my side, which made me sad. Not for myself, but for the two of them.

"Roger Henderson provided us with some other information," Michael said. At my puzzled look, she explained that the operatives who brought him to the safe house asked him some questions on her behalf. "He gave Rukhsana the security setup for the *Supernatural: Debunked* exhibit. She'd heard about the shedim magic on Sire's Spark and had a buyer lined up for it. But someone else had the same idea and beat her to the punch. To add insult to injury, they killed the thief they'd hired, planted the name of one of Rukhsana's crew on him, and bandied it about town that she was responsible."

"Turning our officers' attention on her," Olivier said with a scowl. "And wasting our time."

"Rukhsana allegedly murdered both the thief and his boss in payback," Michael said.

I'd been so blithely trusting in my own abilities to unmask the bad guys that I hadn't seen Rukhsana coming.

And Ezra didn't see Alastair, Cherry pointed out.

Maybe it wasn't some moral failing, simply human nature to want to believe that someone we'd grown fond of was exactly as they appeared.

Self-recrimination was pointless. I'd learn from this and move forward.

"How do we know that Rukhsana didn't switch sides to save herself and is in league with the shedim coming to the meeting tomorrow?" Keira said.

"Rukhsana doesn't like other demons." I pulled up the

photo she'd given me and passed my phone around. "She had some encounter with them in the past that literally left scars that didn't heal."

"That's some dark shit to defy her healing abilities," Ezra said.

"She freed demons for Chandra to sell to Eishei Kodesh criminals as payback for her injuries?" Nasir said.

"Yes."

Though I didn't believe her retribution stopped there. Rukhsana craved vengeance, but she needed more power to protect herself. What better way than having the locations of all the shedim prisons? However, bringing up the brain now would just muddy everyone's focus.

"I'm going to pretend to be the shedim who worked with Chandra," I said. "My guess is that the other demons are eager to learn Rukhsana's identity."

"You'll say you're her?" Olivier asked.

"Not outright. I'll stall until she shows up." I gestured at all the vampires. "Once I get a confession, you all move in."

"You're sure she'll come?" Darsh said.

"I'll make certain of it."

Silas glanced at Cécile and Nasir. "Is pretending to be a shedim a good idea, Avi?" he said carefully.

"It's the best way to keep the situation inside under control," Ezra said.

I gaped at him.

He gave me a tight smile. "I don't have to like it to appreciate the sense of it."

Michael opened her briefcase by her feet, pulled out a small round silver amulet on a chain, and tossed it across the table to me. "This will help sell the disguise. It'll stop your heartbeat from being detected."

Some demons did have heartbeats, but a lot didn't. Likely because they didn't have hearts.

I slung the necklace over my head. It was to my advantage to appear not to have a heartbeat: I wouldn't read as human, nor could anyone use it to detect my fear or anxiety. "Thank you."

Michael and Keira went over a few more details before the meeting ended.

Cécile and Nasir hurried off to return to staking out the gallery.

Keira had put human operatives out there for the duration of the meeting, and both commanders were antsy to get the vamps back on the job in case the shedim made an early surprise appearance.

I tried to speak with Silas and Darsh, but they avoided me and left separately. Darsh added a "Not now, Aviva" in a back-the-fuck-off voice for good measure.

"Whatever is going on," Michael said quietly, coming up next to me, "they're professional enough to put it aside for the duration of this operation."

"That's not what I'm worried about," I said.

"I know. Just like I know you've got this, Operative Fleischer." Then she hugged me, which was weird but wonderful.

Keira was next in line. "I'm sorrier than you can know for my horrible reaction when you shared your truth with me. You're an excellent Maccabee and I'm proud to work with you." She held out her hand.

I shook it. "Thank you."

"Let's do this," she said and joined Michael in the hallway.

Ezra's phone rang. He checked the screen and said he had to take it.

I said I'd get Sach and meet him in the lobby.

One of the elevators was in service to move some office furniture and the other one was packed, so I took the stairs down to the Spook Squad.

I opened the door, which the vamps kept well-oiled because they liked to try to sneak up on each other.

"Going on a tear through a vamp gang last night was a foolish and unnecessary risk," Silas said from the conference room at the far end of the basement. His body language was relaxed, his hands spread wide.

I froze, the door ajar a crack.

"Don't treat me like I'm a feral dog." Darsh wasn't visible from my vantage point, but his hissed comments traveled clearly across the space. "And do *not* tell me how to do my job."

Sachie obviously wasn't down here. I should leave them to their privacy.

I stayed put, one hand on the heartbeat-blocking amulet around my neck. If Darsh was acting out and could compromise our operation in any way, I needed to know.

Silas rubbed his brow. "Leaving vamp parts strewn around, not even killing them? I surely missed that part of the Maccabee training."

"I was sending a message," Darsh said.

"You're not being careful."

"How'd being careful work out for you? At least I'm *stopping* monsters."

"You're trying to provoke me," Silas said. "This isn't about us."

"I'm not going to compromise any mission and certainly not because of you. That's all you need to know."

I was about to close the door and leave, believing that while Darsh was still angry, he'd step up to the plate as always.

Silas punched the wall.

I jumped a foot, feeling the reverberations from way over here in the stairwell.

"Stop acting like you have nothing to lose!" The force of Silas's temper made the hairs on the back of my neck stand up. It wasn't even directed at me, but it edged out all the oxygen down here.

"I don't have anything to lose." Darsh's words weren't flung out. They were delivered with surgical precision. "You made sure of that. Twice."

My fingers tightened on the doorknob.

Silas shoved him. "You have yourself, asshole! Patrin wouldn't want you to use his death as an excuse to destroy yourself."

"You have no idea what Patrin would want."

"If he loved you half as much as I do, then yeah. I sure as shit do. You think I don't understand crushing guilt or death wishes? Fuck you, Darsh." Silas turned away. "Hate me all you want, but go live your best life out of spite."

There was silence for a moment, then Darsh gave a broken laugh. "Why did you have to push and push and force your way in? I didn't want it and I sure as fuck don't want it now."

Silas's exhale made his shoulders sag. He walked toward the conference room door, but Darsh grabbed his shoulder and spun the much larger vampire around.

I leaned forward, both my friends now in view.

"Don't." Darsh lifted his hand off Silas's shoulder and scrubbed it over his face. "I don't know how to do this."

"Because of Patrin."

Darsh looked up at the ceiling. "When you told me about the Ashbishop, I wanted to hate you so badly, but you know what my first emotion was?"

Silas shook his head.

"Terror, because even knowing you played a part in my little brother's death didn't change how I felt about you." His voice cracked and he slid down the doorframe until he hit the floor, knees drawn to his chest like a child. "What does that say about honoring Patrin's memory? What does that say about *me*?"

Silas crouched down beside him. "That you're a man who loves deeply and forever."

Darsh lunged at Silas in a hug, his head pressed to the other vamp's chest and his shoulders heaving in silent sobs.

Silas murmured something.

I strained forward to hear better but caught myself. What was I doing? After easing the door shut, I fled up the stairs.

Sach was the first one I ran into back in the lobby. "You okay?"

I nodded, too overwrought to speak.

Olivier, Ezra, Sachie, and I all crowded into her car for the ride back to our place. This was the first time the guys had been together outside of a work context, and they got along fabulously, comparing their favorite surfing spots.

I let their conversation wash over me, and Sach didn't say much while she drove, but when we got out of the car in the condo's parking garage, she pulled me aside.

"I'm not sure I like them bonding," she said.

Olivier and I had dated briefly. Ezra had not enjoyed learning that. The two of them bonding was the best outcome imaginable. "You'd like bloodshed better?"

Sach perked up for a minute, then heaved a sigh. "No."

Despite it seeming all double-datey, none of us were in the mood to hang out. Olivier and Sach headed into her bedroom with a subdued "See you in the morning."

Ezra and I didn't speak much while we got ready for bed either. I didn't feel like rehashing what we were up against with the shedim, Rukhsana, or Alastair. I just wanted to fall asleep in my boyfriend's arms, and pretend, for one night, that all was right with the world.

My phone beeped with a notification.

Ezra folded back the covers and slid into bed. "What's up?"

I blushed and mumbled, "Nothing."

He curled his fingers over my hips. "Must I deploy tickle torture?"

I shoved his hands away, grabbed my phone, and showed him the screen. "I set up notifications about those dumb photos of you and Irene, okay?"

"Why?"

"To tease you? Some perverse urge to know what people were saying?"

He chuckled, scanned a few comments, then placed the phone on my bedside table, out of my reach.

I poked his side. "What's with the sudden carefully neutral expression?"

"Nothing."

I motioned for him to hand over my phone. When he didn't comply, I raised my eyebrows. "Do you want me imagining what you're hiding when the reality can't be half as bad?"

He gave me the phone. "These people don't matter."

The initial swell of online love had turned to online hate—all aimed at Irene.

Even the ones who weren't bad-mouthing her had reduced her to nothing more than Ezra's latest girlfriend, completely dismissing her many accomplishments as a ballet dancer. The rest of the comments were akin to a pack of wolves ripping their prey apart.

I swallowed down the taste of bile.

This time, when Ezra took away my phone, I didn't protest. "I'll reach out to some people," he said, "and get this scrubbed. As much as possible."

"This is what I'll face, won't I? When we go public."

"Then let's not."

"That's hardly realistic."

He assumed a haughty expression. "I hid being a Maccabee spy from the world for four years. Trust me, sweetheart, I can hide this. And I will. I'll do anything to keep you from being hurt."

I notched up my chin. "What if I want to tell everyone you're *mine*? My world. My heart. My home."

He raised his hands. "Far be it from me to stop you."

I curled into his side and laced our fingers together. "Whatever the future holds, we'll weather it together, okay?"

He kissed my head. "Okay."

Morning came far too soon.

I dressed silently, attempting to remain in the moment and not spiral into dark thoughts, but it didn't help that Ezra sat there tensely watching my every move. I placed my Maccabee ring on my dresser and headed off to breakfast.

Sach had coffee ready and enough bacon, eggs, and pancakes to feed a small army. She hovered over me with a metal spatula that she tightened her grip on whenever I paused eating.

I stared pointedly at Olivier, who stood up and wrestled the implement away from her.

"It's just another day at the office," Ezra said with a completely unnatural hearty cheer.

"Stop it." I wiped my mouth and stood up. "It'll all be fine. Now quit unnerving me." I left the room to put the final piece of my plan into motion.

I grabbed my phone off my bedside table and pulled up Rukhsana's number.

I'd be facing down shedim soon and responsible for Mois's and Linda's lives, yet it was this call that made my hands shake.

In fury.

I was positive I was going to blow it and tip Rukhsana off that the jig was up. The universe cut me a break, though, and the call went to voice mail. "I found Mois," I said in a low, harried tone. "It's bad, Rukhsana. He's meeting with shedim in about half an hour and I don't know that I can get him out of this." I took a deep breath for effect. "But you can get somewhere safe. I haven't forgotten our deal, and you'll have your money today, but I can't get that photo of your scars out of my head. Take your crew and make sure you're clear of this."

It was an utter crock of shit.

I wasn't sending her people—sending Jordy—away with a shedim. I'd announced at the meeting yesterday that they were to be protected, and Darsh volunteered to round them up. Cécile would tail Rukhsana, so we had a heads-up of her arrival at the Lions Gallery.

Rukhsana had always taken care of her people, however she was a demon, and that could turn on a dime. Jordy was sweet and smart and no match for Rukhsana.

I hadn't been either. That changed now.

Chapter 31

Linda hugged me when I slipped inside the dimly lit Lions Gallery. The space was stripped of all artwork, and I couldn't look at the stark white walls without envisioning blood splattered like gruesome canvases.

Mois and Linda had been holed up here for only a few days, but it had a musty, closed-in odor.

Her father stepped forward, a white-knuckled grip on the metal case with the love locks. He was as wan with fatigue and fear as his daughter, the pair in wrinkled clothes that smelled a bit ripe. "I apologize for you having to debase yourself," he said stiffly.

"Debase?"

"You're forced to pretend to be one of those wretched atrocities to clean up my ex-wife's mess."

Linda flinched at the venom in his voice.

I didn't love the anti-shedim bias, however, I didn't require my synesthete vision to understand that their limbic systems were flooding their bodies with a flight-or-fight response. It also didn't help that I was a Maccabee. From Mois's POV, that actually counted against me. Magic had landed him and his daughter in this nightmare.

I cut them some slack. "My team is in position."

They'd commandeered a dry cleaner across the street with a perfect view of the gallery. Ezra, Silas, and Nasir were poised to act on my signal—or if they heard things go wrong through our comms.

Meantime, Michael, Keira, and Olivier waited with them, ready to handle any human complications that might arise.

"The bars on all the gallery windows remain unbreakable," I said. "The security gate is locked in place across the back door, and we've removed the mezuzah off the front doorframe."

"There's no back escape route?" Linda said.

"You can still unlock the door and gate and get out, but it's better to force the demons in through the entrance that my team has eyes on," I assured her. "That way, we have an accurate head count and won't be surprised by others attacking from the rear."

Mezuzahs had been affixed to all the windowsills and doorways inside the gallery, which meant the shedim couldn't portal in. Linda had learned a few things from her mother about dealing with demons after all.

Mois tapped the case. "The sooner I trade this, the better."

"Give it to me," I said.

He shook his head. "I'd feel more comfort—"

"You want to be comfortable? Book yourself into a fancy hotel when we get out of this. Let me be clear, Mr. Aviyente. You are not in charge. Without me and my people, you and your daughter will end up like your ex-wife and Troy. Your deaths will not be swift and merciful. You will suffer for daring to betray these demons."

"We didn't do it!" His face went blotchy red. "It was all Chandra!"

"The shedim won't care," I said coldly.

 Cherry huffed. *There are easier ways to make him fall in line.*

I had to set the pecking order, but I didn't want to contribute to their suffering. I held out my hand. "I'll close this deal faster and safer than you can. Then you and Linda will be done with this. Forever."

To Mois's credit, his stare down lasted a good thirty seconds, but he handed the metal case over.

It felt impossibly heavy, a stark reminder of the dangerous path we trod. I couldn't sense the prison cells, but the memory of their effect on me if I so much as unlocked the case made my hands shake.

"Three incoming," Olivier murmured over the comms.

I nodded at the door to the employee-only area. There was a mezuzah on the frame; the shedim couldn't get to the Aviyentes so long as they stayed behind it. "Into the back room. My team will give one knock followed by a pause and two quick raps. When you hear that, unlock the back exit and go with them."

Linda obeyed, but Mois didn't move.

Before I could force the issue, the gallery's front door creaked open.

Our three shedim visitors dropped their human glamors the second they stepped through the door.

Linda gasped and Mois finally got some much-needed self-preservation, skuttling behind the protective ward.

Interesting that the shedim hadn't arrived in their demon forms, scaring any humans who saw them. Apparently, the rush they'd receive from any panic wasn't worth this meeting being disturbed.

They weren't fucking around.

Neither was I.

The tallest figure, the one in front, was a writhing mass of shadowy forms barely contained in a humanoid outline. Behind it on the left stood a demon with bristly fur, long sharp elephant tusks, and an unsettling grin, while the final one was a blob with countless eyes scattered across its gelatinous mass. That multi-gaze beam was trained on us, gleaming with an otherworldly detachment that sent a chill down my spine.

Fun!

Okay, Cherry. Glad one of us was enjoying this. I dubbed the demons: Shadow, Dumbo, and Eyz. Not the most brilliant nicknames, but it was better than Death!, Death!, and Death!

"You have our locks." Shadow's voice was a whisper of wind that sent its words twining coldly around my limbs.

I held up the case and spoke in my best growly voice. "Exactly. *I* have them. Let us send the pathetic humans on their way and deal together, shedim to shedim."

"Ixnay on the oicevay," Ezra muttered on the comms. Michael shushed him.

The trio exchanged quick glances. Did they buy my cover story of being the one who'd freed the demons, allowing Chandra to sell them to magic criminals?

"The deal," Dumbo said flutily, "has changed."

"Changed how?"

"You have something far more valuable than those two measly prisons." Drool slid out of its mouth and down its tusk. "We want it back."

They were after the brain. One word from me and these shedim would turn their sights on Delacroix.

I required proof that Rukhsana murdered Troy, but to get that, I had to prevent Shadow, Dumbo, and Eyz from slaughtering Mois and Linda until my former informant arrived. Plus, keep Linda from using her white flame magic, which would do nothing against these demons except sign her death warrant.

I held up the metal case. "You're telling me this isn't

valuable? Why'd you waste my business partner if that's true?"

Olivier cursed in my ear, a sharp, shocked noise, and then muted the communication channel.

My gut churned in dread at all the things that could have just gone wrong at the dry cleaner's, but I kept my expression impassive.

"That human overstepped." Eyz's voice filled the room. An impressive trick for a creature with no visible mouth, but creepy as shit.

Still, thanks for the confirmation that they were behind Chandra's murder. Their confession wasn't required for the vamps on my team to get the green light to kill the demons, but it was nice to have that cold case definitively solved.

Eyz floated over, every single one of their peepers narrowing at me. "You overstepped as well, shedim."

The comm crackled back to life.

"We're coming in," Michael said tersely.

"No!" It wasn't enough to kill these demons. Rukhsana had to arrive and confess.

And pay, Cherry snarled.

Eyz leaned in blobbily. "No?"

I took several steps backward. "I mean, it was just business. I don't know about anything other than what's in this case, but if you tell me what you seek, I can help you find it. We can come to an understanding."

The second I told them about Delacroix, at least one, if not all of them, would decamp for the Copper Hell. My prime directive was to stall, because this plan was staying on track.

"Cécile is missing and presumed dead," Michael said insistently in my earpiece. "Darsh rounded up most of Rukhsana's crew and has them at a secure location, but Rukhsana is either on the warpath or she's fled, and either way, I have to concentrate my resources on finding her."

I blinked dumbly at the shedim, barely processing Shadow's response about the brain.

Banish the fear, Cherry said calmly.

Fuck fear. I was going to tear Rukhsana apart with my bare hands.

"Do you have the brain?" Shadow said.

"Five minutes," Michael said over the comms. "Then we come in, kill these shedim, and regroup."

"No," I said sharply. "But I know where the brain is," I added for Shadow's benefit.

"Take us there immediately or they die." Shadow motioned to Eyz.

The demon stood by the threshold to the back room. The mezuzah kept him out, but sadly it didn't keep Mois and Linda in.

The slack-jawed humans lurched toward Eyz like zombies. Or the compelled. Another few feet and they'd leave the sanctuary of that area for the main gallery and be in the demon's clutches.

I sprinted for them but was knocked down, Dumbo's heavy body pinning mine.

Tear out its eyes! Cherry yelled.

I used a Krav Maga move to knock the demon off, jumping to my feet just as the main gallery door crashed open.

"Sorry I'm late to the party," Rukhsana purred. She'd shaved her head, the snake tattoo that freaked Roger out once more clearly visible. One hand was clamped on to poor Jordy's arm.

I had a lot of blood on my hands, but so help me, none of it would be his.

Jordy trembled. "What are those things?"

Linda grabbed her father and slammed the door to the staff area.

"Back door," I whispered into my comms. "But hold."

Hopefully, the mezuzah ward on the closed employee-only door would keep any of the demons from detecting the vampires' presence once they arrived.

I just needed a couple more minutes.

"Who are you?" Shadow demanded. It deployed a wraith from its center mass, the apparition winging its way to Rukhsana.

She let go of Jordy and grabbed the wraith a heartbeat before it enveloped her. Her eyes turned to slits dancing with flames. "Prisoner 32X475, at your service."

My jaw hit the ground. Talk about a mic drop moment.

Rukhsana didn't simply *free* the demon prisoners; she'd been one.

The snake tattoo leapt off her skull. Made of fire, it pounced on the wraith, tumbling with it to the floor.

Jordy bolted to my side.

Rukhsana's tattoo had helped glamor her and without it, her face and body were a wreckage of ropey dark purple scars that twisted her mouth to one side.

I gasped. "Rukhsana? I— You're a shedim?"

The magic snake squeezed the wraith and Shadow dimmed, the demon folding in on itself.

"Well, well," Eyz said, swiveling its gazes to me. "It seems we have an imposter in our midst." Neither it nor Dumbo moved. Demons respected power, and if Shadow couldn't save itself, oh well.

Rukhsana followed his line of sight to me and her face lit up. She gave her throaty laugh whose familiarity made my chest constrict. "Did you truly believe you could successfully pretend to be a shedim? Aviva, you stupid girl."

Chapter 32

I looked at the ground, my shoulders hunched. Cherry scratched at me under my skin, howling at me to show that bitch the truth, but I remained abashed. "You—you're the one Chandra worked with?"

"Return the brain!" Shadow exploded into a flurry of wraiths, all whipping toward Rukhsana.

Her fiery snake tattoo spun like a tornado, capturing and squeezing the life out of them.

Shadow shriveled up and vanished.

I swallowed hard—not an act.

Dumbo and Eyz looked at each other in some silent communication.

Rukhsana sauntered toward me and Jordy. I shielded him with my body, and the shedim laughed. "Such a savior complex."

"Di-did you kill Troy?" I trembled. (Mostly an act.)

"Yeah, she did," Jordy said, beaming at her. "And she was fucking glorious." He tore the metal case from my grip and tossed it to Rukhsana. "Sorry, Avi, but you were suckered."

"Et tu, Jordy?" I said sadly.

"She's going to make me an infernal." He bounced on his toes, a look of awe on his deluded face. "She picked me, a Trad, for this honor."

I pressed my lips together, blinking away moisture at this incredible betrayal. Not Jordy to me, but the lie Rukhsana had fed him.

Suddenly, the door from the employee-only area shattered. Ezra, Silas, and Nasir poured into the main gallery, startling the shedim and giving me an opportunity.

Jordy was stronger than me, though I had training and experience on my side. However, I had to remove him from the game board before Rukhsana sacrificed her human pawn. And I had to do it safely.

There was really only one option.

I busted out my bulked-up shedim body with my frosted scaley armor, crimson hair, and horns, and lobbed Jordy out the door into the street.

He hit the concrete with a curse, rolled onto his back, and lay there, moaning, with his hand to his head.

Nasir blurred outside, flung Jordy over his shoulder, and sped the Trad into Michael's care.

It was such a demon free-for-all in here that no one noticed.

Ezra and Silas were battling the shedim, including Rukhsana. The briefcase had been knocked to the ground, and every time one of the shedim went for it, a vamp was on them.

I ducked behind a pillar as a stray burst of black light, courtesy of Dumbo, scorched the wall beside me.

Nasir rejoined the fight. Even so, my team would have been overpowered by Rukhsana's stupid snake, were it not for the fact that she was also using it to fend off attacks from Eyz and Dumbo.

I crept from the pillar to behind an overturned table with a view of the employee-only area.

Michael and Keira were escorting Mois and Linda out the back door.

Silas roared in pain and fury as Dumbo's tusks raked across his chest.

I descended into an ocean of calm, watching the proceedings with a detachment that spurred me into motion. I sprinted for the metal case, sliding the last few feet. My claws closed on the handle, but I was yanked backward by my hair.

"Oh, chère," Rukhsana said, raking a slow gaze over my half-shedim form. "You should have led with this."

You forfeited an hour of your magic. The sentience from the fortress in the Brink spoke directly in my head. *I have come to collect.*

The words slithered through my skull like ice water, pooling at the base of my spine. My magic writhed under my skin, trying to burrow deeper, to hide.

That fucker had let me ask it for the supplicant's name, then given me a maggot and a memory that almost killed me. Wasn't that enough?

"Please no," I whispered. Every instinct screamed at me to run, but my legs wouldn't move, and my heart hammered against my ribs like a bunny rabbit in a trap. I swear it was making the amulet bounce.

Any second now Rukhsana would see it under my shirt, tear it off, and sense the true depths of my fear.

She dragged me all the way back into the kitchen, tearing off the mezuzahs on the two doors along the way. They burned her hands with a sizzle, but her skin was already so scarred, she barely flinched.

It is time, the fortress fucker psychically said.

A sharp jab pinged through my body, and I deflated in Rukhsana's hold, my shedim armor suddenly gone. My connection to *Cherry* was gone, along with all my Eishei Kodesh magic. I shivered, feeling as vulnerable as a newborn babe. For the next sixty minutes, I had no way to defend myself.

Rukhsana mock-frowned at me. "Scared, are we?"

All the sound beyond the kitchen abruptly cut off.

Act like the Maccabee you are, I admonished myself. I kicked the shedim sideways in the knee and tore free with a wince.

With one eye on the demon, I took a centering breath. Think. What had that forfeit been? One hour of my blue flame magic. I'd learned a thing or two about magic wagers, and I'd learned not to bet everything at once.

Which meant this forfeit was merely a signal disrupter to my shedim side, not a total blackout.

I cast my awareness deep inside myself, rewarded with Cherry scraping at my mind like a kitten trapped on the wrong side of a door. Now to kick that door down.

Rukhsana's snake whirred toward me, bobbing and hissing in front of my face. It was only a demon's tattoo, not even the demon herself, yet it pulsed with a malevolence that was overwhelming.

Even if I had magic, Rukhsana was out of my league.

That didn't mean I wouldn't go down fighting. I imagined smashing my way through to Cherry.

Ezra helped Nasir kill Eyz, then sprinted for me, but he bounced off an invisible barrier in the doorway.

Rukhsana glanced over her shoulder at my boyfriend, who bellowed in rage, though I couldn't hear it. "It'll be a shame to destroy the Crimson Prince. We could have had such fun." She plucked the metal case away from me.

"Did you care about Jordy at all?"

Rukhsana laughed, a chilling sound that echoed inside this bubble she'd created for the two of us. "Spend centuries trapped in unending darkness and pain, and then tell me if you care about anyone other than yourself."

The fucking fire snake feinted left.

I flinched, but my anger at being toyed with put a crack

in the metaphoric glass blocking Cherry from me. While I worked on that, I shoved an actual chair between me and the snake, gripping the plastic tightly. "Did you have fun messing with Roger?"

"Look at you, knowing all about me before I showed my hand. Très bien, Maccabee."

"And Troy?"

She gave a very Gallic shrug. "He knew too much. I should thank you for him, really. You made my job so much easier."

I pushed the guilt aside, focused on connecting with Cherry. "At least give me the villain monologue, Rukhsana. Let me put the pieces in place before I die."

She laughed again. "Why not? You've been amusing enough over our acquaintanceship to earn that. I was part of the team that created those lock cells. And my reward was to be imprisoned in one. When I finally escaped—"

"How?"

Outside the bubble, Silas tore Dumbo in half and Nasir decapitated him. The shedim was dead. They ran for Ezra, who threw himself against the magic barrier to no avail.

There was nothing here to defend myself with. The vamps had to break through before Rukhsana got bored of talking.

She wagged a finger at me. "I must reserve some secrets, chère. Suffice it to say, I was weak when I escaped, stuck here for decades trying to heal."

"Freeing other demons helped that?"

"Not physically no, but revenge can be a tonic. It is always such a delight to hurt those who hurt me."

The snake flared in extension of her rage, hissing fire.

I shrank back, not taking my eyes off it. This chair wasn't going to cut it as a shield. I shifted my weight— barely a step—in the direction of the kitchen door. "Why not release all the prisoners at once?"

"There's a very small window after Maccabees send the shedim into the cells where I can find them. Très difficile. If I don't, they're imprisoned for eternity."

No wonder Bratwurst Demon healed so quickly. She'd barely been incarcerated for any time at all. "What about Quentin Baker?" The man who'd staked Calista. "You let me believe he physically abused you."

"Blame your savior complex. He was my shot at regaining my strength."

I edged closer to the doorway. I could feel Cherry again, which was a huge relief, but I still couldn't access that magic. "The game of dodgeball, all that destruction and misery, it was your idea."

Ezra locked eyes with me, devastation writ large on his face, and flung himself against the magic barrier.

"Every step engineered by me," Rukhsana said. "I couldn't go into the Copper Hell myself, Calista would have detected me, but Quentin was so controllable. That game almost fully restored me."

The fire snake twined around my legs and I froze, breathing shallowly.

Rukhsana kept it from outright burning me, going for a constant wire-thin feed of pain. "You can't escape unless I allow it," she said. "Your turn to answer a question." She narrowed her eyes. "It was so clever of that vampire bartender at the Hell to use Quentin to get to Calista. I wouldn't have thought twice about it until Delacroix paraded his daughter around and made me doubt the story. Funny how similar her infernal form is to yours."

"I don't hear a question, but if it's whether Delacroix will hunt you down if you hurt me, the answer is a vehement yes."

"I doubt that, since he kept you a secret. Same as you've kept your shedim side your entire life. You may not believe me, but my respect for you has actually gone up."

"Considering how little you thought of me before, that's hardly some high bar." There was a tiny click between the Brimstone Baroness and me, like we'd touched pinkies. It wasn't enough.

"True, but now I'm considering you as an asset." She gnawed on her thumbnail. "What if I let you live in exchange for helping me find that brain?"

"For helping you free all the prisoners."

Her dreamy expression was unnerving against all her vicious scars. "That would be fun, but non. We destroy the locks, purge them from the face of the earth. With that one fell stroke?" She sliced a hand through the air. "We decimate the shedim who've been leaching off that power for themselves. They've depended on that boost for so long that their normal magic has withered. You send in your vampires to take them out, et voilà."

"Such a nice, tidy offer." I did a hopping dance to get away from the damn snake slithering around my feet. "Is that where you step into the void?"

She gave me a coy smile.

"Forget it. I might have a savior complex but I'm not a total idiot. You'd never hold up your end of the deal."

"I would if we magically sealed the oath."

"What's the catch? The oath makes me your slave?"

"So dramatic, Aviva. It's nothing so drastic. You simply leave the Maccabees. For good." She held out her arm and the fire snake reared up to lick her palm. "I never toyed with you out of contempt. You always fascinated me. Now more than ever. You may not be a full shedim, but I am curious to see what you would become without that Maccabee yoke around your neck."

"I'd be me. But jobless."

"You'd land on your feet. Think about what I'm offering. Earth without all those demons or those cells. The good to humanity. Nothing else about your life would have to change."

"I'm a Maccabee. Pretty big change." I flexed my left hand and a single claw appeared.

Yesssss, Cherry exalted.

Less than a heartbeat later, that magic vanished again.

My shoulders sagged, exhaustion washing through my fear.

Rukhsana jabbed a finger at me with a sneer. "Your group couldn't even see they were playing into shedim hands for hundreds of years. That's who you want to remain loyal to? Don't you want a chance to find yourself without trying to please some flawed ideal?"

I rubbed my bare right index finger. I'd already taken off my ring—shedding my Maccabee identity wouldn't change who I was. This deal, if it was legit, would let me enact more change than via my current career plans. I intended to steal the brain away from Delacroix anyway. Why not do it with Rukhsana's help?

The air around me shivered. Ezra's fist punched through the bubble, bringing with it his roared fury. Silas and Nasir hacked away at the air, helping to open the breach.

I didn't even have to answer. I could just stand here, let Ezra rescue me, and keep my beliefs intact that I wouldn't join Rukhsana, not for any reason.

The snake rose up, poised to strike.

I stared into the flickering slits of its eyes, a helpless human whose vamp boyfriend remained out of reach.

It was make the deal or die.

Chapter 33

Fuck death and fuck that deal. A stripe of toxic green scales flickered over my skin and with an enraged howl, I launched myself through the flaming snake onto Rukhsana, stabbing my claws into her eyeballs.

She bent double, cursing me in French while the snake whipped around trying to find me.

"I'll locate those prisons and destroy all the shedim involved." I beat at my clothing with my bare hands, my scales gone again. My fingers were burned, my voice was raspy with pain, and my shedim magic felt like a staticky song tuning in and out in faint bursts. "But it'll happen on *my* terms."

There was a noise akin to nails on a chalkboard, and Ezra tumbled through Rukhsana's magic barrier. Silas and Nasir were on his heels, but the Prime had already kicked a table aside to grab Rukhsana in a choke hold.

The snake shot back to its mistress, slithering along her skull to strike at Ezra's face. He grabbed the magic tattoo in one hand, but the snake bit his palm.

A muscle ticked in the Prime's jaw, and he crushed the

snake in his fist, fire spurting out from between his fingers, until an instant later, all that was left were sparks.

Rukhsana's howl was a raw symphony of pain and fury. She sagged in his grip.

"You good here, Ez?" Silas was practically vibrating.

"Yup. Go."

Silas bolted, his phone already in his hand, followed by Nasir.

Ezra shook Rukhsana like a ragdoll. "Your call, Aviva."

Most of Rukhsana's power was extinguished thanks to Ezra doing the heavy lifting and chances were, I could finish her off. Should I say the word, he'd deal the final blow as well so I didn't have to live with any of it on my conscience, but that wasn't fair.

Nothing about this was fair.

I dug deep inside myself, reaching through the static of the magic forfeit with a pained hiss to manifest two single deadly sharp claws.

Then I slashed Rukhsana's throat.

Ezra dropped her to the ground.

Rukhsana pressed a hand against her skin, black goo oozing from between her fingers and out of her ruined eye socket. Even bleeding out, there was a defiant tilt to her chin. Slender tendrils of fire flew off her body and licked at my skin.

I slapped at a dozen smoldering burns, the heat of her assault growing stronger.

She was healing. Enough to kill me without her fire snake?

Ezra stepped forward, but I shook my head and crouched down.

I'd always relied on the magic cocktail to kill shedim, but that weapon had been taken off the table. Physically assaulting her hadn't worked, what else could I try?

Acting on instinct, I shoved my fingers in Rukhsana's neck wound and surged my faint connection with Cherry into the Frenchwoman. My entire body vibrated on a magic frequency that made me grind my teeth and blink away tears.

I created a feedback loop, a resonance that amplified the inherent instability within Rukhsana's shedim magic.

The rush was electrifying. Cherry grew stronger, more present within me.

Rukhsana's face contorted in pain. "Chère, please. Have mercy."

A distant part of my brain reacted in horror, but Cherry rode me hard and I craved vengeance.

The Frenchwoman's human glamor dripped off her like wax and her flames dimmed, until with a final hiss of steam, Rukhsana Gill was no more.

She'd been shedim; there'd only ever been one possible outcome. I'd ended her and I didn't feel bad about it.

Liar, Cherry whispered, already fading away under the combination of my pain, exhaustion, and the forfeit. *But we'll work on that.*

"Avi?" Ezra scanned my face. "Let me heal you."

My skin throbbed from all the scorch marks, and Cherry was locked out again, but I shook my head. "Not yet."

"You don't need to suffer in penance," he said in a frustrated voice.

I scooped up the metal case, cradling it against my chest since my hands were too raw to hold the handle. "I want this job dealt with once and for all. Then I'll let myself be treated."

He nodded. "I'll be waiting."

Exhausted, I trudged outside, shivering from the bite of winter air that speared through me. Oh for my toasty coat, currently stashed in the trunk of my car.

A man on the sidewalk took one look and sprinted around the corner.

The stretchy clothes I'd worn in case I had to let Cherry out were torn, and when I gingerly ran a hand over my head, sooty strands broke onto my fingers, but it wasn't my physical appearance that had sent him fleeing.

Olivier intercepted me when I stepped inside the dry cleaner's. "You okay?"

Plastic garments hung neatly on the conveyer, the air was moist and warm, and the room smelled mildly of solvent. The mundanity of it was a much-needed balm.

"As good as I can be," I said. "Where's Michael?"

"In the back office with the chief constable, going over the details of the Aviyentes' new identities." He grimaced. "They're pretty steamed they have to leave their lives."

I was sympathetic, but if the shedim believed those two were still alive, their lifespans would be pretty damn short. Michael and Keira would ensure the family was hidden under watertight new aliases.

"Any news on Cécile?"

Olivier shook his head. "We found her ashes. I'm sorry."

I hadn't known the Québecois vampire well, but I'd always been amused by how this rule-lover was the first to encourage her beloved Montréal Canadiens hockey team to drop their gloves and brawl.

I gave Olivier the metal case with a heavy heart. Oh yeah. Hearts. I had him remove the amulet from my neck since my burned and throbbing hands weren't up to the task. "Can you please give all of this to Michael?" She'd make sure the locks inside were secured until we had a way to destroy the cells and the prisoners.

"Sure thing."

"What's going to happen to Roger once he leaves protective custody?"

"Probably nothing. The director and the chief constable are adamant that Jared never learn about shedim. Maccabees planted a cover story about a medical emergency for Roger's sister and that he flew out to Ottawa. He called his second-in-command, leaving them in charge of any upcoming events until he's been thoroughly questioned and can return to his normal life."

I didn't feel bad that Roger wouldn't pay for his role. I was simply grateful that so many of us had made it out unharmed.

"Thanks." I leaned my head against Olivier's shoulder in a makeshift hug, my eyes blurring. Partially in pain from my burns, but there was enough emotion overwhelm that I chalked it up to that. "Rukhsana…"

"Yeah. It sucks." He patted my shoulder gingerly. "We heard the offer she made you."

I screwed up my face. I'd assumed the comms didn't work inside her cone of silence. "How'd Michael and Keira react?"

"Once Michael stopped gripping my boss's hand out of fear for your safety, they were both very proud of you. There are a lot of people who have your back, human or half shedim."

I swiped at my eyes with my sleeve. "Okay, shut up. You're making me verklempt and today's had enough feels."

Olivier laughed softly and took the briefcase to Michael.

Before I could leave the dry cleaner's, Nasir jumped into my path.

My muscles locked up on instinct, sending a fresh wave of aches through my already-screaming body, and the noise that escaped me was somewhere between a sigh and a growl.

"Nice work!" He bobbed up and down on his toes. "May I heal you?"

At Nasir's easy acceptance, something righted itself in my chest, and I strengthened my resolve to come out to the other Maccabees ASAP. It didn't matter if they couldn't handle it; I wouldn't walk away. Despite all our setbacks, I believed in my organization, and no one was driving me out.

"That would be great," I said.

There was no high from my brief feed from Nasir's wrist. I wasn't sure if it was because he made it that way or because I didn't have any magic.

Regardless, while the blood tasted gross, it worked.

I cracked my neck, the motion unlocking all the muscles through my shoulders, arms, and back. Heavenly. "I appreciate it."

Nasir bobbed up and down again. "I'll check on Ezra. He'll act all fine after taking out that magic snake, but vampires are stubborn."

I laughed. "That one more than most."

I followed Nasir outside and threw my face to the sky, taking a couple of deep breaths.

Silas found me. "I'm taking Jordy to where Darsh has the rest of the crew."

"Great!" I said too brightly, my heart hammering. Why had I given the amulet to Olivier? "Are things okay between you?"

"We'll get there."

I flashed Silas double thumbs up, which made him frown.

"You sure you're all right? Your heart is—"

"Never felt better." I pushed him away. "Run along now."

He gave me one more doubtful look and headed to his

rental SUV, where Jordy sat in the back, handcuffed to the "oh shit" handle.

The Trad locked eyes with me for the briefest second, then looked away.

I sighed. I'd deal with my feelings about his betrayal later.

I'd almost made it to the gallery doors when Delacroix peeled out of the shadows of a neighboring business.

"Did you rat me out about the brain?" He struck a match and lit the cigarette in his mouth. His hair was wet and he smelled faintly of brine.

"No. Tempting as it was." I was getting goosebumps from the cold, but I refused to wrap my arms around myself in case he took it as weakness. I jammed my hands in my pockets. "Did you know my informant was a demon?"

"Aww, was my eldest child played?" He made a sad trombone sound.

Now he claimed me?

I made that trombone sound right back. "I wasn't the only one. Rukhsana was manipulating Quentin Baker. Thanks to her, Quentin was forced to live in the cracks of his own life, which meant Calista never saw him coming and you lost your partner."

Delacroix's eyes flashed red. "I wouldn't share that information if I were you." He dragged on his cigarette. "Have fun trying to destroy those two locks."

He could have taken them from us during this sting, yet he didn't. Was he planning on moving all of them somewhere to sow chaos in political or natural events? I gnawed the inside of my cheek. He hadn't yet. The Authority would have sounded the alarm.

Besides, that didn't feel like Delacroix's play. All these years that he was earthside, he'd never shown any interest in human affairs outside the yacht. He barely ever left—

They've depended on that boost for so long... Rukhsana's words provided the insight I'd been missing.

My eyes went wide. "You're going to use those locks to power up, aren't you? They're batteries and you're going to plug in. Are you staging a demon coup?"

"If I was, you think you could stop me?"

"Do what you want in the demon realm. The more casualties the better. But use earth as a battleground at your peril. I'll marshal every single resource to destroy you."

The taste of salt water filled my mouth. My pulse spiked, the memory of being drowned overwhelming me, but I steeled myself, jutting my chin up higher.

Delacroix's eyes flashed; anger or pride? He barked a laugh and blew smoke in my face. "This is going to be fun, daughter o mine."

I shot him the finger as he walked away. I'd gather the troops to deal with him and steal back the brain, but for now I was tapped out. I entered the gallery once more and sighed in delight. Central heating was the best invention ever. "Ezra?"

There was no answer. I frowned. Ezra and Nasir wouldn't have left the place unattended. I hurried into the back area and pulled up short.

Nasir sat on the ground in Linda's office, feeding the Prime from a gash in his wrist. "Killing that shedim's snake took more out of Ezra than he realized. He was cold and hungry."

"Can I come closer?" I said. When Nasir nodded, I ran to my boyfriend's side, crouching down to feel his skin. Luckily, he'd already warmed up.

Ezra pulled away from the other vampire and slumped back against the desk. "Did I take too much?"

"Nope." Nasir stood up with a wavery smile. "Cécile..." He cleared his throat. "I'm going back to HQ."

"I'm so sorry," I said. The two had worked closely together.

"Thank you, Nasir," Ezra said.

"Of course." His wrist had already healed.

Ezra listened for a moment after our team member left, his head cocked, then he tugged me into his lap, his arms coming around me.

I relaxed back against his chest. "We should lock up. I want to get out of here."

"Me too, but I need a moment."

I turned my head in alarm. "The blood didn't help?"

Ezra's eyes were clear, and his gaze was steady. "Avi, relax. I'm okay. I just want a second to send you to a locked closet."

I tried to break out of his grip, but he tightened his hold. "You're not serious," I said. "Are you?"

"Depends. Are you going to keep shortening my life-span with these stunts of yours?"

"Your immortal lifespan?" I nodded. "Probably. Your move, Count von Cardoso." I made my voice meek and pathetic. "But the magic from the fortress came to collect a forfeit, and I have no blue flame magic for another forty minutes or so, and I can't sense Cherry again." I slumped against him. "I'm very sad."

"You play dirty," he growled.

Pouting, I twisted my head to look at him. "So sad."

He glared at me, but his hold became a hug and he nuzzled my neck. "Better?"

"A bit." I kissed his cheek.

Ezra stiffened. Black lines exploded like cracks along his skin.

Yelling his name, I wrenched on his arms to loosen his grip, but he didn't respond.

Suddenly, he went limp and sagged to the ground. I got

free and lightly slapped his cheeks, but he was freezing and unresponsive.

A cold sweat broke out over my skin, and every breath was a knife twisting in my gut. "Hang on, sweetheart."

The landline here in the office was dead. Our cell phones were in my car and Olivier had my comm. I leaned over the desk; Ezra didn't have his earpiece.

I sprinted all around the gallery, finding it smashed at the base of a pillar. I ran to the front window, but the transport van we'd taken here had departed, my team headed back to HQ.

I bolted back to Ezra.

The black cracks on his skin pulsed in time with tremors rolling through his body. In the past couple of minutes, his skin had gone from ice-cold to a burning heat. Sweat dripped off his brow and into his eyes, which were fixed open in a dull, vacant stare.

I wrestled him into a seated position against the wall, forcing my wrist to his mouth. "Bite me, Ezra." Even if I didn't have magic, my blood would nourish him, wouldn't it?

His regular teeth scraped uselessly against my skin.

"Come on, baby," I pleaded. "You need to look pretty so we can take a photo together for all your fans."

"Avivaaaaaaa."

I stiffened at the sound of my name called from the main gallery in Alastair's broad British accent.

He couldn't see Ezra in this state.

Making sure my boyfriend was securely propped up, I whispered a promise that I'd be back, and hurried out of the back room.

Alastair, usually so stylish and composed, looked ragged. His tie was a tattered flag askew around a torn collar, buttons were missing from his wool coat, and he had a streak of grease along his stubbled jaw. It wasn't only the hem of his trousers that was coming apart at the seams.

I rubbed my hands together. "I could use Natán's reward money. Might come in handy for future car repairs. Thanks for making it easy to claim, Ashbishop. Sorry. I mean Ash Lite, big-time copycat."

He bared his fangs at me. "I'm not going down to the likes of you, infernal."

I clenched my jaw, but there was no surge of fear at the confirmation that the vampire responsible for murdering my kind knew about me. All my fear was currently occupied with Ezra's condition. "Then we're at a standoff, *dhampir*."

Alastair stiffened, his mouth twisting in a ruthless sneer. "Not quite. You're coming with me."

I snorted. "Whatever gave you that idea? My team is in the back."

Alastair scoffed. "Nice try. There's no one else here. I'd sense if there was."

My heart stuttered. He didn't sense Ezra?

My boyfriend had killed demons before with no ill effects. What had Rukhsana's snake done to him? Had being imprisoned in the lock corrupted her magic enough to affect a Prime?

It took every ounce of control not to look at the back room.

Alastair smirked. "Didn't think a dhampir had that skill?" He blurred toward me and grabbed my arm. "You're going to take a test for me."

My blood ran cold.

The test set by the magic sentience currently in possession of my blue flame magic who turned Shiny Jimmy into a wall and separated Evelyn from her name in maggot form?

I headbutted him. "I'd rather die."

Alastair rubbed his forehead. "You might anyway, but I doubt it. You survived one test at that bloody fortress, I reckon you can survive this one."

Personally, I wouldn't take my odds.

Alastair pulled out a phone and showed me a live video feed of an elderly woman sitting in a garden, staring vacantly at a rosebush.

"Secretary Pederson?"

The vampire flipped to a photo of a slender, almost coltish shedim covered in quills like an armadillo with red glowing eyes. "You remember her nephew, Aleksander."

The half shedim who'd been murdered and drained of all blood on Alastair's orders.

I flew at the vampire, kicking and punching with all my human strength, pouring out my rage that this young boy's life had been stolen from him and desperately trying to access Cherry through the static in my head so I could tear Alastair limb from limb.

He grabbed my arms, twisted them painfully behind my back, and slammed my face and chest against a table. "Too drained to use your magic?" He laughed and slapped magic-nulling cuffs on me. "That makes my life easier."

"I'm not going anywhere with you."

He released me.

My hands were literally tied behind my back but I stood tall.

"Even if you could get away," he said, "I've got a contingency plan. Should one of my vamps not receive word from me within a specific time frame, Secretary Pederson will be killed and evidence will be found that your mother knew Aleksander was an infernal. It's why she sent Ezra to the London chapter to kill Roman Whittaker. Fear and protecting her own mutt."

"That's not what happened." I wrenched on the magic cuffs.

"Dmitri Kozlov will believe this version. Especially when he sees the photo I have of you as an infernal. Your mother will be sent to Sector A. Your boyfriend will be hunted and killed. Silas's escape will be dug into. What about Sachie or Darsh or any of the Vancouver chapter? Who else will end up in Sector A? And you'll get to live with all the suffering you caused, just because you wouldn't assist me." He paused, then mugged. "Until they kill you, that is."

Ezra could die if I went with Alastair.

The other people I cared about could die if I didn't.

My boyfriend's face flashed in my mind, followed by my mother's, each image twisting my gut with anguish.

"Come with me, take the test, and if you get the power word, tell it to me or I destroy everyone you care about. Your choice, infernal."

I closed my eyes, centering myself through the pressure building in my chest. Alastair wasn't bluffing. With Natán hunting him, he needed to power up to survive, and he didn't care about collateral damage.

Even if he had to burn my world to the ground.

Whereas Ezra was a Prime. His healing magic *would* kick in and… And if I didn't go, Alastair's plans would ensure my boyfriend was dead anyway.

"Decide," Alastair said harshly.

"I'll come," I said dully.

"Smart choice."

I had to play Alastair's game—for now.

In order to reach the fortress, we had to go into the Brink. Cell phones didn't work there, and the hour forfeit would be over soon. At that point, it was anyone's game, but I liked my odds. I'd get these cuffs off, get my magic back, and make my move.

I sent a silent prayer to the universe to take care of my boyfriend and accompanied Alastair out the front door.

This vampire was convinced he'd corralled a little lamb, a half shedim whose life was as disposable as the others he'd so callously ordered to be snuffed out. But I'd been forged in iron; once after Ezra left me and again after the trials of the past few months.

I was Aviva Jacqueline Fleisher, level three Maccabee operative par excellence and half shedim fresh out of fucks to give. Woe betide all those who crossed me, because I was finally done hiding.

THANK you for reading DEMON IN DISGUISE.

If you enjoyed this book and want to be first in the know about bonus content, reveals, and exclusive give-aways, become a Wilde One by joining my newsletter: http://www.deborahwilde.com/subscribe

You'll immediately receive short stories set in my various worlds and available FREE only to my newsletter subscribers.

Now, are you ready for Aviva's final adventure in THE DEMON'S DUE (Bedeviled AF, #5)?

Magic has a price, and Aviva's running out of ways to pay.

When an ancient healing ritual goes nuclear and vampires start short-circuiting, the supernatural world begins unraveling faster than you can say "apocalypse now." Aviva isn't just investigating a disaster—she's living in the blast zone.

Meantime, with demon magic threatening her boyfriend's life, Aviva makes a desperate choice: she forges a magic bond with him. Nice idea. Too bad it complicates everything. Now tethered to each other and racing against time, they must find a way to contain the chaos unleashed by the ritual—assuming their connection doesn't destroy them first.

Time to fight fire with fire. Literally.

To save the world, Aviva must embrace both sides of herself: the dedicated operative and the demon who's done playing nice.

Enter Cherry Bomb. The world better brace for impact.

Turn the page for a sneak peek of THE DEMON'S DUE …

Sneak Peek of The
Demon's Due

The Brink tasted like ozone and fear, but I swallowed both as Alastair's fingers dug into my arm. While I might be done hiding my shedim side, I wasn't done being hunted.

I picked my way over patches of ice that bloomed into carpets of tiny flowers with sharp crystalline petals, a lifetime of running over uneven terrain saving me a twisted ankle on the slick ground. Crunching a lopsided carnation —Mother Nature's gas station flower—under my boot, I wondered whether Alastair's head would make that same satisfying noise when I killed him for good.

Operative Fleischer, champion of justice, had vanished the second the bloodsucking parasite blackmailed me into leaving—

I dropped my gaze from the mud-brown sky to the fortress looming ahead of us. The weathered gray stone walls were lined with crenellations and guard towers, while bushes with oversized thorns grew wild in the dry moat. Their barbs coiled like hungry serpents, waiting for unwary flesh to pierce.

Annoyingly, my eyes stung from the stench of pine cleaner that had followed us for the past half hour. The reek made as much sense as the floating reefs of bone-white coral resembling teeth we'd navigated in eerie silence.

Usually, trips to the Brink were anything but quick. Count on Alastair to have some dumb artifact that could whisk us from the rift through the Brink to the fortress like an overeager puppy with a full bladder bounding to its favorite tree.

Though even one second spent in his charming presence was an eternity too long. He'd forsaken any pretense of civility, exposing a man-shaped reservoir of spite and brutishness.

The handcuffs bit painfully into my wrists as he hauled me forward by the chain, his casual flick sending me lurching behind him. My stomach churned with revulsion at being reduced to a prisoner, a possession, while the weight of his control over me made me want to scream with rage, but I refused to give him the satisfaction.

Alastair didn't know it, but the restraints were overkill, given that the very sentience he was frog-marching me toward had already stripped me of my Eishei Kodesh abilities and left my connection to Cherry Bomb on the fritz.

Yes, I'd forfeited my blue flame magic for an hour, but I'd expected the pay up to happen either when I first wagered it days ago or at some random innocuous time. Not that some asshole magic guardian would stalk me and find the exact worst moment to snatch my abilities away.

My captor pounded on the fortress's metal-reinforced wooden gate with an expression of savage triumph, and that old adage about not counting chickens flitted through my head.

I still had a shot. One requiring extraordinary luck, insanely perfect timing, and possibly a minor miracle, but technically, still a shot.

But with my shedim side fading in and out, my Eishei Kodesh magic in absentia, and the nulling cuffs squashing the hope that I'd be able to do anything even if I got my powers back, I was swimming in a catastrophe cocktail. My brain had locked up completely, like a computer with too many fatal errors. No reboot and no strategic thinking.

Sensing my distress, the Brimstone Baroness tore through the staticky barrier separating us. Our link clicked into place like a dislocated joint popping back to where it belonged.

Cherry itched to tear that British bastard limb from limb for orchestrating horrors from his comfortable shadows. I forced the sudden toxic green of my eyes back to their regular light brown and ordered her to shove her hate down, because my jaw still throbbed from Alastair's back-handed blow when I'd attempted to bond over deadbeat supernatural parents.

Who could have guessed that while Calista had hidden her dhampir son, she'd also protected him, visiting as often as she could to not only train him with valuable survival skills, but simply spend time with him.

Alastair had stoked his hatred for the parties he believed responsible for his mother's death like precious glowing coals. To be fair, he had plenty of that emotion to go around, along with a list of every vampire who'd ever dissed or underestimated him.

"They'll get theirs when I have the power of a Prime and they don't," he'd said darkly.

Alastair's hand now flitted to a green camo canteen worn on a canvas shoulder strap, the uncharacteristic accessory first revealed when he lost his wool coat back in the bone reefs. BYOB? Supplies for a tailgate party? Picky about his food? In any case, he hadn't touched it yet, so perchance it was a boutique hemoglobin to be savored in celebration.

So long as he didn't try snacking on me.

Get it now!

About the Author

Deborah Wilde is a global wanderer and hopeless romantic. After twelve years as a screenwriter, she was also a total cynic with a broken edit button, so, she jumped ship, started writing funny, sexy, urban fantasy and paranormal women's fiction novels, and never looked back.

She loves writing smart, flawed, wisecracking women who can solve a mystery, kick supernatural butt, banter with hot men, and still make time for their best female friend, because those were the women she grew up around and admired. Granted, her grandmother never had to kill a demon at her weekly friend lunches, but Deborah is pretty sure she could have.

Smart (ass) heroines. Epic magic. Red-hot romance.

www.deborahwilde.com